# MONTE CARLO
*by*
# MOONLIGHT

**Anton Du Beke** – the King of Ballroom, *Strictly Come Dancing* royalty and household name – is one of this generation's all-round entertainers. In 2018, he realised his boyhood ambition and published the first in a series of bestselling novels set in the 1930s world of the exclusive Mayfair hotel, The Buckingham. He started the new Forsyth Family series with *The Royal Show* (2024).

*Also by Anton du Beke*

THE BUCKINGHAM SERIES

One Enchanted Evening
Moonlight over Mayfair
A Christmas to Remember
We'll Meet Again
The Ballroom Blitz
The Paris Affair
A Dance for the King

FORSYTH FAMILY SERIES

The Royal Show

# ANTON DU BEKE

# MONTE CARLO by MOONLIGHT

ORION

First published in Great Britain in 2025 by Orion Fiction,
an imprint of The Orion Publishing Group Ltd.
Carmelite House, 50 Victoria Embankment
London EC4Y 0DZ

An Hachette UK Company

The authorised representative in the EEA is Hachette Ireland,
8 Castlecourt Centre, Dublin 15, D15 XTP3,
Ireland (email: info@hbgi.ie)

1 3 5 7 9 10 8 6 4 2

A CIP catalogue record for this book is
available from the British Library.

ISBN (Mass Market Paperback) 9781 3987 1021 4
ISBN (Ebook) 9781 3987 1022 1
ISBN (Audio) 9781 3987 1023 8

Typeset at The Spartan Press Ltd,
Lymington, Hants

Printed and bound in Great Britain by Clays Ltd,
Elcograf S.p.A.

MIX
Paper | Supporting
responsible forestry
FSC® C104740

www.orionbooks.co.uk

*For my family,*
*I do everything for you.*

*TUESDAY, 2 May 1967*

# Chapter One

The skies had been heavenly blue over the French Riviera – but somehow, over the glistening white towers of Monte Carlo, they seemed more heavenly still.

The canary-yellow Ford Anglia that followed the sweep of the harbour, through the boulevards where the Grand Prix grandstands were already falling into place, did not exactly fit into the elegant surrounds. The car, battered around the edges and burnished by a hundred long crossings of the Continent, had tarnished even further this long, hot summer – but so had its driver, which was precisely why he didn't jettison the car for some better model. At seventy-one years old, Ed Forsyth – just like this car – had seen finer days. Yet, as he came past the grand hotels and squares, the luxury Casino which drew so much wealth to the city, he got the inalienable feeling that his finest was yet to come.

In fact, as he reached his final destination, he thought it was very probably coming this very weekend.

Bringing the car to a halt, he stepped out into the blistering heat of Monte Carlo.

The Prince's Palace was one of the grandest and oldest buildings in Monaco. Above Ed, its white turrets gleamed against the cerulean sky. The Monacoan flag, striking bands of red and white, sailed in the wind. Beyond, hung the grey crags of the mountain that cleaved Monte Carlo in two. Standing here, dwarfed by both palace and mountain, it was easy to understand why the city was so steeped in history; what had become a pleasure-ground for the wealthy of the twentieth century had once been of enormous strategic significance.

Ed took his cane from the car and picked his way to the rail running around the circumference of the palace grounds. It had felt, in the last six months, as if age was finally catching up with him. Born in the latter years of the previous century, two wars and what seemed several lifetimes ago, Ed was not the sort of man who liked getting old. He understood that some folks simply faded into old age with a kind of contentment, but Ed hated the aches and pains it made of his body. He'd had enough of those to contend with as a young man, just back from the Great War.

But it was funny how much a little beauty could change the way a man felt. It was strange how a little *exhilaration* lifted not just the spirit but the body. There were certain places in the world that did that to a travelling performer like Ed. Stepping into the London Palladium could make an octogenarian feel sprightly. Stepping into the Théâtre Edouard VII in Paris was enough to make a man feel timeless. And a summer on the French Riviera, culminating in an unexpected return to this city of opulence, of wonder, of *starlight*, was enough to crown not just a season, but an entire career.

He was just approaching the rail, expecting to announce himself to the guardsmen who stood sentry here, when a man in a starched white shirt and bow tie approached. 'Monsieur Forsyth,' he said in a heavy French accent, 'there has been a change of plan. If you would, perhaps, step this way?'

4

The man, who Ed now took for one of the palace's personal valets, made an ostentatious turn and presented a vehicle sitting in the yard in front of the palace. Ed had had the honour of riding in a good number of high-class cars before – but this was beyond compare: a gleaming red Chevrolet Corvette, which put him more in mind of the wide open roads of the United States than it did the steep mountain paths of Monaco. Then again, the princess *was* American, and had given up much of her heritage – and Hollywood itself – to come here; perhaps she had asked her husband, the sovereign, Prince Rainier, for a little American indulgence.

'Where to?' Ed asked.

He gazed up at the mountain, wondering what it might be like to see Monte Carlo from above.

'Not so very far at all, sir. Please come – the princess is waiting.'

Who was Ed Forsyth, provincial British performer, to deny the request of a princess? He'd been performing for commoners and kings all of his life. It pleased him to think that she had called him by name – so, without another word, he entered the Corvette and soon felt the wind rushing through what was left of his hair.

It had been seventeen years since he last came to the city. In 1950, the world, and indeed Forsyth Varieties – the Company Ed had ruled over half of his life – had been so different. Europe was still showing the ravages of war; everywhere, the greyness and the desolation of a world putting itself back together. And then there was Monaco. The Principality had taken its own hits during the war, conquered and occupied twice over, but there was something about the French Riviera that still spoke of joy and hopefulness for the future. The shows they'd been performing along the coast, first in Nice and then in Cannes, had ended right here in Monte Carlo. Even back then, there had been no lack of money in the Principality – and no shortage of ways the city's gilded elites might entertain themselves as the sun went down – but they'd flocked to the Forsyth Varieties all the same. A three-week spell of spectacular shows, a dream, an idyll before the greyer skies of Great Britain summoned them home.

But for all the wonders of that month, the one thing Ed treasured most was the night he and his late wife Bella had taken a long stroll along the seafront, sitting to watch the sun come down over the pure white sands of the Plage du Larvotto and revelling in the fact that their dear twins, Evie and Cal, were coming of age in such beautiful surrounds. 'The world's going to be different for them,' Ed remembered saying. 'Perhaps Cal will never truly go to war…' What a dream that had seemed – and so far, at least, it had come to pass.

Bella had passed away six years later, but he felt certain her ghost was walking alongside him as he left behind the grand white turrets of the Prince's Palace. 'We never got invited inside, did we, Belle?' he said to her spirit, as if she hovered in the air all around. 'And it looks like that pleasure will have to wait again. Come on, old girl, let's see what's happening. A lot's changed since we were here. Monte Carlo didn't have its Hollywood princess back then…'

The ride in the scarlet Chevrolet took but a few moments, skirting the edge of the Port Hercule and its rainbow of pleasure crafts until they reached the very head of the bay. Ed was pleased to feel the wind in his hair, but was hardly disappointed when the driver swept the car off the road and the striking grounds of Fort Antoine awaited.

'Sir, her Royal Highness is waiting for you.'

The Fort Antoine had once been an imposing citadel, the first thing raiders might have seen approaching Monte Carlo across the glittering waves. The citadel still stood, but when Ed was led up the stone steps to the top of the imposing edifice, he did not find a formidable military outpost. The only soldiers barricading the top of the stairs were the security officers in charge of the princess's safety – for directly in front of Ed, where cannons had once stood, was an amphitheatre open to the skies, rings of tiered stone seats on one side and, on the other, only the vastness of the Mediterranean. What a backdrop that was going to be to perform against – all the dance and song and magic of the Forsyth Varieties, as a crimson sun sank into the ocean waves.

There were a good number of security men in the stone seating – but only one person stood in the middle of the empty amphitheatre floor.

'Your Highness,' said Ed, as their eyes met.

Princess Grace of Monaco: it had been some years since Ed last saw her, and even then, it had been in a different world. She looked as elegant, now, as she had ever seemed on the silver screen, back in the days when she was just good old Grace Kelly of Philadelphia – but she'd grown into her regal bearing; she'd been married for more than a decade, princess of the Principality for eleven years. She was approaching forty (though who could tell? She looked as timeless as ever). The simple white dress she was wearing was in tune with the pearls around her neck. The ring upon her finger, no doubt the jewel Prince Rainier had gifted her on the day she agreed to be his wife, sparkled like a star fallen from the heavens.

'I think I should like it if you called me Grace, Mr Forsyth, as in days of old.'

They came together in the middle of the theatre floor.

'If that's how it is, your … *Grace*.'

'Your Grace,' the princess smiled. 'Now *that* has a certain ring to it – but Grace will do.'

Ed smiled in return; her laughter was infectious. And hadn't that been one of the qualities that propelled her to stardom in the first place? That infectious love of life that drew audiences to her? Ed still remembered the first time he'd seen her on a cinema screen: Grace Kelly, the star of *High Noon*, scintillating and stunning even in black-and-white.

'I'm glad you could make it, Ed. I couldn't have done this without you. Well... perhaps there was a way, but I wouldn't have *wanted* to. How long has it been? Ten years?'

'Eleven,' Ed replied without hesitation. He knew, because Bella had passed into the next life only a few short months later. 'From the highs of *High Society* to...'

Princess Grace clasped Ed's hand. Funny, but that tiny gesture of affection wouldn't have seemed strange, nor out of place, eleven years ago; yet, now that she'd spent those years as a princess, it felt strange, almost untoward. They'd met at a gala just after the launch of *High Society*. The Forsyth Varieties, hired to perform, hadn't expected to find themselves milling with Hollywood royalty – but there they'd been, after the show, in the company of the greats. It was just like Bella to have struck up a friendship with the young starlet. Just like Bella, who had never lusted for fame but just loved to put on a show, to find Grace drawn to her side. They'd made plans to see each other again, even written letters; there'd been promises of an invitation to Monte Carlo, after Grace was married, after the world *changed*. But fate caught up with Bella and the best-laid plans came to nought.

Until today.

'Sometimes the stars align,' said Ed – and, looking up, thought how brilliant the stars must seem above Fort Antoine on a clear summer's night. 'We've spent this summer on the Riviera. Your letter caught up with me in Cannes. I've got old John Lauderdale

– our illusionist, if you remember? – sitting back home. He's too old to travel now.' Ed looked momentarily forlorn at this; John was one of his oldest colleagues in the Company, but the century was growing old, just like them, and his travelling days were over. 'So we have him to thank for the letter reaching me.'

'I'm just glad it did. Ed, I've been wanting to invite you since the beginning. Ever since dear Bella …'

Ed held up his hand. Bella was more than a decade gone, but sometimes her passing still seemed so vivid. 'She would have loved to have visited you here. She would have loved to perform here, right here, with the sun going down.' Ed gravitated to the citadel's edge and gazed into the distance. 'We're here for you, Your Highness. I promised you once that, when the time came, my Company would put on the very best show we could, to celebrate all you're doing here. I'll do it for you, and I'll do it for my Bella as well. Perhaps she'll be watching, from up there.'

Joining him, Princess Grace said, 'I've been hosting the Rose Ball at the palace every year since I first arrived. There's so much money in Monaco – what better than to get everyone together and make them *give* for people who have so much less? The ballroom will be *alive*, Ed. We'll do so much good. But this year I wanted something just a little bit different. A little bit *special*. That's when I thought of you.' She opened her arms, as if to take in the Fort Antoine. 'They half destroyed this place during the war – or so I'm told. It was used to store explosives – but the problem with explosives is that …'

'They explode,' grinned Ed.

'Rainier knew we had to rebuild, and that it wouldn't be a fortress anymore. So – a theatre instead!' And she clapped her hands. 'Do you know, there isn't a thing I would change about my life, but … sometimes, when I think of those early days in

Philadelphia and New York, taking to the boards for the very first time...'

There were few words to express the rest of that sentiment, but Ed seemed to understand it well enough. 'It gets in your blood,' he said.

'And there it remains. So, while I shall not step out onto a stage again, I couldn't resist it when the idea came upon me. One night only at the Fort Antoine, all of the guests attending our Rose Ball, to be entertained by you, my favourite company of all.' She paused. 'Well, a girl has dreams – and sometimes, she gets to make those dreams come true. It won't be the biggest audience you've played for this summer – but if you get them into a good mood, each and every one, just think how eager they'll be to do some *good* when it comes to the Ball. Just *think* of all the donations we'll receive.' Again, the princess paused. 'How is the Company, Ed?'

'That, Your Highness, is—'

'I thought I told you to speak to me as a friend, Ed. I know an Englishman likes to bow, but I won't be bowed to – not by you.'

For a moment, Ed felt choked. It wasn't just the honour she gave him; it was the memory of why she gave him that honour – the memory of Bella, and the immediacy of their bond. But Bella had always been like that; a mother to every performing girl in the Company and beyond. By God, how they'd missed her. By God, how fractious those years after she left had been. He'd almost lost the Company to the abyss of his grief. He'd almost lost his son...

'Well, Cal went off and did his own thing for a few years, of course.'

'Indeed – I hear he's very highly prized now.'

'Evie's been with us throughout. She's rather the glue that binds us together. And... I'm a grandfather now. Cal's little boy

Sam – he may even perform out here on Friday night. What an auspicious debut that might be!' Ed did a little turn, remembering his own dancing days. 'So, there's a new generation rising up. Grace, it makes a man feel proud to see the generation coming after him – but...' and here he winced a little, 'it makes one feel *old* as well. I'm not performing as much as I was. Sometimes, Cal's been compèring our shows. I wonder – I wonder how long my road lasts. But then I come to a place like this, and I wonder... why would anyone want to do anything else?'

There came a wistful look to the princess's eyes. For a moment, Ed wondered if she was thinking the same thing. 'My children grow up princes and princesses. One day, my son will be king. How do you think *that* feels, Ed, for a young woman from Philly?'

Ed smiled. 'I should like to meet your children, Grace, if the opportunity arises.'

'Why, Mr Forsyth – they'll be right here, front row at the Fort Antoine.' She paused. 'You're thinking of the future, Ed,' she surmised.

'The past, the future... it's all as one in this brain of mine.'

'You're not so old and befuddled yet.'

'Perhaps not – but... it's different in your world, Grace. You look at your son and you know – one day he's going to be king. I look at mine, and...'

'Cal's still wild, then?'

'It isn't just that. Wait until you meet him; he's lost so much of his wildness since he became a father. He's a devil, that's true, but he's working hard. He came up ahead of us, to meet a film director shooting a picture in the city. It's... I don't know what's *next*, Grace. When I ride off into the sunset – when my own body's too creaky for the stage...' and he brandished his cane like a valiant jousting knight, as if to prove he wasn't *quite* there yet, 'I don't know what the next act is going to be. I don't know what becomes of the Company when my curtain falls.'

Grace led Ed along the former fortress parapets. Here, the sunlight spilt across them, lighting up all Grace's beauty for Ed, lighting up all Ed's aged lines for Grace. 'In my world we call it succession planning,' said Grace.

'It's what my father called it in our world too.'

'You feel you have to choose between Evie and Cal?'

'I feel like the *future* has to choose. Cal's got wild talent. He draws the eye. But Evie's a natural-born leader. She's got grit. She's the one who carried me when Bella died.' Ed didn't want to say what next came to his mind, even to somebody he trusted as much as the princess. Cal had come through for the Company, he'd come back to the fold and brought them back magic and *pizazz*. But Ed still remembered, too vividly, the day he'd walked out on them, the twin losses of Bella passing on and Cal – unable, perhaps, to bear the tragedy of it all – striking out on his own. 'But Cal's the one with a child. I see myself in Sam. I see the *future* in him.'

'Evie has no one?'

'She's had suitors over the years. She's got close, once or twice. But … she's been unlucky in love.'

'Sometimes the best of us are.'

'The kings of old always stage-managed a succession,' Ed mused, 'to stop the court from falling apart. But I find myself curiously *lacking* in the talent it needs. I love both my children, with all my heart. But could one ever rule over the other? Is Cal with us forever, or is he just biding his time? Does *he* even know it? His wife Meredith will want more children soon. Is the touring life for her? And … would the troupe really accept Evie? Things *are* changing in the world, but … a woman, in a world of ambitious men? The way her dancing girls look at her, you'd think they'd follow her into battle itself! But without a husband, without children of her own to vest the future in? What's the future of the Forsyth Varieties if you can't gaze down the decades and know that it's going to go on and on?'

There was a silence in the Fort Antoine. In only a few nights' time, these stone tiers would be filled with the great, the anointed, the wealthy patrons of Princess Grace's benefit ball. Music would echo out over the water as the sun went down and the stars came up. Evie's girls would dance to Cal's bombastic piano, while Davith's dogs turned their tricks and Jim Livesey – who'd been studying with the illusionist John Lauderdale for five years and was finally seizing his chance to take centre stage – cast his enchantments over the crowd. But right now, there was a stillness, a quietude in the amphitheatre. The only sound was the gentle susurration of the sea against the rocks somewhere below, and the calls of wheeling seabirds overhead.

'My Company is almost a century old. My family's been performing since the days of vaudeville and music hall. But sometimes, just sometimes, I wonder if I'm the last. My grandfathers kept this Company alive. My father steered it into a new century. We've come through wars together, one generation to the next. But am I, Grace, am *I* the one to lose it all?'

Grace threaded her arm into the crook of Ed's.

'The sun sets on all of us, Ed. But not *just* yet. One day we'll all wake for the final time. We'll kiss our lovers and then never kiss them again. We'll sing one last song, take one last bow, hear one final round of applause. But not tonight, dear friend. Not this time.' She bowed her head to whisper the last, 'I brought you here for a reason. I thought it was just a promise to an old, dearly departed friend. I thought it was time to make good on an agreement from long ago. I *thought* it was for the Rose Ball, and all the good we'll do for those who need it. But now I see that it's more.'

'Your Highness?'

Grace rolled her eyes, but she let this one slide, for she had seen the mischief sparkling in Ed's eyes.

'It's for *you*, Mr Forsyth. So that you might catch a glimpse of what the future might be. And personally, Ed, I simply can't wait.'

# Chapter Two

Champagne corks flew at the Casino de Monte Carlo.

Across the Casino floor, the air pulsated with promise and expectation. Dreams would be made here tonight; fortunes won, or fortunes squandered. From card table to roulette wheel, gentlemen in elegant black marched imperiously with beautiful women on their arms. An olive-skinned titan in a suit of white linen chewed on a fat Montecristo cigar, its reef of smoke billowing out in perfect rings across the table where he cast his dice. Somewhere, a cry of jubilation rose up and set the crystal chandeliers above to tinkling. Somewhere else, security officers roamed, their eyes acutely aware of every single movement in the building.

And at a baccarat table in the heart of the palace, a young man with a bow tie slightly off-centre – as if to suggest that he did not *really* belong here, but he was going to have the time of his life while he stayed – took one look at the cards the croupier was dealing, flashed a devil-may-care look at the tall, gangling figure on his right, and tossed down his chips.

'Luck's my lady tonight,' he said, flashing a smile so pearly white it seemed to draw the light of the chandeliers. Then he reached for another fistful of chips, his entire reserve, and prepared to throw them down. 'Deal 'em, sir. Let's see what's coming to—'

A meaty hand gripped him by the wrist.

One moment there had been the buzz of anticipation around the baccarat table, that beautiful moment in gambling when every eye in the house is drawn to a single person – perhaps a born winner, perhaps one of life's natural born losers, but captivating all the same. Then, in an instant, the anticipation was gone. In the vacuum it left behind there was only shock and horror, as the young man's hand opened up, spilling all of his chips, and whoever had taken hold of him hoisted him aloft.

'I say!' the young man exclaimed, still flashing those pearly whites. 'Is this any way to treat a guest? I'm ...'

Dangling over the seat that he'd moments before been treating like a throne, the young man revolved, only to discover that he was being grappled by one of the Casino's burly security guards. Three others stood in an arc around the table. 'Our apologies, sirs. Our apologies, madams,' the most genteel of them said (though in truth he wasn't very genteel). 'On occasion these things do happen. For the sake of our trusted guests, we must keep the Casino honest.'

'Honest?' exclaimed the young man, filled with indignation. 'Ladies, gentlemen,' he pronounced to those around, 'this is a clear case of mistaken identity. Honesty is my middle name. In point of fact, it *is* my middle name. It's a family name, after my grandmother – a fabulous Frenchwoman, I might add, and ...'

The security guard shook the young man. Out of his sleeve slipped three playing cards: a Jack of Diamonds, a Seven of Spades, and an Ace of Hearts. From a pocket spilt a handful of craps dice, and from his trouser cuff a golden chip.

The young man's smile crumpled, but as he took in the spectators, his eyes still dazzled.

'Of course,' he grinned, 'there's honesty and then there's ... Look!'

The sudden exclamation, which came quite out of nowhere, changed everything. One second, the crowd had been staring at the spectacle of the captured cheater; the next, they swirled round, as if to discover what he was gesticulating at. Even the security guards currently patting their hands all over his body turned.

It didn't matter that there was nothing to see.

In fact, that was rather the point.

The split second it took for the officers to understand they were being duped was all it took. In an instant, the young man was flurrying up out of their grasp. In another instant, he was leaping onto the top of the baccarat table, scattering cards and chips. One more instant and he was vaulting over the other side.

'Stop him!' somebody bawled.

The young man looked back and threw a dainty wave at the security guards. Thick-headed fools – they respected the Casino too much; they were chasing him by going *round* the tables.

The young man had no such compunction. Directly ahead of him, a group of refined older gentlemen were playing roulette. The wheel started spinning, the chips were being placed; the croupier called time as the ball began to skitter madly around. But none of it came to anything, for now he was leaping on top of the table, tumbling off the other side. 'My deepest apologies,' he said to a stunning brunette in sapphire sequins, taking the Champagne flute from her hand, tasting it, then handing it back. 'Something to whet the whistle, ma'am.'

Security guards were streaming at him from every angle now. Over the blackjack tables he cantered, vaulting from one to another. When he reached the last one, the guards charging after him on either side, he cast himself upwards, grappled with the chandelier, swung himself around (knocking two guards aside in the process) and landed – inelegantly, he thought – on top of a poker table. 'Royal Flush wins,' he declared, with a cursory look at the players' hands.

Then his eyes zoned in on the doors up ahead.

Out there lay the ancient streets of Monte Carlo.

Out there: freedom, and whatever came next.

Only one guard stood at the door; the others were too busy scrambling madly through the Casino, trying to hem him in. There might be an element of fisticuffs about this, he decided – but that would do. That wouldn't matter. Not if he got out into the night.

He grinned.

He was about to throw himself forward when, in the corner of his eye, a flash of emerald green caught his eye. Instinctively, he turned. There stood the most beautiful creature he'd ever seen: tall and lithe, her hair a golden cascade, her eyes glittering in exactly the same striking colour as the chiffon that spilt around her.

Mirth played on her lips. She'd been watching him, he thought, since the beginning – and liking what she saw.

Not everybody in this Casino, then, was outraged by the evening.

He lifted his hand to salute her.

He winked – and, in return, she smiled.

The world seemed to slow down.

There he stood, balanced on the table's edge, about to make his mad dash for freedom – and everything froze.

For a split second, there was nothing in the world except that lady.

But the split second lasted too long. A squandered split second was all it took for the guards to catch up. Suddenly, the young man was being pulled down from the table, then pinioned to the floor while fists and boots pounded him from every angle.

All things told, this hadn't quite been the evening he expected.

But there, through the kicks and the punches, stood the woman in green.

She was beaming at him, even through the haze.

'CUT!'

That one word, bellowed through a megaphone, changed everything.

The cameras pulled back. The entirety of the Casino floor took a breath. Applause broke out all around – and Benedict Frey, the dark-haired young man curled up on the floor while the actors playing security guards crowded around him, was helped to his feet by a portly middle-aged man with a significant paunch and big bald pate. 'Ben,' he said in his crisp English tones, 'that's the one. Every mark hit. You sold it, my boy. You *sold it*. We'll reset for pick-ups and reaction shots, but I'm sure we've got this one in the can. Just wait until I get it in front of the studio. Ben, they're going to *love it*.'

Benedict Frey leapt to his feet, soaking up the applause. He'd been rehearsing that sequence for two full weeks while the second unit shot the exteriors and the scenes in which he didn't figure; day after day, vaulting from one table to another, making sure he didn't miss a beat. 'Mr Hines,' he said to the portly fellow, 'we just made *magic*.'

'Wait until it's on the silver screen, my boy.'

Albert Hines, veteran director of *Can't Stop Now*, *Lost in Tangiers* and assorted other pictures for Parker & Parr, whose studios were small but ambitious beyond compare, left his star with a wink and turned away. Benedict was already being mobbed by the backstage crew, his make-up touched up and his costume dusted down for the pick-ups, so Albert would have a little peace in which to think this through.

Deep in thought, he picked his way through the technicians – and all the Casino staff, on contract from the Casino itself to reset everything once a scene was completed – until he reached a table tucked behind the last of the cameras. Here, in front of a boxy black-and-white television screen, sat a black-haired man in his middle thirties. Cal Forsyth was wearing a jet-black shirt, open at the collar, and denim jeans, his brown leather boots propped up on the table while his eyes were buried in the script in front of him. The title page read *MONTE CARLO BY MOONLIGHT*, and the script was annotated with so much scrawl it was almost indecipherable. Regardless, Cal had been following it closely. He looked up now, to see the director approaching.

'That's it,' said Albert, clenching his fist decisively. '*That's* the moment. Our lead is down, no way out – and that's when the music kicks in. That's when all hell breaks loose.'

Cal smiled. 'It really could be quite a moment.'

'Oh, it will be, Mr Forsyth. If I get the right shots, and we marry it with the right sounds – well, that's the *real* magic. All the stars coming together to make a *moment*. You can see that, right?'

Cal nodded. He understood magic. He understood *moments*. He'd never before been invited to a movie set, but he understood the art of the show better than most – for he'd grown up the son of a theatre family, and wasn't that the purest form of show there was? Just the players and their audience, and the magic they could create between them? It seemed to him, right now, that moviemaking was a different sort of business, but so much was the same. The marrying of a movie with music – well, it wasn't so far away from what he'd done before, was it?

'We've got a lot sunk into this production, Mr Forsyth. Now, you might think it grandiose, but I attained the rank of captain during the war – naval captain, you understand – and marshalling this lot to make a movie is not altogether unlike captaining a ship of the line. Both require vast resources, and both require vast manpower. Both require strategy and leadership. And ... *capital*. Parker & Parr have gone all out for this picture, and it's my task not just to bring it in on budget – but to bring it in *spectacular*. I'm a man of my word. I consider it an act of duty.'

'It's a brilliant script, Mr Hines.'

'Yes, well, Parker & Parr spent a lot of time and money finding the right scribbler for this. It might seem simple on the surface, but making simple *sing* is no easy task.'

Cal knew that as well. He was a songwriter by trade, and there was nothing that *sold* like simplicity. You needed joy and pace and panache, but above all things you needed to be understood.

This script had everything. He'd only been permitted to see it two hours earlier, when he first came to set, but already he'd torn through it once, then got stuck into it again. In *Monte Carlo by Moonlight*, a group of young musicians had spent the summer playing music and making merry on the French Riviera, living the young man's dream – live fast, try not to die too young – and falling into countless memorable escapades along the way. But summer was coming to an end, the boys knew they had to make it back to Blighty – well, their lead guitarist *was* getting married, after all – and, in the first scenes of the movie, disaster was about to strike...

'I like how it starts,' said Cal. 'I've been that musician too. Well, maybe not quite so dramatic, but...'

At the start of the movie, the gang were conned out of their instruments, money and the van they'd been touring in – and left, with only the clothes they stood up in, on the beach outside

Monaco. From that moment on, the movie charted their increasingly desperate attempts to rustle up enough money to get them back home – setting them into direct confrontation with the local casino, a particularly truculent mob boss, a beautiful French starlet and an army of infuriating *gendarmes*.

'It's a caper,' Cal grinned. 'Everyone likes a caper. It will light up the summer.'

'Well,' Mr Hines intervened, 'that's where *you* come in. Mr Forsyth, you know why you're here. Now, I hasten to add, it isn't actually my decision – but I'm damn glad you are, because we're *lacking* a certain something, and it's not something any of us here can fix. Music, Mr Forsyth. We've been working with a base set of songs, but they're just not cutting the mustard for the folks at home – and we've got a lot to live up to. Now, I've heard that number of yours – "Runaway ... Runaway Lovers", wasn't it?'

Cal smiled. It was a song he'd written many moons ago, but five years ago – quite by accident, and courtesy of a memorable turn at the Royal Variety Performance – that piece of poetic piano balladry had transformed his fortunes. Since then, the song had been recorded by thirty-seven different artists and performed by many more. It had reached California, featured in advertisements for Cadillacs and scents by Dior; Roy Orbison had sung it on stage at Madison Square Garden (this had, perhaps, been the highlight of Cal's whole career), and Frank Sinatra was known to have said there were very few classics being written in the modern day, but that 'Runaway Lovers' was one of them. If it hadn't turned Cal himself into a star – and it would be wrong to say this had never irked him – it had opened a door through which countless other of his compositions stormed. The decade had been dominated by the Beatles, the Rolling Stones, the Animals, the Kinks, all the British bands taking the music of

Blighty out into the world – but Cal's epic balladry, reminiscent of some earlier time, still captured the imagination.

'And that's what makes you perfect for this picture. You're a good old boy from England, but you *feel* like you could be riding down Route 66 with the wind in your hair, belting out these ballads – and that's what we need.' He lowered his voice. 'Benedict's songs just aren't cutting it. There's American money invested in this picture. If it doesn't break America…' Mr Hines shrugged. 'Sprinkle some magic dust for us, Cal. The studio will pay handsomely if you do. Your manager's spoken to them already?'

Cal froze, but only momentarily. The fact was, he didn't have a manager. He'd never needed one. To begin with, he hadn't been successful enough – there were very few managers who stuck with an act who wasn't immediately successful; such was the way of a cut-throat world – and then, when 'Runaway Lovers' changed everything, he'd been so full of scorn for that class of men that he'd simply asked his wife Meredith to handle matters instead.

'What about him?' asked Cal.

'Benedict?'

Cal lifted himself from the seat. It was miraculous how efficiently the carnage in the Casino was being turned round. The set was almost ready for the pick-ups and reaction shots Hines had planned. 'It seems to me that, if I was in his shoes, I might feel a little out of sorts if another songwriter was drafted in to replace me.'

Albert Hines looked around. For the first time, Cal saw that he wasn't just a movie director, nor just a naval captain – he was an assured politician as well. He put his fingers to his lips, let out a shrill whistle, then called out Benedict's name. On the other side of the set, the young man lifted himself from the make-up chair and sauntered over. As he did so, Hines remarked, 'Making movies isn't like writing songs, just like waging wars isn't like a duel. These are vast enterprises, with hundreds of moving parts. We all play our little role. Benedict will understand. The studio's committed to putting his star in the heavens. The ends will justify the means.'

Benedict soon reached them through the throng of camera operatives, sound engineers and other technicians filling the Casino floor. When Cal had watched him on camera, he'd been scurrilously charming, but he seemed to have lost some of that swagger now that they weren't rolling. He was a wispish young man, perhaps only twenty years old, with a face so cherubic that Cal wondered if he could even grow stubble. The black hair was swept back in a quiff, evidently styled upon the American icons – James Dean sprang to mind, except that James Dean had soulful, glowering eyes, where Benedict's seemed puppyish at best.

'Mr Frey,' Cal said, leaping to his feet and extending his hand. 'Bravura performance! I loved it.'

Albert Hines flashed an approving look at Cal. 'You, sir, are a man I can do business with,' he seemed to be saying. Cal had known a lot of ego-driven performers in his time writing songs for the labels; he fancied he knew how to handle a young man like Benedict.

'Ben, I want to you to meet Cal Forsyth,' Albert began, stretching out his braces. 'You might not know the name, but you'll sure know the work. "Runaway Lovers", perhaps?'

Benedict rocked on his heels. 'I've heard it,' he said, non-committally – but his eyes narrowed in suspicion, as inwardly he tried to make sense of the situation. 'It's nice to meet you, Mr Forsyth. Say, you know I write songs too?'

Cal nodded.

'What are you on set for?' Benedict asked.

There was something suspicious in his voice too, but immediately Albert Hines intervened. 'Cal's not just a songwriter, Ben. He's the star turn with the Forsyth Varieties – you heard of them?'

Benedict shrugged, but at least he was apologetic about it. 'Variety Theatre's never been my thing. Meaning no offence, Mr Forsyth, but my dreams were always different. Screen instead of stage, you see? Hollywood, not the end of the pier.'

Cal bristled. There'd been a time when he'd doubted whether he truly belonged to the Company that carried his name – wilderness years, when he'd wondered if it was the right thing for him – but he'd never doubted its worth. The Forsyth Varieties had a history almost a hundred years old. His grandfathers had founded it, and it had taken them all over the Continent – and even beyond. Five years ago, they'd performed for the king – and soon, very soon, Cal's own son would take to the stage for the first time. There was community, family, history in a company like this. You didn't get that in the all too often fleeting stardom of the silver screen.

'Mr Forsyth's agreed to lend us his considerable talents, Ben. With Mr Forsyth on board, the soundtrack to our picture is going to go stratospheric. Your face, combined with Cal's magical musical dust – it's coming together at last! And with scenes like the one we did today, I think there are going to be some very happy money men back at Parker & Parr. I for one—'

Benedict's face had acquired a stupefied air, but now he seemed to come to his senses. 'Mr Hines, I feel like I'm missing a piece of this picture here. Magical – musical – *dust*? What exactly are you trying to tell me?'

For the first time, Cal felt the awkwardness in the room. He stiffened, set down the script, opened his mouth as if to enter the fray – but Albert Hines was an adept politician, and already he was putting an arm around his young star and saying, 'My dear boy, I'm trying to tell you – you're going to be a *star*.'

Benedict just stared.

'Cal here is just the cherry on the cake. The icing on top! He's going to help you get the best out of your songs.'

Benedict shook Albert off and said, 'What's wrong with my songs?'

'Not one thing!' Albert guffawed. 'Ben, we've got to play the game. You're about to be a star, but Cal here – well, he has a little star power of his own. A little *kudos* in the industry, you might say. The studio have selected him – and they're paying him handsomely – to put a rocket under our soundtrack. We're going to blast off! It'll be your name in lights, Benny – nobody else. Your voice – just with a little extra *pizazz*.' Albert paused; he seemed to sense that Benedict's immediate iciness was thawing. 'You know, we ought to feel very lucky that Cal here just happened to be in Monte Carlo. It couldn't have come at a more opportune moment.'

Benedict turned to Cal and looked him up and down. Cal wasn't sure, but he seemed to sense more curiosity than suspicion in the boy now. 'What *are* you doing in Monte Carlo? If you didn't come especially to rewrite my songs, I mean…'

Inwardly, Cal had to smile; he rather liked the boy's *chutzpah*. In those years when he'd walked away from the family firm and tried to blaze his own way in the world, he'd worked on Denmark Street, churning out as many songs as he could to satisfy a string of managers, all searching for the 'next big thing' – and he'd learnt that, more than talent, *chutzpah* was what took you places. It was a quality, somewhere between confidence and obnoxiousness, and all artists had to have it if they were to succeed in their cut-throat worlds.

'I'm here with the family company,' Cal explained. 'There's a show being pulled together, a benefit at the Fort Antoine. We're to play there in just a few nights.'

Benedict shrugged. Evidently, he didn't even know what the Fort Antoine – that grand amphitheatre high up above Monte Carlo, that mighty military citadel whose war-torn days were over, and which was now given over to the arts – was. But at least his face flickered, perhaps even betraying some sort of wonder, when Cal added, 'Of course, we wouldn't be here at all if it wasn't for the Princess Grace. My mother and she were close, once upon a time. The sort of friendship that burns bright, but never really fades, no matter how many years pass by, no matter how rarely you see each other. She's invited us. The princess couldn't possibly put on this show without the Forsyths leading the charge.'

'So you see,' Albert Hines weighed in, seizing the moment with a film director's talent for how a scene ought to unfold, 'we're in starry company, and we must make of it what we will.'

At that moment, another figure approached the trio – a young man with dusky blond hair, a willowy frame and blue-grey eyes. The sleeves of his linen shirt were rolled up to the elbows, and his fingers sparkled with rings that looked like props stolen from the costume department – which was precisely where he worked. 'I'm sorry sir,' the newcomer began, 'we really must get Benedict set for the pick-ups. This jacket,' and he fingered the black tuxedo sleeves Benedict was wearing, 'is too scuffed up. We're burning through them like firewood! Come on, Ben. You're keeping everyone waiting.'

Benedict waited for Mr Hines's approval – 'Take him, Gideon. Ben, we can talk properly after the shots' – before he departed. His farewell to Cal could not be said to be rude, but there was a certain indignance in the air as he sauntered away. Cal watched as he bowed heads with the fey wardrobe assistant Gideon and couldn't escape the feeling that *he* was the subject of their conversation.

After Benedict was safely out of earshot, Mr Hines said, 'I'm afraid that's how you have to handle the stars, Mr Forsyth. I imagine things are a little more *honest* in your world. Working in the theatre keeps a man grounded. Working with family stops you from believing in your own legend. But in *this* world ...' He shrugged and threw back his head in imperious laughter. 'Benedict will need a little *handling*. He'll need steering through the process like a lamb to the chopping block. But let me be very clear with you, Mr Forsyth. This edict comes from on high – Parker & Parr them very selves. Everybody wants Benedict to ride this wave. We want his name in lights for many movies to come. And it isn't that his songs don't work – in fact, they're perfectly fine. The problem is that *perfectly fine* just will not do. The studio has sunk too much capital into *Monte Carlo by Moonlight* to take risks. Leave alone the idea of "sprinkling magic dust" – it's just a line to burnish the boy's ego. You're to rewrite those songs entirely, if that's what's needed.'

Cal watched Benedict and the young man named Gideon get swallowed up by the crowds on the Casino floor and said, 'You're going to ruffle some feathers.'

'Yes, Mr Forsyth – but *that* is why you are being paid so handsomely. His resentment may be overpowering, and you'll have to wear it – but be under no delusions: Benedict wants the fame that's coming to him, so he'll sing sweetly in the end.'

But something about it still seemed to stick in the back of Cal's throat. 'I know how I'd feel, Mr Hines, if those were my songs being rewritten.'

Together, they began to cross the Casino floor. Inside it was night-time, for that was what the movie demanded – but, when they reached the doors and the set curtains were drawn back, Cal could see the brilliant sunshine that deluged the old town of Monte Carlo. The moment the doors opened, the wave of warmth hit him. The sweet smell of the Mediterranean came over him, the piquancy of salt, the undefinable touch of Riviera air. There were some places in the world that made you feel alive, just walking their streets. This was Cal's second time in Monte Carlo, but you never quite forgot the touch of it. The skies of cerulean blue looked like something from another world. They looked, he thought now, like the Technicolor vistas of a movie.

'Tell me, Cal, are you the sort of man who turns down opportunities for a principle?'

Cal breathed in, luxuriating in the heat. It was only the middle of the afternoon, but he had a sudden craving to sit on the bluffs, overlooking the glittering blue and drink an ice-cold Trois Monts. That was the sort of afternoon that might help him think this through.

'I want to do it, Mr Hines. I think I could do you a good job. I could make your soundtrack sing. And yet—'

'Cal, Benedict will go far. He doesn't know it because he's young, and the young always believe legends about themselves, but he *needs* this. Stardom isn't a gift from the heavens; it's the result of a lot of hard work, and every star has an army behind them. He'll be grateful for your work by the end.' There followed a silence, in which Cal seemed to be ruminating yet further. Then, sensing his mind still wasn't made up, Albert added, 'You know the Varieties can't last forever, Cal. The world changes at such pace. Twenty years ago, there was no rock and roll. What will it be in twenty years' time? They'll flock to this picture, Cal. Your work will be heard by many millions more than you could ever hope to reach in a lifetime travelling from stage to stage. Why, the Fort Antoine itself – the most magnificent, splendid

ANTON DU BEKE

of venues a company like yours could ever hope to perform at, how many does she seat? Three hundred? Three hundred and fifty, at most? Cal, there'll be as many in every cinema. *Every last one.*' Albert Hines turned back towards the darkness of his film set, patting Cal on the shoulder as he left. 'Make hay while the sun shines, Mr Forsyth. None of us know what the future is going to bring.'

Cal was thinking about that as he wandered the stone streets of Monte Carlo's old town. It oozed with history, but there could be few brighter places on earth – for here, even in the city's shadowed streets, you felt as if you were walking on a different plane. Soon, Cal was following one of the steep lanes of the escarpment, up to the city's heights. From here he could see forever: the vast sweep of the bay, azure waters filled with yachts and other pleasure craft – and beyond that, the sun playing upon endless open water. From above, the apartment towers that lined the seafront looked as if they'd been here forever, merging seamlessly with the coast.

High above the old town, he sat outside a bar and satisfied his thirst. Even the beer was better on the Riviera, and in Monte Carlo it was the best of all. The first taste was divine, and as he let it settle, his thoughts turned back to what Mr Hines had said. Was there really a future in the Varieties? Was that where fate would leave him? In some way he'd been wrestling with the same dilemma all his life, and certainly ever since his mother – such a talented dancer – passed away. His father and twin sister Evie were crusaders for the Company, determined to steer it through the long century – but as for Cal...

He thought of his wife, Meredith.

He thought of his son, Sam, now almost six years old – and starting to have dreams for the future himself.

If the Company would one day die, what did that mean for him?

What was his son's inheritance to be, if Albert Hines was right, and the world moved on?

He drummed his fingers on the table, drank his beer and said out loud:

'Make hay, Mr Forsyth. Make hay while the sun shines.'

And the sun truly was shining. Its cascade lit up the rooftops of Monte Carlo in magnificent hues.

That was when he saw them, wending their way through the streets far below: the unmistakeable flash of scarlet that belonged to a London bus, with a multitude of black London taxicabs following it through the town.

His heart lit up, for this was the fleet in which the Forsyth Varieties always travelled – and it filled him up with every good feeling on earth, just like his first taste of Monacoan beer.

Cal finished his drink, flashed a smile (did she really *swoon*?) at the waitress – and, having first left a generous tip at the bar, picked his way back through the streets until he was on the seafront below. Already, many of the streets were being cordoned off, diversions put in place as the grandstands for the Grand Prix were transforming the city, so it wasn't an easy thing for the flotilla to find its way. That was why Cal was the first to reach the grand colonnades of the Hotel de Lyon, pride of place on the seafront, with tall palms swaying gracefully in front. He was lounging beneath one of those palms, enjoying the taste of his first cigarillo of the day, when the red double-decker drew up and its doors scythed back.

Out stepped Meredith, her white-blonde hair cut short – and, at her side, his son Sam.

Sam, the spitting image of his father – sometimes Meredith said that her genes didn't get a chance – ripped free of his

ANTON DU BEKE

mother and was nearly cut down by one of the taxicabs as he
hurtled straight into his father's arms.

'See,' Cal grinned, whirling him around, 'I told you I'd beat
you here!'

Then, to his son's unutterable groans, Cal bowed down to kiss
Meredith. She tasted even better than the beer. 'What did they
say?' she whispered.

'It's happening,' Cal beamed in return. 'I don't know how I'll
juggle it with the Fort Antoine, but... it's for the future.'

And when he looked up, there stood the future – or one
possible form of it – for his twin sister Evie had just stepped
out of the bus. As tall and statuesque as Cal, she hadn't given
in to the temptation of the day to cut her hair short; banks of
black hair rolled over her shoulders as she lifted her face to take
in the sun.

Cal's eyes flashed around. The rest of the Company – the
dancers, the musicians, Jim Livesey the young magician, Davith
Harvard with his two dancing terriers Tinky and Tiny – were
stepping out of the black taxicabs, but of one particular vehicle
there was no sign.

'Where's Dad?' Cal asked, with just a hint of concern in his
voice.

No sooner had he asked it, than the voice of Ed Forsyth
sounded from behind – and, flanked by half a dozen concierges
fanning out to help the Company with their packs, he declared,
'I'm here. I'm here and I'm ready.' Then he opened his arms to
the crowd of his Company, and Cal, Evie and all the rest lined
up to hear what he had to say. 'My friends,' he began – and Cal
and Evie shared a delighted look, for a smile was playing in the
corner of their father's lips again, 'we have our commission. The
Princess Grace herself invites us to create something spectacular,
here in this city of dreams. We have but a few short days – but

we have the most spectacular venue on the Riviera to fill with magic. So I invite you all, now, to settle into your suites – and then to meet me out at the Fort Antoine. Time is ticking by – and we must begin. My friends,' he beamed, 'get ready for something you'll remember until the end of your days.'

# Chapter Three

Last summer, when the Grand Prix came to Monte Carlo, the Hotel de Lyon had lost out in the battle for guests, with so many setting up at the Hotel de Paris, or the lavish suites at the Hermitage, with its striking cupola and beautiful, Belle Epoque stylings. This year, however, the battle for prestige had been viciously fought – and, though the Lotus team were embedded at the Hermitage, and the Ferrari boys were staying out of town, the cunning machinations of the Hotel de Lyon's management had, at least, drawn in the new Talbot-Lago crew. A group of the team's financiers had been in residence for some days already, and innumerable back-up and track staff came and went, occupying the hotel's minor suites. Every porter and concierge had been instructed to go out of their way to make the crew feel welcome, and no guest was awaited with more anticipation than a Frenchman named Charles Laurent.

Laurent had been expected in Monte Carlo the evening before, but he had failed to arrive – and the Talbot-Lago management were *incensed*. His back-up driver – an Englishman named Anstis – had already been in the city for days, claiming he needed to acquaint himself with the roads long before the grandstands went up and the diversions were posted. 'A man needs to *know* where he's driving,' he had loftily announced to the team's nervous financiers, 'to *feel* the living city, before the race begins' – but Charles didn't hold much truck with such old-fashioned ideas, and secretly he believed it was just Anstis's way of ingratiating himself with the Talbot-Lago financiers. Charles himself preferred to come to a race clean, not to wander around brooding for days before he hit the accelerator and took off around the circuit. He'd been racing in competition for years, taking whatever opportunities came his way, and he wasn't about to squander this shot at real glory by pandering to the team officials; Charles Laurent was a racing driver, not a politician.

Even so, as he followed the coast and rose into the mountainous roads of outer Monte Carlo, the Mediterranean mesmerising him on one side and the steep, rugged rock faces on the other, he wondered if he was arriving too late. The grandstands were going up all over the city, and it might have been useful to embed himself before expectation reached its peak. He'd attended the race before, of course – as all eager young Frenchmen did, lining up in the harbour to watch the motorcars rocketing past – and even spent one glorious summer, with an old flame, playing at being wealthy in the bars and clubs of Monte Carlo, but this time was different. This time, it *mattered*.

He hadn't expected an honour guard to be waiting at the Hotel de Lyon, but nor had he expected *this*. By the time he'd passed into the Principality, paused over the harbour where the yacht club was in full sail and gunned down the seafront with the wind in his rich, chestnut hair, he was ready for a glass of something sparkling and one of the cold showers that kept him feeling fresh. Yet, outside the Hotel de Lyon, the strangest, most motley collection of vehicles seemed to have assembled – and the strangest, most motley collection of people seemed to be tumbling out. A red London bus, a double-decker no less, was surrounded by a group of black taxicabs, and one blue-and-white

Volkswagen minibus out of which innumerable suitcases were being excavated by hotel porters. Two little terriers ran in yapping circles while a middle-aged man of dour expression – like a clown without make-up, Charles suddenly thought – was chasing them around.

In the midst of them all, a striking black-haired lady, perhaps a couple of years older than Charles's thirty-two, seemed to be in command. A group of younger girls were hanging on her every word, while the driver of the minibus dangled out of the window and took her instructions.

Charles was staring at her, bemused by the goings-on – and wondering if, perhaps, the Champagne in Cannes last night was still affecting his vision – when she caught his eye.

All it took was a second to be catapulted back in time.

All it took was a single *look*.

Reims, 1953. He'd been a young man back then, a driver with scarcely a race under his belt – and no home team to call his own – but, by God, he'd loved going to the races. Reims still bore the scars of war back then (perhaps it always would); everywhere you looked, you could see the reconstruction, or be reminded by town gossips of who had done what and where when the Nazis paraded through these streets – but, set against that had been the glory of the town's triangular circuit, that long right-hand hairpin that made the circuit so fast, so exhilarating, so spectacular. He could remember every twist and turn of that race, how the Ferrari and Maserati drivers had tussled for the top spot – but, more than any of that, he could remember the girl at the Hotel Lavannes.

He was staring at her now.

*Evie.*

Eve Forsyth.

He was sure of it.

What he wasn't sure of was whether she had recognised him.

Her eyes lingered on his, so perhaps it was so; or perhaps it was just some dim flicker of recognition from the deepest recesses of her brain. He ventured a smile, willing her to remember. Then he thought: fourteen years have passed since then. Half our lifetimes, between one moment and the next. He'd thought of her often in the days since then – but, of course, there'd been other lovers, and surely there'd been other lovers for her as well. Instinctively, he looked at her hand: no ring on her finger, just as there was none on his. But what did that really tell of a life's story?

Her eyes broke away, and suddenly Charles was wondering whether it was her at all.

Then he saw the way she dazzled a smile at her companions, and his certainty resurfaced. She'd always had a glorious smile, as if she was forever revelling in the absurdity of life. As Charles watched, she turned to one of the hoteliers and said, 'Are you *sure* dogs can't stay in the suites? I'm quite certain my father called ahead ...'

Charles could have stared at this show forever, but at that moment one of the hotel valets, dressed in resplendent white and gold, approached him and held out his palm for the keys of his forest-green Lago T26. It was his personal car, a 1950s vintage, and still ran as smoothly as it had in the days when it belonged to his brother, and he never liked handing over the keys – but he did so, all the same. 'Take care of her,' he told the valet. Then he turned back to Evie – but her attention had moved on, to a gangly young twenty-something who was trying to manoeuvre a wardrobe etched in mystical symbols out of the double-decker bus without anybody's help.

Charles grinned: the Forsyth Varieties. He'd never had the opportunity to see one of their shows, but suddenly the stories she'd told, in that long ago summer, were rushing back. Quite how they were as lauded as they were if they conducted all their business with the same level of pandemonium, he didn't know. Weren't theatre companies supposed to be *organised*?

He could only hope his own team had a better handle on affairs. He might have been here to win the upcoming Grand Prix – but, if there was to be any hope of success, the team would have to be working at their most streamlined and efficient. Formula One was a sport in which personal heroics did matter, but there could be no heroics without a team.

As he stepped into the Hotel de Lyon, he looked back once.

He'd had a feeling that destiny was calling this week. He'd thought it was to do with the Grand Prix, but now a new idea was stirring at the back of his head.

He was still thinking about it when, immediately inside the hotel, concierges and porters swarmed to his attention. Evidently, they'd been prepped for his arrival. What cases he had – and Charles Laurent always travelled light – were already being ferried from his car, and the only thing that stopped him from being swept directly across the reception hall was that old man with the dogs, who had now shepherded them inside, only to be met by a barricade of porters, and one particularly aggrieved manager.

'Sir, the Hotel is no place for dogs.'

'But where will they *go*?' the old man protested, in a forlorn Welsh lilt. 'They never leave my side, you see.' Then he crouched down, to let the terriers jump all over him. 'It's Tinky and Tiny. They're my little darlings. Where would you be without your Davith, eh?'

Charles was enjoying this spectacle so much that, at first, he did not hear what the desk clerk was saying to him. He had to be prompted twice, one of the concierges going so far as to touch his arm, before he heard, 'M. Laurent, your rooms are ready – but may we take you through to the Paradise Bar? Your presence is required.'

Charles lifted his sunglasses and ran his hand through his hair. 'By whom?' he asked.

'M. Allard, I believe – and his guest. Please, come this way.'

Allard was the one name Charles knew he couldn't ignore – so he allowed himself to be shepherded across the hotel reception and into the lavish environs of their Paradise Bar and lounge.

The lounge had been designed perfectly to capture the sunlight of a Monacoan afternoon. Open windows allowed the sea breeze to waft across the diners, and resplendent palms stood in every corner. Though it was only mid-afternoon, Champagne corks were already popping – and there, in the middle of the dining floor, sat the man named Raphael Allard.

Allard was senior to Charles by about twenty years, a dignified fifty-something with silver hair and the complexion of somebody who had spent all of his life in the sun. He was a broad man, given to a little fat from his overindulgences, and his piggy fingers were adorned with golden rings. He wore his white linen shirt with the sleeves rolled up, which was in direct contrast to the man at his side. This man had a staider air than Allard, with a hawkish nose and slicked-back grey hair. He was, perhaps, sixty years old – and evidently did not have Allard's vanity, for his complexion was pale, and he wore not a single adornment, not even cufflinks for his shirt. An Englishman, Charles decided, and a sombre one at that. This could only be one of the project's London-based financiers.

'Charles, I'm glad you could make it,' Raphael Allard began, rising as Charles approached. Then hands were shaken and Charles was invited to sit. 'The lobster here is divine. Waiter?'

A waiter appeared, as if manifesting directly from the air. 'A glass for our friend, please.'

'A white, sir?'

Charles nodded. Champagne could wait.

'Charles, allow me to introduce a gentleman of significant import to our prospects this week. You've heard the name Knight? Conrad Knight?'

Charles considered the greying individual. He was, he noted, the only man in the restaurant to be wearing a jacket and neck-tie. The man ought to have been sweltering – and, indeed, beads of sweat kept appearing at his brow and collar to be dabbed delicately away by a red spotted handkerchief.

'Mr Knight,' Charles said, with his most winsome smile. 'It's a pleasure.'

'The pleasure's mine, Laurent, but it ought to have been mine yesterday evening, when I was sitting in this very seat waiting for you. What the devil's been keeping you, man?'

Charles flashed a look between Allard and Knight. Raphael Allard was the head of operations for the new Talbot-Lago team – and, as such, he was Charles's direct superior – but Conrad Knight was the man who'd made it all possible, as head of the London consortium that were backing the bid. It had been sixteen years since Talbot-Lago had last fielded a team in Formula 1 – indeed, it had been eight years since Talbot-Lago last existed, for the French manufacturer had gone out of busi-ness in 1959, only months before its owner passed away. Since then, the Company had been one of those many dormant entities of the business world, a ghost company seeking out someone who might bring it back to life and resurrect its fortunes. Conrad Knight and his City consortium had been the resurrectionists who did just that. 'Talbot-Lago won in Monaco once before, and they can do it again,' the financiers had cheered when the contracts were signed and the Champagne corks were popping. Conrad Knight was determined to be the man who made that happen – but for him, the driving seat wasn't behind the wheel of the new Talbot-Lago Grand Sport; it was at a board table, in front of his ledgers.

'I'm here now, sir,' Charles began, grateful that the wine was at last being poured. 'That's what counts. We'll be race-ready in twenty-four hours – and that's still plenty of time for sightseeing before the pistols go.'

Conrad Knight's face had blanched at the very idea, but Raphael was quick to allay his fears. 'Charles is joking. You're joking – aren't you, Charles?'

Charles hesitated before he nodded; something about the way Conrad Knight's eyes were boring into him had caused him to falter.

'This isn't the moment for joking, M. Laurent. You'll be aware that you weren't *my* first choice to drive our car. I've had to put my trust in more learned minds – I'm a banker, M. Laurent, not a motorcar racer – but my vote was for an Englishman. In other circumstances I'd be keen to be vindicated – a man in my profession *hates* to be told "no" – but, for once, I'm praying I was wrong.' He made a steeple of his fingers and glared at Charles over the table. 'The consortium needs success. Nothing else will do. Much capital – not just financial, but reputational too – has been sunk into this endeavour. If our first foray is anything less than spectacular, there's every chance the whole edifice implodes. I'm a winner in my world. I need you to be a winner in this.'

'You leave the racing to me, sir. If that car's got what it takes, I'll take her there.'

'You can be damn certain the car's got it. No expense has been spared. But I don't just need a win. I need you to leave Ferrari in the dirt. I need you to leave BRM wanting. I need *showmanship* if this firm is to take flight. I don't care what Graham Hill's accomplished these last years. I want him forgotten – and *us* on top. Reputations are made in first outings, M. Laurent.'

'Talbot-Lago carries a little … baggage with it,' said Raphael, more diplomatically. 'Charles, all Mr Knight's trying to impress on you is how critical our first race is. We need to make a mark.' His eyes flashed past Charles, to the restaurant doors – and beyond, where that motley collection of performers were now assembling in the hotel foyer. Apparently, the dogs had been whisked off, because there was no longer any real commotion, but a gaggle of beautiful dancers were waiting at the check-in desks, and there was Evie, deep in conversation with a concierge. Charles couldn't tear his eyes away. The world was so vast, and yet there she was, a memory torn out of his mind, given shape and form.

'We need some of *that*,' Raphael went on. 'They're here, I'm told, to play a show for the Princess Grace. *Showmanship*, Charles! A sense of occasion! A big win! People like an under-dog story. They'll love the story of a team, and a classic car, that's come back from the dead. But nobody will marvel at a team back from the dead, if they come in last … We need *style*. Out of the coffin, and straight up onto the podium with a trophy held high!'

'Which is why,' Conrad Knight intervened, 'I'd hoped you might show a little more dedication to the cause – and arrive in a timely manner. What have you been doing, Charles? Sunning yourself along the Riviera? Drinking cocktails and playing cards? Yes, everyone loves a playboy – but I'm paying you to play for *me*.'

Charles fixed Conrad with a glare. He drained his glass, set it down, rose to his feet. 'Mr Knight, do you know what yesterday was?'

'It was the day you should have been here already, sir.'

'No, sir. Yesterday was the twelfth anniversary of what happened at Le Mans.'

Le Mans, 1955: a day etched forever in the memories of every motor racing fan. How many had perished that day, when the drivers of the Jaguar, Mercedes and Austin-Healey teams reached their deadly collision on the track? One was too many, but by the end of the day, almost a hundred were dead: drivers and spectators, lives torn to shreds, hopes and dreams ended forever, by the debris arcing out over the crowd.

'It's been twelve years since my brother died on that racetrack,' Charles seethed. 'Twelve years since Tobias was cut down forever. Twelve years since this...' and Charles lifted his shirt, to reveal the deep scar across his breast where a shard of debris had scored him that day, leaving him broken and bloody in the stands. 'So I went to toast my brother last night. I went to our favourite beach, and I raised a glass to his memory – and I called out to the universe, for him to watch over me when I race for you this week. And I'll be damned if I'll be criticised for it. I'll win this race, Mr Knight, but I won't do it for you or any of your board. I'm doing it for Tobias. I'm living his dream.'

Charles turned on his heel. Raphael pleaded with him to stay, his eyes flashing between Charles's retreating form and Conrad Knight's incandescent stare, but his words had no effect. After he was gone, he turned to Mr Knight and said, 'It's personal with Charles Laurent. He's a damn good driver, but he's different to the rest. It isn't just the glory he wants. It isn't just riches. It isn't just that he wants to go down in history – though there's all three of those things mixed up in it as well. It's his brother. The whole of his life has been about his brother.'

'I've never been spoken to like that by a subordinate,' Conrad said darkly. His eyes were still fixed on Charles. 'If you'll excuse me, Mr Allard.'

Charles had already left the restaurant by the time Conrad Knight got to his feet. He was already wading through the members of the Forsyth Varieties by the time Conrad Knight made the restaurant doors, then tried to follow him across the reception hall. 'Out of my way,' Conrad snarled at the dancing girls – and, though they parted to let him through, they stalled him long enough that Charles was able to stalk through the doors of the Hotel de Lyon, back into the open air of the Monte Carlo seafront.

'M. Laurent,' Conrad called, as he too emerged from the hotel doors. 'Let's speak. Let's make peace. Let's—'

At that precise moment, the terriers Tinky and Tiny appeared from behind that unsightly double-decker bus, cantered over to Conrad and started scrabbling on their hind-paws to get his attention.

'Sir!' Conrad called out, as Charles headed for the seafront, already sparking up the cigarillo in his hands. 'M. Laurent, let's speak about this.'

Behind Conrad Knight, the revolving doors of the Hotel de Lyon spun around. If only Charles had chosen that moment to look back, he would have seen Evie Forsyth – who he would forever think of as the Girl from Reims – stepping out into the sun. 'Please excuse me,' she said, clicking her fingers at Tinky and Tiny, 'they really are incorrigible.'

'I shall call the management,' Conrad seethed. 'This suit cost two hundred pounds.'

But the dogs seemed to be paying no attention, and it wasn't until Evie started calling out for the decrepit old Welshmen who'd been sobbing over them in the reception hall that they withdrew from Conrad Knight, letting him pass.

'I should have them put down,' he whispered darkly, as he

stalked past. Then, to himself as he marched after Charles, 'This is what happens when you let a *woman* run things.'

At the doors of the hotel, crouching down to mollify Tinky and Tiny, Evie looked up, as if unable to believe what she had heard. For a moment, she paused, head bobbing from side to side debating what she might do. Then, remembering a trick Davith had once taught the dogs, she put her fingers to her lips, whistled twice, gestured with two fingers and told them to run.

This the dogs did.

And Evie Forsyth watched with some modicum of delight as Tinky and Tiny scampered up to Conrad Knight, cocked their legs and proceeded to ruin a suit that, to Evie's mind, had cost the financier *far* too much money.

Conrad Knight flurried up in fury. He turned round to kick the dogs, but they were already scampering away. As for Evie, she simply shrugged – but it didn't escape her notice that the man the financier had been chasing was standing, perplexed, on the other side of the double-decker bus, having watched the whole scene unfold with mounting incredulity.

For the first time in all the years since Reims, across the wide open plaza in front of the Hotel de Lyon, Charles Laurent and Evie Forsyth looked each other directly in the eye.

Yes, thought Charles, *now* she remembered.

He could tell she was caught off-guard.

He could tell a host of half-forgotten memories were surging through her, just as they had for him.

But at least now he *knew*.

He'd left an impression on her that summer as well.

And, judging by the way Conrad Knight was hopping around, incandescent with fury – while Evie acted all innocent, apologising with a twinkle in her eye for the unruly behaviour of those dogs – Evie Forsyth had lost nothing of her forthrightness, confidence or unutterable charm in the years since.

So Charles lifted his hand and waved.

Such a little gesture – but right now, still furious at Conrad Knight, still sputtering with half-buried emotions at the sight of Evie in front of him – it was all the ordinarily calm, collected and suave Talbot-Lago driver could do.

# Chapter Four

Readying the Fort Antoine for a theatrical spectacular didn't take quite as long as readying Monte Carlo for a Grand Prix, but it certainly felt like it.

The Forsyth Varieties had played in a thousand different venues, but staging a show outside was always a particularly interesting technical challenge. The following morning, Ed assembled his players and crew outside the Hotel de Lyon and, pulling a storage crate out of the blue-and-white Volkswagen, levered himself on top of it as a makeshift stage. 'The Fort Antoine isn't far. We'll move in procession – show this city a little bit of the carnival that's coming. The cars are already down there.' The company's backstage crew, the beating heart of the Varieties, were led by Hugo – a former ventriloquist who, though he no longer graced the stage, had remained with the Company throughout. 'You'll see our faithful double-decker is nowhere in sight either. I've had to come to an accommodation with hotel management – and Davith has agreed that he'll be sleeping on site with Tinky and Tiny, to avoid any further complications.'

In the crowd, Evie shrugged. Davith was used to living a little wild – before he joined the Company, he'd travelled by foot and horse-cart all over Wales, taking his various dogs to the most remote of towns to perform for the price of a fish supper – and, besides, the double-decker was more comfortable than many of the lodgings they'd stayed in. It didn't, of course, compare to the Hotel de Lyon – but if there was one person who wouldn't mind slumming it, it was Davith.

'This morning we're focused on lighting rigs and blocking. We're running the same show we've been doing all summer – so there won't be any great surprises. Except perhaps…' Ed's eyes landed on Cal and Meredith standing in the crowd, little Sam sandwiched between them. He gave a great wink, and it was all the little boy needed for a thrill to course up and down his body. 'But we haven't much time, and the venue's unusual. We're relying on the heavens,' he looked above, 'and this one's important. Let's make it a good one. In a week we'll be under English skies again. But we're all going to *remember* this.' In days of old, he'd have leapt off the crate and started the procession himself. But at this age, he had to lever himself down. Then he brandished his walking cane, directing them off along the seafront. *'Allez!'* he declared.

It was Evie, he noticed, who sprang up to lead them. She'd seemed distracted at dinner last night – as if she was lost in some private thoughts of her own. Perhaps it was memories of the last time they'd come to Monaco that were preoccupying her. She'd seemed curiously faraway – and Evie was not, ordinarily, a daydreaming sort of girl. Even so, as soon as Ed gave his command, the dancing girls rallied to her, eager for the promenade. Ed himself waited until the last of the Company were leaving – the young magician, Jim Livesey, bringing up the rear – before he joined the procession.

Only one other person had stayed behind. Cal, urging Meredith and Sam off along the seafront, joined his father at the hotel rail and said, 'I might need to sit this morning out. I'm going back to the set, Dad. I've been turning it over all night – and … I'm going to take the commission. Work with this young actor while I can. It seems like an opportunity that ought to be seized, you know?'

Ed had been expecting as much, though he tried not to show it. Late last night, with the Princess Grace's words circling in his head, he'd lain awake and spoken to Bella's ghost – she lay beside him always; some nights, he could feel her hand in his own – and tried to picture the show they were about to perform. Cal would be at the heart of things, as he always was: his number, 'Runaway Lovers' – the one that had become so synonymous with the Company after the Royal Variety performance in '62 – and all the other songs built around it. For a time, its success had satisfied Cal. But the thing about ambition, real ambition, was that it was *relentless*. Once you scaled one mountain, you had to scale another. Once you'd crossed one ocean, you needed to circumnavigate the globe. Cal had made the Company his home again, but ambition needled at him.

'I'll be back by the afternoon, Dad. I just need to get a handle on things. This young star they've got, Benedict Frey – his nose has been put of joint by them hiring me. I want to settle things. I want to make it work.' Cal grinned – for a little bit of flattery never hurt, even with someone as experienced and all-knowing as his father. 'I learnt that from you, you know. How to handle a personality…'

Ed rolled his eyes. '*I* learnt it from *you*, you must mean. I never had to handle a personality like yours, Cal – not until …' And he opened his arms, as if presenting Cal to an audience. 'Be back by mid-afternoon, won't you, son? We can slot this show together easily enough, but I want it to *dazzle* – and we'll need to run it through to make sure it does.' He paused. 'Your mother would have loved to come back to this place. She would have loved to have seen Grace where she is today – to have met her children ... If she'd lived, I imagine Monaco might have been a second home for the Forsyth Varieties. Think how different things might have been.'

Cal could always tell when his father's wistfulness was tipping over into melancholy. It had taken some time to understand the signs – and Evie had always been better at reading their father than Cal – but he saw it now, deepening the creases of the old man's face. 'I'll be there,' he promised, with a hand on his father's arm, 'for you, and for Mum – and for ... well, for *all* of us, Dad. I'm not going anywhere.'

But by the look of ambition and determination on Cal's face as he set off into the city, Ed wasn't so sure.

The Forsyth Varieties were wending their way slowly along the seafront, taking in the spectacle of all the city's thousand yachts fanning out across the bay's crystalline waters, so it was possible for Ed to catch up. Jim Livesey was straggling behind – 'It'll be hard to make magic out of thin air, without any tricks of the stage, Mr Forsyth, but I'll give it my best!' – and, just ahead of him, Sam sat high on Meredith's shoulders, gazing in wonder out over the ocean.

Ed had to compel his body to quicken so that he could catch them, for an idea had just occurred to him. It wasn't fair, he knew, to dictate to Cal; he'd tried that when Cal was a much younger man, and it only encouraged rebellion. Cal had Bella's rebellious blood. But he had her thirst for family as well. He could have made his way without the Company, Ed felt certain of it, but he could never have made his way without Meredith and Sam.

'I think it's time, Merry,' he said as he drew alongside them.

Together, they stopped at one of the railings to gaze across the water, allowing Jim Livesey to overtake. Up ahead, the dancing girls were turning cartwheels on the promenade – well, *that* ought to get some local tongues wagging – and, blushing, Jim averted his eyes. He'd proven an adept apprentice magician, but sometimes, *just sometimes*, Ed wished he'd grow as much in confidence off the stage as well. He wasn't much to look at, but talent and charm could carry a man much further than good looks – and any one of those girls might have been a future bride.

Inwardly, he grinned. That was how his mind worked. Succession planning – that was what Princess Grace had called it. Courtly politics. *Legacy*. You had to plant the seeds, even if you wouldn't live to see them flourish. That was how you safeguarded the future.

And it was with that in mind that he said, 'Sam's young. As a matter of fact, he'll be the youngest ever to make their debut with the Forsyth Varieties. But sometimes you just *feel* like the time is right. Sometimes, it isn't even you making the decision. It's something else. Something up *there*,' and he pointed to the heavens.

Sam's eyes were goggling, for he'd been begging to join his father on stage since he'd first learnt to talk, but Meredith was not so easily won over. 'You don't fool me, Ed,' she said, not unkindly. Ed liked Meredith for this: she was a straight talker, and never said what she didn't mean. 'You're worried Cal's about to stray again. You're worried he's got his eye on a bigger prize.'

'Oh, I *know* he does,' Ed laughed. 'I'm just wondering how much two worlds can exist together. Can Cal have it all?'

'And you want to remind him what the Company is all about. You want to remind him what it could be, for the future – for Sam, and ...' Meredith cupped her hand around her belly. '...whatever comes next.'

Ed nodded. 'Seeing Sam take the applause might do it for him – but it's about what you want too, Meredith.'

Meredith nodded. She hadn't expected this life – but then, how could you ever expect a man like Cal Forsyth? She'd been with him eight of the best years of her life, and she still didn't know what to expect when she woke up each morning. 'I say we do it for Sam,' she declared, 'and what Cal makes of it is just what Cal makes of it.' Then she softened her voice and said, 'I don't think he's straying too far, for what it's worth. But Cal ... he can be like a big kid. He wants to saddle up and ride, and push at what he can do – but he still needs a home to come back to.'

Ed nodded. 'Then it's settled. What do you think, little man?'

Still perched on Meredith's shoulders, Sam could hardly contain his excitement. 'Is it real this time?' he asked.

'Oh, it's real,' Ed replied.

And Sam flung his arms open wide, as if to take hold of the whole world. 'I'm going to be a star!'

In the same moment that the Forsyth Varieties weaved their way round the harbour and approached the Fort Antoine, Cal was cruising out of the city limits, back over the border into France. Here, at a secluded little cove just beyond the edge of the Monacoan authorities, the second unit of Parker & Parr's *Monte Carlo by Moonlight* had been set up since dawn, capturing some of the movie's quieter, more reflective moments.

He arrived just as one scene – Benedict and his band staring out at the retreating tide and wondering if they'd ever make it back home – was coming to an end. 'By this point, they've had to forgo any luxuries,' Albert Hines explained, as Cal was led onto the set. 'They're camping wild on the beach – not that the *gendarmes* like it – and busking by day ... their getting chased off every patch they start working. It's the quiet of the storm, before their more audacious plans. We're shooting out of sequence, of course – this is actually the morning of the Casino brawl ...'

Cal gazed over the set. Some of the shots had been staged in front of the glittering seascape itself, but the cave where the characters were camping was a temporary construction of imported rocks, wood panelling and craftsmanship; even now, set dressers were arranging mosses and seaweed to better aid the scene. Cast members and crew were waiting around – movie sets seemed to contain an inordinate amount of waiting around – but Benedict himself was sitting, waiting for Cal by the cameras, his guitar slung over his shoulder.

'Remember,' Albert said as Cal approached, 'treat him as an equal – but remember it's just another trick of the silver screen. I need those songs glowing, and the studio doesn't care if they've got Benedict's fingerprints on them at all.' Then he lowered his voice and winked, 'Only *stars* think they've made it alone, Mr Forsyth!'

At least, this time, Benedict was prepared for his coming. Cal had to wait just a few moments, while the wardrobe artist Gideon fussed with his costume, before Benedict was ready. 'At least it's something to do in the downtime,' Benedict said, leading Cal to one of the trailers parked up above the beach. 'You wouldn't believe how little a star actually has to do on a set. You haven't been in a picture before, have you, Mr Forsyth?'

There was a breeziness to Benedict's tone, but Cal detected a touch of superiority now – and it flashed in his eyes as well: the look of a man putting another man in his place. Cal just remembered what Albert had said and followed Benedict into the trailer. Inside, as well as a dressing table and wardrobe racks, several guitars were held in brackets against the trailer walls. 'Choose your weapon,' Benedict grinned – but again, there was a whisper of menace underneath the words, and Cal reminded himself to tread lightly.

'What we really need is a piano,' he grinned. 'I find composing at a piano much more satisfying somehow – don't you? There's a whole orchestra in that instrument.'

Benedict swung the guitar off his back and strummed a simple C major. 'Oh, I think we're past orchestras. I would have thought, by the time 1970 comes around, the only orchestras left will be for the old fuddy-duddies in London. Who needs the Philharmonic when you've got the Stones?' And he brushed back his hair, preening in the trailer mirror as if to suggest that he, himself, had been sharing a stage with Mick Jagger. 'This picture isn't about orchestras. Matter of fact, there isn't a piano in sight. It's guitars and drums, Mr Forsyth. It's rock and roll. Six strings and a pounding beat.'

For the first time, Cal started bristling. He didn't like being lectured, and especially by a boy whose musical knowledge seemed to stretch back to Chuck Berry and not before. What a lot of these young performers lacked was *heritage* – and that was one of the many good things Cal got from being part of the Forsyth Varieties. Benedict played rock and roll – and that was great – but rock and roll didn't start with Little Richard. Bill Haley would never have found his Comets if there hadn't been a generation playing the blues, or even big band swing, before that. Every new kind of music was built on the foundations of the last, like a city that kept being burnt down, then built back up again. A great songwriter would have known and respected that.

'Well, look,' Cal ventured, 'these are your songs – we're just getting the best out of them. Whether that's guitars and drums, or pianos and orchestras, it's all the same to me. I don't care if it's on a *flute*, as long as it's *great*.' He paused. 'So … let's hear them.'

Benedict shrugged and started picking at the guitar strings, sliding his fingers up and down the frets. 'What do you wanna hear?'

There was a set-list pinned to the wall, beside one of the guitars. Eight songs: the soundtrack to *Monte Carlo by Moonlight*. Benedict perused it now, drawing Cal near.

1. 'Open Sea'
2. 'Back to Mine'
3. 'Three Thousand Miles (And I Love You)'
4. 'Digby's Serenade'
5. 'Only For You'
6. 'Can I Put You On?'
7. 'Jam and Bread'
8. 'Meet Me in Monte Carlo (Or Don't Meet Me at All)'

It would be wrong to say that Cal was particularly inspired by looking at Benedict's song titles, but it would be equally wrong to say that he was despondent. By his reckoning (and he'd battled with enough music publishers to be fairly sure of his grounding), no song called 'Jam and Bread' was ever going to the top of the charts – and, despite the Beatles' penchant for walruses, bluejays and yellow submarines, neither was any serenade devoted to a man called 'Digby'. Instead, his eye was drawn to the closing track, 'Meet Me in Monte Carlo'. Any publisher worth his salt (and plenty that weren't) would recommend getting rid of the parentheses, but that could wait for now. This looked like the sort of number that the movie might be remembered by, so he asked Benedict to sing it.

There was just the merest flicker of hesitation on Benedict's part, before he remembered that he was supposed to be the star. Then, steeling himself for whatever comments Cal might make – and trying not to let his resentment blossom too obviously – he began:

*'Six weeks is a long time coming*
*Six weeks we've been apart*
*I've been breaking bones and records*
*But I ain't been breaking hearts*
*So find me on the beaches*
*Find me at the cove*
*Find me, find me, find me,*
*In Monte Ca-ar-lo!'*

There was more of this – much more, in fact, because the song had been written to run over a full six minutes of credits – and it wasn't *bad*. It had a good hook – and, as Benedict had intimated, a driving rhythm – and there was no doubt the boy could sing. There was, Cal decided, a sense that his throaty growl was a put-on – he looked too cherubic, too baby-faced, to pass as a grizzled rock-and-roll star – but that didn't matter. In the context of the movie, it might even help.

But, although Cal could see all that was good about the song, he could clearly see what Albert Hines and the financiers at Parker & Parr had meant when they said it just *lacked* a little something. Nothing wrong with it, but nothing *memorable* either – and wasn't that the same critique that could be made of ten thousand other songs? If songwriters knew how to turn each and every number into a standard for the ages, they would do it every time – but nobody had yet worked out that particular alchemy, so onward everyone soldiered.

'Let's try it a little faster,' said Cal. 'Nothing transformative, but let's ratchet it up. And ... well, let's see if we can find a different way into that chorus. If you've got to build a song over six minutes, it gets repetitive. All those rock and rollers knew it. They were writing songs barely two-and-a-half minutes long: just balls of fire that burnt bright and burnt out. Now, it's not impossible to write a standard that goes on and on. Hell, maybe that's why I'm here. "Runaway Lovers" was as long as this, and look what that did for me. But ...' Cal picked one of the guitars from the wall, taking care to choose one that Benedict might think inferior to his. Then he started strumming. His voice rose up: *'Six weeks is a long time coming ...'*

For some time, Cal and Benedict batted the song back and forth. It worked better faster, and it worked better shorter – but the key to the whole thing would be finding a way to make sure it kept an audience captured for the full six minutes that the credits ran. That meant the song had to change in some fundamental way. No doubt Benedict would hate to hear it, but it would have to work through several different movements – just like one of the orchestrations of old.

'This is the bit,' said Cal suddenly. 'This moment right *here*. Right now, we're just looping back to the beginning: new words, but same old melody. What we need is a change. Change, Benedict, is fundamental to a good song. It's like a feint. You're leading them one way, but then you pull them another – and God, the elation of it!'

So Cal started singing. He changed the key. He changed the words, latching on to whatever came to his mind. He led the song up and up again – and then, when he was finished and he opened his eyes, he realised that Benedict was staring blankly at him with a look of barely concealed contempt.

He strummed his last chord.

There was silence in the trailer.

'I think you're meant to get the best out of my songs, Mr Forsyth – not just write your own.'

Inwardly, Cal groaned. He ought to have kept his eyes open when he sang, and if he'd been on stage he'd have done just that – but there was something about composing that always compelled him to close his eyes and get lost in the moment. If only he'd had his eyes open, he might have seen how scarlet Benedict was turning and stopped right there. 'But don't you see,' he began, scrabbling to out things right, 'that *is* your song. That's what your song can be, if it's really given wings. And Benedict, with your voice – with that *growl*...'

Benedict just turned away. 'Let's pick this up later, Mr Forsyth. I've got scenes to shoot this afternoon, and it's just about time for lunch.'

For some time after Benedict had left, Cal just sat there with the guitar in his hands. The truth was, he'd really started to *feel* that song as he was singing. There was something in it, some scent he had started to follow – and perhaps, if he followed it far enough, it might lead him to something *great*. But he'd have to contend with Benedict first. And he'd have to do this eight times over, for all of these songs pinned up on the wall. Quite what he was going to do with 'Jam and Bread' he didn't know; it sounded like a placeholder lyric – he only hoped it had a killer melody.

He was still turning the song over in his mind when there came a knock at the trailer door, and a young lady of perhaps seventeen years old, with hair as black and wild as Cal's and eyes as glittering blue as the ocean outside, stuck her head round the door.

'Oh, I'm sorry,' she ventured, 'I was looking for—'

'Benedict bolted,' said Cal, with a weary sigh, 'but he promised he'd be back. I think he went down to the cafeteria truck. Scenes to shoot, stomach to fill – that sort of thing.'

The girl hardly looked surprised; it seemed to Cal that Benedict Frey (or was it just actors more generally?) could never be trusted to be where they were told. She glanced around the trailer for a moment, then shrugged and turned away. She was about to depart when she said, 'You know, the cafeteria's closing up soon. If you want something to eat, now's your moment.'

Cal looked at the guitar. He coaxed a few more chords out of it and let that lyric eddy in the air. The lyric too – it was fine, but it wasn't exceptional. It would hurt Benedict to hack away at something that was perfectly good just because it wasn't good *enough*, but it would have to be done.

Just one step at a time …

The girl was almost gone, but Cal slid the guitar back onto its brackets and said, 'You know, a break *would* be good.'

Outside, the sun was directly overhead – and the wave of heat that crashed over Cal was almost overwhelming. For the first time since the Hotel de Lyon, his thoughts flashed to the Company at the Fort Antoine, who'd been working hard in the sun's fierce glare all morning long in preparation for the show. Thoughts of them only redoubled his determination to get something of value out of the day. A little sustenance, a little more work on the songs and he'd head to the Fort Antoine himself. He just needed a *little* breakthrough – no matter how small – with Benedict first.

The girl introduced herself as Brielle. 'I'm not a professional filmmaker, as you might be able to tell!' she laughed, as she led Cal through the cameras, across the set and further along the beach to an area where the cast and crew were all gathered at trestle tables outside a cafeteria truck serving griddled fish, tomatoes, aubergines and more. Her accent, though tinged with French, might have passed for an upper-crust English if they'd met on the streets of London. 'I'm from up in the Principality. It's all I've ever known. Dad works at the Casino there, and I've been waiting tables up and down the port – but then this studio comes along, and they're looking for locals to run errands. Well, sign me up, I said – and here I am! It beats pouring wine.'

It was only when they arrived at the cafeteria truck that Cal realised how famished he was. He and Brielle loaded up plates, then found a spot at one of the trestle tables, where two of the set carpenters were pontificating fiercely in French about their handiwork. As for Benedict, he already seemed to be finished eating – and was prowling up and down the sand with the wardrobe assistant Gideon traipsing on his heels. 'Benedict seems to have a fan club,' Cal commented, before he tucked in.

Brielle just smiled and looked away. Perhaps, thought Cal, she was part of his fan club too – though, given the wearied look she had on entering his trailer and finding him absent, he somehow doubted it. Meanwhile, out on the sand, Benedict was kicking at stones – and Gideon seemed, very much, to be trying to calm him down.

'I'd have thought he had actors to get together with, not wardrobe assistants.' Cal dropped his voice. 'Isn't he a little, you know, *full of himself*, to be consorting with lowly assistants? I thought Benedict Frey was the star around here.'

There was something Brielle didn't seem to want to say. 'It's like my dad says about the gamblers at the Casino. Sometimes you get a player who struts in like he's already won ten thousand francs. He walks with his head held high and he just *exudes* confidence. He acts like the world owes him his victory – and, because he's acting like it, somehow he gets it.' She paused. 'That's like Benedict. That's like all of these actors. They get dressed up like stars, they start to think that they are stars – and, because *they* think it, everybody else thinks it too.'

For a seventeen-year-old girl without any history in show business, Brielle seemed pretty astute. The logic wasn't too far away from the sort of wisdom they passed down in the Company. 'Walk out there like you've walked out there a thousand times before,' Ed would counsel new players, 'even if it's your very first time. You can't expect an audience to believe in what they can't see – so you damn well make sure they see it.'

'That's why all of *this* ...' said Cal, turning in his seat to take in all the industry of the set. '...Ninety minutes on the screen, but nine months in the making. That's why they ...' *Hired me.* He had to finish the sentence in his head, because the enormity of it had only just dawned on him. All of this enterprise, with such ambition and attention shown to every little detail – they hadn't just hired him because of 'Runaway Lovers' and a little bit of kudos; they'd hired him because they truly believed his could be the special ingredient that turned Benedict into a star.

He smiled at Brielle one last time, then got to his feet. 'I've got a lot of work to do.'

Benedict was still idling on the sands with the wardrobe assistant, but Cal broke into a run and made it back to the trailer in a trice. There had to be some way to marshall all these songs and turn them into something greater. He was certain there were seeds; it might take a little brutality, but if Cal could strip them back, rebuild them, take them where they needed to go – mightn't this, somehow, become a soundtrack for the ages?

He picked up the guitar, closed his eyes and started to play.

Who knows how much time passes when an artist is in the middle of some startling creation? Cal certainly didn't know how much time was flickering by. To his mind, this was the greatest sensation in songwriting – those lost hours, when it was just you and the melody, just you and the rhythm, floating together, trying to find form, and the rest of the world just fading into the distance. One hour passed, then two, just Cal, the guitar and some paper to scribble on. None of it was perfect yet, but every iteration was an iteration closer to the finished product. Benedict had an instinct for a song, that much was true, but he hadn't got the chops to harness those instincts. Well, Cal had chops. He'd been writing professionally for years, honing the craft. And now, with just a little bit of inspiration, these songs could be fantastic.

It was a different feeling, working from foundations somebody else had lain. He hadn't expected to find it inspiring, yet that was how it felt as he led one song in a completely different direction, as he sought out what was special in the raw clay Benedict had provided for him to sculpt.

'Meet me in Monte Carlo,' he sang, 'Monaco by night . . . I'll see you by the seafront, in that blue, celestial light . . .' Too flowery, perhaps? Too old? Or . . . perhaps to be epic, to be memorable, you needed just a little ostentation.

Cal opened his eyes.

The trailer door had opened – and there, rather abashed, stood Brielle. It dawned on him, suddenly, that she'd been standing there for some minutes already, just listening to him sing.

'I'm sorry, Mr Forsyth. He's needed on set, but . . .' She faltered. 'Have you *seen* him? We all thought he was in here, working on the songs.'

Cal flashed a look around. A clock on the trailer wall told him that he'd had his head in the songs for two and a half hours, with neither hide nor hair of Benedict Frey.

'We thought he was . . .' Brielle flashed another look around. 'Sorry, Mr Forsyth. I didn't mean to interrupt, Mr Forsyth.'

After Brielle had hurried off, Cal wondered if his silence had intimidated her – perhaps she'd thought he was angry at the interruption? The truth was, he was still a little disorientated from spending so long lost inside the songs. That was something only another songwriter would understand. He tried to dive back into them now, but the spell had been broken – and though he tried, a little pigheadedly, to force his way back in, the moment and the muse had clearly left him.

He was still trying when the trailer door opened again – and, fully expecting this to be Benedict Frey at last, he turned to see the director Albert Hines standing there with his hands on his hips like a disappointed schoolmaster. Brielle was standing nervously just outside.

'I'm afraid I haven't seen him, Mr Hines – not since just before lunch. But, listen, these songs…'

'I know you haven't seen him, Mr Forsyth.' There was a deep, entrenched exasperation in Hines's voice – but it wasn't directed at Cal. 'Our star seems to have been affronted at your work this morning, and he's indulged himself at Chez Mimi, just up the coast.'

Cal's heart sank. 'He didn't seem to be struggling. I mean, I knew he didn't want me here, but…'

Hines just waved his hand. 'I don't care about the source of the problem. I care about the solution. I've a scene that needs blocking. We're fixing for cameras and lights. This one's important – the band play a midnight concert on the sands, and the town goes wild. It's one of the big set-pieces – set to one of these songs, Mr Forsyth, if we ever get them in good order.' Hines had marched into the room and picked up the paper, now decorated with Cal's copious scrawl, on which the soundtrack's titles were listed. 'Ben's going to have to be sobered up. I'll have the sound crew dunk him in the ocean if I need to. But, in the meantime, I need that band on stage so we can fix the camera, the lights, and get the extras drilled.'

At this point, Hines simply turned away and started marching back to his players, leaving Cal beached in the trailer with his guitar. He was still wondering what on earth had just happened – and if every film set was as much of a madhouse as this one seemed to be – when he caught Brielle's eye. She was smiling to herself, shaking her head as if he ought to have understood.

'What?' he asked. 'What?'

'He wants you on set, Mr Forsyth.'

'Me?' Cal asked. 'On set?'

'It's a technical run, and for the extras. As long as somebody's in place, keeping the beats, so the cameras can be set and the extras learn what they're doing … well, it's better if it's Benedict, but you'll do just as well.'

Cal wasn't entirely certain this was a good idea, but his worries melted away as Brielle led him to the set. A half-mile down the beach from where they'd been shooting the cave scenes, a mock-up of a little beachside restaurant had been built by the crew, open to the sea at one side and to platforms where cameras and lighting rigs could be erected on the other. When Cal appraised it from one angle, it looked like any other beachside restaurant along the Riviera; but from every other, it was just a few walls and props cobbled together. The magic of making movies, he supposed. The problem was, in songwriting it just wasn't possible to hoodwink an audience – the only illusion you could conjure up had to come from melody and lyrics, the ineffable *feeling* of a song.

A horde of extras – thirty, forty, perhaps even fifty – had been assembled on the sands and were now milling around, eagerly awaiting their moment to shine. The other principal actors were on the set itself, standing on a little stage with their instruments. When they saw Cal approaching, Brielle leading him through the cameras, they shared a pointed look – but whether this was disappointment in Benedict, or irritation at Cal, he did not know. Nor did he get the chance to ask – for, almost immediately, Mr Hines was rallying everyone together, commanding the other actors into their places, having the extras shepherded onto the sands in front of the bar and issuing orders to each of his cameramen.

Then, at last, he fixed upon Cal. 'Up on stage please, Mr Forsyth – yes, right there, between bass and rhythm. I just need somebody in place while we fix these angles. After that, it's a dry run for the extras.'

As Cal picked his way to the makeshift stage, the actors at least acknowledged him. Perhaps, he began to wonder, they were used to having to 'make do'; perhaps it wasn't so unusual for Benedict to absent himself for hours at a time. Besides, all he had to do was stand here. Any fool could have done that, couldn't they? It might easily have been one of the extras. It might have been Brielle. Somebody roughly the same size and shape as Benedict – so why did it have to be him?

'Right, let's try the first number,' Mr Hines declared, after the cameras were set and the extras assembled.

Cal's eyes flashed around. The other actors only seemed to shrug at him. 'It's for the extras,' the bass guitarist, whose straw-coloured hair was tied back in a red spotted bandana, said. 'Get them in the mood. We're not shooting this scene for real until the sun starts dipping.'

'Benedict ought to be sober by then,' said the stout fellow behind the drums.

'Listen up, ladies and gentlemen,' Albert Hines began, addressing the crowd, 'to begin with these are just the long shots. Some music and dancing – scene setters, before the drama begins. Now, I want you worked up – I want you firing and wild, as if you've been out here for hours already. We'll do a couple of songs to get the juices flowing, and then we'll start shooting.' Hines flashed a look around. 'Ready, boys?'

Cal flashed his own look around. The other actors didn't seem to have blanched at all – they were just readying themselves to play – but something had upended Cal; he felt as if he was floating on a tide which had just, quite unexpectedly, carried him away. 'Mr Hines,' he called out from the edge of the stage, 'what about Benedict?'

Hines seemed to purple with irritation at the mere mention of the actor's name. 'These are for the crowd shots, Mr Forsyth. We'll feed in the song later – once you've scrubbed it into shape. And nobody on Mr Forsyth's face…' he said, nodding stoutly at each of the cameraman. 'Let's get some shots of his hands,' he added, 'but keep clear of his face. We can splice it with Ben when he's seen fit to join us.'

There was such a dark undercurrent in Mr Hines's last words that Cal questioned it no further. Even so, as he waited for the cry of 'ACTION!', he couldn't help wondering how he had ended up standing here, right here, in front of cameras ready to roll. One hour ago, he'd been nothing but the songwriter; half an hour ago, just a double standing in Benedict's place for lights and cameras; now, his fingers were about to strike the first chord of a song he barely knew. '"Meet me in Monte Carlo", right?' he whispered.

The other players nodded. 'It's a pretty simple turnaround,' said the rhythm guitarist. 'They'll be dubbing it anyway. So let's just make sure they dance.'

Cal figured he could do that.

He'd done it a thousand times before.

'ACTION!' bellowed Albert Hines.

So Cal struck the first chord.

He faltered in the first verse. He hadn't quite imagined it with a full band, and the drummer was pushing the song forward at a pace much more lively than Cal had reckoned – but, by the time the second verse came around, he was feeling much more in tune with the other musicians, and even starting to feel the *groove*. Played live, and with an audience reacting as well as they did (Cal had to remind himself they were actors, but they really did seem to be swept along in the music), it was a much more enjoyable number than it had been in the trailer.

Even so, by the time Hines had called 'CUT!', reset every-thing, then had them playing all over again, it was starting to feel familiar. Some of the best songs did – that familiarity became like a comfort blanket that people loved to throw over themselves – but it was never a good sign when a song became stale on the second or third listen. By the fourth time round, Cal thought he'd gelled with the band – but he also knew that his heart was leaving the song, and soon he got to thinking he could see it in the dancers below.

What they needed was something new – a fire lit beneath them, to make sure this dance *flew*.

Cal couldn't help it. The moment he had the idea, his fingers started working of their own volition. By God, he'd have given anything to be in front of a piano right now. With a piano he could have turned this into a symphony – but the guitar would have to do. All he had to do was get lost in the song, like he'd been doing in the trailer. To cast himself into it and let it take him wherever it soared. The rest of the band would keep up – they were functional musicians at best, but there wouldn't be a lot of complexity, not in what they had to do. No, this was a *singer's* song – and Cal led the way.

He closed his eyes.

Eight bars later, he opened them again.

Across the sands, the extras danced and twirled. Lovers took each other in their arms and spun around. A girl sailed up into the air, was caught again by her partner, then found herself airborne again. He could see them moving like waves crashing against a shore. He could see real delight, not the fake delight of actors, colouring their faces. The late afternoon sun was pouring over them – but it might have been midnight in any nightclub in London, for the crowd couldn't keep themselves from the dance.

'CUT!'

Cal carried on playing, even while the rest of the band petered out. Some bars later, when he realised the momentum was gone, he looked around.

But it was not Mr Hines who had screamed out 'CUT!' The whole of the beach was still now, save for Mr Hines himself – who simply stood there, resolutely beating his fist against his palm – but there, in the midst of them all, stood Benedict Frey. The ghostly pallor of his face might have been to do with the drink he'd been imbibing, or it might have been to do with his horror at the scene he'd just seen unfold – because, even now, he was rising onto the tips of his toes, fists clenched at his side, as if trying to repress some terrible feeling.

Cal was suddenly aware that he was standing centre stage.

He was suddenly aware there was a spotlight on him as well.

That was when Benedict Frey started to scream.

# Chapter Five

'Help with the songs?' Benedict seethed. 'Get the best out of them? Mr Hines, you must take me for a fool. You have him right there, up on stage. Writer, is it? Hired help, is it? Well, what kind of hired help is up there, playing my songs, with the cameras on him? Exactly what game are you trying to play?'

The crowd – who, moments before, had been lost in Cal's tempestuous music – parted as Benedict scythed through. If he'd been drunk a little earlier, right now he seemed as surefooted and sober as a priest – though perhaps that was just the fury that was driving him. He planted himself in front of the extras, separated from the stage by two of the camera operatives – and by Mr Hines, who marched into view through the restaurant tables.

'Benny,' the director said, drolly, 'it's nice of you to join us.' Then, with a look up at the stage, he said, 'Let's reset for Benedict. Cal, thanks for the service. We'll take it from the top – and this time,' he added, with looks at the cameras, 'we can get shots of his face, nice and clear and … in close-up.' Then he paused before going on, 'Make-up, can we get onto Ben? And where's wardrobe …'

Gideon had appeared in the crowd as well, though he lingered at a distance. It seemed to Cal that he had the vague, bloodshot eyes of an afternoon drinker as well – but, quite clearly, he was worse at keeping it hidden than Benedict.

'Hang on a minute, Mr Hines – you can't expect me to just *pretend*? Just get up there and carry on, as if this hasn't even happened? What in God's name is that … that *hack* doing up there? You told me he was here to arrange my songs. You told me the studio dropped him on us to give us a fresh lick of paint. Well, if that's so, what in hell is he doing up there, with *my* band?'

The eyes of the cast kept flashing between Benedict and Cal. The sun burnt, merciless, overhead.

Not for the first time, Cal tried to bite his tongue. He could feel every muscle in his body tightening – but he took a series of deep breaths, trying to swallow the desire to bite back. There were very few people in the world who would claim Cal Forsyth was patient – but he was more patient than he'd been as a younger man, and proud of it. That was what becoming a father, and returning to the Forsyth Varieties, had done for him. Even so, he had to keep looking away. Brielle was on the edge of the set, and only by catching her eye could he contain the compulsion to snap at Benedict. She just shook her head and shrugged, as if to say: that's just Benedict; we all know what Benedict's like.

'It's bad enough you send this also-ran to touch my songs – but look at him, Mr Hines! You think he could pass for me? Good God, how old is he?' Then he turned to Cal. 'You had your chance, Forsyth, and you blew it. You don't get to be a star at forty-eight years old, or whatever you are. You missed the boat. This is my chance. Hell, get off the stage! And hand me that guitar. I'm about to show you what talent actually looks like.' Benedict strode forward, past the line of cameras, and up onto stage. Even before Cal could take the guitar strap off his shoulder, he was barrelling him out of the way to stand in front of the microphone. 'You can forget all that footage, boys,' he said to the cameramen. 'And you lot? You haven't seen anything yet,' he said to the crowd – who, after a stilted silence, responded in an uncertain, half-hearted cheer.

As Cal pressed the guitar into Benedict's hands, his eyes strayed to Albert Hines, standing below. The director's face was set in the most rigid of scowls, but he too seemed to be containing his fury. Cal wondered if there was anything a man like Benedict could do to invite a scolding from this movie's producers? If this was the Varieties, there was no doubt about it: talent or no talent, Cal's father would have fired him on the spot. But then, a company like the Forsyths had to endure, season by season, year after year; all Albert Hines had to do was get to the end of the shoot, get the best out of Benedict and then pray their paths never crossed again.

Ego upended a theatre company.

But perhaps ego made movies the monoliths that they were.

Cal stepped away from the stage. 'I'm just here to make you look good, Benedict,' he said, through gritted teeth. It felt dirty, but wasn't this what Albert Hines was doing as well? Appeasing his star, just to get the job done? Making a scoundrel happy, so that they got the best picture they possibly could? 'Just the same as all these good people,' he added, so that the crowd could hear.

'I don't need you to *help* me to look good, old man,' Benedict sneered as Cal jumped off stage.

Cal stopped dead.

*Old man.*

There he stood, thirty-five years old, and already he was *old*. Too old for stardom. Too old to upend the world with his songs.

But not too old, and not lacking in the talent, to light the fire that would send Benedict rocketing to the stars.

He was about to turn round when Albert Hines approached and doffed him gently on the shoulder.

'Same time tomorrow, Mr Forsyth?' he said out loud.

If Cal was spending the afternoon wondering if he ought to have stuck with the relative peacefulness and camaraderie of the Fort Antoine, the rest of the Company were spending the afternoon wondering where on earth he was.

By the middle of the afternoon, when the lights were set and Evie was starting to rehearse her dancers, Ed was sitting on the highest stone tier of the amphitheatre thinking, mopping his brow and wondering what on earth was taking so long.

The morning had been spent in the joyful shared endeavour of setting up the stage. Ever since he'd been a boy, trotting on his father Ted's heels as he inspected each theatre and dreamt about how that particular show might go, this had been Ed's favourite part of company life. Every arrival at a new venue was filled with promise and potential – and the potential of the Fort Antoine eclipsed almost any he had ever known. The sun was blinding right now, but by evening it would have the burnished, faded grandeur of an approaching sunset. The show would begin with dance, move through Davith's dog act and magic – until, at its apex, out stepped Cal. The travelling piano was under the tarpaulins – what a devil that had been to get to the peak of the Fort Antoine! – and needed tuning. Ed himself had once been a singer – and, though he'd lost so much of his nuance and range in the ravages the Great War made of his body, he still had a perfect ear. Ed himself would tune the piano at which his son would sing, timed perfectly to coincide with the sunset over the bay.

In the bowl of the amphitheatre, the young magician Jim Livesey was taking the opportunity to set up his wardrobe, endlessly walking into it, disappearing, and then walking out of it again, while one of the dancing girls inspected it from every angle. Jim was a talented young man – he'd learnt from the best in John Lauderdale – but it was near impossible to make this sort of illusion stick when the audience had such a clear view of you from three sides. What Jim needed, Ed decided, was an assistant of his own – and that was when his eyes lit upon Meredith and Sam.

Sam had been prowling the theatre ramparts all afternoon, peering over the edge to catch a sight of his father's return. Just watching him filled Ed's heart – for hadn't he been the same, once upon a time, clinging to his father and grandfather, wanting to follow wherever they went (especially when he watched them marching out onto the stage)? And now he got to thinking… did Sam's debut really have to be as a song and dance man? The boy had a sweet voice, but it could hardly be said to be powerful yet – he was only six years old, and in a theatre without any acoustics, his song would surely be lost. But as Jim's assistant? Mightn't the boy enjoy a disappearing act? And mightn't the crowd enjoy that too?

While Sam kept guard for Cal's return, Meredith had come to sit with Ed. She'd been travelling with the Company for five years now, but hadn't yet taken a turn on the stage – no matter how much Cal, Ed and Evie cajoled her. Cal had met her in the offices of one of the Denmark Street publishers he'd been writing songs for – and the truth was she didn't feel the draw of performance like the rest of them did. This was not to say she was content to sit on the sidelines, forever a spectator. Six months after joining them, she'd taken up the Company admin-istration – a job that Ed had clung on to for far too long, and which he had found difficult to let go. Yet he was quite certain now that freeing himself of those organisational responsibilities had extended his playing career. The mind slowed down, just like the body did; sometimes you had to make tough decisions.

'What do you think?' Ed asked, after he'd outlined his idea.

'It's every small boy's dream – a touch of magic,' Meredith laughed. 'But Ed, you know he's a song and dance man at heart. And you know *why*.'

They both gazed at Sam, still keeping watch. Evie was with him now, which was the only reason they were sure he wouldn't topple over the edge, so eager was he to catch the first sight of Cal.

'Not just his father,' Meredith said. 'His *grandfather* too.'

Below them, Jim Livesey stepped into the wardrobe – and then didn't step out again. For a protracted moment, only silence came from the amphitheatre floor. Then came the gentle knocking of Jim from within.

'You better go and let him out,' said Ed, hanging his head.

Meredith stood. 'And perhaps sending Sam into that thing on show night isn't the best trick after all…'

In the same moment that Meredith skipped down the stone seating to release the unfortunate Jim from the prison of his own illusion, Evie started beckoning to her father from the amphitheatre walls. 'At last,' Ed sighed, looking at his watch; several hours had passed by without Cal appearing, and he had been beginning to give up hope.

Yet, when he reached the rampart where Evie and Sam stood, it wasn't Cal that he saw approaching from below. A blocky red Citroen was parked between the Company's black cabs, and leaning upon its bonnet was a middle-aged woman with bright auburn curls, cigarette smoke trailing from her constantly fidgeting fingers.

'She's just been standing there,' said Evie, bewildered. 'Just standing and – and waiting…'

'Maybe she's excited for the show,' Sam squeaked.

To a six-year-old this made perfect sense, but neither Evie nor Ed could dismiss it so easily. The Fort Antoine was a destination; it sat at the very head of the harbour, so it was not a place people simply idled by. There was, Evie supposed, every chance she was just a tourist who'd arrived at the Fort and discovered it occupied by a crew of performing artistes – but she'd been standing there for some time, as if she was *waiting* for something. Every now and then her eyes flashed up, then roamed on again.

She was, Evie had counted, already smoking her seventh cigarette – like a woman beset by nerves, doing anything she could to ward them off.

Ed crouched and put an arm around Sam. 'We're going to try you singing, young man. Go on down to the floor now. Let's see how that little voice of yours sounds.'

This simple declaration was enough for Sam to forget the lady loitering below; it was enough, even, for him to give up the vigil he'd been keeping for Cal, and to career quickly down the amphitheatre steps, colliding directly with Jim Livesey as his mother released him from the illusion.

'Wait here, Evie,' Ed said, 'I'll have a quiet word with her.'

So that was what Evie did. From above, she watched as her father picked his way back across the amphitheatre, vanishing from her sight – until, at last, he emerged from the stone steps onto the harbourside below. He looked so aged now, thought Evie – with an air of the wistful sadness she'd been trying to keep at bay for several seasons now. The way he hobbled to meet the old woman filled her not only with love, but with a certain frisson of dread for the future as well. He hadn't said it out loud, but she was quite certain this was to be her father's last foray from English shores. He may yet perform with them in Brighton, Bradford and Southend – but she doubted she would see him framed by the aquamarine waters of the French Riviera ever again.

Down below, the woman appeared most startled to see Ed. Evie watched with something approaching bewilderment – perhaps even suspicion – as the two of them engaged in a conversation much more lively than she'd expected. Evie was too far away to hear what they were saying, but within moments the woman had stubbed out her cigarette, opened the car door and slid inside. The conversation softened now – there were far fewer gesticulating arms, now that she was seated – and her father bowed down to speak consolingly through the car window with her. Then the engine fired, the blocky red Citroen stuttered backward through the Company flotilla and Ed watched as she drove it back into the streets of the Port Hercule.

It took Ed a little longer to get back up the stairs than it had for him to go down. The moment he returned, Sam started calling out for his grandpa – so eager was he to start his singing that nothing else in the world really mattered – but Evie caught up with him before the rehearsal could begin.

'What was that all about, Dad?' she asked.

'Oh, just old faces,' Ed said, with a disarming smile. Then he caressed Evie's arm and said, 'It's nice to know we're remembered from all those years ago – but this show doesn't have an open invitation. This show's for patrons of the Princess Grace.'

But as Ed sallied on to lead Sam in his first proper rehearsal, Evie couldn't shake the feeling that, even though her father had spent his lifetime creating different characters on stage, he really was a terrible liar.

Cal knew he ought to head straight to the Fort Antoine – but the problem with keeping all your fury repressed so well was that it stayed deep down inside you, coiled up, ready to spring.

What he really needed, before he rallied to the Company's cause, was a stiff drink.

He arrived at the Hotel de Lyon just as the fiercest heat was beginning to burn off the afternoon. Across Monte Carlo, the grandstands were finally complete. The city's residents went about their business as if this was an everyday occurrence – and to some of them it must have seemed that way, for the city had been hosting its Grand Prix for almost forty years, transforming the Principality each glorious summer since 1929 – but to Cal it seemed a miracle to find a city so transformed, and all in the pursuit of hedonistic pleasure. He'd only seen a Formula 1 race once, the Forsyths given hospitality tickets to Silverstone by one of their benefactors. Later, there'd been the races in ... Reims, was it? Cal had barely been out of boyhood, those heady days after the war had been won, but he'd understood the thrill well enough. He could still remember overhearing his mother confiding in his father: 'He'll run away to race cars, if he isn't centre stage soon enough. We need to give him something to do, something big, or he'll find his glory somewhere else ...'

Cal's mother had been wrong; he'd run away eventually, but not to race cars. Even so, all these years later – and with the arrogance of youth (at least partially) worn off – he felt a flutter at the thought of the upcoming race. Being in one of those cars, a Maserati or Ferrari hurtling around the city, must carry the same buzz as standing in front of a thousand screaming fans while you raised your voice in song. In a different life, born under a different star, perhaps that might have been for Cal.

He tried not to think of Benedict as he flew into the hotel, found himself a stool at the long, sweeping bar and ordered a long cocktail. Ordinarily Cal was a pale ale drinker – but something about the sunshine and opulence of Monte Carlo demanded he drink a Tom Collins. Actually, because the first one went down so easily, it demanded he drink a second, then a third. By the time he'd drained that glass, some of the ire was starting to leave him. Instead, it was a peculiar kind of hollowness that he felt – for, while his anger was burning, hot as the Monacoan sun, he'd been able to focus solely on Benedict's obnoxiousness, but as soon as that fire burnt out, he was forced to confront the real reason he felt so wild and strung out.

It was because Benedict was right.

Some men had a talent for finding a weakness, then attacking it as viciously as they could. Benedict had spotted Cal's weakness straight away. He'd spent his twenties on the run from his family company, hunting for his own glory in the world. London as a young man with a guitar: what an odyssey that had been! But it hadn't brought him fame – and, until 'Runaway Lovers' was seized upon at the Royal Variety five years ago, it hadn't brought him fortune either. Just the steady, numbing grind of pumping out songs for other singers, and the slow, dawning realisation that history wasn't going to come calling for Cal Forsyth. Too young to fit in with the crooners and bandleaders of his father's generation, yet too old to ride the wave of the sixties: the Beatles, the Stones, the British invasion now taking the world by storm. 'Runaway Lovers' had been the perfect mingling of the old and the new, and it had brought him opportunities only a fool wouldn't seize hold of – but it hadn't been his face on the front of those records; it hadn't been his voice singing that song.

It wasn't his name up in lights.

Even at the Forsyth Varieties, he was just one of many – and, yes, that was how it ought to be; yes, the Company mattered, because the Company was his family, and above all things, Cal was a family man now.

Yet when Benedict had said those things, all the old feelings – of failure, of frustration, of chances missed never to come again – had started rushing back in.

No matter; a fourth cocktail would do the trick. He'd finish those songs for Benedict, take his money and move on. If he got through it without scalding the brat, there might even be more work in it. Benedict would never be grateful, not even if this movie rocketed him to the upper echelons of global fame, but Albert Hines, and Parker & Parr, surely would – especially if they saw him handling their troubled star well. That might lead to something further down the line. And there were bigger stars than Benedict Frey, weren't there? Hell, Elvis Presley himself made movies. Wasn't it possible there was a future where Cal worked on songs that Elvis himself might sing?

'Excuse me, sir?'

The voice came from further down the bar, where a debonair gentleman with rich chestnut hair, a pinstripe shirt rolled up to the elbows and a pair of Ray-Ban Wayfarers hooked around his collar, was propped, luxuriating in the sun that spilt into the bar. The man had the same olive complexion of all who partied and played up and down the Riviera, his striking jawline dusted in carefully manicured black stubble. A silver watch shone at his wrist.

Cal raised his glass. 'To new opportunities, sir,' he declared, and drank it dry.

The man slipped over and, clicking his fingers at the barman, gestured for two more.

'I better not,' said Cal, who was only just strong enough to resist the temptation. 'I've got to drive down to the port.'

'You can walk it from here. Better still – I'll take you.'

Two more Tom Collins materialised; now that it was here, Cal figured it would be rude to turn it away, so he set about drinking. 'You'll take me?' he said.

'You'll have to forgive me if I'm wrong – but a promise is a promise, so I'll take you either way. But ... you're with the players, right? You're one of the performers, with the acrobats and the dancers – and the man with the little dogs who,' he stumbled over the next word, '*pee* on demand?'

Cal spluttered so suddenly that he was in real and present danger of showering gin and lemon juice all over the bar. 'Tinky and Tiny. They do have that remarkable ability, yes. I should add they have a hundred other tricks – ones more appropriate for a family audience. Did they ...' Cal looked the stranger up and down, '...*perform* for you?' he asked.

'Not upon me, but I saw it done.' The Frenchman, for he had a heavy Parisian accent, seemed to be revelling in the memory. He propped himself on the bar with one elbow and extended the other hand to shake Cal's. 'I'm Laurent,' he said. 'Charles Laurent. And you – you're ... Cal, if I remember. Cal Forsyth?'

Perhaps all that talk of being overlooked, having missed his shot, his name never being the one up in lights, had come too soon. Cal puffed himself up. 'You know me, sir! "Runaway Lovers", I presume?'

The Frenchman's face creased. 'I'd hardly call myself a runaway. And I haven't thought of myself as her lover for half a lifetime. In fact, I'm not quite sure I'd ever have used the word. I don't want to presume. And yet ...'

Cal's face creased. Then he started flushing red. He drained the Tom Collins and said, 'It's a song I wrote. I wasn't ...' He put down the glass. 'What *are* we talking about, M. Laurent?'

'Evie,' he answered, plainly.

'Evie,' said Cal, equally plain. 'My sister, Evie.'

'You don't remember me, do you, Cal?'

Cal looked perplexed, so much so that the man named Charles quickly went on, 'Your Company and I crossed paths many moons ago. Reims, 1953. It was a ... different time.'

'I'll say,' said Cal. 'We were still so young.' And his face darkened slightly as he said it: so *young*; so full of *promise*; back when it was still possible that it might have been him, Cal Forsyth, who made it big. 'I remember Reims. There were races that summer as well.' It wasn't long after his mother had died, the same summer he'd upped and left the Company to forge his own way through the wilderness. And it hit him, like a bolt from the blue: 'You were one of the drivers? We were staying at the Hotel ... what was it?'

'Lavannes,' Charles said, easing into the conversation at last. 'The boys and I came to see one of your shows – and then, back at the hotel, well ...' Charles didn't mean to spill the rest of it, but the memories had been hardening in him since his arrival in the city – and now he fancied he could remember every little detail. 'I've always remembered that summer. It was the first time I raced. And now – here you all are again, on the week I'm to take a new team into the Grand Prix. Do you believe in destiny, M. Forsyth?'

'I don't like to,' said Cal.

'Why not?'

Cal wanted to say: because that would mean my destiny is to be the 'second man', the support act, the talent in the shadows instead of in the light. But instead he said, 'You French are more romantic than we poor English. Destiny. Fate. I prefer a little elbow grease and hard work. My father always taught me – legends aren't handed to you; they have to be *made*.'

'Yes,' said Charles, momentarily lost in thought, 'I like the sound of that. We can all make the legends we want out of our lives. Which rather brings me on to … your sister, monsieur. Evie. Might I ask, is she happy?'

'Happy?' Cal started grinning. 'Why don't you come out and ask it?'

But Charles Laurent was too much of a gentleman, so in the end it was Cal who had to say, 'As a matter of fact, she isn't married. And as a further matter of fact, she isn't even close. So, if that's what you bought me this drink for, sir, now you've got your answer.' Cal stood up. 'And now I'll have my ride. She'll be waiting at the Fort, you know.'

Cal began striding out of the bar, grateful to have the whole matter of Benedict Frey pushed out of his mind.

'Are all Englishmen this eager to help along their sisters' romance?' Charles asked, sliding elegantly along Cal's side.

Cal himself was much less elegant, whether there were four Tom Collins in him or not. 'Well, I'm in the family business. That company's been in my father's line for a hundred years – and, right now, the future's just my six-year-old boy.' They had reached the reception hall, but before they passed out into the sunlight, Cal paused and fixed this Frenchman with a look. 'Are you a good man, Charles?'

Charles nodded. 'I believe so.'

Outside, Charles led Cal to his old Lago T26 and opened the door. Cal was no keen admirer of old cars, but something about this one appealed to him. 'You'll be taking something a little more modern out onto the circuit, I should think?'

'Oh yes,' said Charles, 'the new Talbot-Lago Grand Sport's quite a sleek beast. No expense has been spared. But this old girl's been at my side for eleven long years,' he added, stroking the car's contours fondly. 'She's stood the test of time. I won't have a thing said against her.'

The journey round the port, to the imposing walls of the Fort Antoine, was not long – not nearly long enough for Cal's liking. The port road was hardly empty, but there was enough space for Charles to let the engine fly and for Cal, with the window wound down and the wind streaming through his hair, to get the same giddy thrill he'd had all those years ago, visiting Silverstone for the first time.

He had a hundred questions for Charles Laurent, but the wind robbed him of all breath. Then, quite suddenly, they were in front of the Fort's tall stone walls, Charles sliding the car neatly between the red double-decker bus and the line of black cabs that formed the Company fleet.

'How did you find it?' Charles asked.

Cal slipped out of the seat and gazed up at the Fort walls. He ought to have been here hours ago. He could hear the sounds of the Company rehearsing. A sweet, fragile voice was raised in song.

'I'll place a bet on you this evening,' Cal said, looking back at the car.

'I won't let you down, good sir.'

Cal was enjoying this Frenchman's impression of a courteous Englishman very much – but he couldn't wait to see what he was like on a racetrack. 'Of course, this Grand Sport you're driving – it's going to be much faster than this.'

'Undoubtedly. You must come and see it for yourself, before the big day.'

'And take it for a spin?' grinned Cal.

'That I shall have to take under advisement…'

The way into the amphitheatre was up narrow stone stairs, built generations ago. Cal palmed his way up the stonework, emerging into the bright sunlight at the peak. There, through the tiers of stone seats, he saw the Company gathered around the piano they'd set up in the heart of the arena. His father was pounding the keys, but the voice raised in song belonged to none other than his son, Sam.

All of the torment and fury of the past few hours melted away in that instant. So too did the hollow feeling he'd been trying to drive away with all those Tom Collinses. What better salve was there for all that bad feeling but this? What better remedy than the way Sam sang to his grandfather's tune, two generations of Forsyths coming together in a moment of simple joy and beauty?

Meredith was already bounding over. 'What do you think? It'll be you on show night on the piano, of course. Or... you with the guitar, Ed on the ivories and Sam in full voice.'

Cal turned on the spot. 'He has an enormous stage to fill,' he said – for, though the Fort Antoine would play host to only three hundred and fifty guests, the sky above them would be open, and Sam's first audience would take in the heavens themselves. 'But what a memory for the boy. What a debut. What a way to—'

Cal was still turning on the spot to take in the arena, his eyes roaming over Jim Livesey (as he struggled with his wardrobe), Lily, Verity and the dancing girls, Davith feeding scraps to the dogs as they strutted around obediently on their hind-paws – but then he stopped dead. A smile that was nothing to do with Sam, and yet everything to do with his family's fortunes, flourished on his lips. He reached for Meredith's hand and drew her tighter. 'Would you look at that,' he laughed – for, just as Charles Laurent had emerged from the stone stairs behind them, his sister Evie had cantered over to engage him in conversation, and now the two of them seemed, somehow, like old friends who'd just happened across each other, close and familiar as only people who've grown up together ever are.

'An old friend?' Meredith asked.

Cal shrugged. 'He saw us perform years ago, a theatre in Reims.'

'A fan, then!' Meredith grinned.

Cal looked back. 'Oh yes, I think you could call him a fan. But whether he's a fan of the Company or just one Forsyth in particular, I really couldn't say.' He took her hand, then turned back to the rehearsal. 'It's been a day of ups and downs, but I'll tell you about that later. It looks like we're going to end on a high after all.'

They certainly were – for the song was ending, and Sam was stampeding across the amphitheatre to scramble up into Cal's arms. 'Did you hear me, Dad?' he squawked. 'Did you hear?'

Funny, but he was much more melodic when he sang than when he squawked.

'Son,' he said – and saw, suddenly, how happy Ed was that he'd caught the moment as well, 'you're going to be a star!'

## Chapter Six

Evie had dined in a good number of fabulous restaurants – she'd dined in a good number of lay-bys, car parks and truck stops too, for such was life with the Forsyth Varieties – but she'd never quite experienced the opulence of La Toison d'Or.

The seafood restaurant did not have a traditional spot on the harbour. Instead, it sat on the heights above Monte Carlo, resting on one of the manifold bluffs of Mont Agel – beyond the grand, palatial glades of the Monte Carlo Golf Club. The view from here, with the sun going down over the city and the seascape beyond, was just stunning – and Evie and Charles had the best seats in the house. Framed by the open windows, they could see all the way over the city's forest of towers, out across the bay where colourful yachts still bobbed, and into the darkling ocean. The sun was turning to burnt orange, then vermilion red, lighting up the horizon in a glorious array.

But Evie and Charles weren't looking at that; they were looking at each other, across the lobster Charles had just cracked open. Its rich, buttery scent blossomed between them.

And nor was it the only thing blossoming…

'I was sure it was you,' Charles went on; they'd been talking for an hour already, without a single stilted moment. 'Perhaps I ought to have guessed when I saw that double-decker bus.

Well, a London bus, this far from Piccadilly Circus? What else could it mean? But then... there you were, and fourteen years came crashing down. It was like none of them ever happened. It could have been yesterday. You and me, in the bar at the Hotel Lavannes. Then you and me, on that little spot down by the river.'

It was at this point that Evie had to cut him off. She arched an eyebrow and said, 'I remember.'

'But do you know the moment I *really* knew? The moment I really managed to push away all the doubts and believe it was you, Evie Forsyth, standing there?'

This time, when she arched her eyebrow she was not chiding him to stop, but inviting him to go on.

'It was the way you dealt with Conrad Knight – really quite remarkable. I felt it displayed a kind of...' He mulled over the correct description while he separated the lobster. 'A kind of *subtlety*, I believe. A subtlety – but a ruthlessness too. You just whistled and, *voila*, that pompous old fool was brought down to earth.'

Evie had to admit she was particularly proud of the way she'd disarmed the old man. 'When you have a twin brother, and he's got a taste for being the centre of attention, you do have to develop certain *techniques*. Mine was finding ways to score points without it ever looking like I'd done anything wrong.'

'You pass your mischievousness over to a dog, for example.'

'And you hit them where it really hurts. That man looked as if the thing he cared about most in the world was his suit.'

'Actually, he cares about his *money*.'

'And his suit is a symbol of that.'

Charles shrugged. 'It was beautiful. It was divine. He couldn't even lambast you, because he didn't *know*. *C'est magnifique!*'

After that, they raised glasses and set about the lobster in earnest.

'What is he to you, that man?'

'Oh, I suppose you English would say he is my ... *boss*.'

This intrigued Evie.

'Do you remember learning about the old days, when you were sitting at school? In Paris it was Charlemagne or Louis XIV. All of the lords and princes of Le Grand Siècle. All the court running around after them, frightened they'd lose their heads. In England I imagine it was Henry VIII and all of his wives. Well, to me, Conrad Knight's like one of those kings ...'

Evie narrowed her eyes, taunting him. 'It sounds to me like you think yourself part of the king's inner circle ...'

'*Mais oui*, but I *am*. Conrad Knight is like a king, and I am like the king's favourite. I owe my position entirely to him, and if I fall foul of him – for instance, if I instructed some dogs to relieve themselves up against his very smart gabardine suit – I would be cast into exile, or locked in the Tower, or lose my head to an executioner's axe.' Charles smiled; he had the most dashing smile. 'He pulls the purse strings, and in my world, money means power.'

'I think that's true of most worlds,' said Evie. 'But, perhaps, not mine.'

'No?'

'In my world ... talent draws power. If you have what it takes, you start exerting a kind of *gravity*. Things start revolving around you.' She paused. 'But surely, in motor racing ...'

'The same thing, perhaps, but always – *always* – at the mercy of money.' He smiled. 'I am not like I was when we met in Reims. I was full of passion and belief.'

'I remember,' said Evie. 'Those letters you used to send me afterwards. You were going to be King of the World.'

Was Evie wrong, or did Charles almost blush? He hadn't seemed the sort of man who even had the ability to blush back in Reims. He'd seemed convinced of his destiny – as if he was walking a preordained road, and nothing could sway him from it. He wasn't the best driver back then – as Evie remembered it, he was just a charming third-rung rally driver, hanging around the circuit, driving show races while the crowds warmed up for the real thing – but that hadn't mattered to him, because he *knew* where life was taking him.

Was him blushing now a tacit admission that he might have been *wrong*?

'My brother warned me of it. "Charles," he said, "the car is not the only thing that goes round the circuit. The money goes round as well – round and round and round, on and on…" It was good advice. My brother was a fountain of wisdom, for one so young.' He paused. 'Do you remember my brother?'

Evie wasn't sure that she did. What she remembered of that summer was the dashing young Frenchman who'd sashayed up to her in the hotel bar and announced that he'd seen her dancing in the show last night, and immediately reserved tickets to see her again. She remembered their walks down by the river, the first kiss by the cathedral, the talk of his father – lost at war – and the way life seemed to be dragging them both forward into something exciting, unknown, perhaps even dangerous. She vaguely remembered Charles talking of his brother, who was some rungs ahead of him in the racing fraternity, but back then Evie's mind had been focused on other things. For one brief summer, it had seemed as if *her* life was walking a destined path as well – and that it was leading her directly to Charle  Laurent.

'He was a driver, wasn't he? Does he still race…' A memory flashed into her head, something Charles had said on one of those long perambulations around Reims, and it brought a teasing smile to her lips, '…or have you overtaken him at last?'

Charles's face paled.

'Tobias died,' he said, simple and plain.

Evie reached for his hand. 'I didn't know.'

And of course she didn't, because Charles had never told her. After that long stolen summer in Reims, he'd written to her often. She'd sent postcards from whatever far-flung corner of the Continent she was playing in; he'd sent missives from Paris and Rome. They'd made plans to meet in London, that month he came to the races at the newly inaugurated Aintree circuit – but, of course, by then the fates had taken the Forsyth Varieties to Copenhagen, so their paths – which so often felt tantalisingly close – never quite crossed. Even so, Charles always *knew* he'd meet Evie again, just as he always *knew* he'd join his brother in the upper echelons of the racing fraternity.

But then had come Le Mans, the end of Tobias's life, the end of innocence.

And Charles hadn't written to Evie after that. The world had seemed bleak and unyieldingly grey, and Evie a source of such light that, even when he started to surface from grief, he knew that he couldn't burden her with it. The past stayed buried with Tobias, and Charles stepped into the future.

'You should have told me. You *knew* my mother was gone. I would have understood.'

Charles smiled, sadly. 'It was too much for my young soul to carry. I'm sorry. My silence was wrong.'

Now, in the restaurant above the glittering cityscape of Monte Carlo, Evie sensed that the story Charles was about to spill was at the root of whatever argument had erupted between him and Conrad Knight. She tried not to pry; Charles seemed only too willing to let it pour out. By the time he'd told her about Le

Mans, about the fire and destruction and the knowledge he'd gained that a life could be snuffed out as suddenly as a candle is doused, she began to understand that, for him, racing was no longer just a passion; since she'd met him last, it had become a testament to the brother he'd lost.

'When I go out onto the stage,' said Evie suddenly, now that the sun was down and the stars rising up over the mountain, 'I can feel my mother ushering me on. I don't know what I believe anymore. I don't know if there's really heaven above and hell below – but I do know that, when the lights go up and the band strikes its first note, I can feel her in the air all around me.'

Charles leant across the table and took her hand. 'Precisely,' he whispered, with the urgency of a secret being shared. 'The pistol goes. The engine roars. And something possesses me, in that exact moment: if I can go fast enough, if I take the corners boldly enough; if I reach first place and strike out ahead, leaving everyone else in the dust, perhaps I'll meet my brother, out there on the track.'

The ghostliness of the idea overcame Evie. She imagined Charles with his foot on the accelerator, urging his car on and ever on – certain, in some oblique way, that if only he was fast enough, if only he lapped all of his competitors over and over again, he might in some way catch up with Tobias, and drive alongside him.

'That's why you race.'

'I always wanted to be like my brother. Big brothers, they are like gods. And when he died, when his spirit stayed on the track, I couldn't look away. Not until I win. And, if I do win, it will be for Tobias.' He paused, for a waiter had appeared to refill their glasses with the Louis Roederer they were drinking. 'So, you see, I cannot risk upsetting Conrad Knight too much. He did not favour me winning the position of principal driver.

He wanted another. It would take little for him to unseat me. And that's why...'

'You couldn't send two dogs to sully his suit – but *I* could.'

'*Precisement!*'

And they raised their glasses one more time.

In the same moment that their glasses clinked, a flash of white light flared somewhere outside the restaurant, blinding both Charles and Evie as they drank. It took neither of them more than a millisecond to understand what this was; both their professions were *au fait* with photographers. As soon as the flash died down, Charles turned to the window – but outside there was only the rugged darkness of Mont Agel and, in the distance, the starlight playing on the waters of the harbour. Monte Carlo itself was not yet illuminated in the lights of its nocturnal life, though that could not be far away. He could see the silhouettes of the towers, the dark shape that was the Fort Antoine, the hulk of the grand Casino.

But he could see no photographer.

'A smile, if you please.'

Evie turned. So, this was the reason. While they'd been peering out of the window, the photographer – a beanpole of a man, dressed in light tan chinos and a smart blue shirt folded up around his elbows – had marched brazenly into the restaurant. Even before the maître-d' and his attendants could accost the interloper, he had brandished his camera, directed its gaze and taken another snap of Evie and Charles. 'M. Laurent,' he began, 'what is it like to have the weight of such expectation hanging over you? Is this how you unwind, M. Laurent, before a race as totemic as this? In the hills of Monte Carlo with a beautiful bride? *Is* she your bride, M. Laurent?'

'Monsieur, mademoiselle – we must apologise.'

That was the maître-d' – who had finally caught up with the photographer and proceeded, as delicately and artfully as he could, to compel him out of the restaurant. The photographer obviously cared little about being manhandled, but he was determined to protect his camera at any cost – so, mission accomplished, he hurried ahead of the maître-d' and returned to the night. Some moments later, through the open window, Evie heard a car engine firing, its driver guiding it to the winding mountain road.

'That must happen to you often in your profession,' Charles smiled.

'You're very kind, Charles, but I think he was here for you. We aren't stars of the screen. People wouldn't know our faces on the street. We've performed for kings, but ...' She thought of Cal, and how much he had always wanted to be *known*. Evie had never quite hungered for it in the same way. This was not to say that she didn't live for the Company, and that walking out onto stage didn't feel like her calling – because it very much did. But only Cal wanted to go down in *history*, and now he felt as though it was passing him by. Perhaps this movie he was embroiled in might sate him, for a while. 'Do they come after you often, the press?'

'Not until today. But I have driven no bigger race than the Grand Prix this weekend.' Charles looked back at the night. 'The truth is, Evie – and you will forgive me the open honesty of it, even if it makes you think a little less of me – that I have never succeeded before. I am a good driver. I believe I could be numbered among the best. There are men lauded in competition right now that I will overcome. And yet ... the fraternity, it has always thought of me as a little ... *other*. I believe they think I am cursed.'

And again, thought Evie, Charles's mind turned back to his brother.

'Not a soul will say it, but they think I have a death wish. Or that I'll never drive well, because my brother's ghost distracts me. Or... that, when it comes to the crux of a race, when I should hit the accelerator and fly, when the chance comes to take a risk and get ahead, I will remember Le Mans and lose my courage.'

'Talbot-Lago took you on,' said Evie – and instinct told her to take his hand. 'They must believe in you.'

'Aha,' grinned Charles, 'but not Conrad Knight.'

'No, not Conrad Knight.'

Then he stood, still holding her hand and declared, 'Come with me tonight. Tomorrow I shall be locked down. Tomorrow, with the team and drilling the car. And you, I imagine...'

'Leading my dancers through their routines. And... trying to keep my brother in order.'

'Then, one night in Monte Carlo. The photojournalist was right in one thing: there is such expectation in this race, sometimes a man needs to unwind. I remember feeling so peaceful, walking along the river with you in Reims. I remember feeling like the world could be mine. And there is only one place in Monte Carlo where two bright young things might unwind until the sun comes up, and perhaps indulge themselves along the way. Are you prepared?'

Evie decided she liked his way of talking. There was a real depth of emotion to Charles Laurent, but it seemed he had a bit of a devil in him as well. Perhaps you needed both to be a superlative racing car driver. Those two qualities certainly took a performer all the way.

'Lead on, sir!' she declared.

So that was exactly what Charles Laurent did.

*

Cal had been one of the last to leave the Fort Antoine, just as twilight was hardening to nightfall over Monte Carlo, with only Davith and his dogs left behind to parade the empty fortress by moonlight. 'It will be an adventure,' the old Welshman had been saying to his dogs as Cal bustled after Meredith and Sam. 'Camping out wild, just like in the old days.'

Camping out on top of a Monacoan fortress, bathed by the balmy Mediterranean air, was perhaps not *quite* like the old days of camping in Welsh bus shelters and beneath tarpaulins on the outside of towns, but Davith seemed quite happy with his lot – so Cal and his family made their way along the seafront back to the Hotel de Lyon.

Now, with an indulgent dinner in his belly – all courtesy of the Princess Grace, who was footing the extravagant bill for the Company to stay at the hotel – Cal sat in a private bar at the back of the hotel, hunkered over a baby grand piano. Sam – who had refused bed, as he always did – was being entertained in one of the suites by Lily and the dancing girls. They were always so eager to spend time with him, and he with them – Cal had no doubt that he was going to raise hell with the girls before he got to sixteen – that Meredith was free to join Cal. The guitar in her hands had once belonged to him, but now its primary purpose was for Meredith to teach Sam. Cal used to think guitars were the future, but the older he got, the more the piano and its grinning black and white teeth beckoned him to play.

'It's this bit,' Cal said, for what seemed the hundredth time. 'The key change works, but it's ... *predictable*. There's a sweet spot I'm trying to reach – somewhere between predictability and something new.' And his voice rose up. 'Meet me in Monte Ca-a-a-a-arlo ...' He slammed a chord. 'It needs to soar. It doesn't soar. It's harder than I thought, working from someone else's material. You don't have any freedom.'

'Freedom isn't the job. Discipline's the job. Just remember what it was like, back on Denmark Street.'

Cal rarely liked to. That had seemed stultifying too: writing songs to commission, seeing them go off into the hands of singers much less talented than he was; always serving somebody else's endeavour, and repeatedly told that it couldn't be *him*.

'Frey thinks I'm a hack, and he might be right. This is *hack work*.'

Cal slammed an off-key chord and stood up to prowl the empty bar.

'It's only hack work because you say it is,' Meredith returned. She was always the steady hand on Cal's wild tiller; she raised her voice, like she sometimes used to do at Sam if he threw a tantrum, and added, 'Just apply yourself, Cal. It isn't songwriting, not like you know it. This is *head* work, not *heart* work. Treat it like a puzzle that needs to be unpicked.'

'One of the assistants on set told me that Frey's father's in management. A talent manager. That's why he's on screen. It isn't what you can do in that industry, it's *who* you *know*.'

'So what?' said Meredith. '*So what?* That's his life. This is yours. And they came looking for you, Cal – so give them what they want.'

'Benedict's the hack, thrust up there to sing another man's songs.'

Meredith laughed. 'And that's what he's feeling too. That's why he tried to upend you. And look at you, Cal! Just look at you! You've let him into your head.'

Cal quit his pacing, turned on his heel and stared the piano down like it was wearing the face of Benedict Frey. 'I'll rewrite every last one of them. They won't even be his anymore, and he'll know it. There's nothing that will convince him. And he'll carry that, for the rest of his career. He wasn't good enough and...'

Meredith had started laughing. It silenced Cal in a second.

'You know I like it when you get angry. I just didn't know I liked it when you got *crazy* as well.' She set down the guitar. 'Just sit down, Cal. Sit down and play whatever comes into your head. The soundtrack will take care of itself. You can't polish plain rocks into diamonds – so, if you're going to have diamonds, you'll just have to write the songs yourself.'

'I'm not sure that'll wash with Mr Hines.'

'I reckon Mr Hines is more wily than you think. He *knows* what Benedict Frey is like – and the picture comes first.'

This seemed to settle Cal, somehow, but there was still a demon in him as he sat down. 'Well, I've been thinking of something like this. I don't know how it slides into the picture, but it's got a line.'

'I'm listening.'

Cal had made his reputation with a well-wrought piano ballad, six minutes of soaring emotion telling the story of lost lovers. But five years had passed, and five years had changed everything. Even in 1962, 'Runaway Lovers' had felt like a throwback to an earlier era, like a forgotten standard that had only just been rediscovered. The problem since then had been: you couldn't repeat the same trick. Cal knew, because he'd tried – and seen only diminishing returns for his efforts. Besides, a picture like *Monte Carlo by Moonlight* didn't want balladry. It wanted something fun, frenetic, something that burnt and then died out. It could still *soar*, but it had to feel fresher and younger than 'Runaway Lovers'. Cal hated thinking of it like that, because Benedict's words kept coming back to him, but in this, at least, the young fool was right. And, if Cal wasn't a cocksure nineteen-year-old anymore, he could still remember what that had been like.

And he could still capture it in song.

The song he'd been playing around with was called 'Come Running'. He liked that it shared the idea of running with his masterpiece of '62, but this time the story wasn't about running away – it was about finding the person you loved and running directly *to* them when times got tough.

> *'Roads on fire*
> *Don't know what to do*
> *The war's come down*
> *But I'm running to you…'*

The words weren't right yet, but it was bouncy and it was strident – and it seemed to capture a feeling of being in love that he hadn't heard set down in song. He knew he had to build on it – but the core of it had come to him in a second, and he *knew* in his heart (devoid of any ego, devoid of any antagonism) that it was better than that dross of Benedict's he'd been hired to whip into shape.

As he went on singing, Meredith picked the guitar back up and found her way into the song as well.

> *'Running, running, running to you*
> *The world might end*
> *But honey, whatcha gonna do?'*

Then he stood up, kicked the piano stool backwards and played the wildest, most pounding cascade that his hands could summon up. Perhaps this part of the song was a little *too* 1950s – a little too Little Richard, a little too Bill Haley – but, hell, this rendition was just for Meredith. They could fine tune the arrangement afterwards – once he'd figured out what to do with it. Yes, he thought, as he howled out the final lyrics, he'd polish Benedict's songs as well as he could, but *this* he'd keep for something better. Something that was surely coming his way.

'Well?' he asked, breathless by the end, 'What do you think?'

Meredith opened her mouth to reply, but instead a man's voice boomed from the back of the bar:

'I'll take it.'

Spooked out of his skin, Cal wheeled round – only to discover that Albert Hines himself had just stepped through the doors. He looked weary after a long day shooting under the Riviera sun, but there was still a spring in his step as he crossed the empty bar.

'Mr Hines,' Cal ventured. Then, gathering his composure, he said, 'Meredith, this is Mr Hines. He's shooting the picture. He's the one who hired me.'

'Technically that was the studio, but I always take credit for good decisions,' Hines said, then took Meredith by the hand. 'You're a nimble guitarist, young lady.'

Cal had often said as much himself. One day, there'd be a moment when musicians like Meredith could form bands and take centre stage themselves – he was sure of it.

'But what are you doing here, Mr Hines?'

'Well,' Hines said – and, going to the bar, brazenly helped himself to a bottle of brandy standing behind the counter. After taking glasses down from a shelf, he poured three generous measures and shared them around. 'I *was* coming to apologise for the fracas on set today. Benedict is what's known in the business as … an insufferable cretin. But he's an insufferable cretin who just happens to be earmarked for stardom, and it's in my job description to make it happen. It doesn't stop him being insufferable though, and it doesn't stop people like you being caught in his mushroom cloud of insufferability – so...' and he motioned for Cal to drink up, 'my apologies.' Then Hines drained his own glass and went on, 'That's what I *was* coming to say, but now that I'm here, I find that fate had something else in store all along. That song, Cal – how much for it?'

Cal flashed Meredith a look. 'It's just a song, Mr Hines. Just something I'm working on. It wasn't meant to be for the picture.'

'The graves of a thousand dead pictures are built upon "meant to be". In this business, we adapt and seize the opportunities as they come. I like the song, Mr Forsyth. To be perfectly frank, it grabbed me a thousand times more than the ones we've been working with. I want this song in my movie – and I'll have the studio pay to get it.'

While Cal tried to formulate a response, Meredith intervened: 'Benedict won't like that, Mr Hines.'

'No, he will not. But he'll like his first starring role being a flop even less. He'll be written off and be back to the provinces in weeks if that happens. Parker & Parr have invested everything in making him a star. But he doesn't get to be a star unless the movie hits big – and it's lacking.' Hines hesitated. 'Let me put it like this. Can you make every single one of Benedict's songs as immediate, as gripping, as *instant* as that one?'

Cal said, 'That isn't how it works, Mr Hines. It's songwriting. It isn't ... mowing a lawn.'

Where that particular image had come from, nobody knew. Meredith couldn't help herself; she started spluttering with laughter.

'Well, Mr Forsyth? Do we have an agreement? I would, of course, lay it out to Benedict.'

'You'd have *him* sing it.'

'I think that's probable.'

Cal tried not to show it, but Meredith could see he was brist-ling. 'Runaway Lovers' had been recorded in so many different voices; once, just once, Cal wanted it to be *him* – and, after Benedict's tirade today, that feeling was stronger than ever.

For a time, Cal just prowled backwards and forwards. For a time, he clenched and unclenched his fists. For a time, he closed his eyes and tried to imagine 'Come Running' in the voice of Benedict Frey. Was anything worth this?

Then he stopped dead. His fists unfurled. He took Meredith's hand, drew her to his side and smiled at Albert Hines.

'Mr Hines, I think I know what I would want.'

'Say it out loud, Cal. I can call the studio tonight.'

Cal puffed out his chest and beamed. 'Mr Hines, I want to be in that movie.'


The last time she'd visited Monte Carlo, Evie had barely been old enough to step through these doors – but now, with the valet taking away the sports car behind them, she stepped into the Casino de Monte Carlo on the arm of Charles Laurent.

It still felt absurd, to have stumbled upon him again.

But somehow it felt *right* as well.

The building itself was like a palace, dominating the Place du Casino on the seafront, overlooking the yacht club and all the boats luxuriating on the starlit water. Evie had walked into grand old-world ballrooms with less ostentation than this. The atrium was paved in marble, with black onyx columns arranged around its edges like a resolute palace guard. Beyond that, sweeping doors led into the Salle Garnier, an auditorium where Charles said ballets and operas had been performed for generations – what Evie wouldn't have given to perform here, surrounded by such lavish reds and golds! – while, on the other side, the gentle susurration of voices in the gaming rooms could be heard.

'It is like no other casino on this earth,' Charles said as he led Evie through. 'You won't find a Monacoan inside these doors, not unless they're working the roulette wheel, dealing the cards, waiting on tables. The Principality doesn't cater to its own. It only caters to ... us.'

And through the doors they stepped.

This was none other than a prince's palace dedicated to gambling. Chandeliers as vast as small ships hung in the vaults of great chambers, where tables for roulette, blackjack, baccarat and more sat upon a baroque tiled floor. Waiters bedecked in burgundy and gold, looking as if they belonged so intimately to the palace they must have been born and raised here, floated between elegant patrons in evening wear and silk gowns. Drinks flowed at every table. A triumphant cry was joined by applause that rippled across the gaming floor – and, in every corner, doors led to the private rooms where more elaborate games of poker, craps and baccarat were being played.

'What do you think?'

'Well,' said Evie, taking in the splendour, 'it's hardly the back room at the Three Tups.'

Charles looked at her with a quizzical expression.

'It's not like the gambling dens back home,' Evie said. 'Back home, gambling's for pubs and social clubs, horses and dogs. Here it's ... for glamour.'

They started picking their way across the floor; to Evie, it was like walking into a past age of Imperial wealth and splendour. Or like ... walking onto a movie set, she thought, something built just to capture the eye and ignite the imagination. And no sooner had she thought that than she saw, in the corner of her eye, some familiar faces gathered around one of the French roulette wheels. As Charles guided her past, she looked a second time – and this time she was certain; that was none other than Benedict Frey, and a group of hangers-on. She'd seen the same face staring out of a copy of *Modern Screen* she'd picked up at a stand in Cannes, just after Cal had received the call to visit the set of *Monte Carlo by Moonlight*. Dressed in a startling blue dinner jacket, he looked ever-so-slightly out of place in the upper-crust environs of the Casino, but he wasn't letting that stop him having a good time. His hangers-on fawned around him. Two girls, and one particularly effete-looking young man with a mop of curly hair, clung to him as he placed his bets.

Then Charles whisked her on, out of the grand hall into one of the side rooms where blackjack tables were lit up by a smaller crystal chandelier, the light less intense, the atmosphere more convivial and intimate.

'Of course,' Charles said as they joined one of the tables, 'the Casino has always been entwined with people of your world. In a way, it is built for you.'

'What do you mean?'

'This was all Princess Caroline's vision. She was like the Princess Grace – an artiste, a star of the stage, who married a prince. Apparently, if you come to Monte Carlo a performer, you have a good chance of leaving it a princess.' Charles drew out a seat at one of the blackjack tables and, like the gentleman he was, invited Evie to sit. 'Perhaps you might be royalty by the time you leave?'

Evie smiled. There was something teasing about this, though she wasn't sure what. Charles's eyes lingered on her; she felt the hairs on the back of her neck begin to stand on end. No, she thought, she wouldn't leave Monte Carlo a princess this weekend – but something told her she'd leave the Principality with her life irrevocably changed.

Of course, she'd thought that about Charles once before.

This time, she would have to make it count.

Blackjack was a good game to warm up with. The smartly uniformed dealer dealt the cards with a winsome smile – his back upright, his shoulders square, always focused on the honour and dignity of the House. Evidently Charles didn't expect Evie to take part, and made space for her to share his hand – but Evie baulked at the very suggestion. 'Do I come across as a demure little handmaiden?' she laughed, elbowing him in the ribs – and, after that, Charles knew his place. He seemed to like it too. Evie was a bold player, always willing to risk a new card in pursuit of an elusive win. Charles bested her first, but after that it was Evie besting him – and the House as well. A little pile of chips accumulated at her side, the spoils of a successful night.

'Perhaps some … French roulette?'

This did not seem as appealing to Evie, somehow. She had spent many long nights, ever since her girlhood, playing cards with the other members of the troupe. Some of her fondest memories were of the dancers, the acrobats, the magicians and ventriloquists and others who had variously made up the Company over the years, gathered around a fire late at night, light spilling out of the double-decker bus as they dealt hands of gin rummy, canasta, sometimes even cribbage. There was skill in cards – sometimes it was just the skill of courage, but it was a skill nevertheless. In roulette, there was just prayer. 'I prefer a card game,' she said.

'Then the mademoiselle is in luck,' came a voice from behind.

Charles and Evie turned to see that a broad-shouldered, slightly rotund man – bedecked not in the Casino's burgundy and gold, but in a suave black suit – had approached them across the blackjack lounge. 'Excuse me, M. Laurent, but your presence has been requested for a game of poker.'

'My presence? Requested?

Charles gave Evie a look as if to say that this wasn't something that happened all the time, but Evie suspected she knew better.

'This way, sir.'

Charles waited for Evie to thread her arm through his, before they followed the attendant out of the lounge, back across the baroque hall where countless French roulette wheels were spinning, and through a curtained doorway on the opposite side.

Inside, a table was laid out – and a middle-aged croupier with golden hair and moustaches, his body given to a little fat, was already in place. So too were four other players. Of them all, Evie recognised only one. He barely looked at her as he wheeled round to greet his new guests, for he had eyes for Charles alone.

'M. Laurent, I was told you were here!' enthused Benedict Frey. 'Please, please, come and sit down. I've a bet on you for the race, M. Laurent. Fifty pounds on first. But I thought – if I don't win it *because* of him, maybe I can win it *from* him tonight, and come out even either way.' Benedict brayed with laughter. 'I'm joking, Charles. I'm joking! I'm just... excited to see you. You know, if the screen hadn't been my calling, *I* might have been a racing driver.'

Charles was evidently uncomfortable with the young man's enthusiasm, but he received it graciously, and whisked Evie along to their seats at the table.

It was as Evie was settling down that she felt the eyes of the croupier upon her. Perhaps he was just inspecting her as he did all who came to play, but she couldn't help thinking that they held some other odiousness in them. He seemed to be swallowing some emotion as he tore his eyes away and declared to the rest of the table, 'My name is Hector Lambert, and tonight I will be presiding. There will be no rake, no commission, taken on this game – it is all to be courtesy of the House. Instead, it is requested that our photographer be present to document a game attended by such luminaries.' He bowed in turn to both Benedict and Charles.

Evie looked around. The photographer in the corner of the room at least looked more debonair – and more *civilised* – than the one who had snapped them at La Toison d'Or.

'If that is agreed, then let us begin.'

Poker was not a game the Forsyth Varieties had regularly played on tour, but Evie knew the rules well enough to work her way into the game. Charles had provided the stake, and the croupier seemed here only to keep the order of the House, playing very little part in proceedings except to deal cards at the change of each round.

Things started slowly, each player tentative as they sought to work out the others. Poker, Evie noted, was as much a game of character, courage and nuance as it was of luck; it required one to read minds – but nobody needed much guidance to read the mind of Benedict Frey, for he could hardly stop talking, and only grew more and more animated as he won the first hands. As for Charles, he kept folding early – the cards, it seemed, were being unkind to him, offering him no opportunities to sally ahead.

Or, at least, that was what Evie thought – until, several hands deep into the game, with Benedict acting as if he was lord of all he surveyed, just biding his time until the whole pot was his, Charles flashed her a look that said, 'Watch this, mademoiselle.' Then, making a theatrical show of whether he ought to fold or play, he decided to raise the stakes.

By this time, Benedict was so puffed up and confident he hardly seemed to care as Charles steadily raised the wager. The boy at Benedict's side, evidently his most ardent hanger-on, just kept goading Benedict onward and onward – until just about every chip was amassed in the middle of the table, and the game ready to explode.

'Mr Frey,' the croupier ventured, 'please reveal your hand.'

Benedict did so proudly. First he revealed a seven – but that was only the start. Then came the Jack of Diamonds. Then, with the smile deepening on Benedict's face, the Jack of Hearts. The Jack of Spades he turned over with a flourish – and, as he revealed the final Jack of Clubs, he was already on his feet, punching the air. 'M. Laurent,' he grinned, 'I might never beat you on the circuit – but I shall always remember beating you tonight. Shake my hand, sir. An invitation to the premiere will be yours – for you and your lovely lady, as well.'

Benedict was already trying to grasp Charles's hand, but Charles simply smiled at Evie and turned over each of his cards instead.

A four of hearts.

A five of hearts.

A six, a seven, an eight – all of hearts.

Benedict's face soured.

He staggered backwards.

'Straight flush beats four of a kind,' the croupier announced. 'M. Laurent takes the game – and, by the looks of it, the pot. Gentlemen.' And he stepped back, with an unusually dainty bow.

Evie was still disconcerted by the way the croupier kept flashing a sullied look at her, but she didn't have time to think about that now – because Benedict was already remonstrating, 'Are you *laughing* at me, M. Laurent? Are you really *laughing*?'

Charles was smiling, but that was all. Whatever else was inside him, he was holding it in. 'Just the joy of a victory,' he said, as he gathered the chips together, ready to cash in. 'Just the fleeting happiness of a driver who comes from behind and claims victory. Miss Forsyth, shall we?'

Evie stood and took Charles's arm.

'It very much feels like you *are* laughing at me, M. Laurent,' Benedict bawled, and grappled for Charles's shoulder as the racing driver turned to make his exit. 'Laughing at me and walking away. I wouldn't treat you with the same discourtesy, sir. I invited you to this table for the pleasure of your company. I didn't invite you here to be made a fool of.'

'If the gentleman could kindly lower his voice and manage his tone,' intervened the croupier, 'the House would appreciate...'

'Oh, the House is laughing at me too, is it?'

From the corner of the room, the flash of the photographer's camera went off. Benedict spun savagely towards it and said, 'Capturing M. Laurent's glory, is it? Or capturing my...'

'M. Frey,' the croupier began, 'we must keep decorum – or I must summon officials.'

The flash went off again, capturing the rictus of indignation that was Benedict Frey's face.

'Come on Gideon,' Benedict said to the most simpering hanger-on. 'This night's got a bad smell about it now.' His voice sallied after Charles and Evie as, heads held high, they left the private room. 'Laughing at me, Laurent. Well, who'll be laughing on Saturday? Who'll be laughing when that car can't even make it round the circuit? Talbot-Lago? *Talbot-Lago?* You can't come back from the dead, Laurent. It's all a cheap trick – a cheap, nasty trick!'

As soon as they were back on the Casino floor, Charles paused. It seemed he'd been holding something in too long.

Evie thought he was swallowing his anger at the way Benedict had acted – but now, when he finally released it, it was gales of laughter that erupted from him.

It was strange to hear him laugh. He was an elegant man, a serious man, but he doubled over, right there between the roulette tables, and had to cling on to Evie to steady himself. 'Never bluff a rally driver,' he said, when finally he caught his breath. 'The boy had it coming.'

'Are we playing on?' asked Evie.

But Charles seemed to think the night had reached its apex. 'Perhaps a midnight stroll, around the harbour, instead? It is a little more glamorous than wandering down the river at Reims…'

As soon as their chips were cashed in, and with the memory of Benedict's defeat still buoying them along, Charles and Evie marched back through the Casino atrium. There were few finer feelings than leaving a casino wealthier than when you entered; it made you feel as if fate really had favoured you after all.

Out on the Place du Casino, the night air was balmy; the smell of salt from the sea was underpinned with something delicate and sweet – but perhaps this was just the taste of triumph, thought Evie. As Charles hurried to meet the valet and have his car brought round, his fingers lightly trailed hers. For the umpteenth time that evening, the hairs on the back of her neck stood on end – and she thought: no, I will not kiss him, not tonight; let this night be perfect and uncomplicated. The last time I kissed Charles Laurent, it felt like a door was opening to a new life. If I'm to kiss him again, at least let it be *true*. Evie wasn't young anymore – there wasn't time for any more stolen summers. This time, if it was to happen at all, she wanted it to be real.

A hand clasped Evie's shoulder.

'Charles,' she said, startled – for the last she'd seen, he was somewhere off in front, waiting for the valet to return his car.

But when she wheeled round, it was not Charles who gripped her; it was Hector, the croupier, and his face was bunched purple in fury.

'Sir?' she ventured, uncertain what was going on. 'Did we – has something happened? Is it Mr … Frey?'

Her eyes flashed to the Casino doors, as if other croupiers or security guards might be about to march out – but no, there was only Hector, his face deep with creases as his fingers tightened on her shoulder.

'I told your father that if I ever saw your lot back in the Principality, he'd pay for it. That was the promise I made. That was the promise *he* made to me.'

From somewhere out towards the seafront, Charles's voice sounded: 'Unhand her, sir! Unhand her this instant!'

Hector released his grip on Evie and staggered backwards, though his eyes were still as baleful as ever they were.

'That promise is broken now,' Hector seethed as he retreated across the Place du Casino. 'All bets are off. *Null and void.* Your father owes me two thousand English pounds. My blood money, you vagabond bastards, and I'll have every penny. So you tell him that.' Then Hector blew a kiss into the air, turned and started to march back to his station.

Just as he vanished through the Casino doors, Charles caught Evie up.

'What was that all about?' he asked.

'I – I don't know,' Evie stuttered. She took Charles's hand. All the warmth and good feeling of the evening seemed to have evaporated, and suddenly she wanted it back. 'Just a … a … just something to do with Benedict, I think.'

But it wasn't that, she knew, as she followed Charles to his car – and on, to the harbour.

It was more than that.

That man somehow knew Evie's father.

And for the first time that night, she cast her mind back to the Fort Antoine of the afternoon – and the woman who'd been watching them, mysteriously, from her blocky red car.

*WEDNESDAY, 3 May 1967*

# Chapter Seven

Well, *this* was interesting.

Ed had woken early the next morning, for he'd promised to send word to the palace that everything was in order for that weekend's show. The moment he'd folded his letter inside an envelope and handed it to the palace courier waiting at the concierge desk, he found a table in the restaurant and sat down with a pot of coffee, orange juice and croissants. Of the many sad things about reaching old age, and the end of his touring life, was the thought that this would be his final week of croissants for breakfast. Ed loved almost everything about his home country, but he made exceptions for porridge.

Now, savouring the first taste of the buttery pastry, he opened up the newspaper he'd collected at the desk and froze.

He'd been expecting to read about the Grand Prix.

And, in a sense, he *was*.

He just hadn't expected his daughter to be at the centre of things.

On the front page of the *Monte Carlo Matin*, the headline read 'HOLLYWOOD CONTRE FORMULE 1: ALTERCATION LAIDE AU CASINO DE MONTE CARLO', and – though Ed's French was strong, after so many seasons touring the Riviera, not to mention his service years – it needed little translation, for the whole story was spelt out in the photograph which dominated the spread. There, in some gaming room at the Casino de Monte Carlo, the rally driver Charles Laurent was striding away from an apoplectic young film star by the name of Benedict Frey. While Frey's face had been caught in a mask of pure venom, his arms in the process of gesticulating wildly as he frothed out some invective, Laurent seemed a man of high dignity and bearing.

There, on his arm, looking for all the world like she was stepping out with her prince, stood Evie.

Ed spent two invigorating pots of coffee studying this article and its intimate description of the night before. 'Talbot-Lago driver wins big at the Casino, but can he win big for his team?' read the byline. 'Laurent's Secret Beauty' read an opinion piece. 'Who is the beautiful woman set upon stealing up-and-coming Talbot-Lago driver Charles Laurent's heart?' And, 'Might this be a distraction or an inspiration as we approach Saturday's Grand Prix?'

By the time the second pot of coffee was finished, the other members of the Company had started to emerge from their rooms and appear in the restaurant. Ed took one last look at the picture and marvelled at how, for the second time, Monte Carlo seemed to be bringing drama to the story of the Forsyth Varieties. Seventeen years since their last visit, and yet the Principality still had its spell cast over them. You didn't get high stakes romance on a tour to Bognor – but somehow, out here on the Riviera ...

Cal was approaching, sauntering through the restaurant with Sam on his shoulders as if he owned the place. Ed supposed he ought to be cautious with his son – he needed him at the Fort Antoine today, not gallivanting off with this reprobate Benedict

Frey – so, with one last look at the photograph, he folded the newspaper.

Wryly, he supposed he ought to be happy. He'd said to Princess Grace only two days before that he was eager for Evie to start driving her own life forward with the same gusto she gave to the Company; how much he wanted love to be in her future, how much he wanted her to build a family of her own; how much he wanted her to live on in children and grandchildren.

He just hadn't expected her to begin that journey on the front page of a newspaper.

'Grandpa!' Sam called out as Cal crashed into the seat opposite Ed.

Quickly, Ed slipped the newspaper out of sight. Right now, Cal didn't need the distraction.

'Cal, I need you at the Fort today. We'll build the middle piece of the show. I was thinking "Runaway Lovers", with Sam at the piano with you and …'

'Oh, I'll be there this afternoon,' Cal interjected, grabbing some toast and buttering it for Sam. 'I've got to go down to the set this morning. I'll tell you about it later. But first …' Cal bowed his head over the table, eyes flashing from side to side as if to make sure nobody else heard – though Ed noticed that every soul in the Company, who were now flooding the restaurant, seemed to be whispering in the same knowing, secretive tones – and said, 'Hey Dad, have you seen this morning's newspaper? You won't *believe* what Evie did last night …'

There was somebody else who couldn't believe what had happened last night, and right now he was marching up and down in his makeshift office on the set of *Monte Carlo by Moonlight*.

Albert Hines was slow to anger, but when he reckoned with the effects of Benedict Frey on this production, it bubbled up inside him.

At least the schedule was quieter today. A new set was being constructed on the beachhead for the midnight party scenes; at the temporary lot – where Albert now paced up and down, behind clapboard walls with the sound of carpenters, joiners and plasterers working without – a jail cell was being dressed for the scenes where Frey's character was imprisoned for causing a public nuisance. He'd thought to spend this time looking at the storyboards, making sure every scene was being framed correctly as the movie raced towards its denouement – but instead the morning had been lost in furious telephone calls with the financiers back at Parker & Parr. For the last hour, he'd had the telephone unplugged – there it sat, now, taunting him from its place on the table – but, just because he wasn't currently being barracked for it, didn't mean the problem had gone away.

Yes, making a movie really could be like being back in the Royal Navy.

With a derelict ship, a mutinous crew and a hurricane somewhere up ahead...

A knock came at the door.

'Come in,' Hines intoned, his voice heavy with dread.

At least Frey had the decency to look sheepish. He knew what was coming, of course, because gossip spreads around a film crew more quickly than measles on a ship – and, when he came through the doors, he barely had the courage to look Hines in the eye. Hines was grateful for that; if the boy had come in cocksure and defensive, preparing to be outraged at his conduct being called into question, he was liable to hurl him against the wall – which, flimsy as it was, would automatically buckle and cause him yet *another* problem.

'Do you think I like being dressed down, Ben?'

Benedict had taken his seat, but he hadn't been prepared for this question. It seemed to come out of nowhere. 'Mr Hines, you have to know how sorry I am. I had no idea last night was about to become a feature news article. As far as I was concerned, we were just taking in the sights of Monte Carlo. Then that man…'

Hines held up his hand. 'I've spent this morning being *thundered* at by London. They're apoplectic, Ben. *Apoplectic.*' By the vacant look on the younger man's face, he had no idea what the word meant. 'They're *furious*. Do you know what capital they've expended on you? Do you know what they have invested? This picture's meant to capture the feeling of summer. High adventure, high stakes, love and life and laughter. They hired you because you bring all that to the flick. You're emblematic of all of *that*. If they wanted some second-rate James Dean bad boy, they'd have gone out and got one.'

Frey just sat there, shell-shocked. It was just as well – because one iota of protest, and Hines was ready to send him packing.

'Ben, you put us all in jeopardy with this.' He brandished one of the manifold copies of the newspaper piled in the corner – he'd had Brielle and a group of other runners criss-crossing Monte Carlo, buying every single copy they could find – and slammed it down on the desk. 'You're meant to be the *good* boy. That's what we're selling to the world. Somebody clean-cut. Somebody the girls who moon at your posters want to take home – and somebody their mothers, who'll pay for their tickets, might quite like to take home as well. And yet… what do you think last night *shows*? What story do you think it's spinning to the world? And don't tell me it's all down to that rally driver, Ben – because, *look at him*. He's got a smile on his face, his head's held high and he's a beautiful woman on his arm. He's a winner – and you, you're a ...'

Hines caught himself before he said 'loser', because – true as it had been, and incandescent as he was, he still needed Benedict on side.

'I'm trying to protect you, Ben. We're *all* trying to protect you. The studio wants your name up in lights for years to come. But when you behave as you did last night ... By God, Ben, you make it difficult for everyone. We've got to put in a lot of work now. We've got to undo all this madness. Your reputation matters – it's what the world *thinks* about you that's going to sell this story. The studio wants you to make a big donation to this charity ball the Princess is hosting. We'll make a song and dance about it. And you're to keep out of trouble now, Ben. In fact, you're to do *nothing* in Monaco without my direct say-so. There are no more nights out. No more revelry. It's head down hard work from now until the end of the shoot – and if you want to hear that directly from Parker & Parr themselves, well, boy, I'm damn certain it can be arranged.'

As Cal cruised along the seafront, around the harbour and past the Fort where the rest of the Company were assembling, he let the wind blast in through the taxicab windows, making a mess of his wild black hair. He would have preferred to have been driving a sports car for a moment like this – perhaps he might even have borrowed one from the driver who seemed so enamoured with Evie? – but that hardly diminished the sense of *occasion* as he cut through the towers of Monte Carlo and embarked upon the mountain road. A short distance up the

slope, before the expansive golf club, he took a left and followed the trail until he reached the makeshift studio lot. The
thing making movies shared with putting on a good show was
that what the audience saw never quite compared to what went
on behind the scenes. Sometimes a theatre backstage could
be a tight, ramshackle warren of dressing rooms and cluttered
passageways – but all the audience saw was the magic of whatever unfolded on stage. A grand illusion, John Lauderdale used
to call it – the grandest illusion of all.

Judging by the look of the studio lot, it was much the same in
making movies. An old barn had been commandeered to build
sets – and, if it hadn't been for the cameras and the lighting rigs
and the general sense of industry as Cal climbed out of the car,
he might have taken it for any old farmyard in the world.

Brielle was waiting to shepherd Cal within. 'Right on time,
Mr Forsyth. Mr Hines is in with Benedict at the moment, but
I was told to bring you straight to him.'

Brielle led Cal across the yard and through the barn doors.
At least, in here, it felt more like Hollywood. Three sets were
under partial construction – some sort of dosshouse, a prison
cell and an area that looked as if it was meant to stand in for an
outside pier. A backdrop on hanging curtains displayed endless
black water, the breakers of waves shimmering as if in starlight
from above. It would have been a wonderful trick on the stage,
but Cal wondered how it might look on the silver screen. On
the stage, the artifice of it could become part of the show, but
on the screen it had to be disguised somehow. Perhaps it was
all a trick of the cameras and lights.

Mr Hines's office was one of a unit on the other side of the
sets, just a small area of flimsy partitions to afford the illusion
of privacy. They certainly weren't soundproofed – for, even as

Cal and Brielle approached, they could hear the raised voices. 'They call it "reputation management",' said Brielle with a smile and a shrug. 'Don't worry – he knows you're coming. You get used to it on the set. It's almost *impossible* to keep anything secret.'

Outside the office door, the newspapers that Brielle had been sent out to collect were piled up, waiting to be destroyed. Cal looked down at the photograph of his sister he'd first seen at the hotel and smiled. Evie hadn't had a lot of luck in romance, but when it came to her, it brought *drama*. At least, this time, the drama wasn't hers. She and Charles Laurent looked perfect together; if it hadn't been for the image of Benedict, a tantrum-ming twenty-something, behind her, it might have been a perfect image.

In the picture, there was another boy at Benedict's side. Cal hadn't noticed until now, but the look of him was certainly familiar. He shot a look back at the set. Yes, he'd seen him before – yesterday, down on the beachfront when they were shooting the bar scene. Gideon was his name. One of the wardrobe assistants, or make-up, or hair – something like that. Benedict, it seemed, had fervent fans everywhere – for, in the picture, Gideon seemed quite as outraged as Benedict himself.

'I'll let them know you're here,' Brielle said, trying to mask her amusement, 'or this might go on forever.'

She rapped on the door, then slipped inside.

While he was waiting to be called through, Cal gazed back at the sets. Yes, *this* might be the life. In and out of film sets, composing soundtracks, appearing briefly on screen and slowly gathering a showreel – too old to be a star? Well, a man could still dream. And then there was Sam, and what the future held in store for him. It was brilliant he was going to share a turn at the Fort Antoine this weekend – but mightn't the boy want *more*, just as Cal had once done?

Cal wasn't oblivious to his father's hopes and dreams. The company meant everything to Ed, for it had been the sum total of his life. But there was a world out here, a world pulsing with possibilities; if you chained yourself to one thing, you were limiting the story of your life. And that was what Cal had always wanted: a life that was *limitless*.

Now that he thought about it, that was a good name for a song. *Limitless*. The Life Unlimited. A … Love Unlimited? *Unlimited Love*?

The door opened up. 'Mr Hines is ready now,' grinned Brielle as she emerged and brushed past. 'Good luck, Mr Forsyth.'

Cal watched her go. He liked the girl. She had a wryness about her. She seemed to see what was going on around her and revel in its absurdity, rather than being carried along. A girl like that most likely had a brilliant future ahead of her.

Through the door, Cal saw Benedict and Albert Hines. Benedict was seated, Hines towering over him like a headmaster. No doubt fiery words had been exchanged because Benedict looked improbably chastened. 'Come in, Cal,' announced Hines, 'and we'll tell Benedict together.'

Cal stepped through the door and closed it behind him.

'Tell me *what*?'

Benedict's eyes flashed between Hines and the newcomer. He'd been chastened just moments ago, but apparently he hadn't lost his capacity for indignation, because Cal saw it flickering in his eyes.

'Ben, as you know, Cal has been hired to help you get the best out of your songs. I know that has been sitting uncomfortably with you, but I also know you recognise the importance of this picture's success – not just to me, not just to Parker & Parr, but to *you* and to everything that comes after. It only takes one picture to make a name. One hit sets up a half-century of success – you can take that for gospel. So I'm obliged that you've acknowledged his importance to this project – and I'm further obliged that you're working so eagerly with him to really elevate those tracks.'

Cal admired this man's choice of words. He was spinning a trap for Benedict – he already had him in chains after the debacle last night, and now he was feeding him lies as if they were truths, telling him how he felt and thanking him for the privilege – all the while, *daring* Benedict to disagree. It wasn't quite how his father would have handled things at the Varieties, but it was brutal and it was effective, for Benedict could do nothing but sit there, soaking it up.

'So what's changed?' Benedict asked through gritted teeth – the most decisive protest that, under the circumstances, it was possible to make.

'The studio have made a decision. Cal here has been invited to take the part of Donny in the third act.'

Benedict almost flew up out of his seat. 'That part's already cast.'

'Well, now it's been cast again – and poor Mr Nicholls has been paid his severance fee, so everything's straight. Benedict, these things happen in production. Tough decisions have to be made. Hearts get broken, but stars get made.' He paused. This time, when he spoke, he was addressing Cal. 'It's a small role, Mr Forsyth, which is why Benedict won't mind you taking it, but it's a pivotal moment in our production and it needs to *fly*. Donny Reaper is the leader of another band touring the Riviera. Benedict and his boys, here, have discovered there's a competition running at one of the beach clubs – and, if they can win top prize, it's just about enough to get them on a plane back home for the wedding. But Donny … he's *good*. And he's determined to win. The whole thing comes down to a head-to-head,' and Hines looked between Benedict and Cal with something approaching a malevolent glee, 'man to man for the winnings. To the victor, the spoils!'

This time, Benedict did stand. 'Of course, Forsyth, since it's *my* movie, I come out on top.'

Hines seemed to have enjoyed his moment in command. He returned to his desk, where he started shuffling papers, and said, 'Cal, we'll want you singing "Come Running" in the scene – but we'll need it a full band number. We discharged Mr Nicholls, but we've got musicians on set. Go out there and find 'em, and make sure they're ready by noon. Oh, and find that boy Gideon – he's got the wardrobe lined up.' There was a silence, as both Benedict and Cal absorbed Mr Hines's instruction. 'Well, get to it, boys! If we get it right, this scene ought to be electric. Two musicians at the top of their games, duking it out on the stage to see whose song's best? Why, you'll hardly need to be acting at all.'

Benedict hardly spoke to Cal after that. The moment they were out of the door, he stalked off in the direction of his trailer, while Brielle caught up with Cal and led him to the back of the lot – where, behind the jail cell set, a trio of musicians were waiting, tuning guitars and fiddling with drums.

'Boys, this is Cal,' Brielle said.

Cal had expected them to look at him suspiciously, but apparently they weren't as surprised nor disappointed to be handed a new leading man as Benedict had been. The bass player even leapt up to shake Cal's hand. 'Cal Forsyth,' he laughed, 'the runaway lover himself. Who'd have thought it? I'll bet that's got Ben riled.'

The other musicians just laughed. One of them, Cal was sure, threw a wink at Brielle, who immediately flushed scarlet.

'Let's not think about Benedict,' said Cal – who rather enjoyed the feeling of moral, as well as musical, superiority. No doubt Meredith would tell him to watch his tone – she had a better instinct for self-preservation than Cal had ever had; it was one of the many reasons he loved her – but, right now, he was happy (perhaps even eager) to revel in the moment. 'We've got three hours to learn a song.'

'Three hours,' the musicians laughed. 'That ought to leave time for a snooze as well …'

Cal couldn't remember the last time he'd played with a band. There'd been much of it in his wilderness years, churning out songs for others by day and playing the pubs and clubs by night – and it wasn't as if his time with the Forsyth Varieties was devoid of musical collaboration, because he had made the musical numbers there his own ever since he returned to the fold – but there was something exhilarating, even nostalgic, about playing with a band. This lot hadn't worked together before the production, but they gelled well enough, and the song was so fresh that they rather had to make it up as they went along. In the corner, a battered old upright piano stood in for the more elegant model he'd be playing when they went down to the set – but it was enough to fill Cal with glee. Soon, he became aware that various of the carpenters and joiners working on the set kept coming past to listen. That was when he knew he truly had a good thing going on. *That* was when he decided to really start performing.

They had just finished one particular run-through of the song – Cal was certain, now, that it was in good shape – when he looked up to find the wardrobe assistant Gideon standing to the side, with various jackets and trousers draped over one arm, a trolley filled with boots, belts and various other items just behind. The rake of a boy was clearly a Benedict fanatic, for he'd been at the Casino last night, but his face didn't betray any of the actor's indignation. 'We've got to get you fitted, Mr Forsyth,' he said, and soon Cal was being led away to one of the partitions, where Gideon started measuring his waist, his shoulders, his inside leg and shoe size, variously choosing and discarding items of clothing along the way.

'There, that ought to do,' he said at last, when Cal was in costume.

Cal considered himself in the full-length mirror mounted on the makeshift wall. An outfit like this would have been considered corny for the Forsyth Varieties. It would have been considered crude, attention-seeking, faintly absurd. He was wearing a Levi Strauss denim jacket that had been ornamented with flashing sequins, and jeans with leather patches stitched into them, as if he was performing at a flashy rodeo in the American south-west. The boots were snakeskin, there was oil in his hair and rings on his fingers the look and feel of which Cal rather detested. 'Really?' he said.

'Read the character sheet, Mr Forsyth. Donny's not the most stylish character.'

Cal could only stare hard into the mirror. A cinematic debut, and he was to be dressed like *this*?

There was still a half-hour until they were due on set. When he returned to the boys for one last run-through, their laughter moved in gales across the lot. 'Get yourself sorted, Cal. The boy's playing with you. There's no way Mr Hines is letting you on set dressed in *rhinestones*.'

Cal, who was suddenly aware how easily he'd been hood-winked, ripped off the denim jacket and kicked off the boots.

'Gideon's probably sore because of Benedict,' said the bassist, with a knowing look. 'Or maybe Ben sent him off to do some mischief. There are some folks who'll do anything to get close to a star. And Gideon for Benedict Frey?' The musicians started laughing. 'Well, it's like a dog to a bone.'

# Chapter Eight

Conrad Knight prized himself on being a man with formidable attention to detail. One year ago, he'd known nothing of racing cars and Formula 1 – but, as soon as an investment opportunity presented itself, he had steeped himself in the sport's history and nuances, accumulating intelligence from all the most experienced players in the field; and what he'd discovered, after diving so deeply into this new world, was that races were not won on the racetrack. Oh, of course, it *helped*. Of course it *mattered*. A talented driver who had long ago renounced his desire for self-preservation could give the team the edge it needed. But the driver was only a single part of the equation. The car was another. The technical team, the mechanical crew.

And, behind and above it all, eclipsing the importance of everything else: the *money*.

Like almost every other endeavour in the world, it was money that mattered. Whether it was football, movie production or *war*, everything was just a proxy for the real battle: one fund versus another; one man's hoard, duking it out with another man's hoard, to decide who was best. And, because Conrad Knight hated losing, he and his fund had wasted not a penny on making sure the new Talbot-Lago Grand Sport had a chance in this competition. No stone had been left unturned. No variable disregarded. Every penny expended would mean a pound in return when the stars lined up.

That was why, when Conrad Knight stopped for coffee above the spectacular palm trees of the Allée des Boulingrins that lunchtime – an oasis of peacefulness before the upcoming storm of the Grand Prix – his face turned white upon seeing the newspaper laid out for him.

'Is everything to your liking, monsieur?' asked the waiter, a concerned fellow with golden moustaches.

Conrad Knight's hand was trembling, for there – spread across the front page of the *Monte Carlo Matin* – was his prized driver, gallivanting in the Casino with the very same woman who, he was quite certain, had connived with that dog to ruin his suit.

But it wasn't the suit that worried him, not this morning.

It wasn't even the upstart actor remonstrating in the back of the picture.

It was the insouciant look on his driver's face.

The look that said that, with only a few days to go before history – and untold fortunes – were to be made, it was totally *acceptable* to be out on the town with some floozy on his arm, living the high life, acting like a win at the Casino de Monte Carlo meant a *thing* compared to the real game about to be played.

Conrad looked back at the waiter and smiled.

'You may keep the coffee,' he said, in his most imperious English. 'I don't have a second to spare.'

The telephone in Charles's suite at the Hotel de Lyon had started trilling at 7 a.m., but Charles knew better than to answer it. No doubt it was one of Conrad Knight's many personal secretaries – apparently the man wasn't content with anything less than an army of underlings – seeking assurances that he hadn't forgotten the scheduling of the day. But of course he hadn't. By 7.15 a.m. he had been out, taking a run along the seafront; by 8.30, freshly showered and breakfasting on orange juice and coffee in the hotel lounge. By 9 a.m., he had joined up with the Talbot-Lago crew at their staging ground, not far from the hairpin bend in the racetrack, east of the Casino where he'd spent such a wonderful evening. The crew had been eager to get Charles into the driver's seat for the first time this trip, for driver and car needed to be in perfect synchronicity if the race was to run according to plan. Dickie Anstis, the back-up driver, had already had the car on the track that morning. He was a good-natured Englishmen, a dozen years older than Charles – the only reason he hadn't been picked ahead of Charles was that those dozen years had bred a little timidity into him; it was one of the perils of experience – and eager to see what Charles could do in the car.

'We've a few days before the qualifying round,' Anstis remarked, running his hands over the handsome cyan and white car, the lightest thing Charles had ever driven – and nimbler than any.

'But not much time on the track for calibration,' chipped in one of the mechanics.

Charles slid into the seat and tested his weight upon the chassis. He *liked* this car. When she started soaring, it almost felt as if she disappeared – as if it was only him and the racetrack hurtling by.

'We've two sixty-minute practice runs tomorrow. There might be time the day after for some zipping about, but the stands will be full by then for the Formula 2 features. After that – well, Saturday's qualifying, and then it's race day, so …' Anstis shrugged. 'Better get the best out of today, M. Laurent. I reckon she'll fly for you, but you want to be comfortable.'

Charles shook the older man's hand.

'Speed before comfort, Mr Anstis!' he beamed.

By the time evening fell, the first flood of spectators would be arriving in Monaco. Tomorrow, the stands would be open – and the sport's most eager followers would be watching the practice runs, placing their bets, passing judgement and making calls about all that they saw. The sports writers would be here as well – Charles knew for certain that two of the Englishmen staying on his floor at the Hotel de Lyon were writing for the London newspapers. But, for now, there was just Charles and the track.

'Oh, and don't forget the press junket at lunchtime, M. Laurent,' called one of the mechanics, as Charles brought the engine to life and rolled the Grand Sport out of the siding, onto the course.

Charles would have been quite happy to forget that particular engagement, but it was all part of the role. 'How could I ever?' he called back.

Then, for the next half-hour, there was only the unadulterated joy of an engine purring, an empty track and the world turning to a blur all around him.

At the Fort Antoine, now that the sun was at its height, the players had retreated into the shade on the fringes of the amphi-theatre. The breeze rolling in over the azure waters provided a little relief from the burning heat of summer – but only a little. Ed, as had been his wont in the last few years, had been resting for some time in the shade of the mighty bougainvillea which overhung the back of the stone terrace. The brim of his boater hat was pulled down over his eyes, but Evie knew he was not really asleep; as ever, he remained alert to the comings and goings of the Company. She supposed he remained particularly alert for Cal – whose promise was broken by hours now, and for whom the whole company had been kept waiting.

A restlessness had settled in. Evie could tell, for the dancing girls had started playing with Jim Livesey – they seemed to get a kick out of teasing him, but Jim just seemed happy to get their attention – and that *always* meant they were bored. Nor was the sun helping. Rehearsing in conditions like this was always a challenge. Back home in Blighty there was such a thing as a 'matinee', but here on the Riviera, afternoons were for snoozing until the sun burnt its heat away.

Evie wouldn't have minded, except that longueurs had to be filled somehow – and, if they were not filled by rehearsal or rest, they were inevitably filled with gossip. And what else was there to gossip about except *her*? It hadn't been in her plans for yesterday evening to end up featured on the front page of the city newspaper, and of course it titillated Lily and the girls. She'd long been in danger of being an 'old maid' in their eyes – not that one of them would ever dare joke about it – and, of course, she knew they'd been eagerly wishing love into her life for years, but not one of them understood how the weight of expectation, and family responsibility, could tie a girl down. Lily had a boy back home – they were due to be married by Christmas, and who knew what became of her place at the Company after that? – and Verity seemed to have a few boys wrapped around her little finger. Travelling with the Company wasn't conducive to building a solid relationship, not unless you got lucky and fell in love with one of your fellow players (Evie doubted Jim Livesey would have that particular good fortune, but the kid was giving it his best shot – and who knew? Stranger illusions had been performed at the Forsyth Varieties), so a performing girl often left marriage and family until later in life.

But Evie? Evie had left it even later than most, and most nights it seemed like the chance had passed her by.

Most nights, she smiled to herself, but not *last night*.

None of the girls had asked about him yet. The Company changed from year to year, season to season, but if any of them remembered that summer in Reims with the same lucidity as Evie did, she would have been surprised. Nor did she want them to. The idea of Evie with a lover would be titillating enough for the dancing girls, but the idea that she'd rediscovered some lost love would be too much for them to contain. Surely they'd start gossiping about him coming back *just in time*, to save her from her solitude. A knight in shining armour.

Well, Evie had never held truck with white knights.

Then, quite without meaning to, she remembered how Charles had hurtled across the Place du Casino when the croupier had accosted her, the tone of his voice as he'd shouted 'Unhand her!', and how she'd felt as he'd reached her side – like there really was a guardian angel in her life, after all.

Not that she *needed* one, she reminded herself. She'd been rubbing along perfectly well, keeping this Company together when her father's will failed him, marshalling both men and women to a common cause, without any angels or knights to aid her.

But it had been *nice*. She had to admit that. Last night had been fun, but in that moment, she'd felt *protected* – and that was an unusual feeling for Evie Forsyth.

And no sooner had she thought of that, then she felt again that croupier's stubborn grip. She saw his porcine face, and heard his embittered words:

*'I told your father that if I ever saw your lot back in the Principality, he'd pay for it . . .'*

She couldn't help it. She looked at her resting father.

What *promise* had he made?

What *two thousand pounds*?

What *blood money* did he owe?

Ed Forsyth wasn't an angel. He'd had the voice of one, once, and there was much goodness inside him – but life was not an honest race, and there was nothing Ed wouldn't do to keep his family and the Company safe from harm. Travelling players attracted joyous crowds, but sometimes – just *sometimes* – they attracted scoundrels too, and Evie had known plenty of those in her career. Ed had known so many more. She knew there were secrets he kept to himself. He boxed them away, to stop them from corrupting his Company – to keep them, in the ultimate calculation, from corrupting his heart.

Evie hadn't known this, until the very last moment, when her mother got sick, when it was already nearly too late.

Ed had been hiding it all.

So what, she wondered, was he hiding right now?

On the golden sands just beyond the Principality's reach, a final electric guitar chord was struck – and a riot broke out.

On a makeshift stage outside the Bar Meridien – a dignified old nightspot that had received a flurry of capital from Parker & Parr and was now augmented with an outside stage, lighting rigs and around two hundred extras in various states of disarray – Cal threw his head up at the mic and howled out his song's final refrain:

'*I'll come running straiiiiight to . . . YOU!*'

Then he threw his arms open wide, letting the screams and applause crash over him as if they were real.

And perhaps they were – for Cal had rarely felt as exhilarated playing a song, certainly not one that he'd only just dreamt up a few days before. He lifted his sunglasses, looked around at the band – they seemed to be enjoying it too – before he bowed his lips to the microphone and said, 'You liked that? You want one more?'

The crowd of extras threw up their arms in exultation. For a moment, Cal felt like a prophet – and, whether they were acting or not, he hardly cared. Not for the first time, he began to perceive the true magic of the movies – to capture an emotion, for just one fleeting moment, to make something so clearly fake feel *real*.

'CUT!' cried Albert Hines, but Cal wasn't ready to cut. He swung back his arm, played another chord...

...but the effect was mute, for all the amplifiers had been turned off, and in the end all Cal could do was smile laconically at the crowd. 'You wish,' he said out loud.

Cal was distinctly aware of the sun, not just because of the perspiration that ran down his face, but because he knew he ought to have been at the Fort Antoine at least two hours ago. No doubt Evie would be seething at him when he finally arrived – Cal's sister wasn't *envious*, as such, of his activities beyond the Varieties, but she did have *opinions* – but what she didn't understand was that not everything on earth revolved around the Company. The entertainment world wasn't what it had been in their father's day. Change was the only constant in life.

There seemed to be some discussion going on below. Mr Hines had gathered with two of his associates – secondary directors, they seemed to be – and their heads were bowed in deep conversation. Occasionally their eyes flashed at Cal, then to the side of the stage where – just out of view of the cameras – Benedict and his own band were waiting. They'd already shot their three-minute rock-and-roll number that had enlivened the crowd, but hardly set them on fire. Benedict was pointedly kicking his heels, refusing to look at Cal – but he too seemed to understand that some important conversation was taking place.

Eventually, after a protracted debate around the cameras, Mr Hines strode back to the set and summoned Benedict and his band.

Even now, Benedict refused to look Cal in the eye. 'What's the story, Mr Hines?'

'Well boys, it's like this.' Hines put a finger to his lips, which put Cal in mind of a headmaster he'd once had. 'The songs are great. We're making *waves!*' Then his voice dropped an octave, and he added, 'But we've got them the wrong way round.'

For the one and only time in their lives, Benedict and Cal shared the same expression.

'Mr Hines, what do you—'

Hines held up his hand, inviting Benedict's silence. 'I don't need a test screening to tell me how these songs are playing. All I need is *them.*' And he waved airily behind him, as if to indicate the crowd. 'Ben, you did great. You got them *dancing!* But your character's meant to win this competition. Donny Reaper here,' and Hines indicated Cal with his thumb, 'is meant to give you a good scare. He's meant to keep the audience *guessing.* But ultimately, Ben, it's *you* who's got to win. We want the audience whooping when you do. We want their hearts skipping a beat. And right now ...' He turned away. 'Well, it isn't authentic. They won't buy it. We've got the songs the wrong way round – so we'll have to go again.'

Hines was already striding back to the cameras, barking for his crew to reset for another take, when Cal loped after him. 'You want me to *give* him my song. Mr Hines? You want me to *give* him my song?'

'Give, Cal?' said Mr Hines, barely breaking stride. 'Who said anything about give? You're selling us that song, and it's going to make everyone rich. What's the problem?'

Cal could scarcely believe the old man didn't understand. In fact, the old man *had* to understand. There was no other explanation for it: he was being wilfully obtuse.

'I sold you the song so that I could play it.'

Hines stopped and looked back. Over Cal's shoulder, he could see Benedict muttering darkly with his crowd. The moment he opened his lips to placate Cal, the young star started stalking over.

'I'll say this once more – and, if I have to be plain, I'll be plain. Cal, your song is trumping Ben's. Ben's is a flier, but yours is getting under their skin – and I can't have it. This is Ben's starring moment. He wins the contest, he catches the flight home; there are wedding bells, and record contracts, and the whole future opens up for Ben and his band. But it doesn't *wash* if your song's better. It doesn't ring true. So I need Ben singing "Come Running" – and you, Cal, will play Ben's song.'

For the second time that day, Benedict and Cal shared the same outraged look.

'His song's no better,' Benedict snarled. 'I got them warmed up, that's all. We shot it in the wrong order. And … they're *actors*, Mr Hines. Tell those extras to *act!*'

Cal smirked, 'That sounds like you think I've got an edge on you, Ben – if you really think a crowd needs to *pretend* …'

Benedict snorted, 'Mr Hines, let's just go again. I can whip them up. They've got an extra drink into them now.'

'And they're tired and the day gets old,' Hines intoned, his voice growing more severe by the second. 'So let's do this, gentlemen.' Momentarily, he softened. He took a step towards each man and laid one hand on each one's shoulder. 'The art of

the compromise, my good men. Cal's song, Benedict's voice –
and a *moment* in cinematic history is born.'

Another hour had passed before filming was complete. Yet
another hour had passed by the time Cal was flying along
the highway, screaming his frustration into the wind. Forever
captured on celluloid: Cal Forsyth singing another man's song,
and coming in second best. 'Your name in the credits, dear boy,'
Mr Hines had said as Cal took his leave – and maybe that
was some small consolation, but only *very* small. A *moment* in
cinematic history. Well, Cal wanted his moment. He'd felt it
once before in his life, when 'Runaway Lovers' was soaring to
the top of every chart, in the voices of a hundred artists, his
song the soundtrack to a hundred thousand love affairs. All he
wanted was to feel it again – and now…

Now it was Benedict's. Cal the songwriter; Benedict the
showman.

'I'm not happy about it either, Forsyth,' Benedict had said,
after he left the stage, the after-effect of his own rendition of
'Come Running' still rippling through the crowd.

But he'd looked happy enough as he strutted away, borne
along by the tide of applause.

Cal arrived at the Fort Antoine to the sound of Sam singing.
Apparently, the Company had waited for him too long – and
they'd gathered around the piano to give Sam *his* moment. It was
Meredith accompanying the boy where it ought to have been
Cal; Meredith, a perfectly capable pianist, who rolled her wrists
through the ascending melody of 'Runaway Lovers', until Sam's
little voice hit its peak. And, as Cal came up the stairs into the
fort, as he laid eyes on his son enjoying the simple pleasures of
music, thrilling at his little moment in the littlest of spotlights,
something of the fury he'd been feeling melted away.

He caught Evie's eye, across the arena. She was, of course, disappointed with him – but, for the moment, it didn't show; because, in that moment, each twin was thinking the very same thing: how wonderful it was to be starting out on this road in life; how beautiful the feeling of belonging to music and dance and spectacle and song.

How special just to love what you were doing, to be filled with promise and potential, and not be filled with fear for the future, with thoughts about failure, riddled with ambition.

Cal stilled.

'Sam,' he called out – and, in that moment, quite in contrast to everything he'd seen and felt today at the set, he remembered what the Forsyth Varieties were truly for.

The pre-race press junket, one of a dozen Charles was being frogmarched in front of, was held at the Hotel Hermitage, and seemed to have gone on forever. Charles wouldn't have minded as much if the event had been partitioned by team, and the journalists who'd gathered here had all been firing questions at him about the resurrection of Talbot-Lago and the intricacies of the Grand Sport. He wasn't just some mercenary driver for hire – he'd been with the team nine months, following the development of the vehicle every step of the way, road-testing it and pushing the mechanics to their absolute limits as they hunted down perfection – and, consequently, he knew everything there was to know about that vehicle. And nor was it as if he didn't enjoy the feeling of being in a room among so many racing luminaries. But the event seemed interminable, and after a little while the journalists seemed only to have eyes for Denny Hulme and his Brabham team, for Graham Hill – who the bookmakers all said was odds-on to extend his winning streak and take away first place – and Chris Amon, the avuncular Ferrari driver whose red and gold machine the photographers had been lusting after just outside the hotel. There was, at least, a nascent interest in Talbot-Lago. 'Everyone likes a good underdog story,' one of the London press gang ventured, 'but do you *really* think you can go all the way, M. Laurent?'

To which Charles had given his most winsome smile and announced, 'And even further!'

At least they liked that.

They'd write him up as a fearless showman, if nothing else.

But then came the inevitable questions about his brother, and Charles's natural charm ran cold. 'My brother will be proud of me whether we win or lose,' Charles declared, then added, sardonically, 'But he won't let me hear the end of it if I lose. There will be apparitions daily. Objects moved around my apartment. Voices in the night. "Charlie, oh Charlie..."'

There; that gave them something to write about at least. And it was, after all, the truth. Tobias had been dead twelve years, but Charles could still imagine how his brother would have teased him if he came last.

Well, what else were brothers for?

'And M. Laurent,' asked a reporter with a thick French accent, 'how are you preparing for your big day? By gambling with movie stars, perhaps?'

But Charles never got the chance to answer that question, for the event's organiser moved swiftly on – and just as well, because, for the very first time, he had no idea what to say.

He was due back at the staging ground as soon as the junket was over, but that reporter's last throwaway question had turned his mind back to Evie and last night's unexpected sojourn at the Casino de Monte Carlo. Charles was no stranger to casinos. Few racing folk were. There was something about a game of calculated chance that gave him the same heady thrill he got when the starting pistol went off and a race began – but, in spite of his winnings, it was not the thrill that he remembered most vividly from last night. No, it was the woman on his arm; the look of her, gazing out of the windows at La Toison d'Or, her face framed by the beauty of the mountain and the bay down below.

Charles's brother could not come back to life.

There was no second chance for Tobias Laurent.

But it seemed possible, *just possible*, that lost love might be resurrected. That there might be second chances in life after all.

The back-up cars were waiting in the brilliant, cascading sunshine outside the hotel, the world's photographers clamouring to catch them in the most brilliant light. Elegant models, dressed in miniskirts and dark glasses, struck stunning poses. And there was the Talbot-Lago Grand Sport, being fawned over by some coterie from Milan.

Charles slid into the vehicle, bowing to the crowd. There came a ripple of applause and expectation as he brought the engine to life. It wasn't, of course, the done thing to take the car beyond the allotted route – he ought to have driven it directly back to the staging ground – but, as he gunned the engine, he couldn't keep the idea at bay. He'd enjoyed taking his chances last night, hadn't he?

Well, why not another one now?

The Grand Sport zipped back to the roads, Charles waving out of the window and a dozen cameras clicking madly as he took off.

If he was quick about it, the crew wouldn't even know.

Through the grandstands, along the seafront, past the yacht club and over the port. Monte Carlo could feel like a village at times – if your idea of villages included many times more wealth than the entirety of Mayfair – and so it seemed to Charles as he reached the Fort Antoine, then slid the Grand Sport into the parade of black cabs sitting underneath the ancient walls. In a second, he had slipped out; then, promising himself he would not be long, he hurtled up the fort's switchback stairs.

At the top, a rehearsal was in full swing. In the middle of the amphitheatre, Evie and the other dancing girls were performing a routine of such complexity that Charles was quite stunned. Until this moment, he hadn't understood that dance could be a form of acrobatics as well – but so it was, because Evie's girls were balanced on top of one another, moving in perfect syn-chronicity to create wonderful, strange geometric shapes as the troupe leader, the elderly man Charles took to be Evie's father, pounded at the piano.

Quite a family, he thought to himself as he watched.

It was Cal who saw Charles first. His son was on his shoulders, scrabbling to get down so that he might race to the ramparts and catch a sight of the racing car below. Eventually, Cal tumbled, letting the boy take flight, and approached Charles. 'I hear you're causing ripples with Benedict Frey,' he grinned. A copy of the *Monte Carlo Matin* hung in Cal's hands, but apparently Charles hadn't properly seen it – for, when he looked at the front page, his eyes goggled.

'The young man and I crossed paths,' Charles shrugged. 'It isn't my fault if he's a sore loser. I think, perhaps, that *bravado* means a very different thing to a man who's used to being on camera. But real life isn't scripted.'

At the ramparts, Sam was hollering for his father, gesticulat-ing madly at the sports car below.

'Maybe he can take a ride?' Cal ventured when they joined him. 'Once around the circuit, before the madness begins?'

Charles said, 'I think I might lose my sponsors if I did any-thing so reckless.'

'Then . . . what about his father?'

Charles just stared.

'I spend my life driving an old black taxicab,' Cal explained. 'You can't blame a man for trying.'

'Come down to the staging ground after the Formula 2 features on Friday night. I might be able to show you around. It's going to be crazy for a few days, but . . .'

The two men were so focused on keeping Sam from scrambling over the ramparts in excitement that they did not, at first, realise the music had come to an end. Nor did they hear the footsteps behind them until Evie's voice sounded out: 'Actually, monsieur, we don't do private shows. Sneaking up here is probably an arrestable offence.' Then Evie joined them at the edge and looked over the top. Down below, in stark contrast to her father's canary-yellow Ford Anglia, stood the gleaming Talbot-Lago Grand Sport. 'I imagine *that's* an arrestable offence in your world as well. Bringing that car out here! Charles, what on earth are you doing?'

'Cocktails,' he announced.

'Cocktails?' Evie flashed her eyes around.

'Not now,' Charles replied. 'But . . . tonight. There's going to be a lot of madness between now and the race on Sunday. But tonight – well, there are a few spare hours, and I should like to spend them with you.'

Evie looked back at the girls, gathered in the middle of the amphitheatre. Her father, still propped by the piano, was watching her closely.

'Your father, he is very protective of you,' said Charles. 'I am sensing it.'

'Oh, I wouldn't worry about *him*,' laughed Cal, dropping the newspaper as he snatched up Sam and spirited him away. 'He might look like a vengeful father – but inside he's egging you on.'

Evie's jaw almost hit the floor as Cal scuttled off, but when she looked back at Charles, he too was smirking. 'Don't worry. You must remember – once, I had a brother too.'

It was the only thing he could have said to melt Evie's horror. She caught herself and said, 'I should love to have drinks with you. At the hotel?'

'I'll find you there,' said Charles, 'and sweep you away. But until then ... They'll think I took the car and rode into the sunset. Wish me *bon chance*, Mlle Forsyth.'

Evie was still watching the Grand Sport snake its way away from the Fort and back round the Port Hercule when her father joined her at the ramparts.

'I'm sorry Dad – I didn't expect an appearance. He just ...'

'I hardly think M. Laurent is going to divulge the secrets of our act,' said Ed, in good humour. Then, more quietly, he added, 'That young man ... you're behaving as though you've known him all of your life.' Wincing at his ailing back, Ed stooped down to pick up the newspaper Cal had left behind.

'That's not *quite* true.' She paused. 'Dad, do you remember Reims?'

She could tell by his vacant look that he didn't. But then, it had been so soon after losing his wife ...

'Charles was there that summer. Do you ever get the feeling, Dad, that life's *showing* you the way?'

'Sometimes it's like that.'

And Ed unrolled the newspaper, to reveal that striking image of Charles and Evie at the Casino de Monte Carlo, Benedict Frey contorted in fury in the background.

Evie had tried to stay away from this newspaper today. The girls had brandished their copies, but Evie had dodged their questions all day long – until, accepting her resolve could not be broken, they'd ceased their interrogation. Only now did she take the time to linger over it.

And the truth was, she and Charles weren't the only ones in this picture.

Nor were Benedict, that wardrobe assistant and the other players who'd been sitting around the poker table.

Because there, in the background, was the croupier who'd accosted her.

What was his name?

*Hector Lambert.*

Evie looked at her father.

There was a split second in which she thought she should keep it to herself.

But then she whispered, 'Dad, do you know this man?'

At first Ed demurred; only when Evie asked again did he ferret in his pocket, take out his reading spectacles and inspect the image.

Evie watched as his face blanched.

She saw the creases deepen just between his eyes.

Then she saw those same eyes light up, the corners of his lips twitching in a smile, a sudden sparkle animating every inch of his features – and knew for certain that something was wrong, because, right now, her father was *performing*. She'd seen the same flicker on his face a thousand different times: the moment her father transformed from the commanding backstage presence who led the Forsyth Varieties, to the cheeky chappie who bounced out to his audience and compèred each night.

'Oh, it was all a long time ago,' he said – and Evie was sure he was masking some lie. 'How long has it been since we came here? You and Cal were barely out of school, if I recall. Seventeen years! I didn't think I'd see this face again. But then... I didn't think I'd come back to Monte Carlo at all, not until the princess called us.'

It was on the tip of Evie's tongue to ask, '*Why*, Dad? *Why* were we not supposed to come back to Monte Carlo? What *happened* back then?', but Ed was just shaking his head merrily and pushing the rolled-up newspaper into his pocket. 'Has your brother seen this?' he asked, nonchalantly.

'He's been taunting me about the picture all day.'

'Yes, yes, that's right,' said Ed, 'he was chirruping about it at breakfast. But...' Again, he stopped. Again, he threw Evie one of his winsome smiles. But this one seemed to have an undercurrent of warning. This one seemed to be saying: ask no more questions, Evie, and I'll tell no more lies. 'It's a good job I've got one child who stays out of trouble, Evie. It's a good job I can depend on *you*.' He touched her arm. 'Take tonight off. See your racing driver. Who knows when we'll get the chance again? A few more days, one big show, and we'll be gone from Monaco – probably forever. It's best to take your chances while you can.'

And Evie thought: at least *one* thing my father says is true.

# Chapter Nine

Her father's fake smile had been following her all day, so by the time evening came, Evie was grateful to be taking a little time away from the Company.

She left the girls in the hotel bar, and picked her way across the airy reception hall. 'Stay out of trouble until I get back,' were the last words she said to Lily before she departed, meaning to freshen up and join them soon. 'We're here at the princess's welcome, and on the princess's charity. Do you know what I'm saying?' Lily had just grinned and saluted at that. 'You won't find us dancing on the tables, Evie,' she said, with the kind of look that meant, 'Do you remember all those *wonderful* times when we danced on the tables?' Evie only hoped they could be trusted. Her girls were not known as shrinking violets in the provincial towns back home where they took their show – but perhaps the elegance and refinement of the environment might seep into them somehow. Her father would never forgive them if they embarrassed Princess Grace.

Ed cut a rather lonely figure as he disappeared into the hotel restaurant to take dinner alone. Cal, Meredith and Sam were joining him as soon as they'd showered and changed – but, as Evie waited for the silver elevator to open its doors, she couldn't help watching him and feeling a rush of sadness. It wasn't just that the older company hands like John Lauderdale had remained in Blighty – though, of course, that did set him apart. Rather, it was the idea of the secret he was keeping. Until this afternoon, Evie thought she knew everything about her father. Ordinarily, parents had private lives beyond the understanding of their children – and so it should be, Evie thought, for they lived whole lives before their children came along – but with Evie and Ed those borders had long been eroded. Ed had lost a wife; Evie had lost a mother. Together, they needed to keep the Company alive. They'd been intertwined ever since.

*But now…*

There was something lonely about secrets.

She only wished she knew what it was.

The elevator door opened, and Evie slipped inside. Her suite was on the fourth storey, but she was just reaching for the button when another figure strode into the lift alongside her, almost barrelling her aside. It took her a moment to understand that she'd seen him before – but of course it was obvious, for nobody in the whole of the Principality dressed less suitably for the blistering Monacoan summer than this man. Conrad Knight was wearing a lighter suit than the one Tinky and Tiny had despoiled – but that was the only way he paid deference to the Riviera sun. His necktie was still done up tight around the starched collar, his brow still beaded with sweat – and, by the look of his face, there wasn't a thing this man understood less than the carefree feeling of the Mediterranean.

He too reached for the elevator buttons, pressing the one marked '5'.

As soon as the elevator started grinding its way upward, Conrad Knight intoned:

'I imagine, by now, you know who I am.'

Some women might have been cowed by that imperious tone, but not Evie Forsyth. Some women might have felt unnerved at being in an elevator with a man like this, the sense of entitlement and arrogance that he exuded, but not Evie Forsyth. She hadn't known who he was when she sent Tinky and Tiny against him, but she'd known what *kind* of man he was, and that was enough for her. This wasn't the 1800s. This was the 1960s. 1967, by God – and men like this were from a different age.

The advantage of standing in an elevator was that she didn't have to look him in the eye. She remained staring steadfastly ahead as she said, 'You're Conrad Knight – but you haven't asked for *my* name.'

'Madam, that is because I already know it. I make it my business to know everything that may affect the success or failure of my enterprise.' He turned on his heel, ninety degrees so that he was looking straight at her. 'Evelyn, I'm willing to overlook the ruin your dogs made of my trousers. I'll absorb the cleaning fee and not charge it back to your company. I am, at heart, a most reasonable man. But I stop being reasonable when my enterprise is under threat. I represent a body of most powerful men, and we have a vested interest – indeed, the *only* vested interest – in Talbot-Lago succeeding this week. As a consequence, we have a vested interest in Charles Laurent. Too much time and money, not to mention reputation, has been expended on a scheme most of our shareholders considered beyond the pale in terms of the risks involved. Long-shot schemes like ours are not undertaken lightly. We must leverage every last element of control if they are to succeed. Everything is accounted for. Every penny of expenditure, every moment, every foreseeable catastrophe. Every catastrophe except one…'

And, as if he'd been rehearsing the motion all day long, he produced from the small of his back the same newspaper that had been plaguing Evie all day.

Evie tried to resist turning to face him – something in the motion made it seem like he'd *won* – but the newspaper seemed to pull her round, as forceful as gravity.

'Funny,' she said, every muscle in her body turning rigid as the elevator flickered past the third storey, 'but I didn't think last night was too much of a catastrophe. Charles came away on top.'

'I'm not talking about the blasted Casino,' Conrad Knight seethed, his face bunched and purpling – as if he was unable to believe a mere woman had sniped back at him. 'I'm talking about *you*. I'm talking about adventure and romance, and how my prize driver's attention has been diluted. Evelyn, there is a reason why champion boxers are forbidden from seeing their wives before a fight. Women upend the mind. They dilute the senses. A fighter feels sated by a woman, when instead he ought to be filled with lust for the fight. And so it is with my driver. I need his focus on the course. I need the sole attention of his every desire to be on *winning*. Too much has been spent for him to fail!'

'Exactly why are we having this conversation, Mr Knight? Charles is an old friend of mine. Nothing more.'

Conrad Knight's face bunched up, as if to say he knew this was a lie. But what did a man like this know about love? What could he possibly know about second chances? Evie was leaving Monte Carlo in just a few short days; the last time she'd left Charles, she'd not seen him for fourteen years. Who was *he* to tell her who she should and shouldn't spend time with?

'My associates and I have the power to replace M. Laurent. It isn't what any of them want. Not *yet*. But it's within our remit. Winning is more important than one man. If they were to think his attention was distracted...'

The lift came to a halt. A bell rang. Evie turned back to the doors and fought against herself to ignore the shower of spittle which had just cascaded across her.

'Have you made this threat to Charles, sir?'

The lift doors opened.

'It is no threat,' Conrad Knight pronounced, suddenly much more of a gentleman than he'd been when the lift doors were closed. 'It's an explanation. Charles has lusted for an opportunity like this since the day he watched his brother die. Don't ruin it for him, Evelyn. All it would take is a few little words...'

Evie stepped out of the elevator. It was, she realised, suddenly so much easier to breathe.

She straightened herself, gathered her composure, looked back swiftly and said, 'My name is Evie, Mr Knight. My parents christened me Evie.'

Then she waved to him daintily as the elevator closed.

The moment she was gone, her heart felt as if it might erupt. Adrenaline coursed through her body – all the feelings of panic (yes, she admitted to herself, now, that it *was* panic) she'd been holding on to while she was trapped in the lift. Mingled with it all was the feeling of incandescence at being spoken to that way – but panic reigned supreme. It was frothing out of her as she made her way along the corridor, as she took the suite key out of her pocket, as she paused at the door and braced herself against the wall.

'No,' she said out loud.

It was as if she was commanding herself to calm down. Or perhaps she was simply saying no to the universe: *no, I will not do as I am told*.

Charles's suite was on the storey below. She knew because she'd left him there the evening before, high on their winnings from the Casino – with thoughts of the croupier running riot in her mind.

Her mind was running a very different kind of riot as she found the staircase, hurried down one level, then through a palatial hall where a porter was pushing a shining silver room service along, and approached his room. It was still an hour before they were due to meet, but Evie knew he was inside for she could hear him sashaying around. More than that, he was singing. His voice was not melodious enough to make the roster at the Forsyth Varieties, but it was strangely pleasant and charming nevertheless.

She knocked on the door.

When Charles opened it, he was obviously caught by surprise. Indeed, he seemed to have stepped out of the shower moments before – for there he stood, wrapped in a towel, his chestnut hair dark and shimmering. The air was filled with the scent of his cologne. Steam wreathed through the ensuite bathroom doors.

'Evie, I was to meet you in the bar. I'm not—'

She stepped into his suite and closed the door behind her.

'Conrad Knight,' she said, defiantly now that the panic was gone.

A silence extended between them. Charles turned from her, crossing the room to pick up a shirt hanging from an open wardrobe door. Between them, now, lay the grand king-size bed and its crisp white sheets, untouched since the chambermaids had visited that morning. 'Mr Knight?' Charles ventured. There was something here that did not make sense; she was telling him something he did not yet understand. 'But what of him?'

So Evie told him it all, every last word – for they were all imprinted upon her. She could almost hear him seething as she spoke them out loud. 'So I'm to come here,' she said, 'and tell you no. I'm to come here and tell you that we can't take cocktails tonight; that we can't see each other – not until … not until your race is already over, and my family have left Monaco forever.'

'The last time our paths intertwined, your Company left – and I didn't see you again, not until this very week.'

'I know,' said Evie. 'I know.'

Again: the silence. This time, it seemed filled with anticipation.

Charles dropped his shirt.

He strode round the bed.

'And is that why?' he asked. 'Evie, is that why you came?'

'He says I'll ruin you. That I'm the thing that will stop you winning. That it will kill the dreams you had, ever since…'

She had been going to say 'Tobias', but in one last stride Charles closed the distance between them and took hold of her hand. 'It isn't Conrad Knight who's racing that car,' he whispered. 'He thinks he owns me, but he isn't right.'

He ran his finger along the line of Evie's jaw, until she lifted herself and looked into his eyes.

'No,' she said, resolutely, 'nobody owns you, Charles.'

'Not yet,' he whispered.

That was when they kissed.

And if it wasn't the first time they'd held each other, if it wasn't *quite* the bloom of new love, it felt frighteningly like it. Evie remembered kissing him by the river in Reims. That moment, memorable as it was, was practically demure compared to this.

Then they fell to the bed – and after that, everything they did together really *was* new.

Afterwards, with the steam still curling through the room and their clothes lying strewn between the bathroom door and the foot of the bed, Evie said, 'Well, it's done now. Now you'll never win. All that pent-up emotion, all that lust you've just wasted. All that *wanting*. Up it's gone – up in smoke.'

'I'm sure I can summon some more,' said Charles, bowing in from above until his brow was pressed against hers. 'And spend it on you again and again.'

Evie kissed him, deep and long, then lay back as Charles rose, pulling on first his underclothes, then a pair of light tan chinos. She watched him closely as he buttoned up a blue shirt, folded back its sleeves and ran a comb through his hair. 'Where are you going?'

He kissed her again. 'I shan't be long. And then ... those cocktails?'

Evie looked from left to right, taking in the state of disarray in which they'd left the bed. 'I'll think about it,' she laughed.

The moment Charles left the suite, his demeanour changed. There was too much conviction in him to wait for the elevator, so he strode purposefully down the stairs, across the reception hall and through the bar – where the dancing girls of the Forsyth Varieties immediately started pointing him out, whispering as he passed, and the young illusionist looked suddenly despondent at all the diverted attention.

The hotel restaurant was buzzing with waiters flying back and forth, diners filling every table. As soon as Charles entered, the maître-d' approached, trying to offer him one of the few remaining spots – 'Perhaps the window, M. Laurent, overlooking the yachts?' – but Charles only inclined his head, said '*Un moment*,' and marched past.

Conrad Knight was sitting with Raphael Allard in the heart of the restaurant. A coterie of other men, obviously cut from the same cloth as Knight, made up the rest of the party. The wine, it seemed, had been flowing for some time already. Tables were steeped high, either with slivers of rare beef or platters of seafood.

Charles found a vacant chair at a neighbouring table, seized hold of it and forced it in between Conrad and Raphael.

'Mr Knight,' he proclaimed, heedless of the way the other men were looking at him. No doubt these were other financiers connected, in the oblique way of all financiers, to the Talbot-Lago bid. Right now, Charles didn't care. 'We need to speak.'

Conrad Knight looked more startled than Charles had imagined he might.

'You've no business, Mr Knight, intervening in my personal affairs. You've no business strong-arming anyone, least of all a woman, on my account.'

Knight opened his mouth to speak, but Charles pitched forward until he loomed above Conrad's plate, and said, 'I'm your driver. I'm a good one. I'm the best you have, and thank god you found me. But I'm not your possession. I'm not *chattel*. I signed a contract to drive for you. I didn't sign over anything else. Look me in the eye, Mr Knight.'

Knight's eyes had been flashing around the table, seeking either support or outrage from his fellow financiers. Now, finding only shock and horror, he fixed on Charles with a sudden resolve. 'I'll look you in the eye, Charles, and tell you what I told your woman: there is too much at stake in this endeavour for us to suffer an embarrassing loss. We bought your devotion, Charles. We bought your service. Instead, you turn up late, you spend your first night causing some fracas at the Casino – and it makes us, *all of us*,' and again his eyes roamed around the table, 'question your judgement. We've promised you the world, Charles. You're like the lowly parish priest who, suddenly, receives a visitation from the Lord. You're *chosen*, you fool, and *we* chose you. Is dedication a little too much to ask? Is it so presumptuous of us that we should expect you to keep your side of the bargain?'

Charles's glare was unwavering. 'You might have come to me, Mr Knight. Do your associates, here, know what kind of man you are? That you'd corner a lady in an elevator? That you'd try to frighten her into doing what you say? That isn't the act of a gentleman, sir. It's the act of a coward.'

Knight had had time, by now, to find his composure. Pointedly, he lifted his knife and fork and cut at the strips of rare, bloody steak sitting upon his plate. 'You know our covenant, Charles. If you must insist on this reckless behaviour, we will make a fresh calculation. And I believe I can speak for the shareholders,' he waved his arm around the table, 'here and at home, when I tell you not to think you are irreplaceable. We like you, Charles. You provide a *story*. But be under no illusions: there are fail-safes baked into our programme. If we deem you uncommitted, another will take your place.'

'Anstis?' Charles laughed. 'Dickie Anstis? He's a nice man, Mr Knight, but *nice* doesn't win races.'

Conrad Knight dabbed at his lips with his handkerchief and flashed a smile. 'Who said anything about Mr Anstis? A reliable fellow, but hardly cut from the cloth of a winner. No, Mr Anstis may find himself disappointed as well. Another Britisher, as it happens, and he's here in Monaco right now – chomping at the bit to prove himself.' Conrad stopped. 'We would rather keep things on an even keel, Charles. So do play along. You want your glory? Well, let us give it to you.'

Charles stood up, the seat underneath him clattering into the diners behind.

'Now Charles,' interjected Raphael Allard, 'let's not make this any more of a scene. We've already been plastered across the newspapers once this week. Let's save the headlines for the weekend, shall we?'

Charles turned to march away – but, by the time he'd reached the restaurant doors, Raphael had caught him. 'Charles, he's right about one thing. You have to play the game. This woman can wait, can't she? Well, can't she?'

'She waited once before. *I* waited. I let her slip out of my life and I waited fourteen years. Why should I wait again? She'll be gone from Monaco, and then...'

Allard just shrugged. 'I envy your emotions, Charles – but this has been driving you half your lifetime. Is she really worth it?'

There was a stringent, menacing silence.

'I provide you a *story*,' Charles said at last, with gritted teeth. 'What did he mean by that, Raphael?'

Raphael tried to dissemble, but after a few stuttering attempts he gave up. 'It's ever since he learnt about Toby. He's imagining ... the potential. How they'll portray you after you win. The drama of it. They think there's money in it. Something to echo through the ages.' Raphael paused. 'You see the sense in it? You must see the sense in it. It's only business, Charles. He acts like he's a king, but it's just ... business.'

'It's insulting,' Charles countered. 'You of all people must see that, Raphael. That I'd let her, however much she might mean to me, distract me from the mission? That I'd let *anyone* upend all that I've been working towards ever since Le Mans?' His voice lowered. 'I'll meet my brother out there, on the course,' he said. 'I'll fly into pole position. I'll lap the second best, and there he'll be – always just ahead of me, a younger man now but always just ahead, waving me on. And you think I'll lose my focus just because I've ... I've fallen in *love*?'

There it was: *love*, the word all of the financiers had been dreading. Raphael looked back across the restaurant. The eyes of everyone around the table were fixed on him. 'They've seen it before – only, in the boardroom instead of the track. Something comes along to change a man's life and it changes the man himself. Knight's always thought you were too emotional for this. The rest of us, we understand the value of emotion – and we're holding the line against him. Impassioned is everything to us! But help us, Charles. Help us for just a few more days. The whole world could be yours.' Raphael lowered his voice. 'Don't let Mr Knight rob you of the chance.'

Charles said no more. He simply gripped Raphael by the arm, lifted his sunglasses back onto his face and threw open the restaurant doors.

Upstairs, the day's exhaustion – or perhaps the exhaustion of just a single hour ago – had caught up with Evie. There she lay, eyes closed, curled up like a question mark with the bedsheets entangled around her. God, but she was beautiful. She'd been beautiful in Reims – but the years had made her more beautiful still. She'd grown into herself somehow; she looked peaceful, content – or perhaps that was just because she was lying there, curled up in the bed of someone she loved?

He remained there, watching her for some time – and perhaps his longing eyes somehow pierced her veil of sleep, for after a short while she opened her eyes, looked at him drowsily, then slid to the side so that he might join her.

So, thought Charles, there were to be no cocktails tonight.

And perhaps that was for the best – for what more fuel could he add to the fire, than to be seen in some upmarket bar, drinking Martinis with Evie as the sun went down?

He lay beside her.

He stroked her hair.

He thought of his brother's ghost, waiting for him out there on the racetrack.

He thought of this new driver, whoever he was, lined up to take his place.

And he thought about Evie, what the chances were of bumping into her again, what it might mean for the rest of his life.

'Is anything wrong?'

Her voice rose up to him from the deep fogs of sleep, but he just slid down beside her, allowing her to fold neatly into the crook of his arm.

'Nothing, my darling,' he answered – and thought, in that same moment, that however long this relationship might last, it would never be entirely honest again, for he had just told her his first lie. 'Not one little thing.'

# Chapter Ten

Sunset over the Fort Antoine: the sun's final rays setting the ocean alight in waves of amber and ochre hue.

Davith Harvard had not been particularly dismayed when Ed had to tell him that he and his dogs would not be being pampered at the Hotel de Lyon. The truth was, he wasn't – and never would be – comfortable with luxury. He'd been a travelling player, working alone or with whatever itinerant group would have him, since the dawn of the century – there wasn't a bus stop, village church or lonely hillside he hadn't slept in between Cardiff and Llandudno – and all he really needed was some protection from the weather, a flask of black tea and his dogs to keep him warm.

It would be wrong to say that, at the age of seventy-one, he hadn't been flattered by the idea of a big feather bed, a room-service trolley – and all courtesy of the Princess Grace – but, if it meant leaving Tinky and Tiny behind, it wasn't worth a thing.

Besides, he thought, as he laid out his picnic in the middle of the amphitheatre and gazed out over the waters, could any view compare to this? Once upon a time, men must have stood at these ramparts and seen the ships of invaders hoving into view over the horizon. Now, it was just the sun bidding its farewell.

There had been a good number of Tinkies and Tinies over the years. The ones who curled up at his side, sharing bites of a simple cheese baguette (he preferred this to the more lavish offerings of the Hotel de Lyon as well), were seven years old, which meant they had a good number of performing years in them yet. Davith supposed he would retire when they retired. He had enough saved up to buy a little timber shack somewhere on Pen y Fan, the mountain of his birth. The sunsets there could be glorious, when the rainclouds allowed – but, right now, he supposed he'd never see one as glorious as this again.

Solitude...

The company had fawned around him, as if it was the most terrible thing.

But what they didn't know was that Davith was never truly alone, not when he had his dogs.

For some time, as the sun went down, he had them prancing around the amphitheatre. The sets, what few they needed for a show in this elegant arena, were covered by tarpaulins, looking like strange grey monoliths in the dusk – but around them the dogs twirled and danced; and when Davith peeled back the covers on the Company piano and his aged fingers hammered out some honky-tonk, they rose on their hind-paws to sing along in tune.

This show was going to be perfect, thought Davith.

If the timing was right – and Davith *knew* Ed, so he knew it would be – they would reach the show's climax, when Cal's music joined with Evie's dance, and Davith led Tinky and Tiny out into the melee to weave in and out of it all.

What a treasure that would be for the princess and all of her patrons.

What a memory for the Forsyth Varieties themselves...

It was in this contented state of mind that Davith led Tinky and Tiny to the spot he'd laid out his bedrolls beneath the bougainvillea and bade them settle down.

No number of nights in the palatial suites of the Hotel de Lyon could compare to the perfection of falling asleep like this, with the sounds of the sea beneath him and the wheeling stars of the heavens above.

Davith fell asleep in a state of such peacefulness as he'd never achieved in this life.

He awoke to the crackle of fire, the rush of flames, the sudden panicked shrieking of his dogs.

Ordinarily, it took Davith a long time to wake up. Now, he started out of his dreams. For some time, he wasn't certain whether he was still sleeping or not. Surely this vision in front of him could only come from some nightmare. Surely these fandangoing flames and churning pillars of smoke could only come from the most fiery depths of imagination.

He looked around.

Across the amphitheatre, cauldrons of flames bounced and surged. One, two, three – great pyres sent roiling black smoke skyward to merge with the night. Davith heaved himself upward, staggering to his feet. 'Tinky! Tiny!' he cried out, steadying himself against the branches of the bougainvillea. 'Come to me boys.'

The dogs did as they were bid, but such panic coursed through them that they could hardly sit still. No matter what Davith said, they skipped and turned frantic circles around his feet. Their shrill yaps, not nearly as tuneful as when they sang, joined in terrible chorus with the raging fires.

'Come boys,' he said, helpless. 'Come now!'

He meant to lead them around the edge of the amphitheatre, for he was certain he could navigate a path to the stone steps leading down. The fortress itself could not catch fire, so the flames would not chase them. These were the sets that were burning all around them – the sets and, yes, the Company's old upright piano, the one that had travelled with them across continents and served them well for years.

'Go,' said Davith, and swept the dogs onward.

But Tinky and Tiny stayed where they were.

No amount of training, no number of years of dedication, loyalty and love, could override the instincts now driving them. Fire meant fear. Fire meant death. Fire, to an animal, was like the world being torn asunder.

So Davith crouched down and took the terriers in his arms.

He wheeled round to carry them from the flames.

And that was when he saw the figure of shadow darting between the burning sets.

Until that moment, all he'd been thinking about was how to get away. Only now did he wonder *why*. Fires like this did not start by accident. Wooden sets in a grey stone amphitheatre did not suddenly turn to infernos, not unless by the hand of God.

But this was not God.

This was just a man, a spindly man with a mop of woolly hair, and in his hands a canister of what Davith could only assume was petrol. Between the pyres he danced like some odd marionette, until at last he reached the one and only tarpaulin where flames did not yet rage. Davith was disoriented but he was quite certain that, underneath it, stood Jim Livesey's magical wardrobe. That wardrobe had been with the Company generations as well – it had been the centrepiece of so many of John Lauderdale's greatest illusions – but now the last of the petrol doused it; and now, before this blackguard could strike a match and ignite it, a spark from one of the other fires landed on the doused tarpaulin and fresh flames exploded vengefully upwards.

'Tiny, *please!*'

The dog was too petrified. Davith tried desperately to cling on to it as it twisted and bucked in his arms, but in the end it was no use. Though he held on to Tinky, Tiny flurried up out of his arms and hurtled off, he knew not where.

Davith's scream chased after the dog, but for the first time it caught the attention of the shadow man too. Between the burning pyres, he froze. His black, sightless face seemed to turn to take in Davith. Then, casting the petrol can into the fire, he turned and fled.

By the time Davith reached the top of the stone steps, the shadow man was already clattering towards the bottom. 'Stop!' Davith bawled. 'Stop, stop, stop!' But of course a man who had just set the Fort Antoine aflame cared nothing for the plaintive pleas of a Welshman; and, of course, Davith's mind was immediately torn back to the amphitheatre – where, somewhere, Tiny cowered from the flames.

'I'm coming,' he panted, breathlessly.

First, there was Tinky to worry about. He set the dog on the stones halfway down the steps, and commanded him to stay. Now that they were away from the flames, the little dog seemed to have shed some of its panic and Davith knew he would do as he was told. Satisfied, he ventured back above. Stepping back into the amphitheatre was like stepping into the jaws of hell. He paused at the stone arch at the top of the stairs, and all he could see was the flames. What a contrast it made to the splendid ochres, ambers and golds of the sunset before. Dancing flames against the endless seascape beyond.

The smoke was deepening now. Blackness coiled around him, choking his cries. 'Tiny!' he spluttered. 'Tiny!'

But it was no use. He felt as if he was wandering in some labyrinth where the walls kept shifting around him, where the paths kept changing, narrowing with every step. 'Tiny, little one. Tiny, *please*.'

And there he stood, a cowering black shape on the ever-changing pathway ahead.

Davith lurched forward, stumbling in some of the debris cast out of one of the fires. Flames to the left of him, flames to the right, he bowed down to pick up Tiny – but the dog whimpered at his touch, and only when he bore him aloft did Davith see how the fur along one of his flanks had been burnt back to the flesh, how one of his ears was naked and raw, how the dog's back haunch was hot and sticky to the touch.

'Oh Tiny,' he gasped.

A rush of flames deafened Davith. He turned on his heel, meaning to lope straight for the stairs – but the smoke was so thick that he realised he had no idea which way to go. He staggered one way, then staggered another, but all he could see now was smoke and fire – and the fear struck him, suddenly, that he might teeter over the edge, that he and poor Tiny might plummet over the precipice, dashing themselves on the rocks where the waves crashed below.

That was when he heard Tinky.

The dog was yapping, yapping for his master.

Yapping to show them the way.

Blind, gasping for breath, hunched over against the raging heat, Davith followed Tinky's summons – and somehow reached the clear air of the stairwell.

He was still heaving for breath as he reached the bottom of the stairs. There he stood, taking deep gulps of the air, Tiny trembling against his breast – until, at last, with fresh air in his lungs, he gazed around. The fire raged above, but down here there was only the night. The man of shadows had vanished, leaving Davith and his poor dogs behind.

Together they crashed into the double-decker bus, the only vehicle to which Davith had the keys. If only he'd been sleeping here as he was meant to, they wouldn't have been caught in the inferno above. If only he hadn't wanted the sunset, the night air, the sensation of stars overhead, Tiny might not have been injured.

He flung open cupboards and drawers, looking for something to help the little dog. Bandages and water – that was what he needed. He uncorked one of the canisters, doused one of Ed's dress shirts and pressed it to the panting dog. Poor Tiny, he was in such pain. His little black eyes sought out his master's, and Davith held him with a stare. 'You're going to be OK. I promise you're going to be OK.'

But he wouldn't be OK – not unless there was a veterinarian; not unless there were fluids and antibiotics, creams and salves and whatever other potions modern veterinarians might have.

He'd have to go for Ed.

It wasn't far to run around the port.

But Davith Harvard was old, his lungs were aching and he wasn't sure how quickly he could run.

'Oh, I shouldn't,' he said out loud, revolving to face the driver's partition and the steering wheel beyond. 'Oh, but it's been years.'

Nevertheless, he knew where to put the key. Nevertheless, his hands stopped trembling as he twisted it and brought the engine to life. Tiny needed him now – and, if that meant a seventy-one-year-old dog act should drive a double-decker bus through the Grand Prix grandstands of Monaco, well, that was just what would have to happen.

The hardest part was manoeuvering it away from the Fort Antoine. Davith was quite certain the rear end scraped across one of the Company's black cabs as he compelled it away – but he was also quite certain that none of it would matter, not once Ed discovered what had happened above.

But he wasn't thinking about that as the bus juddered and groaned onto the seafront.

He wasn't thinking about who might have started that fire, nor why.

He was thinking only about Tiny and his little beating heart, huddled in his lap as he wrenched the steering wheel round and then round again.

Davith would never know how long it took for him to reach the Hotel de Lyon that night. Time was different inside that bus, as the grandstands flew by. It seemed he was on a quest that took him a lifetime, and yet as if no time had passed at all. Later, when he looked back, the first thing he would remember was ripping the key from the ignition, lumbering off the bus with Tiny in his arms, to be met by a flood of alarmed doormen and concierges from the Hotel de Lyon, who had just rushed out to see the double-decker bus slewing around on the plaza in front of the hotel.

'Arrêtez, arrêtez-vous là!' one of them cried out.

'Stop!' cried another, upon seeing the vacant look on Davith's face.

Davith only reeled forward, heading for the hotel doors.

The doormen trying to stop him seemed so far away.

So, too, did the rest of the world.

That was, until one of the concierges grabbed him by the shoulders, wheeled him round and looked at him – the mad vagabond with the whimpering dog in his arms – directly in the eyes.

'You can't come in here, sir. You can't come in.'

The world rushed back into focus.

'Then bring me Ed Forsyth,' he sobbed, 'and bring him now. Tell him... something terrible's happened. One of our Company is dying,' and he held the little dog tighter, 'and the show can't go on!'

*THURSDAY, 4 May 1967*

# Chapter Eleven

Monte Carlo came alive in Grand Prix season, and today was the day that it truly began. Every hotel, from elite establishments like the Hermitage and Metropole to the mountain houses and apartments that the locals threw open, had filled its rooms last night. As the sun was going down over the Fort Antoine, porters and concierges across the Principality were helping guests to their rooms. As the inferno raged at the amphitheatre, drinks were being spilt, bets were being placed – anticipation rising, from the peaks of Mont Agel to the Pointe de la Veille. At the Monte Carlo Country Club, patrons gathered to debate the relative merits of BRM, Ferrari and the upstart Talbot-Lago. The day's last revellers at Plage du Larvotto made toasts to their teams.

And by dawn, over Continental breakfasts across the city, anticipation for the practice sessions of the day reached its pitch. Today, spectators from far and wide would get to *see* their teams in action. The commentariat would gather to prophesy victories and defeats. Those who'd been watching the reborn team with much interest would get to see Talbot-Lago's new Grand Sport in action – and the bookmakers salivated at the prospect.

But while anticipation built for one iconic event, devastation cast its pall over another.

For, rather than being swept up in the expectation of this glorious morning, Ed Forsyth was presiding over the ashes of the amphitheatre, prowling through the gutted sets, the skeleton of the ravished piano, the struts that were all that remained of John Lauderdale's magic wardrobe, built with his own hands fifty years before.

The ashes of his Company, sticking to his feet as he paraded the stage where, in just sixty hours, they were meant to be performing for the princess.

He'd been woken after midnight by the concierges, and all their urgent talk of the vagabond asking for him below. Ed knew immediately who it was, and reeled down through the hotel to meet Davith in the shadow of the double-decker bus, tending to Tiny as best he could with ice the doormen had brought out of the hotel. A veterinarian had been summoned, Davith whisked away, just as Ed barrelled into the night. By the time he reached the amphitheatre, the fires had lost their first rush of fervour – but that was only because they'd burnt so brilliant, burnt so fast, that they had almost run out of material to consume. The bougainvillea under which Ed had rested in the shade was a fiery emblem against the sky. Now, it was as brittle, black and stark as the trees Ed had marched through at Passchendaele – charcoal branches, where there had once been colour and life.

Evie and some of the girls lingered on the stone steps, ready to take account of everything that they'd lost, but the only figure who followed Ed around the amphitheatre was a young officer who had introduced himself as Inspector Patrice Maragoni. Maragoni was a stout man, broad-shouldered and dark, with keen eyes and the look of a hawk about him. Ed had him numbered as thirty years old, and a small part of him had been disappointed in his appearance; by thirty, Ed had fought in a war and risen to be the leader of his family company, but from his current vantage Maragoni was just a boy, and it beggared belief that the department had sent out a boy for a crime as brazen as this.

They were here at the summons of royalty, for goodness' sake.

'I have to ask, Mr Forsyth,' Maragoni began, down on his knees and running his fingers in the ash, as if he might detect something there. 'Is there anyone you can think of, anyone at all, who might hold a grudge against your Company?'

Ed loomed over the remains of the illusionist's cabinet. Most of the rest could be rebuilt – and no doubt Princess Grace would be able to supply them with a piano for the performance – but this cabinet was beyond replacement. The thought of breaking the news to John Lauderdale back home was almost too much to bear.

'Well, Mr Forsyth?'

Ed came to his senses. 'I can think of one person,' he muttered, darkly.

'We'll need you to make a statement, Mr Forsyth. We're not used to random outbursts of violence or criminality in the Principality. We're not used to anything as uncouth as this. If you have a sense of things, you must tell us.'

'Yes, I know.'

On the other side of the wreckage, Evie heard her father's tone. She had so rarely heard him speak with such sudden force, even venom. Lily and Verity shared a startled look. Not one of them had seen Ed snap like that since the days after Bella died, the days when – or so the Company had thought – he had quite lost his mind.

'Stay here, girls. We'll be able to start soon.'

Evie was not actually sure this was true, but nevertheless she confidently assured the girls and marched through the ruin to join her father and the police inspector. There she lay a hand on her father's shoulder and said, 'We can do this,' though she didn't know that this was true either.

Ed said, 'I know we can do this,' with the air of someone who had been told the opposite.

'Dad, I'm only saying…'

Ed seemed to have forgotten himself, but now he remembered. 'I'm sorry Evie,' he said more softly. 'These things are sent to try us. These things are *always* sent to try us.' He turned on his heel. 'Inspector, we have only sixty hours before our performance. We need to rebuild. How long until we can begin?'

Inspector Maragoni looked to the heavens, as if there lay the answer. 'I'll do what I can. The team's on its way. Photographers. Forensic specialists. We'll take what we can, but it seems pretty clear to me: you were the victim of an arson attack. Where will we find Mr Harvard?'

Evie said, 'He's at a veterinarian's near the Carré d'Or.'

The inspector turned on his heel, reaching for the radio at his waist. 'He's the only one who saw the culprit. Finding who did this may depend upon him. But I have to add, Mr Forsyth, if you know of *anyone*…'

'Yes,' Ed snapped, his vitriol flaring again, 'I told you the first time. I'm thinking. If it comes to me, you'll be the first to know.'

The inspector only glowered, as if he – like Evie – could tell there was some secret Ed was holding back.

'I'm hopeful you may begin by noon. Bear with us, Mr Forsyth.'

Then, with his radio crackling, the inspector marched towards the stone steps leading below.

'Rally them up,' said Ed quietly. Then he took Evie's hand. 'I'm glad you're here, my girl.'

Evie squeezed his hand in return, but a thought was already forming in her mind, and she had to give it voice. 'Dad, do you know anything? It's been seventeen years since we came to Monte Carlo. Can someone really be holding a grudge that long? Did something happen back then that…'

Ed's eyes flashed around. 'Where's Cal?' he asked.

Evie did not know if he'd ignored her pointedly, but she saw now that his eyes were shining, that he was holding in his tears. 'Cal's at the film set,' she said. 'He left before dawn, but…'

Ed lifted himself, turning to face the Company as they assembled. Behind the dancing girls, Jim Livesey looked broken – in all likelihood, there was no place for him in whatever act they could reconstitute now.

'He may as well be there,' Ed said, under his breath. 'Let him indulge himself today. He never was much use with a sweeping brush in his hand.'

Evie bristled. Wasn't that the attitude both their parents had had to Cal? *Leave him to his ambition, while the rest of us put in the hard work…*

The company had lined up, ringed in ash. Ed looked them up and down. 'Well, here it is. The calculation is simple. In sixty hours, this theatre – this wreckage, this ruin! – will be a spectacular. In sixty hours, these seats will be filled. We came here at Princess Grace's personal request – and, by God, we will not let her down.'

Evie's irritation melted away. She had quite forgotten how inspiring her father could be in adversity; sometimes, when she looked back, her most vivid recollections were of the moments he'd struggled – but it was good to remember how he could put on a show.

The dancing girls looked rapt.

So too did all the others.

'You have a morning at leisure. To take stock and replenish what reserves of energy and imagination you must. By afternoon,

I want you all back here to attend to the clear-up. After that, we have a fresh show to devise. We have song and dance – and yes, Jim, *magic* – to put back together.' Then Ed paused and stood, defiant, with his hands upon his hips. 'I'm afraid our time for indulging ourselves in the Riviera sun has come to an end. I'm afraid our time living like lords and ladies at the Hotel de Lyon is over as well. Go back, enjoy your morning – and pack your bags. Tonight, we circle the wagons. Tonight, the Fort Antoine is our home – for we camp out here, beneath the stars, and line up against anyone out there who means us harm. I should never have left it to Davith alone. Tonight, all of us will be here, living and breathing our performance, guarding our space – until, on Saturday night, Princess Grace's patrons file through those doors. We will not let her down.' Ed took Evie's hand again and lifted it with his own. 'And, more than anything, people, we will not let *ourselves* down. We never have before – and, by God, we don't start now. We're the Forsyth Varieties. This is how we live. Ladies and gentlemen, the show must go on.'

There was a place beyond the madness of central Monte Carlo, where a cluster of white stucco houses clung to the foothills of the Maritime Alps. The canary-yellow Ford Anglia crept along the approaching roads, then sat with its engine idling in the shadow of one of the grand carob trees that lined the street. There had been fewer houses here, at the Principality's uttermost edge, seventeen years ago. Ed remembered it as the poor relation of central Monte Carlo – a place of dirt tracks and small stake-holdings that belied the opulence along the port – but seventeen years could change a place. The opulence had spread outwards, as opulence always will. The houses were the same, but they looked *part* of Monte Carlo. The streets and gardens had been tended. The fierce heat had been tamed with sprinklers and irrigation. Colour bloomed, where there had once been scrub.

But, no matter how much had changed, he'd know this house anywhere.

It looked less run-down than it used to do. A city like Monte Carlo cannot abide its poorer places for very long. Ed left the Ford Anglia at the end of the road and slowly picked his way upward, using his cane, until he stood outside the house. Only one storey, with a gabled roof, and terraces for olive trees on either side. There was a doghouse in the yard, but no dog on the chain – and, to Ed's eye, it looked as if there hadn't been one for some time.

No car out front, he noticed, as he crossed the white picket fence surrounding the yard – certainly not a blocky red Citroen – but the windows were open, so he had to suppose that somebody was home.

He knocked on the door.

But there was no answer.

The screen door was loose, juddering in the breeze rolling down from the mountains.

He opened it, pushed at the inner door…

…but this one didn't move, for it was locked tight.

So, then, nobody was at home after all. That posed a problem. He'd wanted to look them in the eye. He'd wanted to glare deep within and know, instinctively, whether it was them or not.

*Seventeen years…*

He'd told her not to come poking around. He'd seen her parked outside the Fort Antoine and he'd gone down to her, as cheerily as he could, and told her they'd come at the princess's summons – or they wouldn't have come at all. 'I couldn't decline her,' Ed had said, 'you know that. But we'll be gone before the week's at its end – and then … well, then *never* really does mean *never*.'

He was still playing the conversation over and over as he paced around outside the house. Perhaps there was another way in – or perhaps somebody really was inside, sleeping off the terrible midday heat. It was what they did in this part of the world. It was what Ed ought to be doing himself, content in the shade of the bougainvillea, if only …

An image of fire streaked across him.

Flames dancing in formation, just like the girls Evie trained so diligently.

And … Evie *knew* something, didn't she? He didn't know how, and he didn't know how much, but it was there inside her. She'd tried to broach it with him, but he'd shut her out. For the first time since Bella died, he'd shut her out of his thoughts – and it hurt him more than he knew how to say.

But all he had to do was get through the next few days.

By Sunday night, the show would be long over, the Grand Prix won and the Forsyth Varieties moving in convoy back across the Continent – back to Blighty.

Back to *home*, and …

Retirement, Ed thought.

Yes, it really was right this time.

His father had once told him that he'd wake up one day and somehow *know* when it was his final curtain. He hadn't understood, not until the past few days. Inferno or not, Ed Forsyth was about to face his last ever audience. He just hoped he could carry the Company until Saturday night, without the whole edifice crumbling around him.

He was on his tiptoes, straining to peer through a window at the side of the house, when there came the sound of an approaching car – and a guttural voice hailed him from the side of the road.

'What in hell do you think you're—'

Ed turned.

It wasn't the red Citroen, and nor was it *her*. A white Renault Dauphine, battered around the edges, had ground to a halt on the other side of the fence – and, out of its window, leered a porcine, moustachioed face.

In the same moment that Ed recognised him, *he* recognised Ed. The two men fixed on each other as the driver unfolded from the car. He was bigger than Ed remembered – and Ed, so many years older, had grown smaller with age. The disparity unnerved him. The man had always been given to fat, but in his middle-age it had conquered him. His fists were like hams as he bowled through the gate, then stood between the olives, glaring as Ed made a tentative approach.

'Of all the places in God's green Earth you ought to be, Ed Forsyth, here you are, standing in my front yard.'

'Now, Hector,' said Ed, softly, 'I didn't expect to be here either.'

It had been like a knife in his side when Ed saw Hector Lambert lingering in the background of the photograph of Evie and Charles at the Casino de Monte Carlo. He supposed, somehow, that this was how Evie knew something was awry – but there was little time to debate that now. He held on to his cane, for he could see the antagonism bristling in the man. Some men thought the idea of a quiet life was beneath them. Indeed, Ed was one of them. The difference was – he chose performance, where Hector chose drinking and violence. He'd been that way seventeen years before, and there wasn't a thing in front of him to persuade Ed that 1967 was any different.

'I told you that, if I ever saw your Company in Monte Carlo again, I'd break bones. And yet here you are.'

'We came at Princess Grace's request, Hector. I couldn't turn her down.'

Hector took a stride forward, scything past the first of the olive trees. 'Did she request that you come to my house as well? Did she request that you come looking in my windows?'

In reply, Ed was silent.

'No, I thought not,' Hector went on. 'You're here looking for Estelle. Don't feed me your horseshit – I can see it on your face. Well, the old bird isn't here. She isn't here and, if she was, she wouldn't be seeing *you*.'

Ed begged to disagree. She'd come out to the Fort Antoine, hadn't she? By the look of him, Hector didn't know it – and, by the look of him, it wouldn't do Ed any favours to tell him. Instead, he said, 'We need to talk.'

'I don't need to talk, old man. I need my money. The past can stay buried, but we had a deal. Two thousand English pounds. I think that was the agreement. I think that was the … levy, on my silence.'

'You've already cost me hundreds, Hector.' Ed stopped. 'It was you, wasn't it? At the Fort Antoine last night, with a canister of petrol? You damn fool, they'll come after you for this. I can lead them back to you and you'll rot for it. That show's for Princess Grace. It's a damn charitable endeavour. You're stealing from the palace. You're stealing from the children they support. I always knew you had malice in you, but I didn't think you were crazy.' Ed stopped. 'I suppose seventeen years changes a man.'

Hector's face was suddenly bunched and purple. 'It's put some senility in you, I see. Petrol? What are you talking about?'

Ed just snorted, 'It's only you and me, Hector. You don't need to act innocent. You burnt down my sets and tried to ruin my show – but I'll put it on regardless, you see if I don't.'

'Check with the Casino, you dog. They'll tell you where I was last night. Dealing cards and counting chips. It's our busiest time of the year, and I was in the thick of it.' Hector laughed. 'You've got your own problems, old man, but it doesn't change a thing between us. Why would I set fire to your show, when I can take what I'm owed from you anyway?' Hector closed the distance between them. Now, up close, Ed could feel the warmth of his breath as he barked out, 'Two thousand pounds, or I'll tell the world your dirty little secret. How does it sound? You remember our agreement, at last?'

Ed lifted his cane – sharp, swift, with a performer's flourish – and felt some inner delight at the way Hector winced, rocking backwards. Yes, the man had violence inside him – but his avarice won out; if he punched Ed now, if it became a matter for the *gendarmes*, he was never going to get his money.

Ed's heart beat wildly as he levered past, through the olive groves, turning his back on Hector. 'You can't hold Bella against me anymore.' Then he pivoted, opened his mouth and snarled, 'She died a decade ago – she died without ever finding out, so it never had to break her heart.' His voice cracked on the last words. He had to pause, to take stock, to gather himself. Then, with his next ragged breaths, he said, 'I didn't come to Monte Carlo to stir up old evils. I didn't come to be reminded of betrayals. I would have stayed away forever, as we agreed, but the princess asked. You must understand that, Hector.' Ed paused. 'If I find out it *was* you who destroyed my sets last night, I'm going to tell everyone what happened seventeen years ago, and to hell with the consequences. Bella's gone, so her heart won't break – but you just see what it does to *your* family, Hector.'

By the time Ed reached the roadside, leaving Hector in the olive trees, a deep, unutterable shame had come across him. It wasn't the first threat he'd had to make in his life, but each one was harder than the last. Sometimes, his father had told him, a good man will have to do terrible things to keep his family safe – but he must always forgive himself, if his heart is in the right place. Well, Ed would try – but his mind was a maelstrom, his heart was in tumult and for the first time ever he started to wonder what was right and what was wrong.

Besides, if it truly hadn't been Hector last night – well, *who* had it been?

As he reached the canary-yellow Ford Anglia, another car rolled along the road – Estelle's blocky red Citroen, returning to the house where Hector waited. Through the windows, their gazes met. Her bright auburn curls bounced around her shoulders. She hadn't aged nearly as much as her husband. Her face was lined, but her eyes still sparkled with the same intoxicating youth of two decades before.

She was wasted on Hector.

She always had been.

And the problem was, *she* had known it too.

All Ed wanted to do was get away, but as the Citroen passed, she slowed down, winding down the window. 'Ed?' she ventured, bewildered. 'But what are you—'

'I needed to speak with him.'

'I don't understand. I came to the fort. You could have spoken to me.' She paused. 'Ed? Ed, my darling, what's going on? Has something…'

Ed slammed the key in the ignition, bringing the engine to life. 'I'm sorry, Estelle. That's between you and Hector now. I've got…' It was so hard to summon the words. His heart was straining in his breast. He was getting too old for the harder edge of things, too old to make the tough decisions, too old to lead his Company through disaster time and time again. But… it would feel better on show night, he told himself. He'd see it come together, as it always did, and remember why they did it. He'd hear the laughter, feel the applause, find himself buoyed by the music and the lights – and know once again, when he saw her in the audience, the reason he had so loved this life. 'I've got to go. I'm due at the palace. I've got to assure the princess … I've got to *promise* her that the show will go on.'

# Chapter Twelve

Charles Laurent was determined not to let Conrad Knight's threats keep ringing in his head as he reached the staging ground that afternoon. He'd barely slept a wink. Evie had lain contentedly against him, her head on his shoulder, his chest banked in black hair, but Charles hadn't been able to attain the same peacefulness – for Conrad's voice kept echoing through him. More than once, Evie woke and asked him what was wrong. More than once, she soothed him with a kiss. But no matter what, that English voice kept intoning in the back of Charles's mind: 'Be under no illusions... if we deem you uncommitted, another will take your place.'

When he woke in the morning, she was gone. A note at the bedside read: 'Until tonight. *Bon chance!*' His lover – yes, after fourteen years he was proud to think of her like that – wishing him well for the practice sessions ahead. Well, Charles Laurent didn't believe in luck; he believed in destiny, but not in blind chance.

Yet now, as he reached the staging ground to find Dickie Anstis and the team already gathered around the Talbot-Lago Grand Sport, he couldn't help his eyes flitting around. A British man, Knight had said. The secret back-up waiting in the wings.

What did destiny have in mind today?

Waves of noise moved across Monte Carlo. The stands had been filling since morning and, as they reached capacity, the noise was like the beginning of a storm. Once he was on the grid, of course, it would fade into the distance, and all that Charles would hear was the hum of his engine as it spirited him around the track. But right now, the cascade was growing in strength. It felt as if a storm was about to break.

'Do you want to walk the course before we get to it?' asked Dickie, as Charles approached the Grand Sport. The back-up vehicle was here too, jacked up while one of the crew lay underneath it, performing his checks.

Charles had never been in favour of walking the course. Perhaps there was a point on race day, when a driver might judge the direction of the wind or better appraise some nuance in the track – but, to Charles, that was all over-complicating one of the simplest matters on earth: he who was fastest won the race.

Today, however, he was feeling nervous for perhaps the first time in his life.

His eyes flashed around. The Lotus-BRM team were assembling a little further down the track. Beyond them, he saw the flash of the red Maserati the Swiss driver was warming up.

'OK,' said Charles. 'This time, let's walk it.'

The sun was reaching its meridian above the city.

In one hour, the first practice would begin.


In the same moment that the cars lined up in preparation, the same moment the drivers settled in, secured their helmets and took their last breaths, in the same instant that the starting pistol sounded and the first practice session began, Ed Forsyth was drawing the canary-yellow Ford Anglia across the Place du Palais and approaching the palace gates.

This time there was no valet waiting to spirit him somewhere else. This time, he was led directly towards the vast white palace, through the dark arch in its imposing face, past guardsmen standing solemnly by, and through a courtyard garden where a colourful array of exotica stood in great terracotta pots. Some time later, after having been left to wait under guard in a plush receiving hall – gazed upon by all the princes and princesses of times gone by – Ed was standing in a small chamber with Princess Grace. The walls here were lined in books, with two simple chairs sitting in a bright window overlooking the Place du Palais. Sunlight glittered over Monte Carlo. The buzz of the practice and its attendant crowds seemed like music soundtracking the city.

'It isn't the first time the Fort Antoine has seen fire,' said the princess, a severity underlining the kindness of her tone. 'As you know, the war was not kind to the fortress.'

'This time there was no war,' said Ed, gravely. 'This time, only the Forsyth Varieties. Your Highness, what happened last night is our fault. I feel sure of it. We were meant to bring an evening of joy and magic to your city. Instead, we've brought—'

'Oh, Ed,' said the princess, 'do be quiet.'

Her abruptness was not unkind, for a smile played in the corner of her lips, but she was also deadly serious. 'My aides alerted me after midnight to the fires burning on the Fort Antoine. I could see them from the palace windows. By now, the whole of Monte Carlo must be aware something terrible happened. But, Ed – and I mean this without belittling the attack on you – not one soul lost their lives last night. Your Company survives. It shoulders losses, but it survives.' She paused. 'You look tired, Ed. You've weathered storms before. What makes this one different?'

'An attack on the Company is an attack on my family,' Ed said. 'Your Highness, I don't want to let you down.'

'Then you shan't,' she said. Apparently, she had given up on convincing Ed not to call her 'Your Highness'; it seemed fundamental to the old man's sense of service, and she did not mean to take that away. 'There are still forty-eight hours between us and the crowd's first applause. I suspect you've staged a show in less.'

'It was meant to be a spectacular. But now . . .'

There was a silence.

'You doubt yourself, Ed. You've never doubted yourself before.'

He hadn't — but perhaps that was part of getting old as well. Perhaps that was what happened when the final curtain finally came.

'Ed, have you come to tell me the show goes on, or that the show is over?'

Suddenly galvanised, Ed got to his feet. 'The show goes on, Your Highness. Quite what the show is, I just don't know — not yet. But perhaps, by nightfall, we'll be back in rehearsal. Perhaps, by this time tomorrow, I could stand here and say we've built a fresh spectacular — without so many of our props.' He faltered. 'I came here to tender my apologies — and to say to you that, if a stripped back show, if a show that depends on the talents of my players more than the tricks of our trade, won't be enough to stun your spectators, I should understand it if you wanted to change plans. There is already such spectacle in Monte Carlo this weekend. Were you to think we were the Grand Prix's lesser cousin . . .'

'My guests are coming to see you, Ed. I shan't hear another word of it.'

Something in this steadied Ed. He'd spent so many years having to cultivate courage and belief in his players that, right now, it lifted his soul that somebody else had such conviction in him.

'Then I have work to do, Your Highness.'

He was already at the door when Princess Grace called back, 'Ed?'

He turned, to find her framed in the glorious light pouring in through the palace windows. Somewhere beyond her the clean-up at the Fort Antoine was about to begin. Ed knew he had to be there with his sleeves rolled up, getting filthy among his players. If he could spread the belief Princess Grace had just given him, perhaps he could yet make it happen.

But if it hadn't been Hector Lambert at the Fort Antoine last night – if it hadn't been the disgrace of seventeen years ago that led him up to the fort to launch his attack – then who *was* it?

They were still out there, he thought.

Still bent on undoing everything the Forsyth Varieties were putting together.

'Yes, Your Highness?'

'It isn't easy, leaving it all behind. Trust me. One summer, you're living the life you always dreamt about. You're on stage or you're on screen, and it feels like the world is yours. The whole world is at your feet, watching what you do. But one day you wake up and you know it's the end. Then you exit the stage and . . . you find the world is very different to what it was before. The anticipation, the expectation, the imagination – everything feels different.' She paused. 'But you find your feet again, and you look at the world in new ways – and, what you finally realise is, the world is this vast and beautiful place, whether you're in the spotlight or you're not.'

Ed smiled. 'I suspect, Your Highness, that you might still be in the spotlight.'

'The lights feel different now,' the princess shrugged, 'as they will for you, when the moment comes. But Ed, I'm looking at you, and I don't see a defeated man. I still see the young man Bella fell in love with. You're tired and you're shocked, still reeling from whatever happened last night. But you've been leading your players out for a generation. I believe, in my heart, that you have the conviction to lead them one last time. And what a send-off that might be, Ed, before you leave the glitz and the rush and the glamour behind. Give me a show to remember, because it's not just *my* memories you're making this weekend. It's the legend you pass on to Evie and Cal – and whoever comes next.'

The dancing girls were sunning themselves at the Plage du Larvotto, but the temptation for most of the Company – while they waited for Inspector Maragoni and his team to finish their assessment of the ashes at the Fort Antoine – was to find a place among the grandstands, or some higher vantage where they might catch a glimpse of the Grand Prix cars rushing past. Evie supposed she ought to have gone to watch the practice laps too, for she had left Charles in a fluster that morning, as soon as she'd sensed the commotion in the hotel and understood her Company was at the centre of it – but instead she was behind the wheel of one of the Company's black cabs, making her way up the mountain road to the lot where Parker & Parr were still hard at work shooting *Monte Carlo by Moonlight*.

It had been a long time since Evie last visited a film set. The Forsyths had been hired, on more than one occasion, to provide the background entertainment in bar scenes, theatre scenes – and one particularly flamboyant circus, which featured in a BBC *Play for Today* – but on those occasions she'd been part of an ensemble, arriving with all the attendant pomp and ceremony the studios arranged. Now, she was just disembarking a black cab on a dusty mountain road, to discover nothing but some great barns surrounded by lighting rigs, scaffold constructions and timber piles where the carpenters' offcuts had been piled high.

A runner met her at the barn doors, introducing herself as Brielle. Strange, thought Evie, but she looked faintly familiar. Her hair was as black as Evie's own, and though her complexion was the same olive as everyone's they'd seen this summer, her eyes were unusually vivid and blue. 'Mr Forsyth's hard at work,' she grinned, when Evie had introduced herself. 'After what happened yesterday, it's like they're fighting a battle without saying a word. Cal hates writing for him almost as much as Benedict hates singing them! But Mr Hines seems very pleased with what's coming out of those doors ...'

Evie was not surprised. It was a quiet moment on set, the scenes for that afternoon's filming still being prepped, so the sounds that came from behind the flimsy wooden partition where Cal and Benedict were working spread far and wide. Cal was pounding feverishly at the piano, but it was the way Benedict sang that really got the song going. 'Last week, that song was ... all right,' said Brielle. 'You enjoyed it, but then you forgot all about it. There are a thousand songs like that. *Ten thousand*. But now ...'

A group of set dressers and other assorted assistants were gathered by the partition, evidently using their lunch hour to listen in. From the middle of them, a young man with a mop of curly hair sprang up at Evie's appearance and, looking as if he'd been caught in the act of something terrible, vanished through a side door. 'Gideon,' said Brielle, shaking her head. 'What's got his goat?'

Evie thought she knew, for it had been that boy – just a wardrobe assistant, she realised now, so what was he doing hanging on to Benedict's coattails? – at the Casino de Monte Carlo when

Charles had embarrassed Benedict. To see Evie approaching must have been like seeing a ghost.

Brielle knocked on the partition wall, but for some time afterwards Cal and Benedict kept playing. Only when the song had come to its rambunctious conclusion, Cal concluding matters with a bluesy stampede, did the door open, revealing Benedict's ruddy face.

'Cal has a guest,' said Brielle, and seemed to savour the look on the young star's face as he too took in the apparition of Evie standing there. Gideon had been able to skedaddle, but Benedict just looked trapped. His face contorted into the same rictus the whole of Monte Carlo had seen in the newspaper – but this time he said nothing. 'I'll leave you to it then, shall I?' he breathed, then bustled past. Evie was quite certain she felt his elbow in her side as he passed, but she paid it no mind; it represented some significant life lessons learnt, if Benedict Frey was suddenly able to contain himself instead of lashing out with venom.

'Listen to this one, Evie,' said Cal, as Evie slipped within. 'It's almost a shame to waste this on Benedict. They've already taken "Come Running". But...' His fingers danced up and down the keys, pounding out a sequence that turned from minor to major and back again, toying with the listener's emotion. 'You know, I've come to some sort of accommodation with him. Some sort of... stalemate, I suppose you'd call it. Neither one of us wants to be here. Each one of us hates the other. But each one of us *needs* the other too.'

Evie rolled her eyes. 'It sounds like a wonderfully simple situation.'

'Oh, he thinks I'm his tool. But *I'm* sure he's mine. This is good work if you can get it, Evie. You get the call, you ride in, you patch up their sound – and then you move on. In, out and a pocketful of cash. It might be...' He stalled. He'd been going to say 'just what we need', but – as always – he seemed to have said something wrong. 'Evie, what is it?'

So she told him. She told him about the fire that had raged while they all slept. She told him about Davith's lame dog, the decimation of the sets, the ashes that were John Lauderdale's magic cabinet, the charred skeleton that was all that was left of the family piano.

And lastly, just as Cal was scrabbling around, shoving his piano scores back inside his satchel, reaching for his leather jacket, ready to depart, she grabbed him by the arm and told him about their father. 'He's hiding something. That night at the Casino, there was a croupier...'

Cal threw open the door and started marching, through all the set-hands who'd been listening, past all the sets, bound for the barn doors and the dusty mountain road beyond – so quickly that Evie stumbled to keep up.

'You should have told me this morning. It's my Company too. I wouldn't have come out here if I'd known. And Meredith, and Sam... where are *they*, if not at the Fort Antoine?'

'She took him to see the races. It's practice laps today. But Cal, you're not listening. There was a croupier. Name of Hector Lambert...'

Cal stopped dead, Evie's hand on his arm.

They were just stepping into the mountain sun, but other eyes followed them too. Upon hearing the name, Brielle cocked her head and listened, blue eyes open wide.

'What did you say?' Cal whispered.

'A croupier, up at the Casino. He was presiding over the game where,' and Evie lowered her voice, 'Benedict lost his head. He accosted me after the game. He said there was an old agreement, called us "vagabond bastards", said that Dad owed him money. Two thousand pounds. He called it blood money.'

'Blood money,' mouthed Cal.

'What if it was *him*, at the Fort last night? I asked Dad about him, but he just waved it away – like he … like he used to when we were children and he didn't want us to know about something. Do you remember after the war? We must have been fourteen, fifteen – in Liverpool for the summer, and … all the rioting going on, all those shop windows broken, that synagogue burnt down. But he had us playing snakes and ladders, while the city was on fire less than half a mile away.' Evie paused. 'He has a talent for it, Cal. He does it to protect us. But it's different now. We're different. *He's* different.'

'What are you saying, Evie?'

'What if something happened, seventeen years ago, the last time the Company came to Monte Carlo? What if Dad made it go away, then swore a blood oath that we'd never return? But now we're here, and this man – this Lambert – *remembers*. So, whatever it is, whatever it's for, he's coming after Dad. The agreement's broken, and he wants his blood.' She stopped. 'Dad wouldn't talk to me, but if we asked him together?'

Cal tore away from her, started marching through the scaffolding and timber piles, bound for the black cab that had brought him here. 'I wish I was driving something better than this. A few more jobs like this one, Evie, and the money could be flowing. Whatever ruin's been made of the gear at the Fort, I could replace it ten times over. I'm doing this *for* the Company, you know. I'm not doing it for anyone else.'

'Cal!' Evie exclaimed.

Cal heaved open the door. Some change had come over him, but Evie wasn't sure what it could possibly be. 'You leave Dad to me,' he said, as he slid into the driver's seat. 'I'll talk to him. If there's anything to answer for, I'll find it out. But Evie – there's a show to do. The Fort is obliterated, and we've a show to put on. Isn't that what we should be focused on right now?'

Evie stood there in the sun's full glare as Cal kicked the engine to life, unable to believe what she'd just heard. 'Cal, you've spent every hour, ever since we got here, pursuing *this* instead of—'

'I'm doing it *for* the Company, Evie,' said Cal, wrenching at the steering wheel to bring the taxi round. 'How much longer do you think travelling theatre will go on? How much longer will jugglers and dancers and dog acts captivate an audience, when they have all *this*?' And he waved at the stark barn walls, behind which movie magic was being wrought. 'We can keep it alive, you and I, if we're clever. But we can't keep it alive how Dad did, or how Grandpa did before him. The century's getting old, Evie. Times are changing.' He glared at her one last time before he sped off down the hillside. 'I'll sort Dad, Evie. Then two more days and we can leave Monte Carlo in the dust.'

If Cal couldn't cut it writing soundtracks, thought Evie, perhaps he could cut it writing movie dialogue – because, with perfect serendipity, the dust billowed up from his back wheels and overwhelmed her as she watched him leave.

For some time, Evie just stood there, caked in dirt. *Two more days and we can leave Monte Carlo.* Well, Evie didn't want to leave. Now that she'd rediscovered Charles Laurent, every piece of her wanted to stay. To leave right now – why, it would be like Reims all over again.

When she turned to reach her own car, she saw that the set-hand Brielle was standing some distance behind, her face screwed up as if she'd just watched something terrible unfold. 'Brothers,' Evie tutted, rolling her eyes. 'If you don't already have one, don't go and get one.'

Brielle stuttered forward. 'Cal's going to be needed. He's wanted on set in the morning – just for a few hours. Mr Hines was hoping he might rustle up some extras from your Company too. Just some dancing girls. Perhaps, *you*, E-Evie ...'

The girl had folded her arms across her chest. Half an hour ago, she'd been frothy and light; now she seemed to be looking inward, somehow, as if she'd heard something she didn't want to hear.

'It was only a family argument,' said Evie, softly. 'It happens all the time. I'll ...' She paused. There was every chance the players would all be needed tomorrow morning, but she supposed there was a chance the boys would be building new sets as well, anything so that they had something to work with by Saturday night. 'I'll see what I can do,' she promised, then started running for her own taxicab. 'The silly thing is, there's more drama outside your movie than there could ever be up on screen ...'

The first practice had come to an end. At the staging ground, the mechanics were scrambling to run their diagnostics on the Talbot-Lago, while Charles prowled up and down. It didn't bother his ego that he hadn't led practice – hardly any of the drivers here treated these laps competitively, no matter what the roars of the crowd might say. These were just exhibitions, to tantalise the crowds, iron out problems and ease the drivers into their tasks. No, what bothered him most was that, even strapped in with the engine buzzing, his mind hadn't been with him in the cab. On the racetrack, he who went fastest won out – but, in the boardroom, the calculation was not nearly so simple. Conrad Knight's words weren't just echoing inside him; they had started to weigh him down.

'He's showboating,' Raphael Allard told him, as the teams geared up for the afternoon's second practice. 'Knight has his own battles to win, just the same as you. *He* might not want you in the driver's seat, but the whole of the board ratified it. It's just put his nose out of joint. It makes him feel like he's lost some element of control. But you have to listen to me, Charles: he *can't* do anything, not without taking the board with him. And there isn't time to convince anyone of that. The time for boardroom dramas is gone. The only drama left is the drama you're built for – the drama of the track. Why, Charles, the only way he could replace you is if you drove the Grand Sport off the edge of the track and, and…'

Raphael stuttered into silence, for he suddenly realised that the image he'd been about to evoke had an entirely different connotation to Charles.

He must have looked suddenly shamefaced, for no sooner had his words petered out, than Charles gripped him by the shoulder and looked into his eye. 'Don't think of it, old man.' Then, turning back to the Grand Sport, he added, 'She was roaring. I could feel her wanting to go further, to go faster.'

Raphael smiled, 'Then *show* it. This time, don't hold back. Put Conrad Knight out of your mind, and put your foot the floor. And, as for that girl? Well, she's got enough to worry about today for herself – what with all that business up at the Fort last night. Let her focus on that, and you focus on—'

Charles had been about to slide back into the car, ready to guide her onto the grid for the second practice round, but Raphael's words stopped him dead. Halfway in and halfway out, he craned backwards and said, 'What business at the Fort?'

Immediately, Raphael realised he'd made a miscalculation. His face sagged. Moments ago, the team's star driver had stepped out from beneath the dark cloud that assailed him; now his face betrayed confusion again.

'Oh, it's nothing. I don't think anyone was hurt. But Charles, I thought you knew…'

His mind flashed back to that morning – Evie had been gone when he woke. 'Raphael,' he said, commandingly, 'what happened up there?'

'We're told it was a fire. There's a police investigation. Somebody – somebody obviously doesn't want a vaudeville act sullying the Fort Antoine.' He shrugged. 'But it's what Princess Grace wants, so the show must go on. I don't know, Charles. Is it any of our business? Is it any of yours? We only have one business, and it's right in front of us.' Raphael saw the way Charles glowered and quickly added, 'I'm not trying to be like Mr Knight. I'm just saying – we have priorities.'

Charles bowed into the car. Some moments later, he received the instruction to guide it onto the racetrack.

By the time he was at the grid and the starting pistol went off, he had accepted defeat: try as he might, he could not keep what Raphael had said from bursting into his mind. He pounded his foot against the accelerator, he deftly took each turn, he navigated the hairpin round the Fairmont Hotel with aplomb (perhaps it was just the caution of a practice session, but the Talbot-Lago seemed to have a true advantage here, for the other cars were taking the hairpin much more slowly than Charles). But, in spite of it all, he couldn't shake the picture of fire that streaked across his vision.

He'd had this same nightmare throughout his childhood, but this time it wasn't Tobias ringed in flame.

This time it was Evie, and it was all his fault.

Because there was only *one* person who'd threatened her since she set foot in Monte Carlo, wasn't there?

Conrad Knight, sliding into the elevator to confront her.

And all on Charles's account…

He flew round the track and emerged from his vehicle to the roar of the crowd – and, despite not pushing the Grand Sport into first, the congratulations of his team. 'She's a flier,' said Dickie Anstis, looking on the car with some envy. 'Qualification's not going to be a problem on Saturday, but we'll want a good placing. We'll want pole.'

But Charles wasn't thinking about that now. The qualifying round, and whoever won pole position for the race, would have to take care of itself on Saturday afternoon. Right now, only one thing mattered.

There was no hope of absconding with the Grand Sport again, so instead, Charles ditched his helmet and racing jacket – in the same cyan and white as the car – with the team, then hurried by foot to the seafront, ignoring the exclamations of the press pack and spectators pouring out of the stands.

Through the crowds he weaved his way, past the yacht club and around the Port Hercule. Long before he reached the Fort Antoine, he could smell the smoke of whatever had happened here the night before. As he careened through the Company flotilla, still ranged around the outer walls of the fortress, his heart was thundering in his breast. That this was his fault was almost too much to comprehend. What was it meant for? A warning shot? Just the way Conrad Knight dealt with those who disobeyed him? Moneyed men thought they were kings and kingmakers – and, like kings, they crushed commoners when they were in revolt.

Charles barely broke stride as he hurtled up the stairs and emerged into the amphitheatre above. The smell of smoke – and, yes, petrol, for it had been a petrol fire – still marred the summer air, but little was left of the devastation. Two dozen players and stagehands were working as one, scrubbing the flagstones, hammering together lengths of timber to make fresh sets. A new piano had been found, and Cal was deep in its guts, tuning every string – and showing his son how to do it, along the way.

And there was Evie, working alongside Cal's wife Meredith and her dancing girls, fixing up new costumes, putting fresh heels on dancing shoes, readying everything for the very same show somebody had tried to destroy.

It was one of the dancing girls, Lily, who saw Charles first. When she nudged Evie, Evie looked up; then, after a quiet word with Meredith, she crossed the amphitheatre floor to meet Charles.

Charles embraced her and would not let go, not until she whispered, 'It's all right. Nobody was hurt. One of the dogs, but… there's hope for him yet. Princess Grace's personal veterinarian is—'

'This is my fault,' Charles declared.

'What?'

'Conrad Knight. The threat he made…'

'It wasn't Knight,' whispered Evie. 'I think it was…' But then her eyes flashed at her father, standing on the very edge of the stage and gazing out to sea, and her words petered away. 'We've decamped from the Lyon. My father wants us here, tonight, under the stars. There's one last chance to put on this show, and he doesn't want to risk it.'

Charles's face twisted in horror. 'Absolutely not,' he declared. 'Stay here, so whoever it was can come again? No, Evie. Not this time. Not tonight. You're coming with me.'

For a moment, Evie was silent. Then, suddenly emboldened, she said, 'I know you're saying it because you care, Charles, but you don't get to tell me what to do. This is my family. This is my home. Where they go, I go. I don't need a knight in shining armour.'

Immediately, Charles realised his mistake. 'Then it's agreed. I shall stay here also.'

ANTON DU BEKE

Together, they turned round to take in the Forsyth Varieties, hard at work.

'You're insane. You're meant to race on Sunday. You need a bed.'

'I know you're saying it because you care, Evie, but ... Where you go, I go,' said Charles, in perfect imitation of Evie just moments before.

Evie rolled her eyes. She took hold of his arm. She looked up at the heavens, and the first slight paling of the sun.

'It's the Formula 2 feature races tomorrow,' he said. 'It's my day of rest.'

'Then you ought to be resting.'

But, 'No,' said Charles, 'I'll be right here. I'll be right where I'm needed.'

*FRIDAY, 5 May 1967*

# Chapter Thirteen

Davith opened his eyes, only to find himself in the same stark waiting room he'd been the night before. The walls around him were tiled, the whiteness broken only by a corkboard bedecked with fliers advertising medicines and explaining surgical procedures. Of all the seats in the waiting room, only his own was occupied. The smell of antiseptic filled the air. Somewhere, on the other side of the walls, gentle footsteps tolled.

In his lap, Tinky curled in a ball, whimpering intermittently through his fitful sleep.

Midnight.

One o'clock.

Two o'clock.

*Three . . .*

Sometime before four, he was roused by the whisper of a nurse. Startled, Davith leapt to his feet. 'Did something happen?' he asked.

Davith couldn't bear to say the word 'die'. He'd seen too many Tinkies and Tinies die over the years; each time, it hit rawer than the last.

His eyes were shimmering brightly as the nurse said, 'Come this way.'

So he followed her, past the reception desk and through a back door, into another room where the air was heavy with antiseptic scent. Past rows of empty cages they went, past another dog recuperating from surgery – until there, in a basket behind bars at the end of the row, sat Tiny.

The little dog was swaddled in so many bandages that they covered half his body. He lay spreadeagled, with his head on his front paws – but his eyes were luminescent, and when they took in Davith, the stub of what was left of his tail (for the burn had claimed so much and the vet taken much more) started beating wildly, even in spite of his pain.

'He might not dance again, but he'll keep you warm on a winter night,' said the nurse.

Tinky set up a merry howl – but, as Davith crouched down to nuzzle Tiny through the bars, his happiness was so consuming that he couldn't make a sound

Dawn over the Fort Antoine. Rosy light rolling in from the sea. Ed Forsyth was the first awake, as he was the first awake every morning, brewing tea on the camping stoves brought up from the Company stores. They'd begun the night keeping close watches, Cal relieving Ed at midnight so that the old man could get some rest on the bedrolls spread out across the amphitheatre, but some time in the night weariness had overcome them all – and the Company had slept as one, underneath the stars. There was strength in numbers, or so Evie said; no interloper would dare storm the fortress while so many gathered between its walls. And wasn't this, Ed thought, like old times? The Company out on the road, pitching camp, waiting for the next show to begin? If he shut his mind to the fire, if he shut his mind to the pressure and his aged body, if he shut his mind to the spectre of Hector Lambert, wasn't this almost... nostalgic?

Then he looked at Cal. He and Meredith slept upon a bedroll pushed up against the amphitheatre steps, Sam curled alongside them, his thumb in his mouth, that raggedy blanket he'd had ever since he was a baby in his arms. And, if anyone had been looking at Ed Forsyth then, they would have seen all the flickers of doubt, all the tremors of uncertainty, vanish from his face. As the sun came up over the Fort Antoine and shed its first light across him, a new resolve was hardening inside Ed Forsyth.

Some secrets, it seemed to be saying, should *stay* buried.

'Show night is almost upon us,' Ed declared, when the rest of the Company had roused. 'Only one night separates us from the curtains.' He looked around with a smile – because of course, inferno or not, there were no curtains at the open-air theatre. 'My friends, we've come this far. We can go a little further. Yesterday was a trial – but we must put it out of our minds, as we would any bad show.'

The company were paying attention now. Up on the stone steps with Charles, Evie wondered how much of the bravado her father was feigning – nobody here doubted his acting talents – but perhaps it didn't matter, for she could see how the dancing girls were perking up and paying attention. She could see, too, how Jim Livesey – whose act had been most ravaged by the fire – seemed brighter. Hugo, who drove the double-decker – and had once joined them on stage with his ventriloquist act – was nodding in fierce agreement, while Valentino, Benny and the other musicians joined in chorus.

All the questions of last night faded as Ed proclaimed:

'This is a different dawn.'

'Can I still sing, Grandpa?' Sam's little voice rang out.

'Does the sun still shine?' said Ed, and opened his arms to the golden orb hanging over the ocean.

Suddenly, Sam was on his feet and beaming. All the doubts he'd had that the show might be cancelled were finally melting away. It seemed that he'd get his moment in the spotlight after all.

Ed was about to continue when the sound of approaching vehicles stirred the Company. As one, they hurried to the top of the stone seating so that they might peer over the edge. If it was Inspector Maragoni and his police officers they were expecting, they were sorely mistaken – for, instead, three sleek black cars flying the Monacoan flag were approaching the fortress. Moments later, staff in the employ of the royal household emerged – and, from the backs of the cars, they brought platters of foods that would put the Hotel de Lyon to shame. Rich, buttery pastries were piled high with rainbows of golden pineapple and succulent melon. Beneath silver cloches sat cuts of bacon and ham, cheeses and baguettes still steaming from the palace ovens. Coffee and tea, honeys and preserves, spiced apple tartines and curls of smoked salmon.

'Courtesy of Princess Grace,' said the footman. 'I'm told to tell you, Mr Forsyth, that spectacular shows are not built upon empty stomachs.'

For the first time in what felt like an age, the smile that came to Ed's face was real.

'You may tell the princess that we are eternally grateful.'

Some time later, when the Company had finally come up for air after getting stuck into the banquet, Ed declared, 'The boys and I will be spending the morning with the sets and the scaffolds, setting the stage with what lights and amplifiers we need. Blocking each act for lights, when the sun goes down.' He looked around them. 'I would ask you all to stay, to find corners and rehearse your segments – but I'm told there might be another *opportunity* for some of you this morning,' and he made eyes at Cal. 'Given this week's unusual circumstances, I see no good reason to keep you from it. Make the most of it, people. Tonight we run the show as if it was real, against the sun going down. We'll assemble here two hours before "curtain". Oh, and Jim – I'll need you here all day, I'm afraid, if we're to find a way to make use of any magic at all.' Ed surveyed his troupe. 'One last time, Forsyths. Let's get through the day and see where the night might lead us.'

Albert Hines and his crew had already been on location at the Bar Meridien, just outside the Principality sands, for three hours when the red double-decker of the Forsyth Varieties careened along the seafront, coming to a halt just above the set. As Cal stepped out of the driver's cab, Sam tumbling out behind him – and Meredith hustling to keep him in check – he could see that the principal cast were also in attendance. Benedict stood among his band at the bar, while set dressers and wardrobe assistants clucked around. That young man, Gideon, was prancing around as if he owned the set, various leather and suede jackets slung over his arm.

But Cal had decided that, for today at least, he would let his rivalries slide.

Let Benedict resent him all he wished. Cal would commit to not caring.

Behind him, the dancing girls of the Forsyth Varieties – Lily, Verity, Betty and all the rest – poured out of the double-decker, then rushed out towards the sands where one of the runners was waiting to receive them. On the bluff above, Cal put his arm around Meredith, hoisted Sam onto his shoulders and said, 'They deserve it. After last night, something like this? It'll clean out the cobwebs. It'll give them new *vim* for the show.'

Meredith looked down on the girls as they rushed onto the beach, turning their acrobatic cartwheels – and drawing the eye of every man on set. Every man except, it seemed, Benedict Frey, who only cast his eyes in the other direction, as if resenting *their* presence as well.

'Did you ever imagine the summer might come to this?' Meredith asked, as they picked their way onto the beach. Gideon and his team had already diverted their attention to the girls, who were being led away to trailers on the other side of the set. 'Monte Carlo and movies…'

Cal just grinned at her. 'I've been telling you, ever since the Denmark Street days. Success like this? *It's…*'

'Yes, I know,' Meredith grinned in return, *'just round the corner.'*

'But it *is*. It always was!' said Cal, skipping forward. Up on his shoulders, Sam swayed wildly from side to side, then started making the sounds of one of the motorcars they'd seen from the stands yesterday afternoon. 'I was right, Merry. All I had to do was bide my time. And, when I was down on myself and dejected and despairing it would ever happen at all, *you* were right. Here we are.' He spun around on the spot.

'Cal, you're going to make him sick!' Meredith cried – but Sam didn't seem to care; he just screamed for Cal to go faster.

They had almost reached the set now. 'It mightn't be star billing,' said Cal, 'and I'm not saying it's the dream I had twenty years ago. But… it's a dream, isn't it? To sit at the piano and thrash out a song, and then suddenly, *suddenly* the whole world's singing? I think I'd rather this than what Benedict's about to have. The whole world knowing his name, but not really knowing his heart – because the songs he sings aren't *his*. Do you know what I mean?'

Meredith told him she did with a gentle squeeze of the hand, but in a whisper, she added, 'You better keep your voice down, Cal. Here comes Mr Hines.'

Albert Hines was lumbering towards them. 'Cal, I'm grateful for the mob you've brought with you. It looks like it might be a lively scene! Now, we need you on screen for this – Donny Reaper, just loitering in the background, giving a couple of dark looks when Benedict and his band take to the stage. This is their crowning moment, you see. One last concert, after the battle of the bands, and then it's on to the airport in the nick of time, to catch the last flight home. I'm sure it won't be too much of a stretch, young man – but you better get suited up.'

Hines drifted on, off to rouse Benedict for the shoot ahead.

'I'm proud of you, Cal,' said Meredith. 'But – just keep your head today. Don't let him rile you, whatever he says.'

'What ever can you mean, Mrs Forsyth?' grinned Cal.

He was taunting her. He knew only too well what she meant.

'Cal?' said Meredith, with the same withering look she gave Sam every time he was standing on the precipice of some mischief. 'We don't need more trouble. After what happened at the Fort…' Meredith paused. 'I've just got a feeling. Sometimes you can feel stormclouds coming.'

Sam looked up at the sky and crowed with laughter. 'Blue skies, Mama!'

'Blue skies,' said Cal, with a wink. 'Listen to me. I'm just going to do my part, have my fun and then we'll get back to the Fort. The other night was just some madman, just kids running wild. It happens in London. It happens in Penrith. It happens in Monte Carlo. But I know Dad needs us there, and I won't let him down. It's just that – he doesn't know it yet; he won't really accept it – but he needs *this* as well. Variety theatre, Merry, in a world like *this*? How many times have we talked about it? What have we always said? The Company can survive, but not as it is. We need to spread our wings. The world's changing, Merry, and we'll have to change with it.'

*

Evie did not like leaving the amphitheatre that morning. It was only at her father's insistence that she joined Charles as he departed for the Talbot-Lago staging ground. 'I shouldn't be seen with you,' she said, as they came round the port, to discover the streets of Monte Carlo already thronged with spectators turning out for the Formula 2 races. 'They'll know where you spent the night.'

But Charles said, 'Let them know. I'll tell them myself. Something Raphael said has been turning in my mind ever since. Whatever battle's going on in the boardroom, it's too late. I'm going to race tomorrow. Only an act of God could stop me.'

Evie couldn't help thinking that Charles sounded a little like Cal. Something about the singular determination of his words, the defiance, the idea that he was hurtling headlong towards his destiny – she'd seen those things in Cal, driving him to peaks of success and pits of despair, ever since they were children. For the first time, she wondered what might happen if Charles *didn't* win the race tomorrow? If Talbot-Lago didn't achieve its fairytale success? She wanted to tell him: life isn't fairytales. There was magic and dreaming in variety theatre, but you quickly learnt that it wasn't about glory. It wasn't about *winning*. It was about loving the work, being proud of your creation, a multitude of little victories and blessings. That was what Cal had never been able to reconcile himself with. If he wasn't standing on top of the world with everyone screaming his name, it didn't count. And somehow, in spite of every setback, in spite of every rejection and passing year, he'd been able to keep the belief that his moment was coming. Right now, she saw that in Charles too. They reached Boulevard Albert, the starting line of the race, and she could almost see the conviction hardening his features. Out on the grid, the sound of the engines of the Formula 2 teams, the swelling buzz of the crowds filling the stands, seemed to change him in an instant.

The Talbot-Lago staging ground was not far away. Charles spoke to one of the attendants, to secure Evie and himself a box above the promenade, that part of the course directly opposite the starting line, and picked his way there.

It was not a day of rest for the citizens of Monte Carlo, and for the drivers and teams competing in the Formula 2 contest it was the day they'd been building towards for long, hard months – but, for the Talbot-Lago team, it was a day to tinker, a day to appraise, a day to take stock of all they'd learnt in the practice sessions and decide upon any changes they might need before the qualifying round tomorrow afternoon. At least, as Charles and Evie approached, there was no sign of Conrad Knight. Nor were Raphael Allard or any of the other financiers from the hotel in attendance. The two vehicles stood on blocks, while the mechanics performed their inspections. One of the engines was open to the air; tyres were being refitted and calibrated.

'Where's Dickie?' asked Charles, glancing around the garage.

The mechanic who'd been buried in the engine looked up, a small wrench in hand. His eyes lit up when he saw Charles. Charles was not certain that he'd seen the man before, though the team had been swelling across the season and it was entirely possible he'd forgotten the face. This man was small, with slight shoulders and cropped red hair. Eagerly, he rushed forward, extending his hand. Before Charles knew what was happening, the man had seized it and started shaking. 'Mr Anstis was taken ill last night, sir.' The young man spoke with a polished English accent, the kind achieved only through elocution lessons or one of that country's elite boarding schools. 'Something he ate, the boys are saying. Well, he's always had a poor constitution. My name's Chapman. Christian Chapman. It's a pleasure to meet you, sir. I've been following your career since Syracuse. I was sixteen, sir. I saw you race.'

Charles was rather caught off-guard by the young man's enthusiastic shaking. Syracuse had been a Formula 3 competition, way back in '61. If Christian had been sixteen then, that made him twenty-three now – but he still had the puppyish look of a teenager about him.

'I'm here with Brabham-Lotus. I'm their back-up driver. Or I was until I got the call about Dickie last night and … Well, I'm at your service, sir.' He gave Charles a mock salute – quite preposterous, thought Charles, but at least it meant he had let go of his hand. 'I couldn't be prouder to be part of the team.'

Charles sauntered over to the vehicles, Evie marching alongside. 'She handled perfectly yesterday. Let's not fix what's not broken, boys?'

'Oh absolutely, M. Laurent,' Christian replied, skipping back to Charles's side. 'We'll have her refined and ready by the time the tracks are cleared this afternoon. Then it's only the qualifying round between you and glory, sir.'

With the team hard at work, Charles and Evie returned to the promenade and entered the clamour of the stands. In the gap behind them, the harbour was amassing with yachts and other pleasure craft. Out on the water, Evie thought, was perhaps the best place to watch the race – for there would be none of the uproar she had in her ears the moment the starting pistol went off.

'Hold on,' said Charles, with mounting anticipation, 'here they come …'

Hemmed in on either side, Evie saw the first cars reach the seafront stretch. One second they were here, the next they were gone, harried on their way by the roar of the crowd. This was a different kind of roar to any Evie had ever known – more sudden, more dramatic, than she had received in any theatre. Some moments later, when the cars lapped again, the roar exploded for a second time. The peaks were sudden, but the troughs did not last long. Again and again, the wave kept coming.

'But just wait until Sunday,' Charles said, his voice barely audible beneath the din. 'Then you'll know what real crowds sound like. Then you'll know what real engines can do. This is Formula 2, Evie – the engine power is capped. But the Grand Sport...'

Charles went on, but his voice was drowned out by the clamour as the cars hurtled by again.

Evie followed them with her eyes.

Then, when they had gone – and she could finally hear Charles again, soliloquising on the majesty of the Talbot-Lago Grand Sport – she looked upward.

The stands on the other side of the track were on their feet, cheering the cars as they flashed past – but, as they all settled back down, Evie's eyes latched on to one person in particular.

There he stood, the same porcine face with the same straw-coloured moustaches, the same thickset body and disproportion-ate gut. Now that he was no longer in the smart burgundy and gold of the Casino de Monte Carlo, Hector Lambert did not look nearly as polished. His fists were closed tight, jabbing the air as the excitement of the passing cars moved on.

Evie was about to tell Charles, when she saw the two women at his side. She'd seen them each once before, but quite what they were doing together she did not know.

On Hector Lambert's left sat the same middle-aged woman with bright auburn curls who Evie had seen leaning against the bonnet of her blocky red Citroen outside the Fort Antoine.

Beside Hector she looked smaller somehow, but Evie was certain it was the same woman. Her fingers trailed a cigarette, just as they had that day at the Fort – but there looked something almost sad about her, something almost defeated, something which had certainly not been there that day when Evie's father went down to speak with her and send her on her way.

On the other side of Hector: the girl named Brielle.

Evie was certain it was her. Even at a distance she was striking, her black hair a silhouette against the kaleidoscope of colour in the stands. Like Hector beside her, she was energised. When the cars next came round, she leapt to her feet – and, like Hector, started punching the air with vigour. On the film set she'd seemed cool and collected, but in the stands she seemed gripped by the same fever as all those around her.

She leant across Hector now and took the red-haired woman's hand, raising it into the air as if to encourage her along.

A *family*? thought Evie.

But never before had she seen a family so wholly mismatched: auburn, golden and black, and not one of them looking like the others.

Not like her family.

Cal and Evie, with the same dark wildness that their father had had.

Charles was trying to get her attention, but all of a sudden, all the tumult and chaos of the grandstands seemed to fade into silence. The world was retreating from Evie Forsyth. Right now, she was no longer in the stands above the promenade, waiting for the cars to thunder by. Now, she was alone, suspended in the air, reeling through her memories of Monte Carlo, seventeen years before. She and Cal, running wild, unable to believe the wondrous sights of the Principality, while their mother oversaw the Company and their father busied himself around town, taking meetings with hoteliers, drumming up an audience, spreading the word of their spectacular show, to be performed right there on Larvotto beach.

What a time it had been ...

*Seventeen years ...*

Through the haze of her memories, she looked again at Brielle: dark-haired Brielle, so unlike the mother and father alongside her. How old was she now? Seventeen, perhaps eighteen years old? Not yet born, the last time the Forsyths came to Monte Carlo ...

Another memory crashed into her: her father, bowing over the red Citroen outside the Fort Antoine, the animated conversation she could not hear; her father's reluctance, afterwards, to tell her what was wrong, or why that woman had been camping outside the fortress.

And last of all, Hector Lambert's words, echoing through her with all the forcefulness and terror with which he'd meant them:

*I told your father that if I ever saw your lot back in the Principality, he'd pay for it ...*

Evie's heart started spinning. It was spinning still as the city of Monte Carlo came back into focus.

Charles caught her as she fell back in her seat. 'Evie, my darling, what's wrong?' he asked.

But she couldn't answer.

Because she thought she knew, now, what had happened seventeen years ago. She thought she knew what secret it was her father was trying to keep. She thought she knew why he'd promised he'd never return, and why Hector Lambert was so wrathful that the Forsyths had stumbled back into his life.

Worlds can change in an instant.

Futures can come undone, and pasts can be rewritten.

She'd always thought her father's love for her mother was beyond compare – but right there, across the racetrack, was the evidence she was wrong.

'That girl,' she said to Charles. 'That woman. Charles, I've – I've got to go …'

The atmosphere at the Bar Meridien was electric.

Sam wasn't quite sure why the movie director had made the band play this song eleven times. To his mind, it had been perfectly good the first time. The second time had been a little lacklustre (he liked this word; it was one his dad used a lot), but the director had given everybody a stern lecture, told them to look like they were having fun and then yelled 'ACTION!' again. After that, the crowd threw themselves around every time the chorus kicked in. The sixth, seventh, eighth times – it was all the same. By the time the ninth take came round, he was more puzzled than he'd ever been in his life – but, when he asked his mother (who was happily joining the crowd scenes, dancing madly with the girls from the Company) what it was all about, she told him it was the 'magic of movies'. To Sam's mind, there was more magic in theatre – when you only got one shot at it, and the audience was right there in front of you. This whole 'movie business' felt a little like cheating.

It didn't feel nearly as much like cheating as what he heard on the eleventh take though.

He'd been told to sit in the director's chair, to keep still and stay quiet throughout each take – but Sam was six years old, and the prerogative of six-years-olds was to be bored at will. Consequently, when eleven takes of fidgeting and squirming was not nearly enough to keep the boredom at bay, he tumbled out of the seat and started pottering around. Nobody noticed as he ventured away from his seat, and this increased his confidence.

There seemed to be a particularly long lull going on – and, a little further away, shrouded by the cameras, the director Mr Hines was pacing up and down, his face etched in gravely serious lines. To Sam, this was intriguing, because it contrasted so starkly with the jubilation everybody was faking when Benedict and his band started to play. In fact, the director's face was much more akin to the way Sam's father was acting every time the cameras started rolling. Sam had grown up around performers, and he knew well enough that his father was playing a *role* – in this case, the role of Donny Reaper, the vanquished star – but there wasn't any reason why Mr Hines ought to be acting. By Sam's calculation, the looks of concern, dismay, frustration – perhaps even *anguish* – that ghosted over his face were *real*.

Most children knew they weren't supposed to go eaves-dropping. In principle, Sam knew it too. But the thing about growing up in the Company was that everyone lived and worked in such close proximity that it was almost always impossible *not* to overhear. And therefore, he'd never really thought that overhearing somebody else's conversation was such a terrible thing to do.

So he trotted over and listened in.

Mr Hines was talking to one of his subordinates. He was younger than Hines, but just as portly, with russet-gold hair and a silver watch hanging loosely around his wrist.

'We'll just go again,' the second man was saying, as if counter-ing some argument they'd been having. 'Light them up one more time. Hell, get some spirits into the crowd if we have to. Gee everyone up, and it'll look like everything *clicks*.'

'The audience are going to see straight through it. Actors are paid to fake enthusiasm, but an audience can smell insincerity a mile off. You know I don't want to do it. You know it's going to cause me no end of problems, but...'

'You know, it needn't cause a flutter.'

Sam watched a flutter of curiosity cross Mr Hines's sombre face. 'What do you mean?'

'Well, there's no reason Benedict need know – not until the premiere, at least. By then, it will be too late. He'll be in the audience with all the rest. His name will be up in lights. They'll be cheering for *him*, so ...'

Hines perked up, 'By that point, what would it matter if the voice coming out of Benedict's mouth wasn't his own?'

Sam ducked down behind one of the camera crates, the better not to be seen. Out in the crowd, the extras were getting restless. The sound of their conversation rose, dulling what he could hear of Mr Hines and his colleague's conversation.

'If the audience love it, what does it matter what Benedict thinks?'

Mr Hines seemed to have made up his mind, but there was still an element of caution as he said, 'I'll have to speak to Parker & Parr before I approach Cal. We'll need to know they approve of it. If they do, we'll need to move quickly. How long will it take?'

'It's as easy as pie. Get Cal into a studio, have him record it – then just dub it in over the top. The trickery's in the sounds of the crowd against it – but it's not impossible, Mr Hines. We have sound engineers perfect for the job.' Mr Hines's assistant paused. 'Do you think he'll do it?'

'Cal Forsyth?' Mr Hines grinned. 'Oh, I'm damn certain he'd *relish* it.'

Mr Hines turned on his heel. Fearful he was about to be spotted, Sam crawled through the sand behind the crates, leapt to his feet and hurried on.

It was quieter round the back of the Bar Meridien. As Sam picked his way there, marvelling at how much it was like being backstage at a theatre, he tried to work out exactly what Mr Hines and his associate had been talking about. Evidently, they wanted his father to do an extra job for them – and it wasn't one that Benedict was going to be happy about. He supposed they were keeping it secret to spare Benedict from being upset, which seemed to Sam a very gracious thing. But why they seemed so sombre, and why they'd grinned when they talked about 'Cal Forsyth', he didn't know.

At least the back of the Bar Meridien wasn't as boring as just sitting around waiting for the director to shout 'ACTION!' There were old props here, and old cameras, and a catering truck with pictures of hot dog sausages and iced creams on the side. This only reminded Sam that he hadn't eaten since the breakfast so kindly provided by the princess, so for a time he stood there salivating at the pictures and imagining the feast he might be having if only the catering truck was manned.

He was still staring at the van when he heard the sound of footsteps approaching.

Startled, panicking suddenly that it might be his mother coming to tell him off for wandering, Sam scrabbled behind the catering truck, caught his breath, then peeped back.

But it wasn't his mother at all.

It was Benedict Frey, kicking a stone angrily as he weaved across the sand – and, coming up behind him, a young man with a tangle of curly mousy-brown hair, one of the young men Sam had seen helping Lily, Verity and the others into costumes for the crowd scene on the beach.

'Ben,' the young man was saying, 'it isn't that bad. Just keep it together, OK?'

'I know you're trying to help, Gideon, but you're wrong. They didn't have me singing twelve takes of a song before Cal Forsyth came along. One, two, three times – and done! Hines wasn't barking at me to lift my head or roar it out, or any of the other horseshit he's been shouting all day.' Benedict spun round to face the man named Gideon. 'He didn't have to tell an audience of *mine* to act like they were enjoying it. I'm already singing Forsyth's song. It's like – it's like they're taking my movie away from my, piece by piece.'

'It's still your name.'

Benedict heaved a sigh. 'I know.'

'It's still your face.'

It was the strangest thing – but, in that moment, Benedict smiled. 'Shut up, Gideon,' he said – though, even more strangely now, it didn't *feel* like he wanted Gideon to shut up at all.

'Forsyth will be gone from Monaco by the end of the week. He's performing that show of theirs tomorrow. After today, you'll hardly have to see him – or any of them – again.'

Sam watched keenly. It seemed to him that, in the silence that followed, the two men moved imperceptibly closer together. 'Gideon, you fool, you always say the right thing,' laughed Benedict. And now there was no mistaking it, for the men didn't only move closer together; Benedict reached up, touched Gideon's shoulder as well, and bowed towards him as well.

'Sam!'

Sam jumped, turning round. Nobody was there; the voice had reached him from round the side of the Bar Meridien, his mother's voice cutting through the hum of the crowd. At once, he tore his eyes away from Benedict and Gideon and started to run. Whether they saw him or not, he did not know – but he rather suspected they were too focused on each other to see a little boy scampering away. As for Sam, a nervousness was coursing through him. Something told him he really ought to have stayed where his mother had told him – and it wasn't just the look on his mother's face as, finally, he barrelled into her arms, allowed himself to be swept upwards, and buried his head in her shoulders. Movie sets, he had decided, were angry, fractious places. He would much rather be among the family of the Forsyth Varieties. Yes, the theatre was the place to be; movies were full of whispers and lies.

'Sam,' Meredith said, when she finally peeled him away from her shoulder, 'whatever's the matter?'

'I want to go back and see Grandpa,' he said, simply.

Meredith smiled. 'Well, you're in luck. Mr Hines just made an announcement. We're done for the day. So it's back to the bus for you, young man.' She started carting him away. 'Oh, and Sam – next time, you stay where your mother tells you. I know this place looks like a fantastic playground – but, trust me, it's safer where you are.'

Evie was almost out of the stands when Charles caught up with her. Her eyes flashed wild, every muscle in her body rigid with tension. 'Evie, what happened? What's wrong?' She was striding through the back of the stands, out onto a plaza in front of a grand, white church, when he caught her arm. 'Evie, tell me.'

She opened her mouth to spill it all, but something stopped her.

She'd only known him three days.

This was a secret that had been festering for half of her life.

'I need to see my father,' she told him, then turned to march away.

But it wasn't her father that she saw. The Forsyth Varieties were approaching, but her father was not among them.

The hulk of the Company's red double-decker bus was standing at a junction some distance ahead, beached there by the crowds and diversions that spread out around the circuit. She could see Lily, Verity and the other dancing girls hanging out of the back of the bus. Cal had been in the driver's seat, but now he jumped off, scouting the tangled road ahead, and heaved a sigh. The whole of the city, it seemed, had come to a standstill. The roads around the circuit were static. The distance from here to the Port Hercule was infinitesimal, but there was no way that double-decker was making it – not unless Cal reversed it and found some other route around the city.

She was thinking, then, of how to tell him.

Thinking of how she might breathe the words, 'Everything we knew is a lie.'

Evie had to close her eyes, just to get a grip. She tried telling herself she was wrong. Tried telling herself there were other possibilities – that perhaps she could only see part of the picture, and perhaps the fuller picture painted her father in the same perfect light in which she'd always held him. But the self-deception was too hard. The pieces fit too neatly.

She felt like she could throw up.

Charles was still calling her name as she hurried across the plaza to the road on the other side. Cal spotted her immediately – but, swept up in his own dreams and schemes as he always was, he didn't seem to realise anything was wrong. 'I thought we might be able to get into the stands and see the last races, but…' Behind him, Sam was putting up a petulant protest. It seemed some promise had been made. 'He's been bored all day. He even wandered off.'

'He's been glum ever since,' said Meredith, carrying Sam off the bus. 'We thought – something to cheer him up…'

Evie was about to seize Cal by the arm, drag him away from the rest and tell him 'We need to talk', but at that moment Charles caught up with her. Apparently, he had heard what Meredith said, because the next moment he was saying, 'I think, perhaps, the stands are beyond us now – but, if the young sir would like, *I* could show him something he'll never forget?', and Sam's face was suddenly lighting up.

'Is it your car, monsieur?'

Meredith beamed, for whatever had been weighing Sam down had vanished in an instant – but Evie, whose eyes flashed madly around, didn't know what to say. She had to stop this hammering in her heart. In a moment, somebody would ask her what was wrong – and then she would blurt it out, in front of all of them. After that, there'd be no coming back. Whatever bonds still held the Company together might not outlast something like this. It was shared history, shared heritage that bound the Forsyth Varieties together. What would become of them, if that history was no more? What happened to a house when its foundations were smashed to smithereens?

Charles cried out, *'Viens avec moi!'* and rallied the Company together. Moments later, Sam had scrambled out of Meredith's arms to stampede into Charles's shadow. Having first locked the bus, Meredith and Cal swept after him, the girls close behind.

Evie took a breath.

Then, telling herself the secret had been buried for seventeen years – and it could stay buried a few moments longer – she followed.

It was some distance to the Talbot-Lago staging grounds, moving against the current in the crowd. Evie felt as if she was battling a tide as she fought to follow. Her mind kept darting back to Hector Lambert's grasping hands, his baleful eyes, the malicious way he'd spoken. *You vagabond bastards.* At least, now, she understood. What man wouldn't be filled with such rage, cuckolded years before – and now coming face to face with the villain who'd upended his life?

Then she thought…

He looked after Brielle, didn't he?

He'd been a father to her all these years?

Yes, she thought, she could understand the bitterness now. This sort of secret could upend his life all over again.

By the time Evie reached the staging ground, Charles and the rest had been there for some minutes already. The place buzzed with activity. Christian and the other mechanics had spent the last hour drilling themselves in the art of the pit stop. Even Dickie Anstis had made a reappearance. He looked ghostly white and kept wringing his hands on one of the oily rags which proliferated about the place, but duty had summoned him from his sickbed. 'I'll not be much good to you, Charles,' he said, wanly, 'but I won't just lie back all day. This is *your* weekend, but we've all worked for it. I want to be there, when you're up on the podium, that cup in your hands.'

'Well, go on young man,' Charles said to Sam, once the wheels were fixed back on the Grand Sport. 'See what it feels like in *here*.' Then, having first looked to Meredith for her permission, Charles whisked the boy into the air and deposited him behind the steering column.

Sam could hardly believe his luck. He reached back, finding an oversized helmet, then dropped it over his face. 'Look, Dad!' he beamed – and Cal, suddenly envious of his six-year-old son, scrambled for the second Grand Sport, the back-up vehicle which sat, wheelless, in the shadows behind.

Cal didn't stop to ask. Perhaps he ought to have done, because the mechanics were about to refit its wheels, but Cal hadn't asked permission for anything in his adult life and he wasn't about to break the habit now. Moments later, he had slid into the driver's seat and, aping the sound of the engine, cried out, 'I'm going to catch you, Sam!'

Such joy in the air, thought Evie. Such fun, such laughter, such…*family*. What right did she have to break the spell? What right did she have, except for the *truth*?

'You know,' said Cal, with a twinkle in his eye, 'it is Friday night. You *did* say I might take her for a spin.'

Sam leapt up. 'Me too?'

Charles only shook his head at the boy, but to Cal he said, 'I believe I said I'd have to take that under… advisement.'

'Just a little run,' said Cal, 'it can't hurt.'

Charles's eyes flashed around the staging ground. The mechanics, it seemed, had either not heard or were diligently pretending. Dickie Anstis just shrugged. 'Allard isn't going to like it. And don't get me started on Knight.'

It was, Evie thought, the final word that made up Charles's mind. 'I couldn't possibly let you take her out there now, M. Forsyth. But perhaps, after hours, just to feel the throb of the engine… She's more powerful than you'll ever have driven, you understand?'

'After hours then,' said Cal, and leapt out of the cockpit. 'Did you hear that, Sam? Your father isn't just a movie star. He isn't just a world-renowned songwriter. He's going to be a racing driver too.'

Sam just squirmed as Cal hoisted him from the seat.

'But first,' he declared, 'we've got a show to rehearse.'

By the time the Company made their way back to the double-decker, the streets were clearing. Cal's mind filled with the fantasy of guiding the Grand Sport around the circuit, as he kicked the double-decker to life. The old girl had served the Company well, but she was a cumbersome beast. He could hardly wait to feel the freedom of the Talbot-Lago. Yes, he thought, this trip to Monte Carlo had been worthwhile after all.

'Cal,' said Evie quietly, as he found his way back to the Port Hercule and the road to the Fort Antoine, 'I need to talk to you. In private, you hear? I've got to …'

Up above them, the stone walls of the fortress rose to the sky. Up on the ramparts, their father was waiting. He hallooed them as Cal guided the bus into port, beckoning the Company to join him above.

Whatever had been plaguing Sam since the Bar Meridien seemed long forgotten, for he was the first off the bus, scrambling towards the fortress wall and the narrow stone steps, desperate to take his place in the show about to unfold above. Meredith hurried after, Lily and the girls scurrying in her wake.

'Can it wait, Evie?' asked Cal, as they began to climb through the shadowy darkness. 'You look frazzled. You look worn out. Look, it's only one more night sleeping wild up here. After the show tomorrow, after it's done, we can get back in the Hotel de Lyon. One last night of luxury before we head back to—'

As Cal emerged into the arena above, Evie stumbled to a halt beside him.

What a spectacle this was. Where once had been ash, now there was architecture. A simple set was festooned with lights, ready to burst with brilliance as soon as the sun went down. The devastated bougainvillea had been replaced with a lattice, through which yet more strings of lights had been woven. Two decorative lampposts dominated the rear of the arena, demarking a space for the musicians. The princess's gleaming white piano stood proud and ready to be played.

There was Jim Livesey, with a new, simple cabinet, painted ebony-black and stencilled with stars.

'It's been a long day,' Ed Forsyth beamed, 'but now we come to it.'

Evie almost shuddered as she saw him walking towards her. She almost cringed when he stepped between her and Cal, then put an arm around each. 'We can do this, *together*. The Forsyths against the world!' The last time she'd seen him, he'd looked devastated; now he seemed almost buoyant. Perhaps she wouldn't have noticed if she herself hadn't been so lost, so low, questioning everything around her.

'One more time, for the Forsyths!' Ed called to the Company. 'Take your places, people. Ready your bodies and minds. We're running this as if Princess Grace herself was sitting before us. Let's make it a night Monte Carlo will never forget!'

# Chapter Fourteen

The sun went down.

The lights went up.

Moonlight bathed the water. Ribbons of fairy-lights rippled around the amphitheatre walls. In the same moment that the lights sparked up, like a constellation of brilliant stars, the whole of the Company came together in song. 'Runaway Lovers', Cal's gift to the world, rang out in two dozen different voices – and there, at the heart of them all, Sam's small voice flourished. As the other voices left the song, one by one, only Sam's remained – until, high on his father's shoulders, he sang out the final words.

There were only two members in the audience tonight: Meredith and the Company driver Hugo, the vast hulk who sat beside her. As soon as the song ended, both got to their feet. The applause might not have been titanic, but it meant the world to Sam.

It meant the world to Ed as well. Evie could see how the creases in his face had faded as the rehearsal took flight. Now, a deeply relieved man, he left the Company taking their practice bows on the amphitheatre stage and climbed up the steps to face and address them all.

'I have always known you to be the most dedicated, professional of units – but you have proven to me, once again, how well you all thrive in the face of adversity. The fire remains unsolved, but there is no calamity, big or small, above which the Forsyth Varieties cannot rise. And tomorrow night, when these stone seats are filled with the palace's esteemed guests – when Princess Grace and Prince Rainier sit right here and applaud you – you will be able to feel it for yourselves. I am proud of you, my friends.' And he looked at each of them in turn. 'Each and every one. Hugo, Merry, perhaps you might like to join them?'

In the stone seats, Meredith laughed, 'I don't think *I* need to take a bow, Ed.'

'Indulge me,' said Ed. 'Please.' Now he winked at Hugo too. 'Both of you.'

As soon as Meredith and Hugo joined the rest of the Company on stage, Ed looked to the heavens, whispered some petition or some prayer – to the stars, to God above, to Bella, nobody knew – and said, 'Before I ask you to lay out the bedrolls, before I ask you to turn in and get your rest – because tomorrow will bring with it one of the most special performances of our lives – there is one more thing I have to say.'

In the audience, Evie tensed. Her eyes flashed at Cal, but he barely seemed to notice; no doubt he was too busy dreaming about his return to the staging ground tonight, the opportunity to sit behind the wheel of the Talbot-Lago Grand Sport and take it out onto the circuit.

'This has been a long and difficult trip. When we set out from home, we did not envisage the summer bringing us here. Indeed, I did not envisage coming here ever again ...'

Evie felt her blood beating black.

'But when a princess summons a commoner to court, he must not decline. And when that princess carries such fondness in her heart for one you loved as dearly as I loved my wife, well, the die is cast. Destiny called us here, and who were we to decline?'

Evie tried to still her fidgeting fingers, for Lily was giving her odd, questioning looks. Ed's love for Bella – it was part of Company legend, but wasn't it a lie? Could you really claim to love someone after you betrayed them? Life was complicated, love its most complicated part, but could the two things really coexist?

'Well, destiny called us here – and destiny has spoken to me in other ways as well,' said Ed. His tone had changed, somehow. He seemed almost wistful, his pride at the Company's performance tinged with something approaching regret. 'My friends, you have known for some years that I have been contemplating the moment when I would leave the stage. When we were invited to perform for the queen at the Royal Variety Performance five years ago, I envisaged it my last – but found a new thirst, that night, to carry on. Well, the century grows old. I grow old with it. We old hands at the Forsyth Varieties are already giving way to new, exciting faces,' and here he winked at Jim Livesey, 'and this week I received some wise advice from none other than Princess Grace, advice that I know I must heed. She told me ...' Ed's voice cracked, and in the audience Evie felt suddenly conflicted – for, no matter what else was going on, no matter what lies had been told, the emotion that clouded her father's face was real. 'She told me that, one day, a performer wakes up and knows it's the end. And the truth is, my friends, that I have had many of those days. Each time, I have rebuffed them. Each time, I have sat down with my conscience and told it to go back to the darkness. *Not today*, I say. *Not yet*. But the time is now at hand. Tomorrow will not only be my last performance overseas with the Forsyth Varieties. It will be my last performance of all.'

There was no time for reaction from the audience – for, in spite of their gasps, their hurried looks, the hands that were gripped and brows that were furrowed, Ed ploughed on:

'And I am leaving the Company in the very best of hands. For the first time in its history, the leadership of the Forsyth Varieties shall be shared.' He paused. 'Evie, Cal, will you join me up here for a moment?'

Evie didn't know what to feel. It was the moment she'd been waiting for for years, yet suddenly she was numb. She found herself being pulled forward through the crowd. Hands were grasping her by the shoulder or patting her on the back. Cal, too, was being swept forward. The look on his face was stunned – but to the other players that was only natural, for Cal had never really envisaged being invited to lead. Not after his years in the wilderness. Not after how much his father fretted about Cal's commitment to the Company.

Soon, the Forsyth twins stood alongside their father, and Ed puffed his chest out with pride.

'My twins,' he said. 'My flesh, my blood. As I inherited this Company from my father, as he inherited it from his, so will you together take the reins of the Forsyth Varieties and lead it into the future – so that, one day, it might be carried by your children, and your children's children, into whatever the future has in store. I have wrangled, for long years, about which of you should carry this Company – but the answer has been staring me in the face all along. Cal, you have the devilry and ambition to bring this Company to greatness, to draw the eye of the world. Evie, you have leadership qualities far beyond my own – the talent to marshall your players, to bring them elegance, refinement and flair. You are, between you, the perfect combination. I could not ask for more.'

Then Ed turned to face the Company again.

'So tomorrow night, we are not just performing for the princess. We are not just performing for the patrons of her charity. We are performing to say farewell – and welcome your new leaders. For, by the time the last song is sung and the bows are taken, it won't be me in charge of the Forsyth Varieties. It will be Evie and Cal.'

If Evie had been stunned into silence, it was confusion that had silenced Cal. He looked at Evie, 'Is he *serious?*' he whispered. But Ed had never been more serious in his life. He took his son's hand and said, 'It's always been your home, boy.' Then he embraced both of his children – and there was nothing either one of them could do but submit to the moment.

There was much chatter after that. Sam, though he under-stood only half of what it meant, raced back into Cal's arms in elation, then started fretting about never seeing Grandpa Ed on stage again. Lily and the girls mobbed Evie, who remained unmoving, while a host of players lined up to shake Ed's hand, to tell him how much they would miss him, to recall the stories of their first days at the Forsyth Varieties – and how it had been Ed who plucked them from obscurity, gave them a chance on the Company billing and led them into new lives.

When, at last, the ripples caused by Ed's announcement were fading away, Cal swept Sam onto his shoulders and declared, 'The night doesn't end here, my boy! Dad, we'll be back.'

Ed watched Cal, Meredith and Sam race for the stairs, a trail of dancing girls following behind them. There was, it seemed, a strange piquancy in the air, a lust, an excitement he didn't understand.

But Evie hadn't followed.

She just stood there, looking almost shell-shocked, her eyes luminous and wide as she tried to take this all in. 'Dad, what changed?' She had asked the question before she thought about it; then she realised, quite suddenly, that she didn't want to know the answer. It had to be something to do with Monaco. It had to be something to do with Hector Lambert, the girl Brielle and two thousand English pounds. Was abandoning the Company, somehow, his way of protecting it? Had some other treaty been signed, some other agreement been made?

Or was it just serendipity that brought him to this decision?

An hour ago, she'd been filled with anger. Now, looking at him, she didn't know whether to feel angry, sad or filled with sympathy. Whatever he'd done, he was still her father, wasn't he? She'd watched over him, looked after him, *carried* him in the years after her mother died? He *had* loved her. She was sure of it. And now…

'I can't believe you're leaving,' was all she could say.

He had taken her hand, but she couldn't look him in the eye. Was ever a feeling as complicated as this?

'I've always been leaving some day, sweetheart. But I'm not going to join your mother, not yet. And this Christmas, when you take the Company back to Brighton, I'll be in the circle, watching you play. What a feeling that might be!' Ed paused. 'Evie, don't be sad.'

'I'm – I'm not sad.'

Ed said, 'You look sad, sweetheart.'

She supposed she did, but quite which part of it she was sad for, she didn't know.

'I've got to go, Dad,' she said, drawing away. 'You know what Cal's like. I can't have him doing anything stupid, not if we're really going to run this thing. It's like you said – it's going to take both of us to do it right.'

Ed watched as Evie turned, hurried across the amphitheatre and vanished into the darkness of the stairwell leading below. Then, with a strange feeling – somewhere between sorrow and pride – rising inside him, he picked his way to the ramparts to look over the edge and watch her going.

Something was wrong with her, he decided.

Something that wasn't to do with taking leadership of the Company.

She'd felt that tension before, he knew – for it had been Evie who stayed with the Company in its darkest hour while Cal marched off on his own to conquer the world, and there'd been a time when to award Cal any inheritance would have been a slight to Evie's hard work and dedication – but it felt different tonight.

Perhaps it was just the feeling of old ends and new beginnings.

He knew how strange it must feel, for there'd been a time when he stood in their shoes, watching his own father ride off into retirement. It was funny how quickly your turn came round.

But Ed Forsyth would not allow himself to feel unhappy tonight.

Tonight was for hope for the future, and pride at a job well done.

Cal was still stunned as he swept Sam along the promenade, past the great stands of the Circuit de Monaco.

The air was sticky tonight. It clung to him as he hurried on, Meredith at his side, the dancing girls scampering somewhere up ahead. 'I don't know what to think. Part of me thinks … he's said it before. It's been part of him ever since Mum passed away. Does he mean it now?'

Meredith said, 'I think he meant it, Cal. He's *tired*.'

They were all tired, but Meredith loaded the word with such meaning. Theirs was the tiredness of a long hot summer; Ed's was the tiredness of a long, full life.

'But … to lead the Company, with Evie?' Cal whispered, as they crossed the Place du Casino, rounded the plaza and came, at last, to the Talbot-Lago staging ground.

Leading hadn't been part of his plan. Oh, he'd grown up thinking about it – strutting around like an heir apparent, dreaming of the day when it was his name top of the bill instead of his father's – but when adulthood arrived those dreams hadn't been the same anymore. By the time he was a young man, Cal's dreams had existed over the horizon. It was Evie who had never detached herself from the Company, Evie who had grown in stature and leadership while Cal was off chasing rainbows …

'I'll have to talk to her,' Cal decided. Up ahead, the girls were already at the doors of the lock-up. 'I'll tell her … I'll follow where she goes. I don't *just* want the Company, Merry. I want … the movies, the hit parade, the …'

'High life,' said Meredith, because it was all Cal had really dreamt about since they first met. 'We've been penniless before, Cal. We were adrift and penniless when Sam was born. I don't want to go back. The Company's a base. We *need* a base.'

Ten years ago, Cal would have scoffed – and whisked her along on whatever adventure he had in mind. 'We can have both, if I talk to Evie. She'll understand. She was made for the Company. I'm made for … other things. There has to be a way.'

'Can you two stop talking?' said Sam, high up on Cal's shoulders. 'I want to see the car!'

Charles was waiting for them at the doors to the lock-up.

Inside, the lights were low – but there, in the middle of the garage, sat the twin Talbot-Lago Grand Sports. Even in the ailing lamplight, the cyan and white paintwork seemed to glitter. Lily and the girls were already gathered around the first vehicle – but Lily was too slow sliding into the cockpit, for within an instant, Sam had scrambled from Cal's shoulders and taken her place. The little boy was delighted to get his hands on the wheel. Eagerly, he looked back at Cal, begging him to come over.

'I'm breaking all sorts of rules,' said Charles, 'but to hell with them. They don't own me. They act like they do, but it isn't so.' He paused. 'Come, let's ride out onto the circuit. With your permission, I shall take Sam.'

Sam's face had opened with delight – was he *really* going to sit in the lap of a racing driver, out on the Circuit de Monaco? – but some flicker of caution crossed Meredith's face. 'You wouldn't go too fast…'

Charles touched his chest, just above his heart. 'On my honour.' Then he crouched and, lifting Sam out of the driver's seat, slipped inside himself, settling the boy on his lap. It wouldn't be the most comfortable of rides out to the circuit, but it would thrill the boy – and it wouldn't be far. 'You know Sam, when I was your age, I used to dream of the same thing. I used to watch my brother flash past and think: one day, I want to be like lightning on the track…'

'Go!' screamed Sam. 'Go, go, go!'

The roll-back doors on the other side of the lock-up were already open to the night. Charles flicked an ignition switch and pumped his foot on the accelerator. Under race conditions, the engine would already be heated up and ready to burst with speed; now, he would just tease it out.

'You know,' he said, mistily, 'one day I should like a son of my own, to take to the race…'

He looked up, meaning to salute Cal and Meredith as they followed him out onto the circuit – but, in that moment, the door behind them opened and there stood Evie. By the look on her face, she had heard every word he'd just said.

The silence seemed loaded. Stranded between Evie and Charles, Cal and Meredith shrank into themselves. The dancing girls looked the other way. To them it seemed, suddenly, as if they had intruded upon some private moment between lovers.

But Evie looked bewildered. Instead of breathing a word to Charles, she looked at Cal and said, 'I'm serious, we need to talk.'

'I know,' said Cal, with more breeziness than Evie, 'but ... not yet, Evie. Sam's about to feel the wind in his hair!'

'I'm serious, Cal. It's about Dad. Something's happening with Dad and ...'

The Grand Sport rolled forward, underneath the roll-back door and into the night. Soon, Lily and the girls were flocking after.

Cal felt the hand of gravity – or was it destiny? – pulling him in the same direction. He snatched Meredith's hand and pulled her along. 'We'll talk, Evie,' he called back. 'We've got so much to talk about. I've got ideas and ...' Outside the lock-up, Sam's shrill cheers split the night. 'Oh, come on, Evie! This is the night. Let's *live*.'

Let's *live*, thought Evie as Cal and Meredith hurried after Charles, Sam and the Talbot-Lago. That had been Cal's mantra ever since they were young: breeze past anything difficult, cast yourself headlong into whatever took your fancy and leave all the important things to her. Well, not this time. This was too important to cast aside for some frippery. If the Company was to be theirs, they had to *know* everything. Whatever secrets lay hidden, they had to be unearthed.

Evie made sure the door was locked behind her, then crossed the lock-up and followed the others out towards the circuit.

It was not far to the first of the grandstands, then to the staging grounds on the edge of the circuit. By the time Evie caught up, Charles was scooting Sam up and down a stretch of the track – and, though he was barely going at the speed of the double-decker bus through gridlocked traffic earlier that day, it didn't seem to have diminished the young boy's excitement. Nor did it seem to be diminishing Cal's eagerness to get in the seat. Sometimes it seemed like her brother had never truly grown up.

'Cal,' she said, approaching him once more, 'I need to tell you something.'

For the first time, something about Evie's tone made Cal pay attention. 'Evie, I know running things together isn't what you wanted. I know it should be *you*. I know I … haven't always been the best brother, or the best son. But I've got ideas. Things are different now. The Company *respects* you. They *like* me, but they respect you. And … I don't want to give up what I've got. This business with Parker & Parr, it's opened my eyes again. To hell with what Benedict Frey says – I don't need to be the star, but I can still be a part of it. It can still be my soundtracks, my songs. I … I like chasing opportunities, Evie. I like stumbling across something and thinking – hey, this could change my life! So … I don't need to run the Company, Evie. I just need to be a part of it. If it's leadership you want, hell, you grab hold of it. I'll support you every step of the way.' He paused, a smile flourishing on his face. 'Well, when I'm not off chasing opportunities. It can work, Evie. Dad never wanted to talk about it, but how long will Varieties last? Well, it can last longer if I'm out there, making money, making waves and bringing it back home.'

Out on the track, Charles brought the Grand Sport to a halt and started beckoning to Cal.

'It's not about that, Cal. We can work that out. We'll have to. It's … Dad, Cal. I need to speak to you about Dad.'

But Cal was already tumbling towards the Grand Sport. 'We'll do all the talking in the world, Evie – but first, I've got to *drive*.'

Cal didn't see the look of mounting frustration, perhaps even despair, that was colouring his sister's face, for he was so intent on sliding into the seat that Charles was vacating that he didn't once look back. He did not see the way Evie folded her hands across her chest, the way her eyes were suddenly shimmering with tears, the way she braced herself and started muttering under her breath, instructing herself – in no uncertain terms – to hold things together.

He didn't hear Meredith ask her, 'Evie, is everything all right?'

And he didn't hear Evie reply, 'I'm not sure it's ever going to be right again', because by that point he was already in the cockpit, with Sam on his lap, and Charles was explaining, 'You have to take this gently, M. Forsyth. The merest touch on the pedal, the merest touch of the wheel. I've seen the London bus you wrangle. The Grand Sport is like a rocket ship in comparison.'

'What do you think, Sam?' Cal asked. 'Shall we take her for a ride?'

'Go, Dad, go!'

The moment Cal depressed the accelerator, he knew he was in command of a beast very different to any he had controlled before. The Grand Sport jumped forward, and he had to ease back just to get the feeling of how she handled on the surface of the road. She seemed to glide. He could hear the engine throbbing, but the car itself seemed so light that it felt as if it was floating just above the surface. He played with the accelerator again.

And again she jumped forward.

'Take it easy, Cal.'

It was Meredith's voice, hailing him from the side of the track. And of course she was right, because Sam was in his arms – so he reached the hundred-metre mark, slowed the car to an infinitesimal crawl and navigated a turn so that he was driving back directly the way that he'd come. 'Arms up, Sam! Cheer for Mummy!'

Sam threw his arms upwards and cheered.

'Take hold of the wheel,' Cal whispered in his ear, 'show her what you can do ...'

'Really, Dad?'

'One, two, three ...!'

Cal let go of the wheel, just in time for Sam to seize it. The boy was thrilled beyond compare, his heart pounding in his chest – but there was never any danger, for by now the car was simply rolling forward, Cal's foot hovering over the brake. With a squeal of triumph, Sam guided the Grand Sport back towards the crowd of cheering spectators.

'Go on then, Sam, hop on out.'

Cal brought the Grand Sport to a stop.

'Once more, Dad?'

'Let me give her a run first, son. Go on.' He helped Sam up and out of the car. 'Is that all right?' he asked, looking up at Charles.

Charles looked doubtful, but eventually he said, 'Don't take her far, M. Forsyth. Keep her in sight.'

'You have my promise, sir.'

Cal turned the Grand Sport round. Now the promenade stretched out in front of him, its great stands on either side. Somewhere up ahead, the night would envelop him – but it seemed a good distance to Cal, enough to feel the wind in his hair, enough to get a sense of what this beast could really do. Enough to be able to imagine, for just a few fleeting moments, that the stands were full, the other cars hurtling around him – and that he, Cal Forsyth, was in pole position at the Monaco Grand Prix.

He threw up a salute, winked at Meredith and Sam, and took off.

Now, *this* was more like it. He'd promised Charles he wouldn't go too quickly, but no matter how much he pressed his foot on the accelerator, the car seemed to thirst for more. Wind thundered past. The stands turned to a blur. He'd barely been moving for ten seconds and already he felt like he was in one of the Spitfires he and Evie used to watch tumbling overhead during the war – moving at some incredible speed, ripping a hole in reality as they thundered on.

Charles's words were in the back of his mind – 'Don't take her far, M. Forsyth. Keep her in sight' – but a little further wouldn't hurt. The car wanted it too. Suddenly it felt as if it was the car goading him, not him cajoling the car. Could that be real? Could a car *want* to go faster? It was like a horse rising from a trot into a canter and desperate to gallop, a horse stabled for far too long and suddenly feeling the power and majesty of its hoofs against the ground. From way behind, above the din of the engine, he thought he heard Charles's voice hollering out – but whether it was real or not, he could not say. Perhaps the Frenchman was commanding him to return; perhaps Cal had pushed it too far. Well, just a *little* further wouldn't hurt. A little further, and then he'd turn round, sated for the evening.

Tomorrow: to perform for the princess and her patrons.

Tomorrow: to inherit the Company from his father.

Tomorrow: to see what the future held with *Moonlight in Monte Carlo*, the open, unending possibilities of Parker & Parr.

Surely, by now, he'd gone too far. The night was rushing past, the straight of the promenade ending at the harbour somewhere up ahead. It was time to bring the Grand Sport to a crawl, turn her round and return.

He took his foot from the accelerator.

He applied it to the brake.

But nothing happened.

At first Cal thought he'd made some mistake. A racing car was not like the black taxicabs he ordinarily drove; perhaps his foot had slipped, or perhaps he'd pressed the pedal too fleetingly. The accelerator responded to the merest caress, but perhaps the brake needed more authority.

He slammed his foot on the pedal.

But still nothing happened.

Cal was not naturally given to panic – and he did not panic now. Not at first. Instead, he kicked at the pedal, pressed it again, looked left, looked right, wrenched on the steering wheel to try to alter the vehicle's course. The car handled smoothly enough, but no matter how much he stamped on the brakes, nothing happened.

He looked back.

By now he'd certainly come too far. Behind him there was only blackness.

Up ahead, the circuit banked a sharp right.

He'd almost reached the Port Hercule. On the other side of the stands, the harbour was filled with yachts waiting for the morning. Somewhere beyond that, the Company were staring up at the stars above the Fort Antoine.

There was nothing else for it.

If he couldn't stop the car, he was going to have to follow the course.

The problem was that, in the darkness ahead, lay the Chicane du Port.

Cal didn't know he had reached the chicane until he was already on top of it. The darkness was stampeding towards him – but then, suddenly, the road changed, banking sharply towards the seafront. On his right, seafront apartments rose starkly upward; on his left, only wire and concrete ramparts separated him from the water.

Cal wrestled with the wheel to keep the car on the course, but it was too fast, the chicane too sudden. Before he knew what was happening, he was up against the harbour fence. Sparks flew as the Grand Sport scored the wire, but somehow Cal wrestled the car back onto the road and burst out of the other side of the chicane.

His heart was pounding, but the thrill had long gone.

He slammed his foot to the brake again, but still there was no effect.

At least this stretch of track was straight. There was, at least, a little time to think. There was, at least…

But then the time was gone.

The next bend was coming.

Before Cal knew, the bend was upon him. Instinct was still making him pound at the brake pedal, but it was in vain. All he could do as the harbour loomed above him was throw his weight behind the wheel, trying to stay dead centre as the world pivoted around him.

Cal hardly knew when the car started to skid.

He would never know if he'd turned too fiercely or not fiercely enough.

One moment, the harbour wall was ripping past at incredible speeds; the next, it was meeting him dead on – and, for one blessed moment, everything felt like a dream, as the Talbot-Lago Grand Sport pirouetted like a dancer in the air.

The world slowed down.

Gravity had abandoned Cal; he hung in the air, the world a violent whirr.

Images flashed through his mind: of Meredith and Sam, of a jubilant crowd crying out for more; all the aeons of his life rushing past, just as madly as the stands of the Circuit de Monaco, just as vividly as the thousand theatres and stages onto which he'd once strutted.

He saw his mother and father.

He saw John Lauderdale and all the old hands.

He saw his sister Evie, on the night they first performed together – and felt, again, that same sense of belonging he'd had on that long ago night, being part of the Forsyth Varieties, for now and all time.

Then gravity released him.

The world rushed in from every angle.

All the images of his past life fractured into a million tiny pieces, to rain down all around – and, after that, all Cal Forsyth knew was fire and pain.

# Chapter Fifteen

The world was on fire.

Searing heat held Cal in its grasp.

Dancing flames hissed and mocked him.

He bucked and turned. One moment, he felt like he was falling; the next, as if he was being borne up on a geyser of rampaging oranges and red. There were screams, then muted voices. A hand held his; then, when it let him go, he plunged down and down, like a mountaineer losing grip and plummeting into a ravine. He saw the night sky wheeling. He saw lights of flashing blue. He saw white tiled walls and ghostly figures hovering above. He floated up, then looked back down – and saw his own body in a hospital bed, his sister and wife at his side.

'Do something,' Meredith was saying, her voice as indistinct and far away as the wind. 'Please do something.'

Doctors clucked around. A line fed into a cannula in the back of his hand, hooked up to bags of fluid suspended above. Half his body was naked; the other half draped in dressings, lotions and ice.

His sister crouched at his bedside, taking hold of his one good hand. 'Cal, you're going to be OK. Hang in there, Cal. You're going to be—'

One of the doctors took hold of her, levering her aside. From above, Cal watched as Evie exploded in fury – only for Charles to sweep in from the back of the room and wrap her in his arms. Voices barracked backwards and forwards in French. Another infusion – blood, he wondered? – was being fed into him now. Next moment, Meredith too was barrelled aside. Nurses took readings. Some doctor prepared a syringe.

'For the pain,' said the remote, hollow voice.

The syringe went into his shoulder – and, whatever element of Cal was suspended above, watching the disaster unfold, felt a strange tugging sensation. The searing heat, the dancing flames, began to retreat; in their place rushed a comforting coolness that started in his shoulder and spread like waves through his body. When it reached his heart, it radiated outwards, coating him from the inside out. Down he floated, down towards his body, down through the doctors and nurses, back into the shell that was lying in bed. For a moment, he was separate; then, he sank into himself again. He looked out through his body's closed eyes – and the last thing he saw, before the cocoon of cold darkness took him under, was the terrified eyes of his sister and wife watching him go.

No doubt they thought it was all his fault.

Reckless Cal Forsyth; arrogant Cal Forsyth; Cal Forsyth, who always takes things too far.

'It wasn't me,' he wanted to tell them.

*It was the car...*

But whatever drugs they'd given him were burying him now – and Cal didn't know if he'd ever breathe a word again.

Outside the room in the Centre Hospitalier, Lily clung on to Sam – whose tears had run dry, whose body was rigid, whose horror knew no bounds. The moment Meredith emerged from

248

the room, she rushed to take him in her arms. 'It's OK, Sammy,' she whispered, over and again, 'Daddy's fighting. They're doing everything they can. We have to – we have to pray for him now.'

Behind Meredith, Evie and Charles emerged, Evie's face streaked in tears. Charles looked impassive, as if his features had been hewn out of granite. For a time, nobody spoke a word. The sounds of the hospital went on around them: the beeping of machines through the walls; the echo of footsteps; the creak of some trolley or wheelchair being pushed into an elevator. Somewhere, a phone rang. Somewhere else, somebody lived on while someone else died.

'What did they – what did they say?' Lily breathed, at last.

Neither Meredith nor Evie would say, not while Sam still hung here, burying his head. They'd all seen the fire rush upwards from the end of the course. They'd all run, as one, along the promenade and around the chicane, to see the wreckage of the Grand Sport and the fountains of flame that lit up the night. Sam's screams; Meredith's screams; Evie, crying out her brother's name – that unholy chorus had tried to get close to the wreckage, only to be beaten back by the overpowering waves of heat. In the end, it was Charles who found Cal. The crash must have come first and the consuming flames after, because he was lying, arms and legs at unnatural angles, further along the course. Whether he'd been thrown from the turning vehicle or somehow levered his way out of the wreckage, they did not know – but it seemed likely, now, that he'd been cast out in the crash, for the doctors said his bones were broken in too many places to immediately measure. Some of the flames must have licked around him, for his clothes were but cinders and too much flesh burnt – but all of this a man might survive. It was whatever was happening inside that would kill him.

'One night at a time,' Charles pronounced. 'He lives. He *lives*.'

Evie wanted to scream at him, 'But for how long?', but somehow she was able to battle back the devil that tempted her. When she looked at him, she did not see the Charles Laurent of today; she saw the young man he'd been when they first met, cheering in the stands at Le Mans, his face overcome with pride – only to see his own brother's life snuffed out on the track.

She reached for him.

She took his hand.

'I've got to tell my father.'

It was, Lily decided, the most 'Evie' thing she'd ever heard. It was the only way she knew how to react: in tragedy, keep marching forward. She'd done it for the Company after Bella died. She'd been doing it ever since. But now…

'I'll go,' said Charles. 'This is my fault. It should be me.'

'Your fault?' Meredith sobbed, still rocking Sam from side to side. 'How could it be your fault? How could it be anyone's fault? Anyone except…'

She stopped short of saying 'Cal', but only because Sam still hung there.

'I should have known better. Cal shouldn't have been in the Grand Sport at all.'

Until that moment Evie had never heard Charles raise his voice in fury; that it was fury directed at himself made it sound so much worse. He braced her by the shoulders, kissed her on the brow, said, 'Be strong for your brother,' and turned on his heel.

In silence, Evie watched him go.

Then, with the smell of smoke and burning still all over her clothes, she went back to the door beyond which Cal lay and stared through the glass.

Her brother, her twin, the other half of her beating heart.

Evie hadn't prayed since the night her mother died – but she folded her hands together now, and whispered an entreaty to God up above.

Charles burst through the hospital doors and gulped at the air.

He'd been swallowing it too long, biting back all the memories of Le Mans which were burning so vividly in his mind. All it had taken was an instant to cast him back to the circuit where his life changed forever. He'd seen crashes since Le Mans – he'd seen cars run off the track, cars go up in flames – but never had it consumed him like this. He'd told Evie he was leaving to fetch her father, and he was – but the truth was that he'd been leaving anyway. The hospital walls were caving in around him. He felt trapped in the wreckage himself, hemmed in by mangled chassis on every side, pinned in the very same place he'd been pinned all of his life.

The night was still sticky, the air heavy with scents floating in from the Jardin Exotique. Charles had no car to travel by, but perhaps that was for the best – for he needed to feel the earth beneath his feet.

Along the Avenue Pasteur he pounded, past the closed gates of the city zoo. He had to circumvent the grandstands, until he was almost at the point where it had happened, before he reached the Port Hercule. On the circuit there were still blue flashing lights. No doubt the officials from the Automobile Club of Monaco were already on site. Charles himself would have to alert the Talbot-Lago team – that is, if they hadn't been alerted already. But if it preyed on Charles, he did not think about it. He barely stopped to take breath until he was approaching the dark towers of the Fort Antoine, skidding between the black taxicabs and double-decker bus lined up outside, and scaling the shadowy steps to the amphitheatre above.

He stumbled upon the Company at rest, crying out Ed's name. By some fortune – whether good or bad, Charles didn't know – the old man was already awake. Perhaps it was anticipation of the show he was to put on tomorrow night that kept him awake – or perhaps it was a parent's eternal instinct to wait up for their children to come back home. Whatever it was, Ed took in his arrival with some mounting alarm – as if he sensed, somewhere deep in his bones, that the only reason Charles Laurent might have arrived here was to bring bad news. From here, Charles supposed, he might even have heard the crash. He would certainly have heard the sirens, their desperate music marring the Monacoan night.

Charles stumbled towards him, waking the other members of the Company as he came. In the middle of the theatre floor, he froze.

Ed looked at him with plaintive, shining eyes.

Yes, thought Charles, he didn't know *what* had happened – but certainly he *knew*.

'Which one is it?' Ed brokenly whispered.

Mere minutes later, he was behind the wheel of his canary-yellow car, ploughing into the night.

At the Centre Hospitalier, a door flew open – and Evie, who'd been prowling the hall, up and down, up and down, turned suddenly round.

She'd been expecting her father, but instead it was the young police officer, Inspector Maragoni, who appeared. Stout and broad-shouldered, with deep shadows beneath his eyes, he closed the door behind him and said, 'I'm told your brother lives.' Then he gravitated past Lily and the girls, past Meredith and Sam – who huddled together upon a chair in the corner – and gazed through the window at Cal, swaddled in dressings, lost in his drug-induced dreams. 'Miss Forsyth, I'm afraid there are questions I need to ask. It's unclear whether a crime was committed tonight – my understanding is that M. Laurent organised your brother's adventure out on the circuit – but the Automobile Club may yet bring a complaint. The Talbot-Lago collective may hold M. Laurent to account for criminal damage and …'

'My brother is dying in there,' Evie hissed, through gritted teeth. In the corner of the room, Sam tensed suddenly in Meredith's arms, then started bleating all over again. 'Fighting for his life,' she snapped. 'If you have questions for me, they'll wait.'

Inspector Maragoni lowered his voice, his eyes flashing at Meredith and Sam. 'Perhaps we might step outside? Perhaps there's somewhere quieter? Mademoiselle, I am not without mercy. I can feel the pain in this room. But I have a job to do and …' He hesitated, as if considering how he might rephrase what he had to say next. 'This is not the first incident since your family came to the Principality.'

Evie's face must have purpled with horror, for quickly the inspector went on, 'This is not to suggest wrongdoing on your part, mademoiselle. Nor to suggest wrongdoing on the part of your family. But the attack on the Fort Antoine was no accident. Your own performer saw the arsonist at work. And now, mere nights later, another tragedy … I would be remiss if I did not ask these questions. I would not be doing my job. Mademoiselle, how certain are you that what happened tonight was an accident?'

Evie fell silent. Quite against her will, her hand was trembling. She gripped it with the other, knuckles whitening as she stared at the inspector. In the corner of her eye, Meredith's face was creasing too. 'Sir, he was driving a car he couldn't handle. How could it be anything but …'

The door behind them flew open.

There, bedraggled and gasping for breath, stood Evie's father.

'Where is he?' Ed panted. 'Where is my son?'

He didn't wait for an answer. He barrelled past the girls, scythed directly through the middle of Evie and the police inspector and pushed open the door to the room where Cal was lying. Immediately, the room blurred. Ed had to paw the tears out of his eyes as he hurried to the bedside, took a seat, and grasped his son's bandaged hand. 'Oh Cal,' he whispered. 'Cal, what have you done?'

Behind him, Evie and the inspector slipped back into the room, closing the door behind them.

'What happened?' Ed asked.

He couldn't tear his eyes away from his devastated child, but the question was for Evie.

'He wanted to feel the car. The Grand Sport. He wasn't meant to go far. He wasn't meant to go fast. Just the sensation of it, he said. Just to know what it could do. And then…'

'Then what?' asked the inspector, when Evie's words petered into silence.

'Then he was,' and her voice broke for the simplicity of it, '*Cal*. Just when he could have stopped and turned round, he went *further*. Just when he might have said *stop*, he said *go*. Just when he might have felt satisfied, he said… *not enough*.'

On the bed, Cal's finger started twitching.

Three sets of eyes turned to watch him.

Was it possible, thought Evie, that he could *hear*?

Ed had started crossing himself, over and over, the old habit of his childhood. Evie hadn't seen him do it so urgently since the days after her mother passed away.

'I'm sorry, Miss Forsyth. I'm sorry, sir.' Inspector Maragoni took a breath. 'Trouble finds some people more easily than others, but I have to ask: do you know anyone here in the Principality who might want to hurt your family? Is there anyone here who might have a reason to mean you harm?'

Evie's eyes fell upon her father.

Ed looked up at her, the pain of too many lifetimes scored in deep lines across his face.

'Dad?' she ventured.

Silence.

Only silence in the hospital room.

Until at last, Evie could take it no more.

'Dad,' she snapped, 'what about Hector Lambert?'

Charles Laurent looked up at the Hotel de Lyon and took a succession of deep breaths.

If this was to be the way his career ended, then so be it. If his destiny was not to meet the ghost of his brother out on the track, well, he would just have to find some other way. In Formula One there was no turning back; out on the circuit, a driver could not suddenly change direction. And so it was for Charles Laurent tonight. All he could do, here and now, was march through the doors.

There were already police constables in the hotel reception. Two of them stood by an empty concierge desk – and Charles could only presume that the night concierge had been dispatched to rouse Conrad Knight, Raphael Allard and other members of the Talbot-Lago collective. Defiantly, he strode past them, making directly for the elevators. If he got to Knight first, at least he could seize control of the situation. There was no turning back, no matter what he did, but he could at least be at the head of the race.

The moment Charles approached the silver elevator doors, they slid open – and there stood Dickie Anstis, looking bedraggled, shocked, even more worse for wear than when Charles had last seen him. 'Charles, you're alive!'

Charles didn't know what he'd been expecting, but it certainly wasn't this. He stood in stunned silence as Dickie went on, 'But there's not a scratch on you. They're saying – they're saying you crashed the Grand Sport, out on the circuit. That you took it out after hours and...'

Hearing it in the voice of another made it so plain how foolish it had been.

'It wasn't me in that car, Dickie,' Charles said, and slipped past him into the elevator.

'But there were ambulances. There were flashing lights. Whoever it was, do they – are they... alive?'

Charles nodded stoutly, for he could hardly bring himself to put it in words. 'Pray for them, Dickie,' he said, and closed the elevator doors.

*And pray for me as well.*

As the elevator started to move, Charles realised that this was the very same space where Conrad Knight had made his threats to Evie. He supposed, now, that this was the reason he'd flouted the rules tonight. Something inside him, something he could not control, wanted to kick back at Knight – and this was *how*.

The elevator took too long to grind its way up the storeys. Charles closed his eyes to try and steady his heartbeat, but none of the tricks he'd learnt for calming the nerves before the starting pistol seemed to be working tonight. He could not keep his eyes closed for long. Fire streaked across the backs of his eyelids – but whether it was the memory of Le Mans, or the image of Cal going up in flame, Charles couldn't tell. Nor did he even want to know. Right now, all the courage he had left was for approaching Conrad Knight. Faced with the mangled wreckage and the geysers of fire, he was nothing but a frightened little boy.

Too much time had passed by the time Charles reached the hall where Conrad Knight's suite sat in the dark. Up ahead, a gentleman in the burgundy garb of the hotel was striding purposefully forward. No doubt this was the concierge sent to summon Conrad Knight. Charles picked up his pace, bustling past the concierge. Then, breaking into a run, he rounded the corner and approached Knight's door.

A glimmer of light under the doorjamb.

Perhaps that meant Knight was already awake.

Charles took a moment to gather his composure, but he could not take long. The concierge would be here in seconds – and Charles knew, in his heart, that it had to be *him*.

He knocked on the door.

It took some time for Conrad to answer. Seconds seemed to stretch on. Time bent wildly out of shape.

Then, as everything rushed back into focus, the door drew open – and Charles looked into Conrad Knight's pallid features.

'Mr Knight,' he declared, 'there's been an incident.'

'I can't ignore it anymore,' said Evie. 'You're sitting there and telling him no – that there's nobody here who might hurt us. "This is Monaco. *Everyone* loves us in Monaco." But you're lying, Dad – you're lying and you're doing it with the straightest of faces, and it's ... and it's breaking my heart!'

The words had come out in a torrent, but Evie wasn't finished yet. The inspector's eyes were flashing, as if he was desperate for this secret to be revealed, but Ed's had suddenly grown dry. They fixed on Evie, imploring her to say no more.

'Hector Lambert, Dad. Do you deny it? You do know the name?'

'Of course I know it,' Ed whispered, with a strange look at the door beyond which Meredith was still cuddling Sam. 'But not now Evie – not *now*…' He reached for Cal's hand, started caressing it, even through the bandages that hid it from view.

'Then when, Dad?' Evie snapped. 'When are you going to tell the truth?' She turned to the inspector, who seemed suddenly stranded between them. 'Hector Lambert. He's a croupier at the Casino. On the night we arrived, he confronted me. He said…'

Ed rose to his feet. 'Evie, NOT NOW.'

She hadn't heard him raise his voice like that since she was a girl. Whatever frailties he'd developed over the years, whatever frailties had intensified this summer, seemed to fall away. He looked at her, as commanding and imperious as the leader he used to be, and in his eyes was a warning.

'Something happened, seventeen years ago – and you've been lying about it ever since. Seventeen years ago, you made a solemn promise to Hector Lambert that we'd never return to Monaco. It was a promise you meant to keep, a promise you would have taken to your grave if only Princess Grace hadn't called for you. And… you couldn't let her down, could you, Dad? You couldn't let her down because of the friendship she owed my mother. So we came… and we put ourselves in danger, and Cal and I, we didn't even know it.'

'Evie, darling, I'm begging you to leave this alone. Not now, not here…'

'M. Forsyth,' the inspector interjected, 'if there's a history we don't know if, if this M. Lambert might mean your family some harm, we *must* know.'

Ed tore himself away from Evie and the inspector. Instead, he simply hovered over Cal. 'Lambert wasn't there on the night someone put a torch to the Fort Antoine. I already made sure of it. He was working that night, at the Casino de Monte Carlo.

Go, Inspector – see for yourself! Whoever attacked us that night, they did it for some other reason. It wasn't Lambert.'

'Lambert might easily have had someone working for him,' Evie snapped. 'He might have commissioned it.'

'But *why*?' pressed the inspector, growing more insistent at last. 'Forgive me, mademoiselle, but I'm not sure I understand the meaning of this. This man, Lambert, holds a grudge against your father. Your father promised he would never return to this city. But *why*?'

Evie took a breath. 'Are you going to tell him, Dad, or am I?'

Ed stared at his broken son, but his words were for Evie, 'Not now, Evie. If you hold any love for me, then *not now*.'

'I do love you, Dad. I always have and I…' She stuttered the next words, though she meant them with all of her heart, '…I always will, even though… even though…' She needed another breath. Then, wresting control of herself (and accepting she couldn't look at her father as she said what came next), she fixed her eyes on the inspector. 'Seventeen years ago, my father met a woman. Her name was Estelle Lambert. I don't know how, and I don't know why, but my father began an affair with her. Hector found out. My father made a promise he'd never return – and paid for Hector's silence. In spite of it all, I believe my father did love my mother. He wanted to protect her from the heartache of his betrayal.'

'Evie!' Ed gasped. 'You don't know what you're saying…'

'Oh I do, Dad. Because I've seen them – I've seen them all together. Estelle Lambert was the one who drove out to the Fort Antoine, the first day we were rehearsing there. The woman with auburn curls who *you* sent packing. And now Hector's scared. For him, it's like the past came back to haunt him. The past, come back to destroy his present. Because it isn't dead and buried, Dad. It never could be. What happened seventeen years ago has been with Hector every day ever since – because that daughter of theirs, Brielle Lambert, who's been working out on the film set with Hines and Frey…? Well, she's not their daughter at all, is she? She's a Forsyth, through and through. Maybe she doesn't know it. Maybe Hector and Estelle kept *that* secret too. But she isn't Hector's child. She's yours, Dad. She's my sister – and us coming back to Monte Carlo, it might rip open Hector Lambert's life all over again.'

The inspector had reached for a notebook. His hand darted madly as he rushed to write this all down. But, as for Ed, there was only silence. Somewhere along the way, he had stopped gazing at Cal and started staring at Evie instead. His face was pallid; he looked suddenly shrunken, disbelieving, aghast.

'There's a daughter?' he whispered. 'A *daughter*? But… how do you know? How do you know she's not theirs?'

'Oh, Dad!' Evie sobbed. 'It's written all over her!' She marched towards him, grabbed hold of his shoulders, looked him in the eye. 'How could you? Mum loved you. Mum *loved* you. Did she know? Dad, before she died, did Mum know what you did?'

Ed still looked wan. He cringed away from Evie, as if it wasn't just her words that were assailing him, as if it really was her fists pounding at him again and again.

'Evie, how could you think that of me?'

His voice was so small that he had to say it again.

'How could you…'

Tears streamed, unchecked, down Ed's aged face.

'You don't deny it, Dad. Why else would Hector Lambert come after me? Why else the fire at the Fort Antoine? Why else… two thousand pounds?'

Ed had to dry his eyes before he could find the words. 'I loved your mother. It isn't like you think. Yes, there was a secret – and yes, I had to pay Hector Lambert off, and *yes*, I promised we'd never return. But I didn't think for a second it still mattered. I didn't think it would lead to this.' His voice cracked; he had to take a moment to gather himself. 'I never had an affair with Estelle Lambert, nor anybody else. I loved your mother more than life itself. And that – that's *why* I had to do it. Oh Evie, it wasn't *me* who had an affair with Estelle Lambert. It wasn't *me* who did something so foolish and risked breaking your mother's heart. It was … Cal.'

For a moment, silence prevailed.

'She was older than him, and he was young and wild and … in love, or so he thought. But it would have destroyed your mother to know. It had already ruined one family. I couldn't let it ruin another. It's the only time in my life that I ever kept a secret from her. The only time I ever told lies. But I did it so that your mother never found out. I did it so that she didn't have to think badly of her son.' Something collapsed inside Ed; he fell to his knees at the bedside, then gazed up at Evie. 'And there's a daughter? Cal has a *daughter?*' His eyes flashed to the door. 'Meredith's sitting right out there, and Sam, and … They mustn't know. Not yet. Please, Evie. The world's ripping apart around us. Let's hold it together just a little longer, please?'

Evie didn't know what to say. A thousand emotions were crashing through her – relief that her father was no blackguard, a release that she finally knew the truth, all of it cutting through the horror and despair – but she couldn't put any of it into words.

The door flew open.

There, his face an emotionless mask, stood Charles.

As the door fell closed behind him, he said, 'Is he …'

'He's still here,' said Evie, and reached out for Charles's hand. 'I don't know if he can hear us, but his heart's still beating.'

If Charles could sense the iciness in the room, he must have put it down to the horror of the accident, for he asked no more as he took Evie's arm and drew her close.

'I'm finished,' he whispered.

'What?'

'The team's finished with me, and who can blame them? Someone has to be held accountable ... and here I stand.' He paused. 'I got to Knight and told him. I thought he'd be horrified – and he was, but there was something else underneath it. He looked – he looked like the cat that's got the cream. And he looked me in the eye and he told me: it's finished. The board could never act against him now. I'm out. I won't race.' Charles paused. 'And I don't care. What would it matter? What could a race possibly mean, compared to all this?'

'Charles,' Evie ventured, 'it isn't your fault. Cal went too fast. He pushed too hard.' She looked at her broken brother. 'It's what you've been doing all of your life, Cal. Oh Cal, you fool. Cal, what have you done?'

'He didn't do it,' said Charles, softly. 'I did. To let him out on the course like that, to take such a gamble – and all to make some point to Conrad Knight. It was me – all of it, every last piece. It follows me, Evie. Disaster just walks in my footsteps. I ought to have known.' He drew in a deep breath. 'But now it's done, and I'm finished with Talbot-Lago. I won't be qualifying tomorrow. I won't be racing at all. I'll ...' He lifted his chin, looked momentarily defiant. 'I'll be right here, with you, Evie – and, with you, Mr Forsyth, if you'll let me. I'll give him – why, I'll give him my blood, if that's what he needs. I'll ...'

But here even Charles Laurent lost the power of speech, and in the strangled silence that followed, Evie said, 'I'm sorry, Charles. I'm sorry.'

'Why?'

After all the things that had happened tonight, perhaps this seemed facile – but, in this moment, it mattered as much as everything else. 'Because it was your dream,' she whispered.

Charles looked from Evie to Cal to Ed, then back at Evie. Even tortured as she was, even pockmarked by tears and exhaustion and pain, she looked so beautiful right now. 'It was my dream ever since my brother,' he said, 'but I have a new dream now – and I'm going to live it.'

'How?'

'By being with you, right here,' proclaimed Charles, 'right here where I belong.'

*SATURDAY, 6 May 1967*

# Chapter Sixteen

Some nights pass in but seconds. Nights of wild abandon, joyous music and dance; nights when you first look in the eyes of somebody you love; nights when the stars line up and reveal, to young lovers, the shape of their lives. These nights pass in instants.

But this night lasted an ice age.

At some point in the blackest watches, Ed, Evie and Charles had left the hospital ward. 'I must tell the Company,' Ed had said, bowing down to kiss his son before they left. 'I'll tell them you're strong, Cal. I'll tell them you're fighting.' Evie had offered to stay, but Meredith knew she was torn – drawn to her father's side just as much as she was drawn to her brother. In the end, it had been Meredith who told her to go. 'You can't help Cal now,' she had said. 'But I won't leave him alone. Whatever happens now, I'll see it through to the end.'

It was in times like these that Evie realised why Cal loved Meredith so much. He'd found someone as strong as he was wild, as headstrong as he was reckless; he'd found his counter-weight in a world where true matches were too rare – and he needed her now, more than ever.

Perhaps it was disloyal, but Meredith was glad when Evie and Ed left the hospital, Charles walking dutifully at Evie's side. For five years now, she'd travelled with the Forsyths. For six years, she'd borne their name. And yes, she considered them family; yes, she knew they would lay down their lives for her and Sam; but sometimes, just sometimes, she ached for her own space in the world. Sometimes, just sometimes, she wanted to know that she had Cal all for herself.

If he was going to die tonight, she wanted to know that she'd spent this time with him.

If he was going to leave her, let her have him for just a few short hours.

The exhaustion had overcome Sam. Stiff plastic chairs sat against the rear wall, and he curled in a ball upon them, a hospital gown for a blanket. Meredith dared not imagine what dreams cavorted through his unconscious mind. Whether Cal perished or survived, this night was stained upon him for the rest of his life.

'Oh Cal,' she said out loud. She didn't know which parts of him she should touch – but she brushed, endlessly, at a lock of his wild black hair. 'If you can hear me, Cal, then …'

Meredith's voce pierced the fog of Cal's consciousness. Deep in the labyrinth of his dreams, where he drove a runaway car through tunnels of fire, he heard her calling his name.

'Cal, just wake up. Wake up and let's go home. Nothing else matters. Not the Fort Antoine. Not Parker & Parr. Not *Monte Carlo by Moonlight*. I just want you home …'

Meredith was trying hard to make sure her voice didn't crack, but so much emotion thrashed about inside her that she could sense the words shattering as she spoke them. Indeed, she might have lost control altogether if, at that moment, Sam's little voice hadn't piped up:

'Daddy's going to miss the dubbing.'

Meredith turned round. She'd hoped Sam was fast asleep, but apparently his sleep had been shallow and fitful – for there he sat, the hospital gown still around him, rubbing at his red raw eyes.

'What did you say, sweetheart?'

'Daddy's going to miss his dubbing. I heard Mr Hines.'

While Meredith was still trying to decipher what he meant, Sam left his seat behind, crossed the room and crawled into his mother's lap. 'Daddy,' he said, 'please wake up. Mr Hines is expecting you.'

Something in this didn't make sense. For a moment, Meredith let it pass; then she asked, 'What did Mr Hines say, Sam?'

'I'm sorry Mummy. I know I wasn't supposed to go wandering. I was just so BORED. I did try to sit there like you said, but they were doing a thousand takes and – and – and it's all because they thought Daddy's singing was better than Benedict Frey's and – and – and Mr Hines wanted Daddy to record it and then they could pretend.'

Was it really only yesterday? thought Meredith. The clock on the wall was inching past 4 a.m. Was it really only yesterday that they'd been on the sun-kissed sands outside the Bar Meridien, and danced and sung? Years seemed to have passed since that moment. The world seemed to have changed.

'Daddy didn't tell me about that, sweetheart.'

Sam started sobbing, 'I don't think he knew. I don't think he'll *ever* know.' He threw himself upward, to dangle from Meredith's shoulders, to bury his head. 'I don't like that film set, Mummy. I shouldn't have gone looking.'

Meredith clung on to him tightly. Sometimes, when words failed, when there was nothing good to say, it mattered just to *hold on*.

'I didn't mean to, Mummy. I didn't mean to see.'

'See what, sweetheart?' She held on even more tightly now. 'Sam, you can tell me anything.'

So he did. He told her how, after he'd heard about Mr Hines's secret plan to lay Cal's voice over Benedict's own, he'd crept round the back of the bar. He told her how he'd been gazing, longingly, at the empty hot dog stand, how famished he'd been, when he'd heard the voices. He told her how Benedict had come round the corner, angry and shouting – and muttering all sorts of horrible things about how Cal Forsyth had ruined his film.

He stopped before telling her what came next, because it seemed to Sam something he *really* shouldn't have seen – but, when, at last, Meredith told him there was nothing he couldn't say to her, nothing that would make her angry in all of the world, he said, 'There was another man with him. He was trying to calm Benedict down. His name was Gideon.'

And Sam told his mother how, when Gideon had taken Benedict's hand, all the anger and shouting had suddenly stopped.

And how the two young men had clung to each other and kissed, right there in the sand.

The sun's pink fingers stretched out across Monte Carlo, the endless expanse of the Mediterranean sparkling under dawn's first touch. That was one more morning Cal Forsyth had survived, thought Evie, as she and Ed emerged from the city police station. One more day when she still had a family to call her own.

Her father looked cadaverous in the early morning light. Evie supposed she looked gaunt and haunted too, for neither had snatched a wink of sleep all night. Having first gone back to the Fort Antoine, roused the troupe and shared the frightful news, they had repaired to the police station to rejoin Inspector Maragoni and deliver their statements on the night's events.

Now, standing on the promenade as the city woke, they could only soak up the silence. Yesterday morning had dawned with such hope; this morning brought only despair.

Charles was waiting for them at a nearby café, stoking himself for the day ahead with a pot of bitter, black coffee. The moment they arrived, he abandoned the drink and joined them out on the roadside as the sun revealed itself overhead.

'We're meant to perform tonight,' said Ed, darkly. 'I've already attended the palace once to share disaster. Princess Grace already put me back on my feet. How am I to go to her now and tell her – disaster continues, Your Highness. You brought us to Monte Carlo, and we repaid it in fire and devastation.'

Evie could sense Charles's discomfort. She took his hand, but it did nothing to assuage his guilt. Eventually, if only to break the spell, Evie said, 'I'll go to the palace, Dad. I'll speak with the princess.'

'It isn't your job,' said Ed, and started marching.

'No, but by tonight it will be. By tonight,' and she felt treacherous as she said the next words, for Cal wasn't dead, not yet, 'it might be me alone at the front of the Company. So, Dad, I'm starting now.'

Ed just looked lost. He nodded, then started to walk.

Evie made to follow, but Charles squeezed her hand and drew her back. 'Let him go. He might need his silence.'

Evie knew it made sense, but as she watched her father diminish along the promenade, bound for the Fort Antoine and whatever reception awaited him there, she felt a sudden desperation to follow. Last night, she'd wrestled with the idea she and Cal might inherit the Company together; last night, she'd thought her father might be a scoundrel. Now, everything was different.

'Cal has a daughter,' she said.

'What do you mean?'

'Cal had an affair, the last time we were in Monte Carlo. We were barely more than kids, but … that's the secret my father's been hiding. That's the secret behind the fire at the fortress, I'm sure of it. Cal has a daughter, and he doesn't even know.' She held herself. Too much emotion was a terrible thing. Ordinarily, she was so accomplished at sending it away. She shook herself now, like a dog rising out of a river. She needed strength – but what little strength was there, after a night like this? 'I must go to the palace,' she said. 'Charles, what will you do?'

'I'll find you at the Fort Antoine.' He bowed down to kiss her. 'Right now, I think it wise if I collect all my things and make myself scarce. The whole city's expecting me to be in the practice session this morning. They're expecting me in the qualifier this afternoon. To hell with them,' Charles spat, 'but I'd rather not look them in the eye. Not today.'

At first Evie did not want him to leave, but after he had gone she seemed to find her equilibrium. Somehow, the solitude was cleansing. Her family was fractured, but at least she had a job to do. There was strength to be found in that. There was purpose. She stopped only in the bathroom of a local café, where the staff were gearing up for the flood of spectators, to make herself more presentable, then made her way to the palace.

It took some considerable time before the palace guards permitted Evie into the same waiting room where Ed had, only days ago, awaited his audience with the princess. For Evie, the moment came with much more trepidation. The beauty of the parlour, the elegance and dignity of the palace, the rich sense of history from the tapestries and portraits whose eyes gazed down upon her, were as nothing to Evie. Every minute that passed by was just another minute in which she wasn't sure whether Cal survived, or whether he lay dead in his hospital bed. Every minute that passed brought the moment when the princess's patrons began arriving at the Fort Antoine fractionally closer.

Every second...

*Every heartbeat.*

'Miss Forsyth, you may come this way.'

The voice of the princess's attendant broke the pall Evie had been casting over herself. Not for the first time that morning, she composed herself, shook away every bad feeling and paid attention to the task at hand. Soon, she was following the attendant along a lavish corridor, then through a stark white arch. Here, through the final doors, she emerged into a palatial chamber with vast, vaulted ceilings, marble floors, and walls that glittered with mirrors, portraits and other paintings bordered in gold. Chandeliers sparkled over an antique desk and glistening rosewood chairs.

The ostentation in the room was dazzling – but as Princess Grace turned to receive Evie, she radiated refinement, beauty and understated class. It was her welcoming look that put Evie at ease, though she knew straight away that it was tinged with the knowledge of what had befallen her family the evening before. The Principality of Monaco was too small to keep secrets, but at least it meant Evie would not have to recount the devastating news.

'I'd been anticipating your father this morning – but Evie, you are more than welcome.'

Evie performed a small curtsey. She'd been presented before royalty before – she'd met no less than the Queen of England – and knew how she ought to behave. But Princess Grace seemed eager for the formalities to be over. She stopped short of embracing Evie, but by the look in her eyes Evie could tell that her sympathies ran deep. 'You look so much like your mother,

Evie. It's been a decade and more since I last laid eyes on you. I never noticed it before.'

A decade, thought Evie, in which everything had changed – but she could still remember that gala, just before Grace Kelly left Hollywood behind, and how much the princess had admired her mother. 'People say Cal's the one who takes after her,' she ventured. 'That I'm my father's daughter, through and through.'

There was a silence. It was saying her brother's name that had done it; it seemed to evoke some deep, yawning horror.

Then the princess pronounced:

'I'm told Cal survives. That his burns and his breaks are bad, but the surgeons identify no major damage to his organs.'

Evie stuttered as she replied, 'I – I didn't know that. I haven't been at the h-hospital since…'

This time, Princess Grace closed her hand over Evie's, breathing with her until Evie had assimilated the news. 'He may yet be OK,' said the princess.

But changed forever, thought Evie. If he does wake up, if he can pull through, if the pain and the infections and the rot can be battled away, he'll still be changed.

'Evie, the last time your father came to visit me I asked him if he had come to tell me the show must be cancelled, or whether the show went on.' Princess Grace paused. 'But that was then, and this is now – and a fire that consumes some props and wardrobes is nothing compared to a fire that consumes a loved one. Evie, under these circumstances, I have asked my secretaries to begin contacting our patrons. I could not ask you to perform at the Fort Antoine tonight. My conscience would not allow it. You must look to your brother, now. You must look to your family.' Princess Grace paused. 'I know it may sound foolish, but I must bear some responsibility in this. I invited you to Monte

Carlo, but I had no idea such terror might happen right here, in this city I love.'

Evie wavered. The truth was, she was not certain she could rally herself for tonight, not certain she could rally the girls, not certain she could rally her father from the ravine where he was lost. That old mantra, 'The show must go on' had been following her all of her life. Somehow, they hadn't broken stride, even when they said goodbye to her mother. The Forsyth Varieties were like the North Star: the constant guiding presence in life. But how did you sing and dance, conjure illusions, perform tricks and acrobatics, when one of your members was fighting for his life?

How did you do it when there was still somebody out there who meant you harm?

'Somebody in Monaco means us harm, Your Highness. Somebody attacked my family at the Fort Antoine, and ...' She paused, for somehow this next thing seemed so foolish. 'It's hard not to think that what happened to my brother is part of a pattern. I'm afraid that, if we were to perform tonight, we're asking for more. It's like black clouds massing. The squalls keep breaking over us, but I wonder if worse is yet to come.'

'Evie, I assure you, that from now on the Fort Antoine will be the most protected place in Monte Carlo. My security will make sure of it. I wouldn't put any of my guests – and I include you in that – in danger.'

'We're not used to having enemies, Your Highness. We're players. We live to entertain. But ... somebody wants to destroy us.' She paused. It was not, she knew, circumspect to spill it all, but somehow it felt safe right here, beneath the princess's gaze. 'I found out last night that, last time we came to Monte Carlo, my brother and a local lady began an affair. I found out that he has a daughter, living right here in the city. Neither of them know it, but ... doesn't that seem a secret worth fighting to keep? My father's been keeping it secret for seventeen years. If I was that girl's father, I might do anything, *anything*, to keep it secret as well.'

Princess Grace was silent while she absorbed the information. 'If one of our citizens means you harm, Evie, you must let our police force find them.'

'Oh, they know – they found out in the same moment that I did. But... the man I'm thinking of, as angry with my family as he is, has an alibi for the night the Fort Antoine was put to the torch. And last night, Cal got into the car of his own volition. It feels like more than one man. It feels like... a destiny, of sorts. A fate that's catching up with us.' She remembered, then, seeing Hector Lambert in the stands as the Formula 2 races hurtled by.

Princess Grace took Evie's hand and caressed it kindly. 'You haven't lost your brother yet. Your family is down but not defeated.'

'You're right.'

'What help do you need, Evie?'

Evie drew back, took a deep breath, lifted her head up high. 'Your security at the Fort Antoine would be most welcome, Your Highness. And you should know...' She looked the princess in the eye. 'It won't be necessary to cancel the performance.' Her voice started cracking, but she went on regardless – for a new notion had entered her mind, and she could not shake it. 'Because you're right – my brother isn't dead yet. He may yet open his eyes. And if he *does*, by God's good grace – if he *does* come back to the fold – I'll... I'll never hear the end of it,' she laughed, 'if he knows we cancelled a show.'

'Evie,' said Princess Grace, 'you really do remind me of your mother.'

She'd gone into the meeting filled with doubt, but somehow she came out of it filled with conviction. By the time she emerged from the palace, some of the old feeling had come over her. 'The Forsyths don't give up,' she whispered out loud. Somehow, she felt, if she kept telling herself it was so, she could make it happen.

By now, the city was waking up, the sun reaching its height. Spectators across Monte Carlo were already leaving their hotels to head to the circuit for the morning's final practice. No doubt the news about Talbot-Lago was already rippling across the city, but Evie tried not to think about it now. She murmured a prayer for Cal and hurried along the long harbour road to the Fort Antoine.

As she rose up the narrow stone stairs into the amphitheatre, she expected to find her father already marshalling the Company – but instead all she found were the dancers, the musicians, Jim Livesey and the rest scattered around in disarray. A clamour of voices sailed out to her. 'What news?' Lily was asking. 'Evie, is there any news?'

There, among them, stood Meredith and Sam.

Meredith's face was scored with such deep lines that, immediately, Evie feared the worst.

Why else would she have left Cal's bedside?

Why else would she have abandoned her vigil?

Meredith crouched, whispered to Sam, then left him with Lily and hurried to meet Evie in the shadows at the top of the steps.

Evie could hardly bear it as Meredith began to speak. Suddenly all the fresh conviction she'd received from the princess seemed to melt away.

But it wasn't Cal's death that had brought Meredith here.

And when Meredith told Evie what Sam had seen and heard, suddenly she started thinking that it wasn't only Hector Lambert who had reason to want Cal out of the way after all.

\*

Ed really had meant to go to the Fort. As he left the police station behind, his only plan was to go and wake the Company, to breathe some hope into their tired, hopeless forms – and perhaps, by doing so, to breathe some life into his own – but somewhere between the police station and the Fort Antoine, a new idea gripped him. That was why, having approached the Fort Antoine only to slide behind the wheel of the canary-yellow Ford Anglia, he was now trundling through the white stucco houses nestling in the foothills at the Principality's edge, his eyes on the house where Hector and Estelle Lambert had made their home.

Where, unbeknownst to him, they had raised his grand-daughter, Brielle.

Perhaps it was wrong to think of her as a granddaughter, but ever since the hospital Ed hadn't been able to shake the feeling. He'd come to Monte Carlo knowing he was harbouring a secret, the one and only secret of his lifetime, but he hadn't imagined, for one moment, that a deeper secret was being kept from him.

He parked at a distance from the house – the Ford Anglia was nothing if not inconspicuous – and set about waiting until there was some sign of movement from within. The privations of the night must have caught up with him, because intermittently he awoke to discover that he had fallen asleep at the wheel. One hour had passed, then two, then three. He knew he ought to go back to the fortress – somewhere in the city, the last practice for tomorrow's Grand Prix was being run; somewhere else, the princess's patrons were beginning to contemplate the evening of entertainment ahead – but the next time he awoke, he saw that there was now only one car sitting outside the white stucco house, where there had once been three. Only Estelle's old red Cortina remained. This, he supposed, was his cue.

There'd be no sneaking around this time.

There wasn't time left for sneaking and spying.

So he knocked on the door.

It took some moments before the door opened. The moment it did, he wondered if he was doing the wrong thing. But there stood Estelle, auburn hair cascading around her shoulders, eyes that had faded to grey pulsating in shock to see the old man on her doorstep.

Ed stepped forward, putting a foot inside the door. 'We need to talk.'

At first, Estelle seemed to resist. She braced herself against the door – and, when Ed saw how defensive she was, he relented, opening his hands in petition. 'Turn on your radio, Estelle.'

'My radio? What do you—'

'Have you listened to the news this morning? It must be a headline story. The accident, on the circuit last night? The Talbot-Lago crash?' She looked at him quizzically, but he could tell that she'd heard; she just didn't know what its relevance might be. 'It was Cal, Estelle. Cal was in the car that crashed on the edges of the Chicane du Port. He's fighting for his life right now, in the hospital on the Avenue Pasteur. So *please*, let me in. We need to talk.'

If Estelle had been alarmed to find Ed on her doorstep, she was more alarmed to think of Cal trussed up in some hospital bed, his life slipping away. She staggered backwards, allowing Ed within – and now Ed saw why she had been so resistant on the doorstep, for she was still in a bathing robe, steam billowing in waves from a bathroom somewhere down the hall.

'What happened? W-what happened?' she stammered.

'I think it was just Cal being reckless. I *think* it was just Cal being Cal.' Ed looked her up and down. 'He never did think of the consequences, did he, Estelle? My son never did think more than one step ahead. He's lived his life like a whirlwind! Just like seventeen years ago.' It was on the tip of his tongue to ask about Brielle, but there was something he needed to ask first. If he asked about Brielle, it was all they'd talk about – or she'd send him away, tell him never to return – and, above all else, he needed to know. 'You know about the fire at the Fort Antoine? You must know about the fire.'

Estelle just nodded.

Ed wondered if there was any shame in her expression – perhaps a hint of guilt flickering across her face?

'I know Hector was at the Casino when my Company was put to the torch.' He took a breath. 'But where were you, Estelle?'

'*Me?*' she baulked.

'Please don't act innocent,' Ed said. 'Someone in this city meant to hurt us – and you and me, we've been keeping secrets since 1950.'

'You can't seriously be accusing me of—'

'Hector already went after Evie,' Ed snapped. 'Our first night in the city, he accosted her outside the Casino. Do you know about that? Well, Estelle, do you?'

Estelle retreated from Ed, wrapping her arms around herself.

'I didn't,' she said, voice cracking. 'I *wouldn't*. I don't mean you harm. I don't mean any of you any harm. I never did. Or have you forgotten?'

Ed just stared. 'You came down to the Fort Antoine, the day we first arrived.'

'I heard you were back in town. I wanted to …'

'Catch a glimpse of him,' Ed concluded.

'1950 is so long ago, but in case you've forgotten, I loved Cal once. Ed, I wanted to *be* a Forsyth! How in God's name can you possibly think I'd creep up there and … set fire to it all?'

There was a moment in which Ed didn't know what to say.

There was a moment in which he knew but didn't dare say it.

But if it was lies that had led them here, it had to be truth that set them free.

'Because you have a secret you needed to keep, Estelle? Because you wanted us driven out of the Principality before we found out? Because you've built the last seventeen years on a lie, and you couldn't bear it to be undone?'

'Ed, please ...'

'You have a daughter, Estelle. I'm told she's called Brielle. A beautiful daughter, working at the same film set where Cal's been working. They've already met!' Ed's own voice started fraying, such was the emotion erupting inside him. 'Is she Cal's daughter, Estelle? Is she a Forsyth?'

Estelle just whispered, 'You've got to go.'

'Not until I know,' Ed said, his own voice just a whisper now. 'Is she ...'

'Of course she is!' Estelle blurted out. 'She's Cal's second coming. She's wild and she's reckless and she just *loves* life. But ...' Estelle's eyes darted around. 'I made a mistake. I know it was love and I know it was real – but it doesn't stop it being a mistake. Do you remember that summer? It was long and it was hot. It felt like the air didn't move. It stretched out in front of us, like it was ... full of possibilities, or full of peril, or both. But Hector spent every night that summer working, or out all night drinking, and me? I was rudderless and lonely and wondering if this was what my life was meant to be ... And then there was Cal, and – and it seemed like a second chance, you know? It seemed I was being told I could start again. Oh God, it seems so stupid now – but it was heady and it was free, and it was what I *needed*. And then ...' She caught hold of herself. 'You know the rest.'

Ed remembered it too vividly, though he'd tried to forget. The moment when he understood what was going on. All the warnings he'd made to Cal, to end it before it got out of hand.

The moment Hector found out, confronting Cal down on the seafront.

How fearful Ed had been that Cal might get himself killed. And the pact that he'd made never to return…

'I didn't know I was pregnant, not until you were already gone. Well, what was I to do? Chase after you? Give up everything I had?' She stopped. Some of her panic was ebbing now. 'The strange thing is, it *sorted* us, somehow. You think Hector's a bad man, an angry man, a possessive man – well, maybe he has been, but it isn't *all* that he is. He's been a good father. He's never once held it against her. He raised her with all the love in the world, more love than I ever thought he had in him, and… She wouldn't be the girl she was today, if it wasn't for him. Oh, she's got Cal's blood pounding in her. She's restless and free-spirited, and I don't think she'll stay stuck here with us, not for much longer – but she's the way she is because of Hector as well. Hector's a good man. He didn't do this to you. He wouldn't. He isn't vengeful.'

Ed snapped, 'He was vengeful when he took money from me seventeen years ago. He was vengeful when he said he'd tell Bella, unless I coughed up.'

'That was seventeen years ago…'

'It was two days ago as well. He came after us, the moment we reached the city.'

Estelle fell silent, until at last she said, 'I – I didn't know.'

'Well,' said Ed, and turned on his heel, 'it seems there are no more secrets anymore.'

Ed was walking away when Estelle reached out for him. 'Will he live, Ed? Will Cal live?'

'That's in God's hands,' said Ed, flatly. 'Pray for him, Estelle, if you've any prayers...'

The sound of a car engine backfiring ricocheted across the house, silencing Ed. He left the sentence hanging, readied himself to leave – but a look of horror had come across Estelle's face, and suddenly she clawed past Ed, making her way out to the hall and the front door.

Ed hurried after her. There, in the open doorway, Estelle was staring at a thick cloud of dust being kicked up in the street. At its heart, a clapped-out black Ford was turning a sharp arc, then ploughing up the mountain road, banking away from the skyscrapers of downtown Monte Carlo.

'What is it?' Ed demanded. 'Estelle, who *was* that?'

Estelle wrapped her arms around herself. To Ed, her expression was frighteningly familiar. It was the same expression he'd worn when Charles had arrived at the Fort Antoine last night: the one that meant the sky was caving in, that there was nothing you could do to stop it.

'She was meant to be at the film set an hour ago,' Estelle uttered. 'She must have come back. She must have left something behind. She must have...' She dared to look around. Through shining, disbelieving eyes, she looked at Ed. 'It was Brielle,' she gasped. 'It was my baby Brielle.'

Charles Laurent always travelled light.

It took him but moments to sling his shirts, his Chelsea boots and sports jacket into a bag, then duck out through the hotel halls. The valet had already been instructed to bring his brother's old Lago T26 round and there was nobody at the reception desk, so he just hurried back to the daylight spilling over the plaza. One week ago, he'd been cruising along the Riviera, anticipating a day that would change his life; he just hadn't known that the moment would come early, and in the dead of night.

He'd hoped the valet would have brought the car round already, but no such luck: the plaza was empty, a barren stone plain under the cerulean blue of the Mediterranean sky. Little wonder – because, over the neighbouring buildings, he could hear the swelling chorus of the spectators gathering in the stands. The practice session, it seemed, had drawn the eye of every soul in Monte Carlo, as he had known that it would. Right now, he ought to be sliding into the cockpit of the Talbot-Lago Grand Sport, fixing his helmet while the crew performed all the statutory checks. Instead, he was impatiently staring at the corner of the hotel, desperate for the valet to appear.

At least Conrad Knight, Raphael Allard and the other financiers would be at the circuit – standing imperiously in one of the private boxes, no doubt. At least he wasn't liable to run into any of them.

'Charles?'

Charles turned on the spot, fearing fate was playing games with him – but it wasn't Conrad Knight, nor Raphael Allard, who had called his name. There stood Dickie Anstis, looking ruddy and out of breath, his own bags in hand.

'Dickie,' Charles ventured, eyes flitting from side to side, as if in disbelief, 'but aren't you at the course?'

'I'm right in front of you, Charles – for a few seconds longer. I'm leaving, old boy. This old man knows when the time's right – and so should you.' Dickie came closer, then dropped his bags at his feet; it seemed that he, too, was waiting for a car.

'Aren't you driving this morning, Dickie?'

Dickie snorted, 'Fat chance. I've been relieved of my post.'

Charles just stared.

'They're at panic stations. Allard's pulled them out of the free practice. Right now, the crew's all over the second car, checking it for mechanical faults – the Automobile Club won't let them into the qualifier this afternoon unless there's a clean bill of health.' Dickie stopped. 'Charles, what in hell happened?'

Charles didn't answer that question. He might have done, if the practice's starting pistol hadn't suddenly gone off, piercing the skies above Monte Carlo.

The sound of the engines reverberated over the city.

But the two Talbot-Lago drivers stood, beached together, outside the hotel.

'I was a fool. That's what happened.' Charles stopped. 'I'm sorry, Dickie.'

'They've put the London lad, Chapman, in the driver's seat.'

'You didn't deserve that, Dickie.'

Dickie just shrugged. 'What Knight wants, Knight gets – but you should know, Charles, there's something else he wants too. He wants your head on the chopping block, and…'

In the corner of Charles's eye, his old Lago T26 appeared round the corner of the hotel.

The valet waved from the window.

'He already got what he wanted. I'm already out of the team.'

But Dickie grabbed his arm. 'No, Charles. You misunderstand.' He took a breath. 'They're going to arrest you, M. Laurent. They're going to hold you culpable for whatever happened last night. Criminal damage, endangering life – corporate espionage, as if you did it deliberately to undermine the bid!' Dickie shook his head. 'I'm getting out of the Principality. So should you. This got too messy, too ugly, too *fast*.'

The Lago T26 came to a halt in front of them. The moment the valet stepped out, Charles palmed a two-hundred-franc note into his hand, then rushed to throw his bag into the boot. 'I appreciate your candour, Dickie.'

'Knight's been gunning for you from the start, hasn't he, Charles?'

Charles nodded. 'I suppose he has.'

'Then look after yourself now. The border's a stone's throw away. They won't be able to touch you in France – not straight away. Buy yourself that time.'

Charles cast himself into the driver's seat, closed himself inside, then looked up at Dickie through the window. 'You've been a very loyal friend. I'm sorry you're mixed up in this. I didn't mean for it to touch you.'

'I was only ever your understudy, Charles. It was never going to be me out on the circuit. But…' He paused, for he had seen the look of grim defiance on Charles's face. 'You're not leaving, are you? You're not getting out of the city?'

Out on the circuit, engines roared.

'Evie's brother is in hospital on my account. I won't turn tail and flee, not while he lies there, *dying.*'

He brought his own engine to life.

Dickie just looked at him, hopeless. 'She can join you in France. Charles, think of what it might mean…'

But Charles appeared to have lost all capacity for rational thought. He extended his hand through the window, shook Dickie's stoutly, then pulled his sunglasses down and took off.

He had to take the long way through the city, cutting a deep arc away from the harbour and the striking skyscrapers that dominated the seafront. The roar of the crowd was duller here, but at some point the roads became entangled – and, having sat at a crossing for too long, waiting for a gap to open ahead, his eyes were drawn to a news stand in the shadows of a single Aleppo pine tree growing out of the roadside.

The traffic was not moving. Charles could afford a few moments. Leaping out of the car, he palmed a few coins into the hands of the street-seller and unfurled his copy of the *Monaco Matin*. As his eyes took in the front page, the knot in his stomach only hardened. A stark, black-and-white photograph showed the wreckage of the Grand Sport scattered across the end of the Chicane du Port. The ambulance that had taken Cal away stood with its flashing blue siren illuminated in a blur of white. He could not see himself, nor Evie, nor any of the others, in the picture – but his name was emblazoned beneath the headline. 'MIDNIGHT CRASH ON THE CIRCUIT DE MONACO' read the headline; then, underneath: 'THE CURSE OF LAURENT RETURNS. TALBOT-LAGO RESURRECTION OVER BEFORE IT BEGAN'.

His eyes roamed the story, but such was his fury they only took in one word in three. Not that it mattered; the gist of it was clear. The 'curse' that had been following his family since Le Mans, the familial scourge of recklessness, hubris and a cavalier attitude to life and death that had compelled his brother to hit the accelerator when he should have hit the brakes, was back in full force. Charles Laurent had never been the right driver for the Talbot-Lago bid; Charles Laurent brought too much unpredictability to a long-shot enterprise; men of Laurent's talent were rare, but had the team properly considered the risks of his character?

Horns were blaring behind him.

Charles looked up.

Evidently, he'd been too engrossed in the article, because he hadn't spotted that the traffic had started moving.

Casting the newspaper aside, he hurried back to the T26, hands flailing out apologies, and took off.

The practice session was still being run as Charles finally approached the harbour from the opposite end – and, knuckles whitening on the wheel as he sought to fight away his frustration, took the long road to the Fort Antoine. Somehow, just seeing the red double-decker and the fleet of black taxicabs steadied his heart. He'd only known this family days, but something about them put him at ease.

Swinging the T26 round, he hammered his fist against the horn, then leapt out and looked up at the ramparts. High above, a figure appeared: Sam, looking red-eyed and weary. Charles's heart skipped a beat. If Sam was here at the fortress, did that mean Cal was *gone*? If Meredith and Sam had abandoned their vigil, did it mean Cal was dead – and that he, Charles Laurent, had ushered him there?

Sam ducked away, but only for a second. When he reappeared, Meredith and Evie were at his side. Charles hardly dared ask about Cal, so instead he just waved.

He imagined they might wave back. He imagined Evie might duck away, then reappear from the shadowy steps that led to the bottom of the fortress. That they might beckon him to join them. But instead, their faces creased, and they seemed to look over his head, back down the straight barrel of a road he'd just followed.

Charles turned round.

Two police cars were approaching, slewing to a sudden stop only metres away from where he stood. Out of the first stepped the inspector who'd attended the hospital last night – Maragoni, wasn't that his name? – while, out of the others, several brutish officers who appeared to be under the inspector's command.

Charles looked back at the ramparts. Up there, Sam had vanished from view – but Evie stood, statuesque against the sky, staring straight at him.

He wasn't sure what emotion filled those eyes. Bewilderment, disbelief, horror – or perhaps just a simple solicitation to stay strong, to hold his head up high, to stay true; that none of this, not one thing, was his fault.

'M. Laurent,' began the inspector, 'I'm truly sorry, but I'm going to have to ask you to come with me.'

Leave the Principality while you still can. That's what Dickie had said.

Charles looked left. Then he looked right. There was no way past them, no way except the ocean – and, behind him, only the dead-end of the Fort Antoine.

The police officers fanned around him now. Perhaps they'd been told he was about to take flight – or perhaps it was just that they knew that, if he got back into that car and somehow forced his way back to the harbour road, there was no way even a trained police officer could outsmart him.

He'd already waited too long.

They were already upon him, and Charles Laurent did not mean to fight.

He looked back once at Evie, alone on the battlements, and gave her a wink.

Moments later, he was in handcuffs.

And somewhere in Monte Carlo, the practice session came to an end.

## Chapter Seventeen

Ed Forsyth knew that something was wrong the moment he returned to the Fort Antoine – for there, parked at an unruly angle in front of the Company flotilla, was the vintage Lago T26 that belonged to Charles.

If his aged body had let him, he would have cantered up the stairs to join the troupe. As it was, by the time he levered himself to the top, he was out of breath and desperate for answers. His eyes flashed around, but they did not find Evie – only Meredith and Sam, who scampered over to embrace his grandpa, while the rest of the Company waited in anxious groups, desperate for some indication as to what the day might bring.

It fell to Meredith to explain. 'They just swarmed him, the moment he arrived. I don't know if they'd been following, and I don't know if they were lying in wait, but...'

'Something changed,' Ed muttered. 'I saw Maragoni this morning. He said nothing about Charles.' He clung on to Sam. 'And Cal?' he whispered.

So Meredith explained what revelation had driven her from the bedside – and, as she did so, the knot in Ed's gut tightened yet further. 'You have to go back,' he said. 'Cal needs you now.' He gazed at the Company, all those dozens of expectant faces.

'I need to rally the troupe, but you need to be there if…' He caught himself and quickly said, '*when* Cal wakes.'

Meredith asked, 'But where have *you* been, Ed?'

There weren't any words for this. The image of Brielle's black car engulfed in dust was still playing on Ed's mind. He simply squeezed Meredith's hand – and then, with Sam still dangling around his shoulders, limped out onto the amphitheatre floor. In days gone by, he might have marched out there – but, right now, this faltering body was all he had.

'My friends,' he announced, 'I cannot begin to explain the events of the last twenty-four hours. We have already risen from the ashes once this trip – and now we must do it again. I must ask that we dig deep within ourselves, that we set aside our heartaches and the uncertainty that bedevils us – and that, for a few short hours tonight, we think of nothing but the spectacle.' He paused. 'Many of you were with me in the year my Bella passed away. Many of you will have seen me undone. But the curtains still drew back, and the spotlights still shone – and there was still music and dancing, and by God, I still made them laugh.' Once more, he fell silent. This time, he let the silence linger, making sure that he looked at each of his players in turn. It didn't matter, right now, that he hardly felt what he was saying; he was an actor by trade, and never had he put on a better performance than he did right now. 'While Cal still holds his head up, *we* will hold up ours. While Cal still fights, so do we. We may need to make some adjustments. The musical numbers will have to be restaged; we'll sing them together, every last one of us. And Meredith,' he said, fixing upon her alone, 'we won't put Sam in the spotlight. Not now. Not for this. It wouldn't be fair.'

In Ed's arms, Sam started bucking. The old man still had some strength, but apparently his grandson was stronger – he crashed out of Ed's arms and stood facing him on the amphitheatre floor. 'If you're all singing for my dad, then so am I,' he declared.

Ed crouched down. 'Little man, you don't have to do that. There'll be a time for you – when your father's back here, where he should be. When it's his fingers on the piano, and your voice raising the roof.'

But Sam just shook his head. 'I heard you, Grandpa. I heard what you said. While my dad still holds his head up, we'll hold up ours. While my dad still fights, so do we.' Sam's luminous eyes flashed at Meredith, but only for a second. Then they returned, exactingly, to his grandfather. 'It's for my dad...'

Ed had used up all the spirit he had left in rallying the Company. When he looked at Meredith, she just gave a hopeless shrug. But that hopelessness wasn't meant for Cal; it was meant for Ed and the Company, for how could they ever deny a young man with such strident conviction?

'You really do take after your father,' said Ed, opening his arms.

But Sam did not rush into them, not until he knew for sure. 'We'll sing for him until he wakes up,' the boy said – and, across the amphitheatre, a great cheer rose up.

Meredith rushed to him. Lily, Verity and the others all rushed in too. One moment, Sam had been standing alone on the floor, a tiny figure facing down an indomitable tide – but now he was being borne aloft, and it seemed to Ed, in that moment, that there really was no choice after all.

The sun hung directly above the city.

In seven hours' time, the show would begin.

Brielle was still shaking as she guided the clapped-out black Ford through the rising Monacoan hills, then took the little dirt track that led to the barns where the studio sets were waiting. She was late already – inside, Mr Hines had certainly already gathered the production to take them through the day's schedule – but for some time she simply sat there, head bowed over the wheel of the car. She'd stopped at one of the hillside convenience stores to pick up a copy of the *Monaco Matin*, and now she reached out to the passenger seat, where she'd cast it in disgust. The picture on the front was merely the mangled wreckage on the circuit last night. The article focused on the omens of disaster that had, for more than a decade, dogged the Talbot-Lago driver and his family. It was only in a sidenote that the man injured in the conflagration was named as Cal Forsyth, travelling singer. Nowhere did it mention the family with whom he'd come to Monte Carlo.

Nowhere did it mention the secret family he didn't know he had.

Brielle realised her hands were trembling. She tossed the paper aside again, then pulled round the rear-view mirror and tried to make her flushed, tear-streaked face presentable with a little of the powder she had in the glove compartment. How was a girl meant to react? What was a girl meant to feel, upon hearing the conversation she'd just heard? She'd only swung back to the house to pick up her comfortable shoes. Two minutes, she thought – that was all it would take to dash into the house, then dash out again.

She hadn't thought to discover Ed Forsyth standing there.

She hadn't thought to hear her mother talking about the long, hot summer before she was born; about her father Hector's drinking; about her *true* father, and what that summer had wrought…

She didn't know why she was crying. It wasn't anger or upset, though certainly both those things were bubbling within her. Perhaps it was just the shock of the unknown, the sensation that her feet were no longer on the ground, the dawning realisation that nothing was as she thought it was and never would be again.

Or perhaps it was because she liked Cal. She liked the confidence he carried. She liked the way he provoked Benedict – that pompous, obnoxious prig. She liked the way he made his talent work for him, the way it had carried him through his life – the very same thing she dreamt of doing for herself.

And now he lay dying in hospital.

Above all these things, Brielle knew she had to pull herself together. Part of her wanted to drive back home, to scream at her mother, to demand some answers – but another part of her couldn't bear the thought.

She got out of the car, bit down on the inside of her lip to jolt herself into seeing some sense and hurried inside the barn.

Brielle had been right: Mr Hines had already gathered the production together between the sets. Benedict and the band were at the head of the crowd, but arrayed around them were all the cameramen, sound technicians, lighting riggers, carpenters, set dressers, wardrobe assistants, make-up artists and runners that made up the crew.

She knew, straight away, that this was no ordinary production meeting. If Mr Hines had gone through the schedule for the day already, he must have blitzed through it before moving on to more sombre fare – because every face in the cavernous room was either turned downward, etched in deep lincs of shock, or pallid and grey.

'I'm sure Mr Forsyth would agree with me, however, when I say: The show must go on.'

Hines's voice boomed out across the room. So, thought Brielle, he'd already heard the news, already relayed Cal's accident to the crew. Looking around now, she marvelled at how much it had moved them – but, she supposed, that was down to Cal. He lit up the room, and he was really her father and…

She had to stop that train of thought.

Thank God that Mr Hines was still speaking, for it helped her battle it down.

'To make this work, we'll have to employ a little old movie magic. We were still due to shoot Cal as Donny Reaper in a couple of crowd scenes. That's a relatively straightforward fix – we'll use a stand-in and shoot at oblique angles. With a decent fit, and a good pair of sunglasses, we'll get away with it easily enough. But as for our soundtrack…' Hines's eyes landed on Benedict, who alone seemed to stand tall, his chin jutted out, his head held high. There was something imperious about him, thought Brielle, as if he was daring Mr Hines to criticise his music. 'Cal and Ben had been working feverishly over the last few days to bring our songs together. Did they take them as far as we wanted? No. Has what they come up with been *transformative*? Well, Ben, I think you'd agree it has. Ladies, gentlemen, I don't know what will become of Cal Forsyth. I don't know if that young man will live or die. But I do know the contribution he made to this movie. I do know that we're the better for his coming. And I do know that, come the night of our premiere, if Cal Forsyth should be with us – with you and me, Benedict, watching from the middle front row – then I should like him to gaze up at that silver screen and think: *I had my hand in a masterpiece.*'

There was a moment of silence in the room.

But all it took was one person to begin the applause.

Brielle heard it swell, until she too felt compelled to join in. Then, when at last it started to fade, she watched Mr Hines lift his hands and declare, 'We're in the final furlong, people – but we've got work to do, and so much of it. Let us pray for Cal, but let us do as any showman of his quality would want: keep our eyes focused on the task at hand, and make our picture the best it can be.' He clapped his hands for a final time. 'We've one hour before the day's shoots begin. People, let's make today count.'

As the crowd began to disperse, Brielle kept her eyes fixed on Mr Hines. The moment he stepped away from his crew, he seemed to heave a deep sigh – perhaps it was relief at having got through his rallying speech, or perhaps it was a quiet, private admission that Cal was leaving them with his job half-finished, and there was no way of putting it right. There wasn't a single person on the production who hadn't witnessed, firsthand, the transformative power Cal had had on the songs. When he'd stood up and sung 'Come Running' at the Bar Meridien, it wasn't just the scene that had felt different; it was the very energy on set.

The cast and crew buffeted around her, but Brielle remained stock still.

The sadness for Cal was overpowering – but, when she let herself languish in it, a new, second sadness seemed to rise up, and suddenly she was thinking of her father, of Hector Lambert, of the pain he must have felt in carrying that secret, of the fresh pain he might feel if he ever found out that Brielle *knew*. Secrets were destructive. Secrets were corrosive. But how could she ever let this secret go? Wasn't it better to hold on to it? Wasn't it better to suffer in silence?

She loved her father.

He was all she'd ever known.

He was her *life*.

And yet… how could she pretend? Could she really dig a deep hole inside herself and bury the secret down there? Part of her thought it was impossible, but part of her knew it was what she ought to do. It was the good thing. It was the kind thing. It would be done out of love, the very same love Hector had shown her by burying the secret himself.

Then she remembered the other thing she'd heard: how Hector had tried to extort money out of Ed Forsyth; how he'd turned the secret into a weapon, then tried to turn that weapon into a profit.

Now she didn't know what to think.

One of the production assistants approached her, but he still seemed so far away. 'Brielle?' he asked. 'Brielle, you look peaky. Brielle, is everything OK?'

She just choked out a 'Yes', then added, 'I've got to get ready' – though what she had to get ready for, she did not say. What she really needed was a place to compose herself – a hole, somewhere, to hide away. All around the barn, the production crew, the set dressers and lighting technicians, were preparing themselves for the day's first shots – but there was one corner where she might find some solitude. The corner where Cal and Benedict had been composing, the piano hidden behind wooden partitions, would not be being used – and never would again.

Brielle picked her way there and reached for the handle. The tears were still filling her eyes, but she didn't know who she was crying for – whether it was Cal, trussed up in his hospital bed, or Hector, whose life was about to be blown apart for a second time, or whether those tears were for herself and all the life story that was unravelling behind her.

She was about to slip inside when, suddenly, she heard a chord on the piano within.

Fingers picked out a simple melody.

It was 'Come Running', stripped back: just melody and chords, reduced to the rhythm of a nursery rhyme by whoever was picking it out.

ANTON DU BEKE

Then, over the music, Benedict's voice rang out: 'I didn't want him dead. The man strolls in here and takes over my movie, but I wouldn't wish him…' He gave a guttural sigh. 'I just wanted him away from my movie, that's all.'

Another voice joined Benedict's. Of course it belonged to Gideon. There wasn't a person in this production who didn't know why Gideon trotted around after Benedict. Some secrets were kept in a locked chest and buried six feet under the earth – but others were flaunted so incessantly that they ceased being secrets at all.

'You don't need to lose any sleep over this, Ben. It's just the way it is with some people. Most people go through their lives without a whisper. Then there are some that things just *happen* to.'

Brielle tensed. Was it right that she bristled so much in Cal's defence? Whatever blood ran through her, she hardly knew him.

She reached for the handle.

She wanted to burst through.

She wanted to shout out, 'That man was my father!'

Loyalty to Hector stopped her – because, of course, Cal wasn't her father, not in any way that mattered and, besides, wasn't this *her* secret to keep now? Didn't she need to bury it and stand a close guard – not like Benedict and Gideon and their young, rash love?

Then she stopped.

Because Benedict's words echoed through her.

*I didn't want him dead…*

*I just wanted him away from my movie, that's all.*

Brielle reeled back from the doorway and started to run.

*

298

Evie stood up and, exasperated, marched to the counter.

This was the second time she'd visited the Poste de Police today, but it was the first time she'd been kept waiting. At dawn there'd been a private room, the inspector's associates to take a statement, a pot of coffee and pastries brought in from a local delicatessen. Perhaps it was because the Forsyths were visiting Monte Carlo as the princess's personal guests, or perhaps it was just the shock and severity of the situation, but this morning it had seemed there was nothing Inspector Maragoni and his subordinates would not do to help the Forsyths.

But now, for almost two hours, she'd been in a narrow waiting area, alternately sitting on the hard plastic seats or pacing up and down. Intermittently an officer appeared at the desk, but only ever gave her a cursory glance before returning to his paperwork or vanishing into the station's deeper halls. A clock on the wall kept ticking. Somewhere outside, the roar of the spectators reached fever pitch, then died away. Time kept marching on, every hour bringing Evie closer to the moment when the show began at the Fort Antoine; every hour bringing Cal closer to the moment when he either opened his eyes, or breathed his last breath.

At last, Evie could take it no more. She marched to the desk, rang the small bell sitting there, then – with mounting impatience – rang it again, until at least a hoary old officer, with a balding pate and fringe of white hair, reappeared.

'I need to see him, sir. I need to see him now.'

'I'm sorry, mademoiselle – but nothing's changed since the last time you asked. M. Laurent is in custody here. He isn't permitted house guests.'

Evie pitched across the counter. 'I didn't mean Charles,' she said, through gritted teeth. It was hard not to barrack the man for his condescension – but, as she'd often told Cal, you won more battles with smiles than you did by sniping. 'I'd like to see Inspector Maragoni. You can tell him – tell him I have new information about the crash last night.'

It had been going through her head ever since Meredith arrived at the Fort – but whether it was new information, or whether it was just gossip and innuendo, she didn't know. Nor did she care, for it seemed to do the trick of manifesting Inspector Maragoni. Soon, she was sitting in the same inter-view room where she'd given her statement this morning, and Inspector Maragoni was staring at her across a cup of coffee curling with steam.

'This is a serious matter, Mlle Forsyth – and I'm afraid it would be a dereliction of duty if we didn't pursue it. The Automobile Club has been clear that we should act with the full force of the law. They've been in constant contact with my commander. You must understand how important they are to the Principality. Were we to be seen to be treating this matter lightly...' The inspector opened his hands. 'Let us just say: it would not reflect well on those of us who live here. Meanwhile, Mr Knight, of the Talbot-Lago team—'

'We've run into one another,' said Evie, darkly.

'—may pursue this as a civil as well as criminal matter. It seems clear that M. Laurent acted out of contract in permitting Cal to drive that car – though, whether it meets the threshold for a criminal case, the courts will have to decide.' Inspector Maragoni paused. He was not, Evie knew, acting in any spirit of unkindness. He seemed as hamstrung by the situation as Evie felt. 'We haven't laid official charges against M. Laurent yet, but I'm afraid it's a formality. He'll stay with us tonight but, by tomorrow, I expect we'll be ready to formalise things.'

Time was running out. Running out for Cal, but running out for Charles as well.

'What if I told you it might not have been an accident last night? What if I told you that somebody was holding a grudge against Cal? What if somebody else had a vested interest in making sure Cal was *indisposed* today?'

Inspector Maragoni dwelt upon this before he said, 'Do go on, Mlle Forsyth.'

So Evie told him about *Monte Carlo by Moonlight*. She told him how Cal had sashayed in there and upended the production. About the songs and resentment, about Cal's expanding role, about how Mr Hines had planned, in secret, for Cal's voice to overlay Benedict's.

'And he ought to have been there, right now, making the recording. He sent shockwaves through that set. He provoked its stars. He did what Cal does best and ... *disrupted* the whole endeavour. And, if he wasn't lying in a hospital bed – with nobody quite sure whether he'll live or die – he'd have been muscling Benedict Frey even further out of his own picture.' Evie had become breathless, but now she stopped. 'You're the one who came to us, Inspector Maragoni, and asked us how certain we were it was an accident. *You're* the one who stood there, in that hospital room, and asked us if we knew of anyone here who might mean us harm. Well, here it is.'

Inspector Maragoni shifted uneasily. 'You must understand, mademoiselle, this race weekend is, perhaps, the most crucial weekend in our calendar. Had a murder been committed, had there been a brutal attack, we might be able to deploy resources – but the Automobile Club have been clear that the act of an irresponsible man must not be allowed to mar the weekend. The incident reflects very badly on them. A registered driver, no less, and an outsider on the track. You can see how this might look. Stories would be written, and they wouldn't be about the glory of the Grand Prix. They'd be about a fateful accident the evening before. And…' At least, thought Evie, the inspector had the decency to look despairing. 'It doesn't help that M. Laurent is in the middle of this. After what happened to his brother, it gives any journalist of some dramatic flair the opportunity to spin a story. The Automobile Club have been very clear – the only crime we have documented is one of criminal damage, perpetrated by M. Laurent himself. My department is left with little choice but to attend to that matter, first and foremost.'

Evie's face was a stony mask.

'I didn't know the Automobile Club ran your department, inspector.'

She stood up, turned on her heel, marched to the door.

'Mlle Forsyth?'

Evie looked back.

This time, when he spoke, the inspector did not seem so haughty.

'I like your family, Evie. If things were different, I should have liked to see you perform tonight. But, right now, all you're giving me is gossip. You've given me a motive, but what I'd need is … *evidence*. Because, right now, all I'm looking at is a tragic accident – one Charles brought on you all. He's sitting in my cell, and we're ready to close the file.'

'Cal's been undermining Benedict since we got here. Oh, he says he doesn't mean to – and maybe he doesn't – but I *know* my brother, and I *know* he's been enjoying it. Inspector, isn't it enough to think about? Isn't it enough to slow things down and…'

Inspector Maragoni sighed. 'The Automobile Club are very important to this city. If I was going to set M. Laurent free and start chasing somebody new, I'd need more than *this*. I'd need more than a *why*. I'd need a *how*.' He gestured to the door. 'Without it, all I've got is a man in our cells whose negligence nearly cost your brother his life.'

\*

A glittering red Ferrari burst across the finishing line – and, in an instant, the final practice session of the Monaco Grand Prix was over.

All around the Circuit de Monaco, spectators were leaving the stands in search of sustenance. Cafés filled up. The hotel bars became hubbubs of activity. For now, the local restaurateurs and bar managers made merry – but, in two hours' time, the stands would roar again as the starting pistol of the qualifying round rang out.

'And we'll be there,' declared Raphael Allard, standing on a crate in front of a packed crowd of mechanics, financiers and other technical crew at the Talbot-Lago staging ground. 'Through disaster to glory, gentlemen. We brave few have always been like phoenixes from the flames. They *said* Talbot-Lago was finished, but we valiant few brought it back from the dead. They *said* we'd never make it to Monaco, and yet here we stand. Time and again we've proved our doubters wrong, and now we must do it again.' Allard paused, surveying the crowd. In the middle of them, standing over the gleaming Talbot-Lago Grand Sport – which had spent the morning undergoing the most strenuous of tests, as the mechanics examined its every component – stood Christian Chapman. Already dressed in his race leathers, his helmet tucked under his arm, he looked ready for anything. 'Gentlemen, let us not pretend that the last twenty-four hours have been ideal. Our plans have been thwarted. Our expectations shattered. We have been the most terrible victims of circumstance and …' His eyes flashed at the roll-back doorway, where Conrad Knight stood in his starched shirt and necktie, '…dare I say, *skulduggery*. A man lies in hospital, another in a police station cell; our second vehicle lies in scorched tatters. And yet … *here – we – ARE!*'

It was Christian Chapman who led the cheer. It rose up around him, filling the room – until Raphael Allard, grinning, compelled the crowd to silence again.

'Ours is a beautiful sport. The true test of courage in a world where courage can, too often, seem a thing of the past. We have lost M. Laurent in the most taxing of ways possible. Our faith and unity has been tested. But we are, all of us, better for the adversity we have been through. We are, all of us, stronger, more united, more determined. It is darkest before the dawn, but here we stand, in the baking sunshine of Monte Carlo.' He tapped his watch, then let his eyes rest upon Conrad Knight for one last time. 'Two hours, gentlemen, before we make history. The clock is ticking.'

It wasn't easy to get away. Brielle had fled, meaning to scramble straight back into her car and take off – but, before she'd reached the barn doors, one of the production crew had sent her on an errand, and the moment she completed that there was yet another errand to be run. It wasn't until Mr Hines called 'ACTION!' on the first scene of the day that she managed to slide out of the barn doors and reach her car. Inside, Benedict was filming one of the later low-key scenes, the interlude that shifted *Monte Carlo by Moonlight* from its second to third act, but all she could hear were the whispers he'd shared with Gideon.

The car backfired the moment she turned the key in the ignition. That was the curse of this rundown old deathtrap – and surely it had caused Mr Hines to yell 'CUT!' within – but she turned the key again, then a third and fourth time, willing the engine to start. The moment that it spluttered to life, one of the other runners appeared out of the barn doors and started gesticulating to her. Brielle didn't care; she simply averted her eyes from the rear-view mirror, forced the Ford over the dirt and scrub, and slammed it back onto the mountain road.

Then she was gone, foot pounding at the accelerator.

She had to tell herself to breathe. She had to tell herself that, last night, the man who was really her father had almost died – perhaps, for all she knew, had *already* died – in an automobile accident. She knew these roads like the back of her hand – she'd cruised them after dark, off to mountain haunts with her schoolfriends and whichever boys they were romancing – but she forced herself to slow down. A few seconds might save her life, and the secrets she was carrying were too precious to waste.

To reach the heart of Monte Carlo she would normally pass through the suburb where her own house lay. A kind of gravity seemed to pull her towards it – was her mother there now? Was Ed Forsyth still behind those doors, settling some argument that ought to have been settled long ago? – but Brielle fought against it, taking the long road to the city and the Port Hercule.

Too many of the roads in downtown Monte Carlo were closed. You stayed away from the city during Grand Prix weekend. If you weren't part of the racing fraternity, if you didn't want to soak up the atmosphere of that frenetic weekend, you made for the mountains, or went out along the coast, leaving the Principality behind. The streets around the palace were either closed or bogged down in traffic. It would, Brielle decided, be quicker by foot.

It was difficult to find a place to park the car, for every street and side road was already snarled up. In the end, Brielle was near the Centre Hospitalier when she found a spot. Inside those walls, Cal was still fighting for his life – although it occurred to her that she might burst in there, take his hand, spill every secret she'd learnt directly into his ear, she was determined enough to start running in the opposite direction. From somewhere, over the rooftops, she heard a starting pistol being fired, then the chorus of engines that told her the circuit had come to life. At this time of day it could only have been the qualifying round, the true beginning of the Grand Prix. Brielle was not ordinarily immune to the thrill of the race, but it did not touch her today. She took the long way round the palace, faltering only when she'd been running too hard and felt suddenly short of breath – but, in fits and starts, she came at last to the west end of the harbour, and the long road to the Fort Antoine.

She staggered along the waterfront.

She gasped for breath as she approached the tower.

But she could go no further – because a cordon had been erected around the fortress. Cars flying the Monacoan flag were arrayed in a horseshoe around the looming walls – and, everywhere, security officers marched.

Not policemen, thought Brielle.

This was palace security.

She looked up at the battlements. Even at this distance, when the roar of the engines faded in the city behind her, she could hear voices raised in song.

In spite of everything that had happened, it seemed that the Forsyth Varieties were going to put on their show. The security swarming the fortress might have been put in place for them, or perhaps it was here for Prince Rainier, Princess Grace and all the esteemed guests who would soon begin filling the amphitheatre above.

*I didn't want him dead...*

A voice hailed her from the cordon

'Excuse me, mademoiselle.'

Brielle turned to face the voice. An officer, as wide as he was tall, was knuckling towards her. She took in the long black baton at his belt, her eyes flitting to the firearm in the holster on his opposite hip.

'I need to get above,' Brielle said, her voice a whisper.

'I'm afraid that's not going to happen. Mademoiselle, I need to ask you to vacate this area.'

'I can't,' said Brielle, more boldly now. 'They need to know. The Forsyths need to—'

The officer drew closer. 'Mademoiselle, this is a high security area. My officers and I have been given explicit instructions. The palace is hosting a charitable event at the Fort tonight. My instructions are clear, and I have to ask you to . . .'

Brielle took a step back.

She tilted her face towards the ramparts.

'Evie!' she cried out. 'Mr Forsyth!'

But whether the Company heard her cries before the officers swarmed around and started barrelling her away, she did not know. Some moments later, a hand pushing forcefully in the small of her back, she was being marched back along the harbour road, back the way she had come.

'If it's the princess you're keen to catch sight of,' the officer said, depositing her at the end of the road, 'my recommendation is to wait here. The guests will start arriving within the next two hours. Stake out a spot. You'll see them sure enough.'

Brielle had loved to catch a sight of Princess Grace when she was a girl, but that hardly mattered today.

The officer turned to march back towards his mark – but Brielle just turned her face to the fortress, while inside she howled.

Tonight, the Forsyths sang and danced for the city, while Cal still fought for life.

And not one of them knew who had really wanted him dead.

*

307

In his cell at the Poste de Police, Charles lay with his eyes closed and focused only on breathing.

Directly outside the cells, a radio buzzed with commentary in French, the Grand Prix qualifier being played out in the rising and falling hyperbole of two increasingly excited commentators. Charles heard their voices, but he could hardly make out a word. To him, it was as formless as the sound of the engines as they ripped past outside, each lap of the circuit crashing like a wave over the station.

He did not sleep.

Occasionally he heard one of the officers slide back the little hatch in the door to look down upon him; they thought that he was sleeping, but no – Charles Laurent just wanted to shut out the world.

Then, at last, the engines died.

The sound of spectators faded to a background humming, and for the first time Charles could hear the tinny voices counting down the names of the teams who had qualified for the Grand Prix.

Ferrari and Honda.

Brabham-Repco, BRM.

Eagle-Weslake, Matra-Ford.

Cooper-Maserati.

*Talbot-Lago*.

For the first time, he opened his eyes.

He got to his feet, started prowling like a caged animal, started wringing his hands to rid himself of the adrenaline which had suddenly surged.

In the face of adversity and disaster, Talbot-Lago were through to the final race.

What a legend that might make if they won.

But all Charles Laurent could do was wait here and rot.

*

There was a different feeling in the city, now that qualifying had come to an end. The sun began its descent in the west; the stands emptied, and all of those spectators who had lost themselves in the excitement fanned out to find new haunts in the restaurants and bars. Down on Larvotto beach, Champagne corks flew. Out at the Monaco Country Club, teams were dissected and wagers placed on the events tomorrow might bring.

And at the harbour, where Ed Forsyth's company had retreated into the belly of the fortress to await the arrival of their audience, the anticipation was palpable. The long road to the fortress was bedecked with photographers and newspapermen. The red double-decker, the canary-yellow Ford Anglia, the whole flotilla belonging to the Forsyths had been shuttled away – and in their place, on the fortress approach, a red carpet had been laid. Security officers swarmed the harbour. The convoy of vehicles making the short journey from the palace arrived. On his last foray to the amphitheatre above, Ed risked a look over the battlements – and saw a gleaming black limousine beset by photographers, as out of it emerged Prince Rainier, with Princess Grace on his arm.

Ed returned to the darkness of the fortress interior. In here, it was impossible to know whether it was night or day. A messenger awaited him on the steps, to relay the news that Cal slept on, with neither sign of his condition worsening nor some miraculous recovery. Ed stalwartly shook his hand, then swept on into the chamber where his Company were gathered.

'The princess is here,' he announced, to the banks of waiting faces. 'The guests are making their way above.' When Ed listened closely, he could even hear them making their way up the narrow stone stairs, to emerge into the splendour above. Their footsteps, their voices, resounded around the fortress. 'My friends, this is what we came for. Let us do Cal proud.'

As the Company lined up, ready for the call, Ed gravitated towards Evie and Meredith. There stood Sam, decked out in his miniature tuxedo, a bright yellow bow tie for a hot summer's night. It was cool inside the fortress, but up above the air was sticky and humid.

'We can do this,' he told them.

Evie took his hand. 'Dad,' she said, 'we already are.'

Half an hour passed before word came that the audience were settled. For the final time, Ed rallied the troupe. Then, they began their ascent.

It was the musicians who went first, to take their places around the edge of the stage. After they had gone, the Company awaited the first notes of their opening number. The hum of the audience was silent, the music rose up above the bay – and, when it reached its zenith, that was Ed's cue.

He squeezed Evie's hand. He winked to Meredith – who was now down on her knees, whispering encouragement to Sam – and turned on his heel.

Then, alone, he started to march.

He had hoped the day would slough off him as he made his way up the steps, then saw the portal of light above. There had been many times in his past when he had to summon the spirit to perform, but there was always a moment – somewhere between his dressing room and the stage – where the world *transformed*, and whatever he'd been dealing with just melted away.

Not so this evening.

Even as he stepped into the sunlight above, he was thinking about Cal.

Then, suddenly, he was standing centre stage, gazing at the tiers of stone steps brimming with Princess Grace's patrons.

Ladies bedecked in silver and gold finery rose to their feet to receive him. Men in fine jackets, with slicked-back hair and perfectly sculpted moustaches, brought their hands together in applause. The Forsyth Varieties had played for paupers and princes, and never made any distinction between the two – but in this moment Ed was overawed.

He'd promised it would be his final performance.

His eyes landed on Princess Grace, a bright white flower in her hair, lemon-yellow gloves stretching past her wrists, pearl earrings catching the light from above. She caught his eye as he summoned a smile and waited for the music to end.

Applause swept the amphitheatre.

Sam could hardly stand still.

Evie rallied the dancing girls.

Jim Livesey performed the opening moves of his illusion, over and over again.

And, up above, Ed Forsyth announced, 'Ladies and Gentlemen, let your evening begin!'

For too long Cal had been lost in the labyrinth of fire. For too long, he had turned and run, dodged the falling rafters, cried out for help as the walls of flame grew ever nearer and the heat too terrible to bear. He'd screamed for help, tumbled down crumbling stairs, heard the guttural roar of engines, felt the world listing underneath him.

In and out of those dreamscapes he had plunged, up and down, round and round…

And then, suddenly, there was only blackness. He could still feel the fires, but no longer were they wreathing around him. The heat was fading. Fearsome reds and oranges turned into a low amber glow.

He would never know how long he was adrift in that blackness. Time had no meaning to Cal, as he lay in that hospital bed. He might have been there hours, or he might have been there for centuries untold.

Then, amidst the blackness, he saw *white*.

The first antiseptic smells reached his nostrils, cutting through the stench of oil, smoke and ash.

Somebody was touching him.

Yes, *touch*. He remembered that now.

He opened his eyes.

'Merry?'

The voice wasn't his own. It sounded older, weathered and cracked. It sounded, he decided, like he was having to choke up the words, like the words had jagged edges.

'Cal,' gasped a voice, 'you're awake!'

Even in his helpless fugue, Cal knew this wasn't Meredith's voice. Meredith's voice: he would recognise it anywhere. He tried to turn, searching out this figure, whoever it was. He realised, at last, that he was in a hospital – perhaps it was a doctor, or perhaps it was a nurse – and no sooner had he realised that, than a hailstorm of other memories started crashing over him.

The Grand Sport...

How incredible it had felt as he put his foot on the accelerator.

How terrible when he'd put it on the brakes and felt not a whisper of resistance.

He couldn't turn. His body screamed. Already, there were footsteps clattering around him. 'Mr Forsyth,' came a second voice, this one the deep baritone of a man, 'I'm glad you're back with us. Something for the pain...'

A coldness was rushing into his arm. Whatever they were administering was numbing the edges of the world again. His fingers flexed on the hand that had been holding his own – and, in the few sacred moments he had before the morphine blurred all that he could see, he managed to cough up the crucial few words still lodged in his throat:

'It wasn't an accident. It was the brakes. Somebody – tampered – with – the *brakes*…'

Waves of applause sounded above.

Evie looked over the girls, waiting for the applause to break and the next musical number to kick in. Lily looked fearless; Betty and Verity looked ready to pounce, like athletes at the starting line of a race. At least, Evie thought, the girls were focused. Ed's words had worked their magic upon the entire company. They were sallying out there with Cal in mind.

Evie only wished she could achieve the same sort of focus, but her thoughts had been fractured, her mind persistently distracted, since she'd left the Poste de Police that afternoon. The knowledge that Charles was still there weighed on her. The tone of Inspector Maragoni's voice as he impressed upon her the importance of the Automobile Club, and the pressure he was under to tidy things away, still seemed to echo all around. She'd returned to the Fort, not knowing what she should do – but the hours were cascading by, the palace security had arrived, and now here she stood, ready to lead out her girls.

How many times had she done this before?

Thousands, she thought. Too many to count.

But she'd never before had her heart and mind somewhere else.

Behind the girls, Meredith was still cuddling Sam. Their eyes met. Evie knew she felt she ought to be at the hospital – damn it, it was what Evie thought too – but the determination on Sam's face could not be denied. In the same moment that Evie heard the band strike up with their big band version of Sam

Cooke's 'Twistin' the Night Away', she gave the boy a salute. Sam liked that. He returned the salute with flair.

'Come on then, girls,' said Evie. 'Now's the moment.'

In procession, they sailed up the stairs.

The sun was still in the sky as Evie and the girls erupted into the amphitheatre and took in their first sight of their lauded guests. Evie's instruction to them had been clear: 'Do not seek out the princess,' she had told them – though now that she was up here, in a venue so intimate where the guests were so close to the performers, it was an instruction Evie herself found it almost impossible to obey. For the first time – and only for a fraction of a second – she felt freed from the events of the day. For the merest instant, Charles wasn't in a prison cell; for a single flickering moment, Cal didn't hover on the edge between life and death. The sensation was gone in a second, but it had been so powerful that it carried Evie into the dance.

The girls fanned around her.

They tumbled and cartwheeled, built towers of their bodies, came apart, then reassembled once again.

The Forsyth Varieties were out here, doing what they did best – and, though nobody could forget the journey that had brought them here, there was a beautiful simplicity in just being here, doing what they were put on Earth to do.

Now that Evie was in the arena, things felt as if they were flowing. Soon, the dancers withdrew, as Jim Livesey took to the stage and performed his vanishing illusion with his new wardrobe. A simple piece of sleight of hand, it wasn't easy to get right – not so close to the lauded guests – but Jim swallowed his nerves, summoned up the spirit of his mentor and soaked up the applause. The space where Davith's dog act ought to go was filled with Ed's patter, while the dancers and musicians came together – and, with the sun now dipping over the horizon, the stage lights came up.

Now was Evie's cue. Leaving the girls behind, she slipped back into the shadows beneath the arena. Only two souls were left in the chamber underneath. Meredith, who never performed with the Company, was holding Sam's hand. The boy had lost a little of the defiance he'd shown earlier. He shifted from foot to foot, eyes darting, saying nothing.

'He's nervous,' said Meredith.

'I'm not,' Sam snapped.

Evie went to him and got to her knees. 'You're the best of us, Sammy. I was much older than you when I first went out *there*.' She grinned. 'I'll be right beside you. We all will. Every last member of the Forsyth Varieties – they're willing you on, Sam. And…' Evie was not certain if she should go on, but the words flowed out of her nevertheless. 'Right now, your father is in his hospital bed, dreaming of this show. Everything we do out there, it's playing across the backs of his eyes. Playing in his dreams…'

Sam ceased his fidgeting. 'Like a movie projector,' he said.

'Exactly like a movie projector,' said Evie.

Sam let go of Meredith's hand and took Evie's.

'And your mum's going to be watching from the stairs,' she said.

Together, the three Forsyths made their way back to the arena. There was no time for goodbyes, and perhaps that was for the best – perhaps it meant Sam had rid himself of all his sudden nerves. Meredith remained in the shadows, as Evie and Sam proudly marched into the heart of the Company, taking their place around the piano where Ed was hunkered, hammering at the keys.

The song rose up.

It was 'Runaway Lovers'. Meredith had listened to this song so many times. She had known this song long before the rest of the world. She knew it when it was just a fledgling melody, when Cal was piecing it together on old pianos and guitars in the bedsits and flophouses where they used to live. She knew it when it had different words, when the chorus was unfinished, when the lyrics were but placeholders, things Cal saw around the house.

She'd known this song when it was languishing, unsung and unrecorded.

She'd known it when only she and Cal knew it.

All of that was long before it found its place in the firmament.

And now, here it was, the whole Company in chorus – and Sam's voice rising out of them all to sing, alone, its very last lines:

*'Runaway Lovers, just running for cover…'*

Her heart felt too full. Her eyes filled with tears. The crowd were already on their feet – and, though there were only three hundred and fifty of them, it seemed to Meredith that the whole world was giving her son an ovation – the whole world celebrating her husband's song, in the voice of their child.

After that, fireworks exploded above the Fort Antoine. The crowd demanded an encore – who wouldn't, after a performance like that? – and Meredith watched again as Sam sang his heart out, borne up by the dancing girls so that it seemed the whole arena was for him alone.

After that, Ed led the Company through its bows. The applause chased them back down the stone steps and into the chamber – where, breathless and spent, they waited for the amphitheatre to empty.

Some time later, the night now deep and vast, Ed permitted the Company to return above. The stage lights still dazzled on top of the Fort Antoine, but there was no doubt the festivities were over. The peacefulness left behind drew everyone to the stone steps, where they lay down to breathe deeply of the nocturnal air.

The dancing girls were in repose, Jim Livesey looked fit to crawl inside his vanishing cabinet and sleep for a hundred years, but Evie was already changing out of her performing clothes and hurrying to join Meredith and Ed at the stairs.

'We must go to him now,' Ed told the Company, 'but our work here is done, and you'll be pleased to know that your suites are waiting, at the Hotel de Lyon.' The Company had looked so exhausted – but at the thought of deep feather mattresses, pillows and hot showers, each one of them perked up. 'I'll find you there, my friends. Pray that we bring good news with us.'

Neither Ed, Evie, nor Meredith, wasted any time in hurrying down the fortress stairs. The last of the guests were already gone, the red carpet and cordons long since tidied away, but a scattering of palace officials remained. As soon as Ed appeared, one of the burlier guards turned to him and said, 'I'm sorry, sir. She's been waiting all night. She came down before the performance, but we thought she was just a well-wisher, someone keen to see the princess, so we kept her at bay. But …' The security officer shrugged. 'She's asking for you by name. It isn't the princess she wanted to see, sir. It was you.'

Ed looked along the narrow harbour road. There, shrouded in darkness, stood Brielle.

Ed hobbled forward. 'Stay here,' he said to Evie. 'Stay *right* here,' he said to Meredith.

He tried to ignore the flustered look on Evie's face as he tottered forward to face Brielle. The bewilderment on Meredith's face was even harder to bear, for he knew that, some day soon, the secret would have to be shared with her, that all her notions of the past would have to be rewritten, just as it had been for Evie and Ed. At least, Ed thought, there was no betrayal in it. Cal's world would be rocked in concert with Meredith's and they'd sail through it together – and that was what mattered.

He reached Brielle and looked upon her for the very first time. No, there was so little doubt. It wasn't just that she looked like Cal. Somehow, she radiated his presence.

Quietly, he said, 'You know who I am.'

Brielle nodded.

'You were there, at the house, when I was with your mother.'

Brielle winced. 'I didn't know that she knew. I haven't been back. I haven't spoken to them. Haven't seen my...' She was going to say 'father', but on the word she stalled. 'But it's not important now,' she said, drawing herself to her full height, trying to summon her courage. 'Sir, I tried to come before, but there was so much security, so I went to the hospital – and Cal, and Cal...'

Every muscle in Ed's body turned rigid.

'He's awake.'

Ed could hardly bear it. It felt as if the world was listing. He reached out and took her hand.

'I know who did it,' she said, starkly. 'I was at the set today, and Mr Hines was breaking the news to the crew – and then... Benedict,' she declared, 'he said it as plain as day. *I didn't want him dead. I just wanted him away from my movie.* And Cal said—'

Evie and Meredith had waited long enough. They surged forward now, flanking Ed the moment they heard the words.

'What did Cal say?' Evie gasped.

As for Meredith, she was too stunned to say a thing.

'He said it wasn't an accident,' came Brielle's tremoring voice. 'He said somebody cut the brakes. He'd been bragging at the studio about taking out the Grand Sport. They knew he was going to try the car that night. Benedict's been griping about Cal since the beginning, and he found his way to settle it, once and for all. They cut the brakes. They tried to kill Cal.'

*SUNDAY, 7 May 1967*

# *Chapter Eighteen*

## MONACO MATIN

### SUNDAY 7 MAY 1967

## ARREST MADE IN CASE OF GRAND PRIX SABOTAGE

The extraordinary events of the evening of Friday 5 May took another twist in the small hours of this morning, with the arrest of rising British movie star Benedict Frey. Frey has been based in Monte Carlo since the start of May, filming new movie *Monte Carlo by Moonlight* – and has quickly become a fixture after-hours in the city, regularly frequenting Maona, the Café de Paris, and ending each night at the roulette wheels of the Casino de Monte Carlo.

And it was here that his errant behaviour – which has al-ready seen him featured on the front pages of this newspaper, after an altercation with Talbot-Lago racing driver Charles Laurent – caught up with him. At approximately 12.30 a.m. on the morning of Sunday 7 May, officers of the city police appre-hended twenty-three-year-old Mr Frey at the blackjack table of the Casino de Monte Carlo, and arrested him on suspicion of attempted murder. The alleged victim, Cal Forsyth, is said to be in a critical but stable condition at the Centre Hospitalier, after he was involved in a near-fatal car accident on Friday night. Subsequent investigation, and the testimony of Mr Forsyth, has concluded that the brake line of the Talbot-Lago Grand Sport, which Mr Forsyth was driving, had been cut in an act of deliberate sabotage.

How Mr Frey accessed the vehicle has not yet been established, but his motives appear to be clear, and a private confession appears to have been instrumental in the case made against him. This newspaper understands that, since the moment of his arrest, Mr Frey has maintained his innocence – though, how long that can last with such brazen testimony against him, this editor cannot say . . .

In the meantime, it is our understanding that M. Charles Laurent of Lyon, France – who had been held in custody connected with the same crime – is this morning to be released from the city Poste de Police. Stripped of his role with Talbot-Lago, he may yet face a civil prosecution for criminal damage – but, for Charles Laurent, it seems that Mr Frey's exposure has come just in time . . .

The first thing Charles Laurent knew of the revelations concerning Benedict Frey was when, some time after dawn – with the summer sun scudding in through the narrow grille at the top of his cell – a key fumbled in the lock, and the heavy door drew back to reveal a wan, exhausted Inspector Maragoni standing there with his hands on his hips.

Maragoni said almost nothing as Charles was led from the cell. Indeed, it wasn't until he was in a holding area, signing paperwork and being given back the boots, belt and other accoutrements they'd taken from him at his arrest, that he understood he was not being transported to some bigger, longer-term facility, but being released. 'Monsieur, what changed?' he ventured – but neither the inspector, nor the other station officers, had the authority to say.

It was race day in Monte Carlo.

His world had changed twice in as many days.

At first, he didn't know what to do. Soon, spectators would start flocking out of their hotels to seize the best seats in the stands. Already, the teams would be gathering at their staging grounds, the drivers running through whatever pre-race rituals they'd developed in their careers. Charles reached into his pocket for the wallet they'd just given back to him and, opening it up, looked at the grainy old Polaroid picture of himself and his brother, just boys in their homespun jumpers, back on their grandfather's farm. The idea that he might see Toby again, somewhere out on the track, was for the birds now – but perhaps he'd made his peace with it already, for the person he was thinking of most vividly now wasn't Toby after all.

It was Evie, so he started to run.

His old Lago T26 was still at the Fort Antoine, shuffled off into a siding for safekeeping, but of the Forsyths there was no sign. His heart told him they could not have left Monte Carlo, not with Cal in such a desperate state, not with Charles himself in a cell – so he slipped behind the wheel of the T26 and quickly, before the city was flooded, gunned his way to the Hotel de Lyon.

Inside, the hotel was beginning to buzz. Some of the concierges eyed him oddly as he strode through – but Charles had long ago learnt that a little confidence went a long way. As long as he kept moving, he wouldn't be stopped. With a self-assurance he did not really feel, he marched towards the check-in desk and was about to ask them if Evie Forsyth had returned to staying here, when he caught sight of Lily and one of the other dancing girls scampering towards the breakfast lounge. Lily eyeballed him in surprise, then mouthed 'I'll fetch her', and vanished.

'Sir,' said the check-in attendant, 'may I help you?'

Charles would have replied, but his eyes had been drawn to the pile of newspapers waiting by the desk. Only now that he saw the front page of the *Monaco Matin* did he truly understand what had happened last night, and by what good grace he'd been released from the Poste de Police – for there, spread across the front page for the second time in a week, was a picture of Benedict Frey in the middle of a fracas at the Casino de Monte Carlo. This time, however, it wasn't Charles and Evie he was remonstrating against; it was Inspector Maragoni and the officers sent to arrest him.

After some time, a shadow in the corner of his vision drew Charles's attention. Thinking it was Evie, he looked up – but no, it was Conrad Knight, Raphael Allard, the rest of the Talbot-Lago financiers striding as one out of the breakfasting lounge, making for the hotel doors with the air of warriors off to do battle. Quickly, Charles bowed his head, determined not to be seen.

Then Evie spoke his name.

Suddenly, she was at his side – and, whether Conrad Knight and his followers had noticed Charles was here, he could not say. Evie smothered him in her arms. 'It's going to be all right. Cal's going to be all right. The brakes were cut. They were trying to kill him, but he's going to be—'

'Trying to kill him,' Charles whispered, 'but why?'

'Because he's Cal, and they thought he was taking over – and … it's as plain as day. Brielle heard them talking. Benedict as near as confessed. And Cal had been boasting about taking out the car – because, well, he's Cal and that's what he does, and …'

Evie stopped. 'Leave with me,' she said. 'As soon as Cal's out of the woods, leave with me. I'm going to take the Company back to England. We've already booked end of summer shows, and I can't let them down – not now I'm to be in charge. But I want you to come. I know it's not your world, and maybe it never could be, but I don't want a continent between us, Charles.' She paused. 'You ought to leave Monte Carlo. Leave it all behind, and start something new.'

Charles silenced her with a kiss. 'I'll come,' he said. 'This city's got too dark for me.'

Somewhere behind them, in the breakfasting lounge, Lily and the girls had started to cheer.

In the Centre Hospitalier, still swaddled in dressings, still hooked up to tubes that fed him fluids and drugs, Cal ran his one good hand through Sam's hair and listened to the little boy regale him with his stories of the Fort Antoine. If he closed his eyes, now, he did not see the rampaging oranges and reds of the accident, only his son singing his heart out in front of all the Fort Antoine's honoured guests.

When Sam was tired of the telling – it took a *long* time – and Cal needed rest, Meredith swept Sam up and cuddled him against her shoulder.

'What I don't understand,' Cal said, 'is *how*. I understand *why*. Benedict had that madness about him from the second I laid eyes on him. Evie knew it, from that first night at the Casino. He didn't want me to touch his songs, but it wasn't his choice – and then … the dubbing? I'd have done it, if I'd known. I'd have leapt at the chance.'

'You'd have rubbed his nose in it too,' said Meredith. She was carrying her own weariness this morning, and it was starting to show. 'You don't know when to stop, Cal.' It was only because

Sam was still pressed against her shoulder that she didn't let out the sob she'd been swallowing all night. 'Out on the circuit, or at the set … you don't know when to stop. Cal,' and she dropped her voice to the barest whisper, so that Cal had to strain to either lip-read or hear, 'we have a child. You have to slow down. Please. From now on, please slow down.'

Cal could see the pain etching itself onto her face. There he lay, body broken and burnt, morphine flooding his bloodstream, but it was Meredith who seemed most in pain.

'I promise,' he said. 'But I'm serious, Merry. Benedict had it in for me from the start … but *how*?'

'People like that have power,' said Meredith. 'They have followers and lackeys – like that wardrobe assistant, trotting around after him all the time. People like that call in favours. They find a way. I suppose the investigation will uncover it all.'

Cal still wasn't convinced, but right now silence was the best of all options. He was about to close his eyes, to let sleep restore him just a little bit more, when the door opened. There stood his father.

'Fresh from a victorious show, I'm told,' said Cal woozily, his eyes still half-closed. Then he saw the sombre look on Ed's face and, suddenly, he was awake again. 'What happened? Dad, did something else happen?'

Cal was trying to sit up, but his broken body would not allow him.

Ed came to sit by the bedside. 'Something *did* happen, son, but not last night. Something happened seventeen years ago, and not one of us knew.' Ed looked warmly towards Meredith and Sam. 'Merry, Jim's waiting just outside. He has a deck of those trick cards of his. Maybe Sam might like to see some magic, just for a few moments?'

Meredith's face was a mask. 'You sound so serious, Ed.'

'Well,' Ed sighed, and marshalled his thoughts, 'I have some news I really ought to share. It isn't bad news, not really, but it might take a little getting used to. It might just... change the world. But I've made myself a promise, and because I mean to keep it, it's better that we share it right now.' Ed looked at them both. 'No more secrets,' he said. 'Not a single one.'

Then, when Sam was happily out in the hall, Ed looked at them both and said, 'Well, you've both already met Brielle...'

Albert Hines had been awoken at three o'clock in the morning by a call patched through from the reception of the Hotel Metropole where he was staying. Being past his physical prime, it took Hines a little time to understand what news the lady on the hotel switchboard had been relaying; the truth of the situation didn't even dawn on him when her voice cut off and, in its place, came the frenetic voice of Benedict Frey. The young man had sounded garbled. He had *seemed* drunk. 'Benedict,' Hines had snapped, 'I want to see you on set tomorrow, but I don't want to see nor *hear* from you before.' Benedict's voice had exploded in a riot then – and Hines had been about to slam the receiver down when a more gravelly, altogether less frenetic voice took over from Benedict. 'Mr Hines, you must excuse the hour. My client Mr Frey has asked me to—'

'Client?' Hines had roared. 'Do you mean to suggest I'm being called at...' he checked the clock, '...3 a.m. by Benedict Frey's *agent*?'

There was a long, fat pause before the voice returned:

'Mr Hines, I'm afraid it's a lot more serious than that...'

After that, he hadn't slept a wink. His personal assistant had had to be raised. The hotel had afforded him the utmost support by loaning him the use of an office, and in those scant few hours before sunrise he had had to organise calls with Parker & Parr, with Benedict Frey's management team, with the crisis experts and lawyers kept on retainer by the studio. Not one of them had been trained in how to proceed if their star was suddenly arrested for attempted murder, so there was much scrabbling around that needed to be done – so much so that, by the time Hines got to set that morning, prowling the relics of his ruined production like an archaeologist excavating a tomb, he still had no idea what the studio back home were planning to do.

'It seems they have strong grounds for keeping him in custody,' one of the studio associates had relayed by the time the sun was coming up. 'The word from the station is that one of our own production runners overheard him confessing as much to the wardrobe assistant.'

It was those words that kept preying on Hines. By the time the first set dressers and cameramen had appeared, they were boiling inside him. Until then he'd been raging at his own lack of foresight, for it seemed plain as day now that introducing Cal Forsyth to the production had been like tossing a match into a cinder pile and waiting for it to ignite – but the reality was that the cinders had been alight long before.

'Bring me Gideon,' Hines demanded one of the production runners. By now, the morning was getting old. All over set, the whispers were turning to a torrent.

'I'm sorry sir,' said the production runner, 'but the crew want to know – do we even have a job?'

Hines glared, as implacable as a dictator.

'It's not like losing Cal, is it, sir? We can't film at angles and use doubles for a star.'

'Bring me Gideon now,' Hines intoned – and, after that, nothing more needed to be said.

The problem was that Gideon didn't arrive on set. The sun scaled its heights, the mountaintops were awash with radiant light, the stands in downtown Monte Carlo grew wild and ferocious with the roar of the Grand Prix's expectant crowd – but, when the moment when they ought to have been filming came, and the weaselly wardrobe assistant still wasn't here, Hines's certainty only grew. 'He knows what happened.'

'Like the rest of Monte Carlo, sir,' said one of the set dressers, brandishing the *Monaco Matin*. 'We're finished, aren't we?'

Hines opened his mouth to roar, but something told him to swallow the ire. 'Where were Gideon's digs?' he snapped. 'Somebody must know where Gideon's digs were.'

One of the make-up artists did. 'He's boarding over the border, sir, with a bunch of the crew. The apartment building at La Colle.'

Hines opened his arms to the whole of the crew. Half a hundred startled faces stared at him.

'Did anyone see him?'

In return: only silence.

'This morning!' Hines bawled. 'Did anyone see him this morning?'

The silence intensified, until at last Hines thundered, 'Who else is boarding there?'

One of the other wardrobe assistants raised his hand. 'He was there last night, sir. But by the time morning came round...' He shrugged. 'I supposed he'd made his way here. But he's run away, hasn't he, sir? He saw the *Monaco Matin* and he's run away. If it was him Benedict confessed to, the police might be after him too.'

Hines mopped wretchedly at his brow. Under his breath he uttered, 'Then I know exactly where he is.' He turned to stomp away. 'Somebody get me the Forsyth girl. Somebody get her on the line. I don't care who, and I don't care how, but do it *fast*. If I'm right, I might just save this picture. And, if I'm right, Cal Forsyth's life might not be so safe after all.'

Charles had already forsaken his room at the Hotel de Lyon, but by good fortune Evie was yet to check out.

The door flew open.

In walked Charles, Evie's hands in the small of his back.

The door slammed behind them.

Evie stared, hungry and intent.

She had sometimes thought that it wasn't only Cal who had wildness inside him. Evie had inherited wildness too; she just knew when to hold on to it and when to let it fly free. Now was the time it should fly, just the two of them behind locked doors. She reached up to kiss him. His hands were in her hair. He smelt of the jail cell, of old aftershave and stale sweat – but what did that matter? It wasn't just Charles's shirt opening up in front of her. It was the rest of her life.

They had just fallen to the bed together, thoughts of the future rapidly being forgotten in favour of thoughts of right now, when the telephone on the dresser rang.

'Ignore it,' said Charles, holding on to her.

'It might be the hospital,' said Evie. 'It might be about Cal.'

It took willpower to leave Charles on the bed and reach for the telephone, but any notion that it was her father calling about Cal, or perhaps some doctor at the hospital, was immediately disabused.

'Is this Miss Forsyth?' came a brusque English tone.

'Who is this?' Evie asked.

'This is Albert Hines. You don't know me, but perhaps you know the name. I'm—'

'The director. The man who hired Cal.' The telephone receiver tucked between shoulder and ear, Evie turned to give Charles a puzzled look. 'Mr Hines, why are you calling?'

'I'm going to cut to the chase, Miss Forsyth. I don't know how much time we have. I'm afraid I've reason to believe my star is innocent. And if I'm right, it means that whoever tried to kill your brother is still out there.'

'Mr Hines, I'm not sure what you mean. Benedict *confessed* ...'

'I don't give a damn what they're saying. Look, Miss Forsyth, have you a pen and paper?'

Evie scrabbled for one on the counter.

'Take down this address.'

Evie started scribbling. 'But that's in ... Nice?'

'Precisely. It's where we put them, to keep them out of the way.' Hines paused. 'Is it really worth ignoring me, Miss Forsyth? If somebody meant your brother dead, do you really think they've just scuttled back underneath a stone?'

Evie breathed, long and hard. All around her, the world felt as if it was listing again. 'What do you need?'

'I'm heading there now. Get in your car, Miss Forsyth. Meet me at the address. And, for God's sake, get on the road quickly. The city's about to shut down for this blasted Grand Prix. There isn't a second to spare.'

And the line went dead.


Brielle knew she ought to have gone home last night – she knew how desperately worried her parents would be – but somehow it hadn't felt right. At first, she'd thought about visiting one of her old schoolfriends, begging a bed in an attic, or a sofa, any corner where she might close her eyes and sleep. In the end, however, she'd decided it against it; those friends would only tell their parents, and their parents would telephone her mother – and then all hell would break loose, before Brielle was ready. That was why she'd spent the night on one of the bluffs above the city, at the end of one of the lonely mountain roads, just her and her claptrap of a car, the stars wheeling so beautifully above Monte Carlo by night.

But the dawn brought with it the stark reality of life.

And she knew she had to face it.

Parents had sixth senses, whether they were the ones whose blood ran through your veins or not; the moment that Brielle's car turned into the sweeping crescent where the Lambert house was waiting, there were hands at the curtains, a face in the window glass. Before she'd parked up, her mother was in the doorway; then she was cantering over, almost dragging Brielle from the car in her desperation to wrap the girl in arms.

The last time Brielle had stayed out all night (there had been several occasions – Monte Carlo by moonlight was too tempting for any girl to stay locked up inside, listening to records), Estelle had sternly begged her to understand that the city wasn't really as much of a playground as it seemed. But now there were only arms around her and tears on her shoulder. 'My baby girl, I'm sorry,' Estelle was weeping. 'I'm sorry.'

Sorry for the lies, Brielle supposed, and perhaps that was right – except that, sometime in the solitude of the night, Brielle had wondered if, thrust into the same situation, she mightn't have made exactly the same decisions. She said nothing, just squeezed her mother and held her tightly. For now, and for both of them, that was enough.

She had never before questioned the fault lines in her parents' marriage; never before, if truth be told, thought of them as a young couple, without the responsibilities of a daughter to bring up. Ought she to be angry at her mother – for one hot summer, a whole lifetime ago, when she had strayed from her marriage

334

vows? Ought she to be angry for the lies that had surrounded her, the treaty of silence? Did she really have to rethink every treasured memory? Was her curiosity about Cal a treachery of its own? What would her father, Hector, think if he'd known she'd sat with him in the hospital, holding his hand, teasing him back to consciousness?

All of those questions and thousands more would have to be reckoned with in the weeks to come. But right now, when she stepped into the kitchen, she found her father bent over the stovetop, making pancakes in the same pan he'd been making pancakes in ever since she was small. He turned to her as she came in, and she realised she had never seen him look as uncertain, perhaps even scared, as he was in that moment.

She ran to him.

He swept her up.

He'd been doing that since she was a baby as well.

'We'll tell you everything, darling. Your mother and I have been talking, and we'll tell you everything.'

Estelle stood in the kitchen doorway. 'I rather think she already knows.'

'But you must have a lot of questions.'

There were hundreds, but Brielle's heart was full and she didn't voice a single one – not until, when Hector was beginning to plate up the pancakes, she suddenly blurted out, 'He woke up last night. Cal woke up. He's telling everyone that the brakes were cut. It wasn't an accident. Somebody tried to kill him. They've arrested Benedict and …'

'We know, darling,' said Estelle – for a copy of the *Monaco Matin* was already on the breakfast table.

Hector shuffled it away as he settled down. He shared a pointed look with Estelle as he said, 'I guess that means you

335

don't have to be on set today.' He handed her a knife and fork. 'So where should we start?'

There was one question that came suddenly to the tip of her tongue. 'Do you two love each other?'

Hector and Estelle both reached for her hand.

'We do,' they said together.

'And one day,' Estelle added, with her voice cracking under the pressure, 'you might understand how love tests us all. How it defies us all. How this whole business of life is never really very straightforward.'

'Just like families,' Hector remarked.

Then there was peacefulness in the kitchen.

Peacefulness, and pancakes.


Charles slammed his hands against the wheel.

No traffic had been moving in downtown Monte Carlo. By the time they reached the border, then slipped past the invisible barrier into France, almost an hour had passed. At least, from here on, the road heading west was clear. Heading back into the Principality, the highway was a mass of spectators eager to soak up the atmosphere of race weekend – but out along the coast, directly ahead of Charles and Evie, there was open road.

'You can slow down,' said Evie. 'You're not on the circuit now.'

Charles just set his face, determined, and leant into the accelerator. It was the pull of the empty road that did it. 'No,' he said, grimly, 'but I should be.'

The distance markers flashed by. Nice: forty kilometres. Nice: thirty kilometres. Nice: twenty, ten …

Albert Hines must have escaped the city sooner than Evie and Charles; by the time they reached the address, an apartment block just inland of Nice's sweeping pebble-strewn seafront, he was already there, waiting impatiently outside the forest-green

Rolls Royce in which his driver was sheltering from the midday heat. Some short distance away, a plaza filled with restaurants and bars was beginning to buzz. Through one of the open apartment windows, Evie could hear the sounds of the Grand Prix commentary on a local television station.

'Why are we here, Mr Hines?'

Hines wasted no time. There was already a set of keys jangling in his hand, and he started walking towards the door. Evie and Charles hurried to keep up.

'We've had a lot to deal with, making this picture. I don't just mean the usual problems of making a film. I don't just mean marshalling men and locations, budgets that aren't worth the paper they're written on, rewrites and scrapped scenes and endless notes from the studio board. No, I mean ... our *star*.' Hines reached the apartment door. He looked up at its tall white façade, before he slipped a key into the lock. 'I have to be fair to Parker & Parr. The studio didn't foresee the problems with Benedict – and, when they came around, they didn't throw it back at me to handle alone. They've staked a lot on making Ben a star. They didn't want to see everything crumble. So, when it transpired that Benedict had certain ...' He chose his words very carefully, '*romantic interests* that do not dovetail very nicely with attracting legions of screaming girls to our audiences, we had to make plans. I trust you know what I'm talking about?'

'Benedict has boyfriends,' she said, simply.

Hines nodded. 'It's not unusual in our world. I daresay it isn't unusual in yours. I daresay the world will one day wake up and realise it's not *unusual* any God damn place – but we live in the here and now and, in the here and now, it's the sort of thing that could land Benedict locked up in prison. More importantly to me, it's the sort of thing that could sink a movie that ought to take the world by storm. Well, by the time anybody understood where Ben's allegiances lay, contracts had already been signed, money had already changed hands. The studio was faced with protracted legal battles if they backed out – and damn it, there's nothing worse in the world for causing legal trouble than an actor's agent! The only other option was that we somehow *managed* the situation.' Hines turned the key and opened the door, shepherding Evie and Charles straight through.

'Benedict must be used to hiding himself away,' said Evie. 'He must be good at keeping secrets?'

'He ought to have been better. But he has an ego the size of a mountain – and, pretty early on, we knew it was going to cause trouble. Benedict had just been selected, out of thousands, to star in this picture. The gods of Parker & Parr had chosen him alone – and, well, the boy doesn't have a humble bone in his body. He seemed to think he was anointed – and, if he was anointed, he could damn well do as he pleased. We went to Saint Tropez for the first week of shoots. Of course, in a place like that the drink flows too easily and the press fawn over their stars – so it's perfectly natural that a boy like Benedict would grow too big for his boots. But, when he stopped trying to hide his love affairs, something had to be done.'

'What did you do?' asked Charles.

'Look around you,' said Albert Hines.

The lobby of the apartment building was small and cool. Albert made for the elevator and summoned a lift.

'I don't understand,' said Evie.

'We couldn't tell Benedict to stop. You can't say it to a man. It isn't fair or right. But to ask him to conduct his business in secret, away from the set? Well, that seemed like a compromise we might all make. We'd already organised a three-month stay in Monte Carlo. What were the odds Benedict wouldn't strike something up while we were there? We couldn't have it interrupting our flow. It was a problem we didn't want to deal with. So, here we are.' The lift opened, and the trio stepped inside. 'The idea was: give Benedict a place to take his lovers, far enough from our production, and we might get through without any of it causing an issue. Of course, I didn't reckon on him taking up with that wardrobe assistant. I could have strangled the wretch. I'd have fired him if I could, but the studio were worried it would put Benedict out of sorts and … Here we are!' On the third storey, Hines had led them to a door marked '7'. He rapped on the wood. 'If I'm right there's a good chance that—'

At once, there came a clattering and commotion from the other side of the door. Hines hammered his fist against the wood again, but the clattering only continued.

Evie lunged for the handle.

Whoever was inside hadn't even locked it.

By the time Evie marched through, Gideon had the balcony doors of the palatial apartment open and was hoisting himself onto a fire escape ladder that scaled the side of the building. Golden light cascaded all around him. The glittering seascape on the other side of the plaza framed him as he froze, abandoning his escape.

The wardrobe assistant had evidently spent a good deal of time sobbing, for his face was streaked in red. 'I – I thought you were the p-police,' he stammered.

Charles marched to his side, seizing him by the arm and manhandling him away from the balcony. Only once Evie had closed the balcony doors did Charles let go of him. Gideon reeled, tumbling onto the red leather chaise longue that took pride of place against the apartment wall.

'Now Gideon,' said Albert Hines, 'you might have used a little more imagination. If you really wanted to hide away, mightn't you have chosen somewhere we didn't know about?'

'This is B-Benedict's apartment,' Gideon stammered.

'It's leased by Parker & Parr, and only loaned to Benedict. Didn't he tell you?'

Gideon only stared.

'Gideon,' Hines intoned, 'I know you know they've arrested Ben. I know you know they're about to charge him with an attempted murder. But I also know...'

'Know what, sir?'

Suddenly, Albert Hines lost his patience. 'Half a million pounds has been invested in our picture. Half a million pounds, and here you are, *snivelling*. Look at me, boy. Just look at me!'

At last, Evie thought she understood. The look on Albert Hines's face was growing incandescent; she reached out and touched his arm, hoping to calm him down. 'Gideon, Brielle heard you talking to Benedict. She *heard* him confess to hurting Cal. "I didn't want him dead," he said. "I just wanted him away from my picture."'

Gideon had started shaking. 'It wasn't him. Ben didn't do anything to that car. He couldn't. He wouldn't know how.'

'And you, Gideon?' Charles intervened.

Gideon shook his head, ferociously.

'It wasn't either of us,' he bleated. 'I know it wasn't, because...'

Hines rushed towards the boy, snatching him up by the collar. In a second, Charles had leapt forward to wrestle him back. 'He's talking, Mr Hines. Let him finish.'

'You're destroying this movie, Gideon. You're bringing it crashing down. Just spit it out, boy.'

But in the end, it was Evie who said, 'You were here, weren't you? On Friday night, you and Benedict, you'd come out here?'

Gideon nodded, madly, despairingly, desperately pleased that somebody else had said it.

'I'm not – I've never...' The words gave up on Gideon. 'Benedict's my first,' he said, at last.

'You need to tell the police,' said Charles, stoutly. 'Benedict's a fool, but he doesn't deserve to rot for something he didn't do.'

'But you can't, can you?' Evie realised. 'Because, if you tell them you and Ben were here, together, on the night Cal crashed that car ... you'd have to tell them the real meaning of what Brielle overheard. You'd have to tell them – Benedict didn't sabotage that car, but he *did* set fire to my Company at the Fort Antoine.'

Gideon shook his head feverishly. 'He didn't do that.'

Evie heaved a sigh. Now, at last, she understood why he had run. '*You* did.'

'I just wanted to send Cal a message, you know? He was undermining everything Benedict did. He was taking over. It wasn't going to be Ben's picture anymore. It was going to be Ben, singing Cal's songs. Ben, mouthing Cal's words. And I thought – if I showed him what I could do, well, maybe Ben would appreciate it.'

'Maybe he wouldn't pick you up and throw you away like he does all the rest of his love affairs,' snapped Hines. 'Gideon, you're getting in the car with me.'

'I – I can't,' Gideon panicked.

'Do you love Benedict?' Evie asked.

Gideon's eyes strayed from one to the other. Then, without words, he nodded.

'Then it's only you who can get him out of that cell,' said Evie.

'And it's only you who can save our picture,' Hines snapped – but Gideon didn't seem to hear; he was too engrossed in what Evie had said, staring at her with wide open eyes, to notice.

Slowly, Gideon picked himself up from the chaise longue. 'I'll do it,' he whispered, brokenly. 'I'll – I'll do it, for Ben.'

\*

In the hospital room, while the city outside sweltered and the grandstands swelled with a legion of spectators, Cal and Meredith sat in stunned silence. Intermittently, Cal whispered, 'Meredith, it was years ago. Merry, I didn't know' – and, intermittently, Meredith reached out to squeeze his hand. There was no betrayal in it, no regret, no recrimination – but that didn't mean the world wasn't suddenly reordering itself around them.

Then, when one of the silences had stretched on painfully long, the door opened – and there stood Sam, beaming, with Jim looking apologetic behind him. In Sam's hands was a little silver radio, trailing a length of black wire. 'Daddy, do you want to listen to the races?'

If Sam understood that his parents' worlds had just changed, he did not show it. He simply scampered in, setting the radio down on the bedside and searching, in vain, for a plug underneath the bed.

'One of the nurses gave it to him,' Jim shrugged, looking to Ed for some support. 'I'm sorry, should I take him away again? We can do some more tricks if I find my coins.'

Cal looked at Meredith.

Meredith looked at Cal.

'Darling,' she said to Sam, 'Daddy might not be in the mood for fast cars right now. Maybe we should just—'

But Cal cried out, 'No – fast cars! Yes... *fast cars*. Find him a plug, Merry. Let's get this on.' He gave Meredith a crumpled smile. 'Well, anything's better than painful silence, right?'

The radio burst into life.

The Grand Prix was almost ready to begin.

'Of course,' said Charles as he wrenched the T26 back onto the seafront in Nice, hammering on the horn to send the seaside stragglers scattering, 'all he's done is find Benedict an alibi. All he's done is save his picture. It doesn't explain who sabotaged that car.'

'Who set a trap for Cal,' nodded Evie, darkly. 'Who wanted him dead.'

Outside the city, the Lago T26 burst into life. The Riviera road was emptier now that the deluge of daytrippers had already reached Monte Carlo, but every time Charles pressed his foot to the accelerator some logjam up ahead made him slow down. A little ahead, Albert Hines and Gideon were being ferried back into the Principality in the forest-green Rolls Royce.

'We need to get a message to the hospital,' said Evie. 'Tell Cal that…' She faltered, for an image had forced its way in among her other crowded thoughts. 'Do you remember that day at the race? When the Formula 2 drivers were competing? That's when I saw them, up in the stands. Brielle was there, with her family.' She gripped Charles's arm. 'Hector Lambert, he was there too.'

Charles breathed no words, just pounded the accelerator.

'Don't you see? We've been forgetting all about him, just because he had an alibi for that night at the fortress. But he's wanted us gone since the beginning. He wanted us run out of Monte Carlo, never to return. *Two thousand pounds*. He's a desperate man. His story was unravelling – but if Cal was gone, if Cal wasn't a part of things anymore, then he might keep his secret.' She slammed her hand onto the dash. 'We've got to get to the hospital. Hector was there at the track. He might easily have known what Cal was doing. He might easily have taken his chances. Well, Charles? I'm right, aren't I? Hector Lambert? It's been looking us in the eye, ever since the beginning.'

Evie was waiting for Charles to agree, but instead, the Frenchman fell silent. With one hand still on the wheel, he reached out and took Evie's hand.

'Oh, it's been looking us in the eye,' he said, 'but we've been looking straight past it, trying to bend it into every possible shape, just to make it fit.' He took a breath. 'Just because your brother's been bulldozing his way through this city, just because he's got a superlative talent for making enemies, just because there are people in the Principality who couldn't wait to take him down a peg or two, it doesn't mean that car was sabotaged for *him*.'

This time, it was Evie's turn for silence.

'I'm sorry, Evie. It appears I've been a bad omen for you all along. After this is done, I should understand if you never want to see me again.'

'Charles, I'm not sure what you're saying.'

'I'm saying it really *was* my fault that Cal was nearly killed. They were trying to get to me, Evie. They were never trying to kill Cal. They were trying to run me off the track, so that I couldn't compete. It's what Conrad Knight wanted since the beginning. He said it to my damn face. Allard convinced me there was nothing he could do – so, when he came after you, I took *delight* in pushing back. I wasn't going to let him tell me not to see you. To let him make me his puppet.' Charles slammed his hands on the wheel in fury. 'It's the *how*, Evie. There are plenty of people who wanted rid of Cal, but not one of them could engineer something like this. Don't you see? That was their plan. I wasn't supposed to get in that car until yesterday morning, the third practice round. It was *me* who was supposed to be in that car. It was *me* whose brakes were meant to fail. It was *me* who was meant to go up in flames. It had to be me – and we've been too damn obsessed with whoever's been hunting your family to see what was staring us in the face all along.'

Up ahead, through the windscreen, Evie could see the towers of Monte Carlo hoving into view. There was still traffic along

344

the main highway leading into the city, but Charles wrenched the Lago T26 onto the lesser northern roads, entering the city further inland. Where the Rolls Royce bearing Gideon and Hines was now, Evie did not know. She wrung her hands in frustration, praying for gaps in the traffic – until, with the verdant greenery of the Jardin Exotique just up ahead, she threw open the door and scrambled onto the pavement. 'I'll make for the Poste de Police,' she said, as a wave of sound crashed over Monte Carlo. No doubt the first cars had just appeared on the grid, engines being warmed, slow laps being performed in anticipation of the starting pistol to come. 'Find a place to ditch the car and follow me. Do you hear?'

Charles watched her go and forced the car onto the pavement ahead. The news stand where he'd grabbed his copy of the *Monaco Matin* had closed its doors – no doubt its owner was now up in the stands, waiting for the chorus of wild engines to begin – so he thought nothing of leaving the Lago here, blocking the path.

Time mattered now.

It had never mattered more.

He slammed the door behind him, broke into a run, his arms and legs pumping like pistons as the towers of Monte Carlo rushed past.

No starting pistol sounded in the skies above, but surely the cars were already lining up.

There was every possibility he was already too late.

But Charles Laurent reached the Poste de Police, into which Evie had just slipped, and didn't break stride.

He just kept running.

'Gentlemen, it's time.'

In the grandstand above the promenade, Conrad Knight took his seat among the other Talbot-Lago financiers – and, for the first time any of them had ever seen, removed his jacket, then loosened his tie. Raphael Allard tried hard to show he hadn't noticed, but by the look on Conrad Knight's face he *knew*. 'It's a day for all sorts of miracles, Mr Allard,' said Knight, then settled among his associates.

Down on the track, the drivers' reconnaissance laps were well underway. A flash of cyan and white burst past: the Talbot-Lago Grand Sport, under the expert stewardship of Christian Chapman.

'They'll close the pit lane in ten minutes,' said Allard. 'Then it begins.'

'And be assured, Mr Allard,' crooned Knight, 'that this is *only* the beginning.'

The Grand Sport had proven its worth in yesterday's qualifying round. The Brabham BT19 had taken pole position, sharing the headstart with Ferrari – but behind them came Honda, alongside the Grand Sport itself. Over a hundred laps, there was no reason that slight disadvantage couldn't be completely negated; no reason why Talbot-Lago mightn't come out on top.

Somewhere out on the circuit, a bell rang.

'That's it, sir. It's starting.'

The cars running their reconnaissance laps all slowed. As each reached the rear of the staring grid, the cars slowed to a halt, disgorging their drivers so that teams of mechanics could wheel the cars out to their starting positions. Christian Chapman unfolded himself from the Grand Sport. He was smaller than Charles had been, lighter too. These were the metrics, thought Conrad Knight, on which the success and failure of this enterprise would be made. Chapman turned his helmeted face to the stands, raised a fist and listened to the cheer of encouragement come crashing down.

In the stands, as they watched him go – back towards the Talbot-Lago staging ground – Conrad Knight swelled with pride.

'It's been a long time coming, sir,' said Raphael Allard. 'We've battled to get here.'

'Indeed we have. Sacrifices have had to be made.'

But every sacrifice was worthwhile.

Especially when the sacrifice was not your own...

The security officers were not difficult to navigate. Charles had the confidence of a man who belonged at the Monaco Grand Prix – which, in this moment, he was certain he did. The only man who challenged him as he picked his way through the teeming photographers, journalists and racing aficionados withered under his stare. 'If I was guilty of anything, monsieur, why am I standing here, a free man?' he snapped, swiping away the officer's grasping hand. 'I might not be the team driver, but they're still my team. I'm due at the garage right now. Monsieur, the race is about to begin!'

A little bit of confected outrage always did the trick. Charles ignored the next man who questioned him, slipping past the cordons and over the barriers, until he reached the staging ground back door.

Without another hesitation, he burst through.

No car waited in the garage – just the familiar faces of the team mechanics, all pulling on their leather gloves, tightening their bootlaces, bouncing up and down on the spot to get their blood flowing. Not that there was any need; the adrenaline in the room spiked the moment Charles appeared.

At first, nobody said a word. Charles's eyes flashed around, seeking out the driver – but Chapman was nowhere to be found. That could only mean the car was already on the grid, and that

Chapman was out there too – not with the car, not yet, because the countdown hadn't started, but somewhere in the pit lane, counting down the seconds.

Charles loped towards the roll-back doors, and the roar of the stands beyond. Before he'd emerged into the cascade of sun over the circuit, one of the mechanics hailed him. 'M. Laurent, but we thought you were—'

Charles snapped, 'I know you've had a busy morning, my *friends*, but if you'd paid a little attention, you might have known I wasn't being held in custody. But then, that wasn't the instruction, was it? That wasn't the plan. I wasn't supposed to be in custody. I was supposed to be in the hospital – or, better yet, the morgue.' Charles knew he ought to charge outside, somehow make it to the pit lane, remonstrate with Chapman, but his fury was still rising. 'Which one of you was it?' he said, facing each in turn. 'Which one of you set me up to die?'

A door at the back of the garage opened.

Out of the toilet stall behind, where he'd been taking a final break before the race began, stepped Christian Chapman.

'M. Laurent,' the racing driver stammered, 'but what are you doing here?'

At this moment, the mechanics seemed to gravitate towards the walls – and whatever indignation Charles had been holding towards them melted away. These mechanics were *his* team, weren't they? He'd worked with them throughout. There was nothing to be gained for them by the wreckage of Friday night – everything to lose, but nothing to gain. No, it seemed clear now, how it had happened: Conrad Knight's preferred driver had been crashed into the team at the very last minute, Dickie Anstis ejected and Charles Laurent set up.

Charles strode towards him. 'It will go better for you, sir, if you just confess it.'

'Charles, there's a race about to begin.'

'*Mais oui*, a race I was meant to drive. A race I've spent my life preparing for.' Charles took a stride towards him. 'I know how it must have felt, Christian. Your ambition gets the better of you. Your hopes and dreams feel like they're slipping by, while other, less talented people get their due – it gets so that it's all you really think about. You wonder if it's ever going to happen – and then a man comes along and says, "Well, I can anoint you. I can make it happen. All you'll have to do is perform me this one little service…"'

Christian craned to look past Charles, out through the doors to the circuit beyond. 'I have to be out there. I'm meant to be on the grid.' Then he looked, accusingly, as the banks of mechanics. 'We're *all* meant to be out there. Won't somebody get rid of him?'

At first Charles hoped none of the mechanics would rally to Christian's call – after all, before they'd been Chapman's, they'd been *his* – but when one of them ventured, 'I can call security, Mr Chapman? I could dial the police?', he only grinned and said, 'Please do. Then we can settle this once and for all. Then it can be the right man in a prison cell and the right man taking the win out there. You see, gentlemen, the accident out here the other night? The one that nearly killed Cal Forsyth? It wasn't meant for him. It was meant for *me*. And the man you're all serving is the man who did it. At Mr Knight's behest, I assume.'

'I'll fetch someone, Mr Chapman.'

One of the mechanics leapt from the wall, as if to make for the door and alert security – but Charles just let him go. He only shrugged at Christian, as if *daring* him to stay silent.

'No, *stop!*' Christian barked.

'Now we see how it is,' said Charles, as the mechanic floundered to a stop. 'But it doesn't matter, not really – because the

349

police are already coming. Evie went to fetch them, the moment we came back to the city. They're coming here right now.'

Around the room, the mechanics shared disbelieving looks. Christian started, as if he too might bolt for the door.

'Yes, that's right,' Charles said. 'There may yet be time for you to escape. Over the border and into France, off along the Riviera. You might yet reach London before they catch up with you. But they *will* catch up with you. This isn't just about your hopes and dreams, you desperado. It was a man's life. Any way you look at it, it was attempted murder. Knight gave the order, but you cut the brakes. You're not a racing driver, Christian. You're a hired killer.'

Christian sprang forward, throwing himself at the door. Charles would have let him go, if one last thought hadn't stampeded through his mind. Instinctively, he put out his foot and Christian collided with it, toppling to the floor.

'You're not running anywhere,' snapped Charles, 'not without leaving me that helmet. And that jacket too.' He wrenched them out of Christian's hands, left him lying on the stone at his feet, and rounded on the mechanics spread around the room. 'Whatever happens out there, boys, this is the end of Talbot-Lago. But what do you say we try and win this thing before it all comes crashing down?'

Out on the circuit, the klaxon sounded for the ten-minute warning.

Those drivers not already with their vehicles left their teams at the pit lane and marched down to the grid.

Up in the stands, roars rose up like volcanic eruptions every time one of the drivers appeared.

And here came the Talbot-Lago team, dressed in their uniforms of cyan and white. Mechanics poured into the pit lane – and out of them, walking like a titan, came their driver.

Funny, thought Raphael Allard in the stands up above, but he didn't look quite as slight as he had some moments before, when the reconnaissance laps were done.

He looked bigger, broader, more statuesque.

And he was walking with a more purposeful step.

There'd been a knotted feeling in his stomach all along. In that moment, it started to spread.

The moment Charles slipped into the cockpit of the Talbot-Lago Grand Sport, the outside world faded away.

This was how it always was, in the moments before a race. In one of their quieter moments, Evie had said that, when the curtains opened at one of their shows, when the stage lights went up and the band struck up, nothing else existed in the world except the unique connection between audience and performer. Well, Charles knew what she meant. He hit the ignition, let the engine purr. The mechanics were performing their final checks around him – but, almost as one, they scattered, just like the mechanics attending all the other cars, back to the pit lane. Ahead of him, he saw the Ferrari shuddering – like a bridled horse ready to break free. The Brabham BT19 was shaking as well. Behind the visor of his helmet, Charles just concentrated on his breathing.

The two-minute warning came.

Engines flared all around him, even while silence settled in the stands.

There were so many errant thoughts Charles had to shed, so many conflicted feelings he struggled now to cast aside. He tried to blot out thoughts of Christian Chapman – who had fled through the staging ground doors the moment Charles took the helmet. He tried not to think of Conrad Knight, and the three days that had changed his life. But, most of all, he tried not to think of Cal racing down this very same promenade, heading for the very same chicane, and the ball of fire that came after.

*Toby*...

In the final seconds before the starting pistol went off, Charles tried to bring him to mind. 'I'm coming,' he whispered, and – while there was still time – he closed his eyes. For many long years he had practiced diligently at summoning up his brother. Through months and years of hard labour, he was able – more often than not – to push away the vision of Le Mans and remember older times, better times, happier times.

'Charles!'

For a second, he dreamt he'd heard Evie's voice. For a second, he thought he saw her appearing behind his closed eyes, striding over to the memory of Toby and taking him in her arms. They would have liked each other, thought Charles – and that was the most calming feeling of all.

Then the starting pistol went – and whether he'd heard Evie's voice in the waking world, or whether it was all a figment of his imagination, he would never know – for the race had begun.

The desk clerk had taken too long to summon Inspector Maragoni. They'd taken too long to listen to her at all. 'I'm afraid the inspector is already in an interview,' they had said, when Evie barrelled into the Poste de Police. 'Yes,' she replied, her tone unwavering, 'he's interrogating Benedict Frey. The only problem is, he's interrogating the wrong man.'

It wasn't until the station door burst open, revealing Albert Hines trailing Gideon behind him, that the desk clerk listened at all. By then, Evie feared, it was already too late. Somewhere over the rooftops of Monte Carlo, she heard a klaxon sounding. Then, in the same moment that Inspector Maragoni appeared, the starting pistol scythed through the hubbub pulsating all over the city.

The Grand Prix had begun.

'Inspector,' Evie pronounced, 'you've got to listen. Benedict's innocent. He's a braggart and a blowhard, but he's innocent – and Gideon here, he can prove it. But you've got to come quickly – because the men who almost killed my brother, they're getting away with it. They're getting away with it right now!'

Charles roared through the Chicane du Port, the Ferrari still ahead of him, the Brabham in the lead, the Honda slipping back behind. It wasn't possible to go fast round the chicane – hadn't that been the lesson hard learnt by Cal? – but on the other side the straights opened up. Eighty miles an hour. Ninety. One hundred. Around the harbour hurtled Charles, down the long straight barrel of the Casino's approach. Somewhere in that first lap, the rest of the city became a haze. Even the stands turned to a blur. By the time the second lap came round, the world had reduced itself to a few points of colour on the circuit: just Charles and the cars against whom he was meant to compete. Everything else existed somewhere far beyond the limits of his sight, far beyond the limits of his thought.

Here came the Chicane du Port again. Charles dropped his speed, sailed round it, then leant hard as he reached the harbour straights. The Honda disappeared behind him. Now, for the first time, he raced abreast of the Ferrari.

Foot on the accelerator...

One lap strobing rapidly into the next.

If the other drivers had the advantage of having just run the reconnaissance laps, it did not show. Charles gave in to his instincts. Holding his breath, he came round the hairpin at the

Fairmont Hotel. Gulping back air, he scythed into the long, eerily lit darkness of the circuit tunnel.

Ten laps became twenty, and he was still holding his nerve.

Twenty laps turned into thirty – and somewhere on the Portier curve he edged in front of the Ferrari.

Now only the Brabham separated him from first place.

On the long straight of the promenade, the Grand Sport reached one hundred and thirty miles an hour. He leant into it. The speedometer was a blur, trembling up and ever upwards, but Charles saw it only in the edges of his vision. The world was streaking past, reduced to a helter-skelter of geometric shapes – and he, Charles Laurent, was plummeting into it.

Then, when he reached the dark stampede of tunnel once again, he saw the silver shadow up ahead.

The car kept going, Charles tensed behind the wheel, but the silvery shape kept pace with him – always ten metres ahead, always hovering on the very edge of his vision.

It was, he realised at last, the image of his brother.

'Toby,' Charles gasped, out loud.

For there he hung, suspended in imagination and time, beaming idiotically like he always did, his hand beckoning to Charles, telling him to hurry, to keep thundering onward, to join him – join him out there on the track.

The Grand Sport burst out of the tunnel, into the dazzling Monte Carlo light.

The ghost of Toby had not disappeared. There he hung, still grinning, still gesturing to Charles – except that, in the sunlight, it suddenly seemed that he was not *beckoning* Charles at all; he was merely waving, merely saying hello, merely saying 'I'm still here, little brother.'

The world had been a blur for so many laps already, but suddenly it blurred yet further. Charles had to release his grip on the wheel to wipe the tears from his eyes – and, in that moment of weakness, the Ferrari raced past him again. The Honda drew abreast, then inched into the lead.

Charles kicked at the accelerator.

Up ahead, the chicane came back into view.

And, for the first time, he heard Toby's ghost calling.

'It's OK, Charlie,' said his brother, from some space on the other side of time. 'You don't have to do this. You never did. I'm here. Win or lose, race or not, I'm *always here*.'

Charles let go of the wheel. He knew he ought to brake hard into the chicane. Parts of his body were doing it by instinct, but some other part was rebelling.

'What do you really want to do?' asked Toby, from wherever he remained. 'Do you even want to race? Do you want them to win? They tried to kill you, Charles.' Toby's voice; he'd almost forgotten what it sounded like. Now here it was, like long-forgotten music in his ears. 'You don't have to do it for me. You never did, little brother. I'm here. I'm *here*.'

But then, in a flash, he was gone, his ghost dissipating into the air above the circuit.

The pit lane was coming up. Somewhere beyond that, another lap would start afresh. There was still time to make up everything that he'd lost. He had the instincts. He had the talent.

But, he realised now, he just didn't have the hunger anymore.

Because, when Toby had asked him that question, 'What do you really want?', it hadn't been victory he'd thought of. It hadn't been glory. It hadn't even been to meet his brother, out where speed transformed the world into blurs of unreadable colour.

No, the thing he'd really thought about had been *her*.

Here came the pit lane now.

In rolled the Talbot-Lago Grand Sport.

*

In the stands above, Conrad Knight and Raphael Allard watched the car screech into the pit lane. The team mechanics were upon it in seconds. Seconds later, it ought to have burst back onto the circuit to continue its irresistible flight towards destiny.

*And yet...*

'Why is he getting out of the car?' asked Knight. Suddenly, the financier was up on his feet, remonstrating with his fist. 'Why in God's name is he climbing out of the car?'

Conrad Knight was right. In the pit lane underneath the stands, the Talbot-Lago driver had unfurled himself from the cockpit and turned towards the crowd.

Allard felt a sickness rising in his gorge. He could barely look at the other financiers as the driver reached up to take off his helmet.

It wasn't Christian Chapman at all.

There stood Charles Laurent.

The Frenchman turned his face to the heavens, kissed his fingers and sent that simple gesture of love flying above. Who it was for, Raphael Allard had no time to debate – for, around him, all of the Talbot-Lago team were on their feet in wild panic. 'He's forfeited the race,' somebody whispered. 'He's *sabotaged* the race,' somebody else crowed. 'What have you done? Mr Knight, what have we...'

Then silence fell. The Talbot-Lago team had been staring as one at Charles Laurent – but now, for the first time, Charles Laurent's eyes seemed to have found them. As the race thundered on, the Frenchman looked up and past the financiers, urging them to follow his gaze.

Conrad Knight turned.

Was he mistaken, or were those police officers coming directly for *him*?

Down below, Charles Laurent turned away – but, no matter what they'd done to him, it wasn't disgust on his features. It was, the journalists would later say, a strange relief that seemed to be colouring him as he walked away from the Talbot-Lago Grand Sport, away from the team of mechanics, away from the pit lane – and, the world would later understand, away from the world of motor racing itself.

In the stands, Conrad Knight was still standing when Inspector Patrice Maragoni reached him. The Englishman looked imperiously upon the Monacoan detective, but Maragoni did not wither. The past week had, perhaps, been the most eventful of his career – but, like the drivers who hurtled by underneath, he had been preparing for this all his life. 'M. Knight,' he began, 'I'm afraid I'm going to have to ask you to come this way.' Then, before Knight could put up one of his haughty complaints, Maragoni added, 'We can do this with dignity and good grace, sir, or we can do it so that all the stands can hear. Either way, monsieur, I'm arresting you on suspicion of conspiracy to commit murder. It is not something we take lightly, here in the Principality…'

Charles knew there were a thousand questions for him. By the time he reached the Talbot-Lago staging ground, where he cast aside his helmet and jacket that marked him out as a company man, his name had already been called two dozen times. When he stepped into the burning sunlight beyond the stands, it only got worse. Apparently bad news travelled more rapidly than the cars competing on the circuit, for the next chapter in the story of Talbot-Lago's entry into the Monaco Grand Prix was already being told among the journalists and photographers gathered outside.

Charles did not care.

He didn't answer their questions now, and nor would he ever – for this part of his life was finished.

And there, where the sunlight reached the water, framed by the mirrored surface of the Mediterranean and the multitude of yachts out on the ocean, the next part of his life was waiting to begin.

He raced to Evie.

He kissed her, there and then.

'But it's not over,' she gasped. 'The race isn't done.'

'Mine is,' said Charles.

Some time later, Inspector Patrice Maragoni led Conrad Knight out of the stands, his officers shepherding Raphael Allard and the other financiers to their vehicles to begin their investigation, but neither Charles Laurent nor Evie Forsyth were there to see it – for, when one story ends, another must always begin and, like the ghost of Charles's brother out on the track, the future was beckoning them forward, urging them to follow.

*Several Days Later*

# Chapter Nineteen

It still hurt to sit up, and his sleep was so fitful that, every night, the doctor came to administer drugs – but each morning, when Cal woke, his body felt a little bit *looser* than it had the evening before, and when the nurses arrived to redress his burns, take his temperature and shuffle him around so that his various pipes and tubes could be changed, he felt a little more alive to their presence. By the end of the third day, he was even able – through lips still swollen, livid and red – to crack a joke. And the fact he was being as brazen as this, said Evie, meant that there was no doubt her brother was returning.

This morning she was the first on the ward, and Cal was already awake with the nurses fussing around. One of them was feeding him *purée de pommes* with a spoon, which reminded Cal of when Sam was a baby. One of his arms had just soft tissue damage, and the break in the other was the least serious of his injuries. It was the breaks in his legs that the doctors were worried about, not to mention the fracture in his spine. According to family legend, Cal Forsyth had been riding his luck ever since he was a toddler – and it seemed, somehow, that the luck hadn't run out. More than one doctor had told him he was fortunate to be alive – but Cal was already dreaming of the songs this tragedy might inspire. His legs could take as long as they needed to heal; it was the use of his fingers, for guitar strings and piano keys, that Cal was more worried about.

Evie sat by his bedside and rolled her eyes at one of the nurses. To Evie's mind, this nurse seemed to be enjoying feeding Cal *far* too much. She took the spoon out of the nurse's hand, sent her on her way, and started feeding Cal herself.

'They're almost here,' she told him, while the spoon was still in his mouth. 'Do you understand?'

Cal had more strength than Evie thought; he managed to spit the spoon out, even while she was feeding him. Inwardly, she grinned. That was a good sign.

'Get the nurses,' he said, 'they can get me out of this bed.'

Evie cocked her head, questioningly.

'Just do it, Evie,' Cal laughed, then winced when the laughter shook his battered body too much. 'I might as well make myself presentable.'

None of the nurses were enthusiastic about helping Cal out of the bed, but the doctors had advised it was possible – so, with the help of pulleys and harness, Cal was moved into a reclining chair by the window. As they shifted him, Evie tried not to be reminded of the haulage firm who had come to clear the wreckage of the Talbot-Lago Grand Sport from the circuit, but the fact was the two looked frighteningly alike.

'Cal, I spoke with Dad last night – and we've made a decision.'

'I thought *I* was running the Company with you now?' grinned Cal.

Evie shook her head wryly. 'You were easier to talk to when you were unconscious. Seriously, Cal.' She paused. 'We're going to get on the road.'

Cal's eyes widened.

'The end of summer shows at Brighton are coming into view,' Evie went on. 'It's our first run in charge, Cal. We can't cancel the bookings. We've got to think of Lily and Verity, of Jim and Hugo, all of the Company. It's their livelihoods too. I'm going to go with them and lead the shows. God knows who'll compère. I don't have Dad's patter. Charles is going to come with us, but I can hardly put him centre stage! No, he'll be better for lugging sets and boxes.'

'Or driving that double-decker. He'd get you back to Blighty in no time.'

'We'll just have to make it up as we go along – at least until you're ready.' Evie looked down at his legs, for who really knew if Cal would ever be up to strutting around the stage again? 'Dad's going to stay here, in Monte Carlo. The princess is loaning him an apartment, for Meredith and Sam as well. And for *you*, when we can get you out of here.'

Somewhere along the way, Cal had stopped looking at his sister and started looking at his fingers instead. One after another, he flexed them, as if plucking at the strings of some guitar. 'How long do they say I'm stuck here, Evie?'

Evie just shrugged. 'As long as it takes. But, you know, it's not as if you should be in a hurry to leave anyway. It's not as if there isn't something else you should be doing. One day, you might even think it's a blessing that . . .'

'All right,' snorted Cal, 'let's cut that all out. A blessing, me in that fire?' He paused. For the first time, Evie thought she saw the nervousness flicker on his face. 'Is she here yet?'

Evie looked at the clock on the wall.

'Any moment now.'

Outside the Centre Hospitalier, the blocky red Citroen banked out of the traffic and found a parking spot among all the other cars lined up in the visitors' yard. From the overhang at the hospital entrance, Ed watched as Hector Lambert emerged. Soon after, out stepped Estelle.

And there, her face betraying all her nerves, was Brielle.

At Ed's side, Meredith shifted uneasily. It was a good job, Ed thought, that Sam had stayed behind with the girls. Right now, they were luxuriating on Larvotto beach, waiting for the moment when the convoy would take out on the long journey north. Sam was going to miss the Company so it was good he got to spend time with them – and, besides, it wasn't right for him to be here in this moment. There would come a time when Sam had to be told, but that time was not today.

'How are you holding up, Merry?' Ed ventured. Brielle had already thrown them a vague wave, the caution on her face reflected in Meredith's own.

'It takes some getting used to,' Meredith said, plainly, 'but I think I'm getting there. I always knew Cal was wild. I always knew he wasn't to be tamed. I suppose I'd just imagined that we were finished with secrets – but I suppose that's what Cal thought too. He won't say it, but I think he's almost... excited. He doesn't want to tell me, because he thinks it might hurt me somehow, but it's Cal. He embraces the unexpected.' The family were almost upon them now. There was just enough time for Meredith to add, 'I suppose I'll have to embrace the unexpected as well,' before they reached the hospital doors.

It was Brielle who approached first, but Hector and Estelle were putting on a good show – wide, open faces, without any flicker of hostility. It would have been too much to say that Hector looked contrite – but, before anyone said a word, he had put out his hand to shake Ed's, holding the old man's stare as he did so.

The silence lasted just a moment too long. The momentum that had carried Brielle and her family across the car park and up to the hospital façade stopped suddenly. 'You can go on now,' Estelle told her. 'They're waiting.' But it wasn't just nervousness that held Brielle back. She was looking at Meredith with an almost apologetic air, as if somehow she was the one responsible for recasting the story of Meredith's life as well.

Meredith took a breath. Ever since Evie and Ed had broken the news, she'd been wondering what this moment might be like, but now that it was here, she realised that nothing could prepare her. Who would have known that, upon seeing her, all the bewilderment would simply melt straight away? She stepped forward, put her arms around Brielle and said, 'I'll take you through.'

Brielle scurried backwards, wrapped herself around Hector and Estelle, and then followed Meredith into the hostpital.

'I'm sorry,' said Ed.

Just two words, but they seemed to have a transformative effect on Hector. He rocked on his heels; he took Estelle's hand; he drew a deep breath. But, before he could return the words, Ed went on, 'You don't have to say it. It's all in the past.'

'And in there's the future,' said Hector, nodding at the hospital doors.

Estelle tightened her hold on her husband.

'I've been frightened of it all my life,' said Hector, at last. 'What she'd do, if she found out. How the future might feel, if ever she knew. I suppose – I suppose we're about to find out.'

Ed thought, 'Which one of us can ever know the future?' for he'd been blindsided by it so many times. For the first time in his life, he didn't know what was waiting for him when he finally returned to England. Davith had already announced that he'd be joining Ed in retirement. John Lauderdale had performed his final illusion. One generation gave way to the next – and, unless Cal made some miraculous turnaround, Ed wouldn't even be in the audience for the Forsyths' first show without him. The only thing that was certain was: the world kept turning. The curtains opened, then the curtains closed and each show was a little different from the last.

'No more secrets,' he said to Hector, with the softest of smiles.

'Not one,' said Hector.

And the sun spilt suddenly through the clouds.

Cal had his eyes fixed on the door. The first person he saw was Meredith. There she stood, framed in the pane of glass – his beautiful wife, who had borne so much. She'd been with him in his wilderness years; she'd been with him when he was dirt poor, unsuccessful, feverishly writing songs and kicking out at the world. She'd given him a son, thrown herself into his wild life – and now, there she stood, shepherding the daughter he'd never known to his bedside.

The door opened.

In walked Brielle.

She'd been so much more breezy and confident on the film set. Now, however, she was silent, hesitant, taking tentative steps into the room. For a moment, she simply stood there. Only when Evie rose to greet her, vacating the seat next to Cal, did she speak. 'You look…' She stopped. 'I was going to say *well*. And you do – you do look well! Well, better than you did when you were lying in that bed on Saturday night. You look… *alive*.' Her voice cracked. 'Cal, I'm glad you're alive.'

Evie had floated past Brielle, to join Meredith in the door.

'It sure beats being dead,' said Cal, wincing as he smiled.

The silence returned. In the doorway, Evie and Meredith were beating a steady retreat. 'We'll leave you to it, Cal,' said Evie. 'We'll be right outside.'

Evie turned and left, and the last Cal saw of Meredith before she too vanished was her mouthing the words 'Be nice.' They were the very same words she said every time Cal played too roughly with Sam.

Now that they were alone, the silence felt different.

'So,' said Brielle.

'So,' said Cal.

Now that the introductions were made, the silence felt different again.

'One of us should say something,' said Brielle.

Cal said, 'I don't know what to say.'

Brielle thought upon this for some time, before she replied, 'There must be a thousand things. I don't know anything about you. You don't know anything about me. I suppose I want to know it all.'

So did Cal. He wanted to know what it had been like growing up in Monte Carlo. What were her dreams? What were her ambitions? Which friends did she like? Which did she loathe? Had she ever been to London? Had she ever been in love?

'But maybe we should start with something small,' he said. 'Something we both have in common.' An idea occurred to him. Behind his mask of bruises, he laughed. 'Benedict Frey,' he beamed, 'was he *always* such an insufferable chump?'

Brielle spluttered in reply. 'Cal,' she laughed, 'I'm glad you're not going anywhere, because if you really want to know how insufferable Benedict Frey was to work for, this might take a while...'


By late afternoon, the Company were assembled. On the plaza outside the Hotel de Lyon, the double-decker was packed. The flotilla of black taxicabs were all loaded, fuelled and ready.

Davith's dogs sat obediently at his heels, Lily and the girls played one last round of hopscotch with Sam, and Evie and Ed looked out over the glittering waters beyond.

'We'll be all right, Dad,' said Evie. 'You don't have to worry.'

She had sensed it all afternoon, but now Ed said, 'It isn't worry. I just don't like goodbyes.'

This one felt more final than any. In a few moments' time, he would watch his daughter step aboard the red double-decker and take off along the Riviera, to drive through the night and reach Paris by tomorrow at midday. The Company would voyage without him, for the first time in his life. 'I was born on that bus,' he said – and, though it wasn't strictly true, it might as well have been, for years of his life had been spent on the road with the Forsyth Varieties. 'Evie, I can still remember the day my father handed me the Company and went off into the sun. I was proud and I was excited, hungry to show the world what we could do – but I was scared as well. Oh, I wouldn't admit it – not to my father, and not to your mother, not to anyone around me. But it hit me, that night, that I would have to carry the Company now. Through foul weather and fair, I'd be their leader – and not one of us could know what the future might bring.' He paused. He loved the sound of the Company playing around him. He wondered if he'd ever get used to their absence. 'Well, for me, the future brought those hard, lean years of the '30s, when so few people had money to spend on fripperies like ours. It brought the War, and that might have ended the Varieties forever. It brought those lean years afterwards, when the world seemed so cruel and grey. But it also brought… you,' he said, 'and Cal, and it brought magic and spectacle, and crowds cheering our name. It brought laughter and love, and it took us on long hot summers to Cannes and Nice, Madrid and Milan. What I'm trying to say is…'

'There'll be hard times ahead.'

'But...'

'But oh for the good times,' said Evie – and, for one of the first times since she'd been a girl, she laid her head on her father's shoulder.

Then another figure appeared, through the doors of the Hotel de Lyon.

Charles Laurent lifted his sunglasses and swept out to join Evie. 'I'll take good care of her, Ed,' he said, as he swung up onto the bus.

'M. Laurent,' Ed replied, 'don't deceive yourself. It's she who'll be taking good care of you.' He embraced each of his players as they boarded the vehicles, and quietly added, 'It's she who'll be taking care of you all.'

As soon as the engines flared, Meredith and Sam joined Ed on the plaza, arms waving frantically as the convoy took to the promenade. It would be mere minutes before they were in France – their journey beginning, while Ed's came to an end.

'So, Grandpa – what now?' asked Sam.

What now indeed, thought Ed. First, there would be the apartment – graciously loaned by Princess Grace – to attend to. Then there would be a long, languorous summer of idleness: visits to Cal, bringing Cal home, taking him out for walks as part of his recuperation, making certain he stayed out of trouble – because if any man, riddled with burns and broken bones, could find a way to raise hell, it would surely be Cal.

Life was about to get very fast for Evie, thought Ed – but he had little doubt she would cope.

Life was about to get much slower for Ed. He had a little less faith in himself, but it was time to give it a go.

But first: the sun had not yet set over Monte Carlo; the balmy evening beckoned them on.

He tousled Sam's hair.

'Ice cream,' Ed announced, 'and a visit to Larvotto beach.'

Ice cream, thought Ed, and then the rest of his life.

# *Acknowledgements*

A big thank you to booksellers and my readers all over the world, for being such fantastic advocates for my books. I am so grateful for all your support from reviewing my books online to attending events; you are the reason I tell stories. I loved returning to the world of the Buckingham Hotel at Christmastime, and hope you love this book too.

Much love,
Anton

# Credits

Anton Du Beke and Orion Fiction would like to thank everyone at Orion who worked on the publication of *Monte Carlo by Moonlight* in the UK.

**Editorial**
Sam Eades
Anshuman Yadav

**Copy editor**
Francine Brody

**Proofreader**
Alex Davis

**Audio**
Paul Stark
Louise Richardson

**Contracts**
Dan Herron
Ellie Bowker
Oliver Chacón

**Design**
Charlotte Abrams-Simpson

**Editorial Management**
Charlie Panayiotou
Jane Hughes
Bartley Shaw

**Finance**
Jasdip Nandra
Nick Gibson
Sue Baker

**Marketing**
Lucy Cameron

**Production**
Ameenah Khan

**Publicity**
Sarah Lundy

**Operations**
Group Sales Operations team

**Sales**
Catherine Worsley
Esther Waters
Victoria Laws
Rachael Hum
Ellie Kyrke-Smith
Frances Doyle
Georgina Cutler

**Rights**
Rebecca Folland
Tara Hiatt
Ben Fowler
Alice Cottrell
Ruth Blakemore
Marie Henckel